GRAND CENTRAL
PUBLISHING

LARGE
PRINT

The Jason Bourne Novels

The Covert-One Novels

The Paul Janson Novels

Also by Robert Ludlum

The Scarlatti Inheritance
The Matlock Paper
Trevayne
The Cry of the Halidon
The Rhinemann Exchange
The Road to Gandolfo
The Gemini Contenders
The Chancellor Manuscript
The Holcroft Covenant
The Matarese Circle
The Parsifal Mosaic
The Aquitaine Progression

The Icarus Agenda
The Osterman Weekend
The Road to Omaha
The Scorpio Illusion
The Apocalypse Watch
The Matarese Countdown
The Prometheus Deception
The Sigma Protocol
The Tristan Betrayal
The Ambler Warning
The Bancroft Strategy

Also by Eric Van Lustbader

NICHOLAS LINNEAR NOVELS
Second Skin
Floating City
The Kaisho
White Ninja
The Miko
The Ninja

CHINA MAROC NOVELS
Shan
Jian

OTHER NOVELS
Blood Trust

Last Snow
First Daughter
The Testament
Art Kills
Pale Saint
Dark Homecoming
Black Blade
Angel Eyes
French Kiss
Zero
Black Heart
Sirens

ROBERT LUDLUM'S™

THE
BOURNE
RETRIBUTION

A NEW JASON BOURNE NOVEL BY
ERIC VAN LUSTBADER

GRAND CENTRAL
PUBLISHING

LARGE PRINT

Grand Central Publishing
Hachette Book Group
237 Park Avenue
New York, NY 10017

www.HachetteBookGroup.com

Printed in the United States of America

RRD-C

First edition: December 2013

10 9 8 7 6 5 4 3 2 1

Grand Central Publishing is a division of Hachette Book Group, Inc.
The Grand Central Publishing name and logo is a trademark of Hachette Book Group, Inc.

The Hachette Speakers Bureau provides a wide range of authors for speaking events. To find out more, go to www.hachettespeakersbureau.com or call (866) 376-6591.

The publisher is not responsible for websites (or their content) that are not owned by the publisher.

Library of Congress Cataloging-in-Publication Data
Lustbader, Eric.
  Robert Ludlum's the Bourne retribution : a new Jason Bourne novel / Eric Van Lustbader. — First Edition.
      pages cm
  ISBN 978-1-4789-7952-4 (audio CD) — ISBN 978-1-4789-7951-7 (audio download)
  1. Bourne, Jason (Fictitious character)—Fiction. 2. Intelligence officers—Fiction. 3. Terrorists—Fiction. I. Ludlum, Robert, 1927–2001. II. Title.
  PS3562.U752R648 2013
  813'.54—dc23
                                        2013018525

ISBNs: 978-1-4555-5095-1 (hc); 978-1-4555-7859-7 (int'l pb);
978-1-4555-5097-5 (ebook); 978-1-4555-8110-8 (lg print)

For Ziva

THE
BOURNE
RETRIBUTION

Prologue

IN ALL ITS eleven years of existence, La Concha d'Oro had never witnessed the likes of the security now firmly in place. Armed *Federales* stalked, eagle-eyed, the perimeter of the exclusive resort's land side, a motorboat patrolled the water that paralleled its crescent beachfront, and wherever the two VIPs—for whom the resort had been emptied of guests, vetted, and made secure—went, their bodyguards floated like clouds of bees, busy doing nothing but tending their respective flowers.

About those flowers: They consisted of two men, Carlos Danda Carlos, newly appointed chief of Mexico's anti-drug enforcement agency, and Eden Mazar, Mossad's anti-terrorist specialist. Mexico needed all the help it could get to fight the entrenched corruption and fear that kept the three most powerful drug cartels' grip on the country inviolable, which was why, the Director of Mossad had explained to Jason Bourne not three days ago, Carlos Danda Carlos had reached out to Mossad.

Carlos Danda Carlos was a new breed of Mexican, the Director had explained, educated in the United States, a fearless reformer, a determined general in the fight to free his country from the death grip in which it found itself.

"Los Zetas is far and away the most dangerous cartel," the Director had said, "mainly due to the fact that it was created from a cadre of elite soldiers who deserted from the Mexican Army's Special Forces." The Director had put his hand on Bourne's shoulder. "Nevertheless, there will be so much security, for you it will be a milk run. Just look after Eden Mazar, and, in between, get some sun and relaxation."

"I don't work for you. I don't work for anyone, ever," Bourne had said, rather ungenerously considering the way the Director had treated him ever since he had come to Israel, following the death of Maceo Encarnación.

The Director's smile was tinged with both sadness and regret. "Rebeka was like a daughter to me. It's been a month since her funeral, but you show no inclination to leave. This is not like you."

"I'm no longer me," Bourne said. "Something

inside me has changed. There is nothing that interests me."

The Director watched him for a moment. He was a small man with a halo of wild white hair, the sort of man for whom every line etched into his leather face seemed to represent another death or disappointment. His large cache of victories was hidden out of sight. "I thought this...trip would help take your mind off—"

"Nothing's going to take my mind off her death," Bourne said harshly.

The Director nodded. "It's too soon. I understand completely." He looked around the harborfront. "Well, you can hang around here for another month—or as long as you like."

Bourne scoured his words, looking for a hint of irony, but failed to find any. Apparently, the Director meant what he said.

Then he paused to consider his limited options. "On the other hand, maybe you're right. Maybe an assignment is just what I need."

And so he had met Eden Mazar, had traveled in the same private Mossad jet with him and his contingent of bodyguards, had disembarked at the small private airfield exclusively reserved for La Concha d'Oro guests, which the Mexican *Federales* had kept in security lockdown for forty-eight hours prior to landing.

Now here he was, standing six feet away from the two exotic flowers and their bodyguards, scanning the area for trouble that surely would never come. The trouble was he was back in Mexico, and though he was far from Mexico City, where Rebeka had been killed, his mind was still filled with the sight and scent of her death in the taxi's backseat, driving down apocalyptic streets.

Perhaps the Director hadn't anticipated Bourne's reaction to his swift return to Rebeka's land of death, or possibly his suggestion had been deliberate. Getting back on the horse that threw you was often the best medicine.

Not this time.

Without his fully knowing it, Rebeka had pierced his Bourne armor, penetrating to the core of him. Her death throbbed like an internal wound that refused to heal. *I have met other women like her*, he thought. And then, inevitably: *There's been no one like her*.

Such black thoughts were not typical of his psyche, which had been hardened in crucible after crucible until he had been quite certain that nothing could affect him for long, or even at all. But Rebeka's death, piled upon all the deaths of those others who had tried to get close to him, was a loss that threatened to suffocate him, plow him under the earth. And why not? His life had been little more than a living death from the moment he had been pulled from the black waters by Mediterranean fishermen and realized that he had lost his memory, his past, his life up until the very moment when he had opened his eyes in unfamiliar surroundings.

Eden Mazar, coming out from beneath the gaily painted wooden overhang of the octagonal gazebo set overlooking the Pacific, reminded him that he was once more in unfamiliar surroundings. But this time, he felt lost, a sea captain who has forgotten his charts and how to steer by the stars.

"These people are to be pitied," Eden said to him in a rumbling undertone. "They either lack the will or are too corrupt to take on the cartels in any concerted manner. Either way there's nothing more for me to do here. The government no longer controls Mexico; the cartels do. We'll be leaving this evening after dinner."

Bourne nodded.

Eden turned away, then hesitated and came back to Bourne, a wry smile playing across his lips. "Are you bored yet?"

"What makes you think I'm bored?"

Eden grunted. "I have read your face. Also, your file."

Bourne was alarmed that the Mossad had a file

on him, but he wasn't surprised. He only wondered how accurate it was.

"There's nothing for you to do," Eden continued. "But really, this isn't your thing, is it? You're infiltration and excision. That's what the Director likes so much about you."

"I didn't know I was a current topic of conversation inside the Mossad."

Eden smiled kindly. "You were close to Rebeka. That kind of thing didn't happen with her."

Suddenly Bourne understood. "And I'm the Director's only living link with her."

"She was a special human being, as well as a remarkable agent. We miss her, but we'll never be able to replace her. Her death dealt us a terrible blow. We will demand retribution."

"That's the Mossad way, isn't it?"

Mazar chose not to answer. "I've got to get back to Carlos. He's not a bad sort, but when it comes to change, to making the concerted effort needed to rid Mexico of the cartels, his hands remain tied. As I said, pitiable."

Bourne considered a moment. "Why are you here? What's the Mossad's interest in Mexican drug cartels?"

"This is something you failed to ask the Director?"

Bourne realized he should have; maybe he hadn't been thinking clearly.

Mazar smiled. "But you don't really need to ask anyone that question, Jason, do you?"

Bourne watched him mount the steps back up to the gazebo, where Carlos and his cadre of muscle were waiting patiently in the shade. A cool breeze off the water started up, ruffling Bourne's hair, stirring the hair on his forearms. What did Eden mean? Was the Mossad aware of the links among Encarnación, the Mexican cartels, and the Chinese government Bourne had discovered? Had Rebeka been working on that connection even before she had met him? He determined that, one way or another, he'd pry the answer out of Mazar.

Hearing a whining insect-like drone, he looked up, saw a small plane high in the sky. Squinting as it came closer, he could make out the pontoons. A seaplane then. Shading his eyes, he saw that the crew of the patrol boat had spotted the seaplane as well. There was movement on the deck, the flash of gun barrels.

Bourne saw that Eden's bodyguards, being under the gazebo, were blocked from the scene. He started up the steps in order to warn Eden when Carlos Danda Carlos's men, wielding machetes, sliced off the heads of Eden's two bodyguards.

Eden turned as blood spattered him. Bourne reached for him, but Carlos, aiming a .357 Magnum at Bourne, shook his head. Eden was in the process of turning his head to look for Bourne when one of Carlos's bodyguard swung his machete with such force that Eden's head, severed from his shoulders, arced out onto the beach, where it rolled down the gentle slope until it was kissed by the turquoise waves lapping onto the warm sand.

Bourne took a chance, made his move, leaping onto the machete-wielder. Snatching the weapon from his hand, he drove it into his sternum, piercing skin and flesh, shattering bone.

Then an enormous percussion sounded in his ears at almost the same instant he was slammed backward by the powerful bullet plowing through the muscle of his left shoulder.

He grunted, toppled over the gazebo's striped railing, tumbled down onto the beach.

Hours later, when he was able to rouse himself, the sun was close to setting, turning sky, sea, and sand the color of blood. He lay close to Eden's head, which bobbed in the water like a child's toy, striped with black blood, abandoned.

Bourne turned his head, blinked blurriness out of his eyes. Not a figure could be seen. So far as he could tell, the entire resort was deserted.

The gentle surf bumped Eden's head against

him, turning it slowly, as inexorably as the earth rotates from day to night. Eden's eyes, already filmed over, stared at him accusingly. Bourne opened his mouth, as if the accusation had been verbal, but all at once he was inundated by a wave of violent pain, and quickly he passed into merciful unconsciousness.

Book One

———

Ten days later

1

INTERNALLY, THE DIRECTOR of Mossad was traditionally known as Memune, "first among equals." Not Eli Yadin. "I have a name," he would say to the new recruits whenever he met them. "Use it."

Yadin was normally an optimistic man—in his line of work you were either optimistic or you blew your brains out inside of eighteen months. But today he was unhappy; worse, his optimism had failed him. Possibly that was due to Amir Ophir, the man sitting opposite him, aboard his sailboat, the most secure spot in Tel Aviv—all of Israel for that matter.

Ophir was the head of Metsada, Mossad's Special Ops branch. Through Kidon, its wet-work group, it was in charge of conducting assassination, sabotage, paramilitary, and psychological warfare projects. Unlike the Director, Ophir was dark of both skin and hair. His eyes, set far apart in his face, were pitch black, like the pupil of a raven's eye. Yadin often thought Ophir's soul was the same color.

"Honestly, Memune, I don't understand you." Ophir shook his head. "When he was up and running, the man was a liability, an albatross, even. Now he's finished, done. He goes out with the trash. The Mexicans not only killed Eden, they desecrated him. This is totally unacceptable. They must be made to pay."

"Are you telling me my job, Amir?"

"Of course not, Memune," Ophir said hastily. "I am only voicing my outrage—the outrage of our entire family."

"I share your outrage, Amir. And believe me, the perpetrators will be made to pay."

"I will design a counter to the Mexicans that will—"

"You will do no such thing," the Director said sharply.

"What?"

"Ouyang Jidan is behind the Mexicans. A larger plan has been set in motion."

Ophir's expression grew dark. "You have not told me about it."

"I just did," the Director said blandly.

"Details."

"Compartmentalization."

Ophir appeared offended by this blatant rebuff. "You do not trust me?"

"Don't be absurd, Amir."

"Then—"

The Director looked him in the eye. "The plan involves Bourne."

Ophir made a derisive sound through pursed lips.

The Director raised a hand. "Ah, well, you see..."

"Memune, listen to me. Wherever Bourne goes, death follows. First Rebeka and now Eden. What I cannot fathom is why you've brought him into the center of our family."

"I know how close you were with Eden."

"Eden Mazar was one of my best men."

The Director could see that Ophir was getting heated more rapidly than usual.

"I feel your pain, Amir," the Director said, "but Bourne is of great strategic use to us."

"Bourne is burned out. He's of no use to anyone."

"I disagree."

Ophir raised one ebon eyebrow. "Even if you're right, which I seriously doubt, is that use worth Eden Mazar's life?"

"Amir, Amir, it is for God to make such a judgment."

Ophir snorted. "Yes. God is everywhere, and nowhere at all. The fact is, God has nothing to do with our chosen profession. If there is a God, there would be no need for Mossad or Kidon."

Unfortunately, the Director knew what Ophir meant. It was times like these—when terror clamped Eli's heart and was slowly squeezing the life out of it—that felt as if God had abandoned his chosen people. But such thoughts were counterproductive.

"I would prefer we leave God out of our discussion," the Director said. It wasn't spoken as an order, and yet it was. This, too, was the Mossad way.

"You're mistaken to pin the two deaths on Bourne," he went on. "He was their harbinger, but certainly not their cause."

"He failed to protect Rebeka."

"Rebeka didn't need protection," the Director snapped. "You of all people know that."

"And what about Eden?"

The Director stood up. The wind had changed directions, and he spent some time adjusting the sails accordingly. When everything was secure and to his liking he returned to his seat and stared into Ophir's raven eyes.

"Amir, we find ourselves in a situation that I fear is quite beyond us. We need help."

"I can get you all the help you need."

The Director shook his head. "I think not. Not this time."

"Memune, please. Bourne can't be trusted." Ophir's eyes grew dark and dangerous. "He's not us; he's not family," he said emphatically.

Leaning forward, forearms on knees, the Director put his hands together as if in prayer. "And yet, for better or for worse, it's Bourne, Amir. Only Bourne can help us now."

Jason Bourne, sitting in ancient shadow, stared out at the sunlight chopping the Mediterranean into diamond shards. He imagined each shard to be a leaping fish, went through the exercise of visualizing what each fish looked like as it leapt from the water. Instead he saw Eden Mazar's decapitated head flying over the gazebo into the edge of the surf.

Diamond shards became flecks of blood, raining down on him. He saw Eden's veiled eyes admonishing him. He closed his eyes, but that only brought up images of Rebeka in Mexico City, dying in the backseat of a taxi.

Above him rose the arches of the ancient aqueduct built in the first century BCE, during King Herod's reign. Three hundred years later, with the city of Caesarea greatly enlarged, it was extended, bringing cool, clear water from the springs of Shummi six miles away at the foot of Mount Carmel. Now the modern resort of Caesarea, adjacent to the ruins of the old city, was run by a private corporation.

At some point he became aware that a figure had entered his island of shade, and he grew annoyed, wanting, more than anything, to be alone. He turned, about to voice his displeasure, when he saw the Director, clad in one of his usual lightweight linen suits. His one concession for the beach was highly polished leather huaraches.

"It took me some time to find you," the Director said, "so I imagine that's the way you wanted it."

When Bourne made no reply and swung his head to look out again at the sea, the Director stepped closer and sat down beside him.

"I understand you left the hospital prematurely."

"Opinions differ," Bourne said dully.

"A doctor's opinion—"

"I know my body better than any doctor," Bourne said curtly.

For some time, the two sat in an uncomfortable silence. Young women in tiny bikinis ran, shouting with laughter, into the surf to interrupt their boyfriends' game of water Frisbee. Someone was taking photos of the aqueduct. A mother herded her two children up the beach, rubbing a towel briskly over their dripping heads. The salt tang was overlaid with the scents of suntan lotion and clean sweat.

"How's your shoulder?"

"My shoulder's fine," Bourne said. "Is that why you're here? To check on my health? I don't need a shoulder."

"I don't have a shoulder to give," the Director said brusquely. Then he sighed. "You may want out, Jason—"

"I don't want out. I just want to be here."

"Doing nothing but thinking of her."

"It's none of your business what I'm doing."

"Sitting on the beach day after day isn't for people like us."

Bourne remained mute.

"We'll rest when we're dead," the Director observed drily. "Anyway, I didn't come here to debate the merits of the life we're in. I came to tell you that your enemies are still searching for you."

"Eden's death is proof I'm not ready."

"No one could have saved Eden, not from a betrayal by Carlos. Recall, if you will, Eden had his handpicked bodyguards with him. They were killed instantly. You did your best."

"I should have done better. In other times—"

"This isn't other times," the Director said. "And the past is the past. You and I have to deal with the now."

Bourne's eye was caught by two of the Director's grim-faced men coming down the beach. They bracketed the man who had been taking pictures and hustled him away.

"It didn't take me that long to find you," the Director said. "It hasn't taken Ouyang Jidan long, either."

Bourne squinted through the harsh sunlight. Was the photographer in custody Chinese?

The Director produced a cigar but made no move to light it, simply rolled it back and forth between his fingers like a magician's wand. "Don't for a moment imagine Ouyang hasn't been monitoring the entire situation, Jason." The Director's face held a measure of solace for Bourne. "You embarrassed him, caused him to lose face. He's going to strike while you're most vulnerable."

Bourne swung his head around. "Did Rebeka know about Ouyang?"

"What? No."

"Who did, besides you?"

The Director heaved another sigh. "My head of Metsada. Amir Ophir."

"Then why did Ouyang order her killed?"

For a moment the Director stood stock-still. A pulse beat in his right temple. "Encarnación gave the order."

"No," Bourne said. "He didn't."

2

GOOD." QUAN, THE wushun master, almost casually tossed a *jian*, a slender double-edged sword, traditionally used by gentlemen and scholars. As Ouyang Jidan caught it deftly by the hilt, Quan said, "White Snake Form."

Ouyang stood perfectly still in the center of the training facility. The three men against whom he had been fighting for the past twenty minutes, using the Red Phoenix open-hand style, now picked up their own swords. Unlike Ouyang's, theirs were *dao*, short, single-edged broadswords. All the weapons were carbon steel, rather than the traditional wooden training swords. Ouyang had moved beyond those years ago. There were twenty-nine levels in his chosen wushun discipline; he was fifteenth level.

Quan, a tiny man, looking no more than a wisp, was old in the manner of all great wushun masters. That is to say old in years only. He moved like a thirty-year-old, but his mind was filled with the wisdom only long decades of experience could produce. He was twenty-ninth level.

"Now," Quan said to the three men, "attack."

Ouyang moved not a muscle as the others advanced, an oasis of utter calm in the eye of the approaching whirlwind. The three men—tall, medium, and small in stature—came at him one by one, in the gliding, stretched movements of the Chinese straight sword form.

The small one struck first, an overhead blow meant to split the skull. Ouyang countered without moving his legs or torso in the slightest. Just his arms blurred, steel struck on steel, a lightning flash of sparks, and then the short man, shaken, stepped back at the precise moment the tall man lunged in with a strike meant to penetrate all the way to the spine. With a flick of his wrists that was neither disdainful nor flamboyant, Ouyang guided his opponent's *dao* aside.

The medium man's approach was entirely different. He was an expert in Sacred Stone, the same form Ouyang was using. For almost five minutes the two men stood toe-to-toe, with only their arms and weapons moving, until Ouyang, employing an unorthodox strike, swept his opponent's legs out from under him.

The three men now spread out and simultaneously attacked Ouyang from different directions, the medium man switching from the immobile Sacred Stone to the fluid Fire Dance. For long moments, the endless clang of steel on steel, sparks like lightning, blurs like a mist clouding the interior of the building. Again and again the men tried to defeat Ouyang. Again and again, they were deflected, and then, in a breathtaking flurry, disarmed, defeated.

Well," Colonel Sun said, when it was over, after Ouyang had been elevated to sixteenth level in a brief ceremony, "even I am impressed."

Ouyang looked at him, sword blade lying against his hairless forearm. "Perhaps you wish to take me on."

Colonel Sun chuckled, shaking his head. "You are old school, Minister. I never studied the straight sword forms."

"Too low-tech, I imagine." Ouyang sheathed his *jian* with a reverence the younger man would never grasp. "So there is a gap in your expertise."

Colonel Sun chuckled again, but there was an undertone of uneasiness, an unanswered question of failure. He was young to be such a highly ranked officer—in his midthirties, a handsome man, with a slight Manchu cast to his eyes and cheekbones. Ouyang had mentored him, brought him along, overseeing his swift rise through the military ranks. Sun was intelligent, inquisitive, like Ouyang, a visionary—one of the young upstarts that, Ouyang hoped, would help bring the Middle Kingdom the world hegemony it so richly deserved.

"I have altered my mind-set," Colonel Sun said, "of Ministers who sit in offices and shuffle papers as they make decisions."

"Only me," Ouyang said with an impish smile. "Only me."

Later, the two men sat in the private dining suite at the Hyatt on the Bund reserved exclusively for Ouyang. They drank Starbucks coffee and ate the American breakfast Ouyang insisted they tolerate, if not enjoy, as part of their preparation for world hegemony. Outside the windows stretched Pudong and the glittering arc of the Bund, for centuries one of the world's most famous waterfronts.

Colonel Sun, having had enough of the foreign substances, put aside his fork and said, "One of our people has been taken into custody at Caesarea."

Ouyang scowled. "That is most unfortunate."

Colonel Sun, clearing the tastes out of his mouth with a gulp of water, nodded. "Jason Bourne was with Director Yadin."

"He's like a fucking cockroach," Ouyang said. "Impossible to kill, as you yourself found out in the catacombs of Rome. You tried twice and failed both times."

Colonel Sun winced. "Everyone has failed. That does not mean I'll fail again."

Ouyang nodded. "An outcome that would please me, Sun. And also, I might add, lead to another promotion." He wiped his lips. "Now, about the Mexican operation."

"A mistake was made at Las Peñas." Colonel Sun spat. "Mexicans! They can't be trusted to think for themselves. Though, in the past that has worked in our favor." He hesitated a moment, as if unsure whether to voice his next thought. "And then there is Maricruz."

Ouyang stiffened visibly. "Maceo Encarnación's daughter is an exception to the rule."

"And yet," Colonel Sun said, "she is the one who brought us into contact with the Mexicans."

"In the past that has worked in our favor," Ouyang said, deliberately parroting his protégé.

"The failure at Dahr El Ahmar to obtain the Israeli laser process for enriching uranium has not only set back our plans in Africa, but also given Cho Xilan the ammunition he needs against our long-range path for China."

Cho was the secretary of the powerful Chongqing Party, Ouyang's chief rival in the Central Committee. The Chongqing was also known as the Pure Heaven party for its conservative view of continuing the Middle Kingdom's long-standing policy of isolation and non-engagement with the West. The rift between conservative and liberal factions of the government had been blown open by the very public purging of Bo Xilai and the subsequent arrest of his wife for allegedly murdering a Westerner.

"Listen to me, Sun. Now that the president has decided to convene the Party Congress, everything has changed," Ouyang said. "In two weeks we will finalize plans to hand power to a new generation of leaders.

"I am determined to be one of those leaders. I am just as determined to ensure that Cho Xilan is not one of them. He was elevated when Bo Xilai was purged. We must find a way to implicate him in conspiring with the former head of the Chongqing Party."

Colonel Sun considered. "That will not be easy. Cho has many powerful friends."

"Nothing we do is easy, Sun." Ouyang's fork

paused on the way to his mouth, hanging in midair. "Listen to me now. The Mexicans could not be expected to deal with Jason Bourne, a man they know nothing about. Carlos did what he was ordered to do, and, as a result, Mossad has been dealt another blow. First the powerful agent Rebeka, and now Eden Mazar."

"Well then, it's no wonder Yadin is talking with Bourne."

"The question is, why is Bourne listening?" Ouyang chewed meditatively on a bite of egg and bacon. "Why was Bourne in Las Peñas protecting Mazar? Bourne is a loner. He loathes and distrusts government agencies." He shook his head, staring out at the glimmering high-rise skyline of Shanghai. "Something vital has changed. We need to find out, Sun."

The colonel shook his head. "I don't understand."

Ouyang pursed his lips. "Bourne is a wild card, Sun, he always has been. We cannot afford to let him or Mossad interfere with us."

"I don't understand why you're still worried about Mossad. Their agent Rebeka is dead."

"Given what we know, Sun, there is every possibility that Mossad's Director has talked Bourne into following in Rebeka's footsteps."

"I still don't—"

"You know as much as you need to know, Sun." Ouyang turned away. "Focus on Bourne. He's your target now."

Bourne had booked himself into an anonymous motel on the seedier side of Caesarea, away from the posh tourist center where the rich came to play. Its whitewashed stone looked abused, as if the past had beaten it up. It was, however, not so anonymous that a man dressed as a tourist, carrying an overnight bag, wasn't able to find it and book himself a room, paying cash for a one-night stay. While the clerk turned his back to fetch his room key, the tourist checked the computer terminal for Bourne's room number.

The tourist had an entirely unremarkable face. In fact, minutes after he had checked in, the clerk had forgotten what he looked like. Meanwhile, on the third floor, the tourist stopped outside Bourne's room.

He set down his overnight bag, unzipped it, and removed a vinyl sheet that, when shaken out, deployed as a suit, into which he stepped. When he zipped up the front, his body seemed to disappear. He slipped plastic booties over his shoes, then snapped on latex gloves.

Inside Bourne's room, he observed everything

with a cold clinician's eye. He went methodically through every drawer, shelf, checked behind every picture, underneath the bed—making certain to replace everything in the precise spot and angle in which he'd found it. Finding nothing of interest, he stepped into the bathroom. He felt behind the toilet's water tank, lifted the porcelain lid to peer inside. From the side of the sink, he picked up a water glass. Holding it at rim and bottom, he sprayed a fine white powder on the curved side. Immediately several fingerprints were revealed. He placed a short length of a specially formulated tape over the fingerprints, then carefully peeled it off. The prints were perfectly preserved on the tape.

A moment later, silent and ghost-like, he slipped from the room. Stripping off the vinyl suit and booties, he stowed them in his bag. He kept the latex gloves on. Descending two flights of metal stairs, he exited unnoticed through the rear door, vanishing into the white noonday glare.

3

M Y WORLD," Director Yadin said as he stared out at the cerulean water breaking onto the beach, "is made up of black and white. I leave the shades of gray to other people. I am compelled by my job to see the world in two camps: heroes and villains—those who will help me and those who plot my downfall. Here, we do not have the luxury of being undecided, we do not have the luxury of hesitating, because destruction is always waiting on the other side of night."

The young men and women, finished with their sexual horseplay in the surf, came running back up the beach, bronzed bodies both hard and lush.

"You know," Yadin observed, "it's only when you reach a certain age that you can fully appreciate the bodies of the young." He turned to Bourne.

"It's part of my job to put those beautiful bodies at risk, and I don't even have time to consider what a pity it is. My only mistress is necessity."

Bourne, chin resting on his folded forearms, said, "How does this relate to my history with Ouyang Jidan?"

The Director grunted. "Despite what I've just said, for every generation there comes a person whose skills, ingenuity, and danger fall outside the parameters of my universe. You are such a man. And so is Ouyang Jidan. So I suppose it's not at all surprising that the two of you have a shared history. Somehow, in some mysterious way, you sought each other out, if only because opposites attract."

The Director stopped rolling his cigar between his fingers, poked one end into his mouth, and took his time lighting up. His eyes glittered eerily in the brief flare-up, then the two men were briefly engulfed in a bluish cloud before the sea breeze blew the aromatic smoke away.

"Ten years ago Ophir and I were running an operation in Syria," the Director said. "In those days, we were both Kidon. This op was top secret, very perilous not only for us, but for the state itself." He laughed unexpectedly. "We called ourselves the Assassination Bureau. What a pair of idiots we were!"

His expression sobered quickly enough. "So, then. We had been sent in to infiltrate and to kill. Your specialties, Jason. As it turned out, we weren't the only ones."

He paused for a moment to contemplate the end of his cigar, which glowed with what seemed to be an infernal heat. "You remember Brigadier General Wadi Khalid? He was the head of Syrian military intelligence or, as we dubbed him, the Minister of Shitholes."

The Director puffed on his cigar, then pursed his lips to expel the smoke. Instead he abruptly turned away and began to cough. Released smoke wreathed his head before wafting away.

"Khalid, you may recall, was the architect of the so-called Torture Archipelago, the network of underground torture chambers spread around the country," the Director continued when he had recovered. "They had to be destroyed, of course, but for obvious reasons, not the least of which was an abrupt reversal of morale among the Syrian military, Khalid had to be exterminated first."

Yadin coughed again, less violently this time, and cleared his throat. "As I said, in those days Ophir and I were hotshots. We made mistakes—small ones, but they were enough."

Far out, beyond the shore, a dark blue sailboat, its mainsail ballooned outward, tacked before the wind. Down the beach, a baby started crying. The young women were spreading out a picnic while their boyfriends played cards or sunned themselves.

"So you didn't get Khalid," Bourne said, after a time.

"Ophir and I were lucky to escape Damascus with our lives." The Director stared at his cigar. He no longer seemed interested in smoking it. "But we did return with a startling bit of information. The Syrian military was being taught their interrogation techniques by the Chinese."

This got Bourne's attention, as the Director must certainly have known it would. "The Chinese..."

"Ouyang has been whittling away at us for some time." The Director's eyes met Bourne's. "Now it's cyber warfare, trying to steal our secrets through viruses and Trojans, but it amounts to the same thing. He wants the advanced technology we have."

"So Ouyang is coordinating all the attacks against you."

It was Yadin's turn to look out to sea. "Ouyang's hatred and fear of us started decades ago. He had been sent to Damascus by his then masters. He was the one mentoring the military intelligence in esoteric torture techniques."

"Wait a minute, when was this?" Bourne said.

"Eleven years ago. We got out on November fifth."

Bourne shook his head. "I remember Khalid was killed on November fourth of that year."

"Two bullets from a long-range rifle—one to the chest, a second to the head."

"If you didn't do it—"

"I suppose," Yadin said wryly, "you don't recall pulling the trigger."

"*I* killed Khalid?"

"Indeed you did." The Director nodded. "And Brigadier General Wadi Khalid was our friend Ouyang's premier asset in Syria, one he'd carefully cultivated for years. You blew that operation up. Imagine his loss of face."

Maricruz Encarnación had the face of Mexico's conquerors—the high Castilian cheekbones and the imperious air—but with her huge coffee-colored eyes and long waterfall of hair she also might have been an Aztec princess. In either case, she radiated power like the sun.

Minister Ouyang Jidan, sitting next to her in the limo on its way to Shanghai Pudong International Airport, smirked without letting her see his expression. It amused him no end that she infuriated and terrified both his friends and his enemies. She was an outsider—a Westerner; no one understood her, they couldn't read her and, therefore, had no way of predicting either her requests or her desires. *Lăo mò* was what they called her behind his back, a Mandarin ethnic slur against Mexicans so stupid he refused to acknowledge it, let alone confront the perpetrators. Yet inside him, a cold fury mounted, multiplying like rats. He never told her, however. He was well aware of her murderous temperament; it was one of the things he found wondrous in her. She was as fierce as a Royal Bengal tiger, as independent as any man he had met.

"Do you think this is wise?" he said now. Though he knew her answer, he felt it incumbent upon him to ask her one last time.

"My father and brother are both dead," Maricruz said in her musical alto. "If I don't go, the business will be balkanized. Worse, the executives of the legitimate side of his business will come under increasing pressure from the drug lords my father's power and influence kept under control."

"I scrutinize the news from Mexico as thoroughly as you do."

"Jidan, I very much doubt it."

"Without Maceo Encarnación," he said doggedly, "the war between Los Zetas and the Sinaloa cartels has escalated to such a pitch that, if not controlled, it will plunge the entire country into civil war."

"Nevertheless, I must go."

"I think you are underestimating the level of danger you'll be walking into, Maricruz. I don't think it wise to insert yourself between the two factions."

"You are afraid for me."

"Once you leave China I cannot protect you."

Maricruz showed her small white teeth as she smiled her tigerish smile. "I am my father's daughter, Jidan." She put her hand on his thigh. "Besides, you don't want your lucrative connections severed, do you? Between the opium and the chemicals for meth production we ship to Mexico, we pull down over five billion dollars a year."

"What I don't want, Maricruz, is for you to be separated from your head."

"I won't forget that," she said, laughing, as she spread her legs, the lemony shantung silk of her skirt riding up her powerful, burnished thighs, and mounted him. She wore no underwear, and her nimble fingers quickly unzipped him, freeing him. Then she lowered herself onto him. It was easy; she was already wet.

Ouyang let out a puff of air. Hands flat against his chest, she could feel the fierce beating of his heart as if it were a minor seismic event.

She rose and fell on him in a tide-like rhythm. Ouyang's eyes half closed in pleasure.

"You believe the Encarnación name will protect you."

"Jidan, please. I know Mexico; I know the cartels."

He struggled to keep his thoughts from dissolving in the swiftly rising pool of ecstasy. "Los Zetas are different," he said thickly. "They're defectors from the army's special forces. They're vicious and cruel."

"Mercenaries are, by definition, vicious and cruel—this has been true no matter how far you go back in history." She smiled, as if at a memory. She seemed wholly unaffected by their intimate joining. "But the one thing they all have in common is their lust for money. I'm going in prepared. Trust me, Jidan. I will be fine." Then she gave a little groan, her sole concession to the forces that crested in her. "Everything will be fine."

Ouyang sat staring after her, drinking in the last shred of her image—her erect, dancer's carriage, her long, strong legs, her impossibly firm buttocks—as she walked through the door of the departures terminal. His heart constricted, collapsing in on itself. He felt her absence the way a freezing man feels the absence of fire. His mobile phone rang, but he left it unanswered, not trusting himself to speak.

You screwed Ouyang six ways from Sunday," the Director said, "and after that, Ouyang lost his chance to worm inside the Syrian government. He's never forgotten that defeat. It's why he's after you now; he won't stop until you're dead."

Bourne fingered Rebeka's gold star of David. "I don't care."

"Remember that she—"

"Rebeka was killed by Maceo Encarnación's son. I killed him and Maceo, that's over and done with."

"But it isn't, Jason," Yadin said. "Ouyang Jidan was Maceo Encarnación's partner."

"This isn't news to me."

"But the scope may be." The Director produced a sheaf of onionskin papers from his breast pocket, unfolded them carefully, and handed them to Bourne. "See for yourself."

Bourne didn't want to look; he wanted no more involvement with Yadin, Mossad, Ouyang, anyone from the short life he could remember, for that matter. If the future looked black, then the only patch of gray, the only way out for him, was to choose another path entirely. What that might be, he had no idea. He could return to Georgetown University, resume his professorship in comparative linguistics, of course, except he knew from experience he'd grow bored within the space of a semester. What else was there for him? His Treadstone training had made him uniquely qualified for only one thing.

Reluctantly, with a sinking feeling in the pit of his stomach, he looked down at the first sheet, began reading chapter and verse detailing Ouyang's growing wealth from his periodic shipments of opium and chemicals that, taken together, could only be bound for the meth labs owned by Encarnación's cartels.

"Starting five years ago, Ouyang became Encarnación's sole supplier," the Director said. "And why not? As a senior Minister, Ouyang was one hundred percent reliable. As you can imagine, he was also a leakproof source. No wonder Encarnación not only bought exclusively from him, but kicked back twenty-five percent from the sales of the finished products."

By this time, Bourne had finished reading the pages. He now returned them to Yadin. He felt something old and dangerous stirring inside himself. "Have you been tracking Ouyang's movements?"

"For years," Yadin said, nodding. "He's currently in Shanghai."

"Has he ever traveled to Mexico?"

"No."

"Anywhere close?"

Yadin shook his head.

Bourne gazed out at the somnolent sea, thinking about unfinished business. He couldn't let Rebeka's death go unavenged, and he had nowhere else to go. That thing inside himself sprang to life, and his mind began to shake off the blackness, to work again as it was meant to.

"What doesn't track," he said, "is how the two men hooked up in the first place. They were on opposite sides of the world, they moved in entirely different spheres."

"Not entirely. Don't forget, Encarnación was the CEO of SteelTrap, the world's largest Internet security firm. It's possible they met through the Chinese increasing involvement in cyber espionage."

Bourne shook his head. "I don't buy it. I knew Encarnación. He was scrupulous in keeping his legitimate business separate from his criminal activities. For SteelTrap any hint of business with the Chinese would be pure poison. No, there has to be another connection we don't know about, a connection it's vital we find."

The Director carefully put away the papers. In

their place, he handed Bourne a sealed packet. When Bourne opened it, he found ten thousand dollars, a first-class ticket from Tel Aviv to Shanghai, and a passport in the name of Lawrence Davidoff.

"Welcome back," Yadin said. "You leave tomorrow night."

He waited a moment, perhaps to see if Bourne would return the packet. When he didn't, Yadin rose and, without another word, stepped out of the shadow of the stone arch, making his way toward his bodyguards, who waited patiently at the land end of the beach.

4

As soon as the plane taking him to Tel Aviv had reached cruising altitude, Bourne rose from his seat, went back up the aisle, and locked himself inside one of the two toilets. Taking out the passport Mossad had prepared for him, he slowly leafed through the pages, checking each one edge-on. He found nothing unusual, but when he looked at the back, he thought he spotted something.

Holding the edge up to the light, he detected a tiny bud of glue. Using a fingernail, he picked off the bud, to discover, just beneath, a hairline slit. He looked around for something to use. Opening the trash bin, he saw that someone had stuffed in a plastic glass, cracking it in the process. He drew one half out, laid it on the metal counter, and smacked his fist against it.

Plucking out a shard best suited to his purpose, he drew the tip against the edge of the back cover, over and over, until the slit opened. Slowly and carefully, he drew out what had been inserted between two layers of the board.

He found himself staring at a tiny wafer-thin rectangle of silicon circuits.

Having been in Tel Aviv for some weeks, as Director Yadin's guest, Bourne had absorbed the bulk of the Director's schedule. For that reason, he was surprised to see Yadin exit Mossad headquarters at lunchtime. He usually worked through the midday hours, occasionally consuming a premade sandwich one of his assistants brought up to him from the underground canteen.

Yesterday, though, Yadin, dressed oddly casually in a white guayabera shirt, shorts, and boating shoes, got into an unmarked Mossad vehicle. He was alone, no bodyguard in sight. His usual armored car sat vacant and guarded somewhere below the building.

Firing up the motorcycle he had bought to get around the traffic-clogged city, Bourne followed Yadin as he nosed his car out into traffic. By the way he was dressed, Bourne guessed that he was headed for the marina and his beloved boat, but as soon as Yadin turned toward the center of the city, Bourne knew he was wrong.

Twelve blocks away, the Director pulled into a parking spot near a bus stop. Bourne nosed his motorcycle in toward the curb. A Dan Line bus was slowing, its air brakes sighing as it headed for the stop. Bourne glimpsed Yadin standing in line. The Director looked like an old man as he shuffled along in line, a bent-backed pensioner on a too-meager income.

Bourne followed the bus as it heaved its bulk out into traffic, waiting patiently at each successive stop to see if Yadin got off.

He finally did, at the Weizmann Street stop. Bourne observed him cross the street, walk down to an enormous faceted glass-and-steel building with an immense circular structure on the roof. It looked like one of the CIA buildings in DC.

Bourne gunned the motorcycle forward, parked it at the curb, then followed Yadin between pillars, up a pedestrian ramp. As Yadin entered the building, he was brought up short by the sign: TEL AVIV SOURASKY MEDICAL CENTER. Immediately he thought of the Director's coughing fit on the Caesarea beach, his half-smoked cigar. From the evidence, it seemed possible that Yadin was ill and didn't want anyone to know. If that was the case, Bourne decided he would honor that wish.

Heading back down the ramp, he got on his motorcycle, wheeled around, and drove away.

The Yemenite jewelry shop on one end of Mazal Dagim Street, in the Old Jaffa Bazaar in Tel Aviv, was an unprepossessing storefront, old by the looks of it, with an exquisite hand-painted sign hanging above the door. Inside, the silver jewelry sparkled with the intricate filigree work typical of Yemenite culture. The artistry was exquisite. The Ben Asher family had been working at this address for many years, their craft honed ages before Israel had come into existence.

Apter Ben Asher, current patriarch of the family, was the man Rebeka had told Bourne to seek out should he need to purchase anything in secret.

"*Anything?*" he had asked her.

"*Anything at all,*" she had replied with the enigmatic smile he saw in his mind's eye as he stepped across the threshold from late-morning sun into the cool, dim interior. He had spent two restless nights in a Tel Aviv hotel, and early this morning, making certain no one was following him, either another of Ouyang's men or handlers sent by the Director, he had at last proceeded to the silversmith's.

The shop was illuminated by spotlights strategically placed for viewing the array of jewelry in waist-high glass cases that ringed the rear and side walls. It was filled with customers bending over, peering at the wares, asking to try on a necklace or a bracelet. Straight ahead, behind the cases, was a narrow door that presumably led to the workshop.

Bourne waited for an opening, then asked one of the young salesgirls for Apter Ben Asher.

When she asked his name, he said, "Just tell him a friend of Rebeka's is here to see him."

She gave him an odd look, before nodding perfunctorily. As she headed back to the rear door, she threw a quick glance at him over her shoulder. Bourne was sure he saw a flicker of fear cross her face like heat lightning.

Several moments passed while Bourne admired the silver work. When he looked up a small, rather roly-poly man in a heavily scarred leather apron had appeared in the doorway. He sported a full beard, shot through with a shade of gray that matched his hooded eyes. He had a wide face and thick lips. Rather than step out into the shop proper, he beckoned to Bourne with one long finger.

He said not a word of greeting as Bourne stepped past him into the workshop. Closing the door securely behind him, he crossed to a wooden stool and sat, studying Bourne, hands clasped in his lap.

"So you are the man she spoke about," he said at last. "What can I do for you?"

Bourne handed him the passport the Director had given him.

Ben Asher took it, flipped to the first page, swiveled around to peer at it under a bright light using a jeweler's loupe. At length, he grunted, then turned back, holding out the passport.

"It's gratifying to see that Mossad's expertise hasn't slipped."

Bourne gave him a wry half smile. "You'll have to repair the back cover."

Frowning, Ben Asher swiveled back around, placing the passport in the center of the circle of light. He found the slit right away.

"What was in here?"

"A tracking device."

"Ah." Ben Asher swiveled back to Bourne. "So you want a new name and electronic code for this."

"No," Bourne said, taking back the passport. "I want a new one."

"In other words, an entirely different identity."

"That's right. It needs to look used—immigration stamps and so forth."

"Naturally."

"Including one for Shanghai that's dated tomorrow."

Ben Asher stared at him for a moment. "What time is your flight?"

"Eight thirty this evening."

"Doable, certainly." Asher tapped his forefinger against his lower lip. "Now, what nationality should you be? Too bad you don't have any Asian blood in you; a Malaysian businessman would pass unnoticed in Shanghai." He studied Bourne's face. "I could make you Syrian, but that would only stir up trouble."

"How about Canadian?"

"Perfect! Bland as consommé. Do you want to choose the name, as well?"

"Let's make it Carl Halliday," Bourne said. "How much?"

"Now you offend me."

"All artists should be paid for their expertise."

Ben Asher smiled and shrugged. "Yes, but you see, you are the man Rebeka loved."

5

IT WAS A SAD homecoming for Maricruz. She could not help thinking that the traffic-choked crawl from the airport to smog-shrouded Mexico City—slow, tedious, never ending—was like a funeral procession.

The mansion on Castelar Street, in Colonia Polanco, overlooked Lincoln Park, where, she had been told, Jason Bourne had dragged the Mossad agent, whom her brother had knifed, after escaping from the house. She had never set eyes on Bourne, didn't know what he looked like, though she had a clear picture of him in her mind's eye. Bourne had killed her brother and her father, that much she knew—that much and no more. Her brother's demise was no great loss, but her father—well, that was another matter entirely.

She had expected the house of her childhood to look old and worn, cracks showing where it was in need of restuccoing, but the building that lay in front of her, surrounded by sparkling flower beds and riotous sprays of bougainvillea, gleamed in the wan sunlight as if just polished. The stone had been repointed and the stucco recently painted.

Inside lay bigger surprises still. She was met at the front door by Wendell Marsh, SteelTrap's lawyer, who had been handpicked by her father. More than that, Maceo Encarnación had put Marsh through school, sponsoring, then mentoring the orphan. He was now a de facto member of the family, though that would never occur to him.

"Maricruz." He embraced her. "So good to see you. It's been, what—?"

"Too long." Maricruz stepped back to look at Marsh. He was a broad-shouldered man with stark features, thick, swept-back hair that was almost entirely white. Marsh had been born a pessimist, a quality he had never been able to shake.

"I'm sorry for your loss," Marsh said now as he led her through the foyer and into the densely furnished living room. "I expect you'd like to have a look around. Take your time. When you're ready there are papers to sign."

She nodded absently, barely aware of him fading

away. She had always read that when you returned
to your childhood home it looked far smaller than
you remembered, possibly more shabby. She was,
therefore, somewhat taken aback at how huge the
rooms appeared, how dripping in expensive artwork, rugs, crystal chandeliers, and silver- and
gold-worked pieces that, to her eye, belonged in a
museum. Money was everywhere to be seen, but
her father was not. Jason Bourne had erased him
from the scene with the thoroughness of a professional. And yet so much of her father remained,
calling to her as she went from room to room, then
up the stairs to the second floor, down the hall to
the right, at the far end of which was her father's
bedroom suite.

Standing on the threshold, she pushed the door
open but did not walk in. Staring at the round bed,
she wondered how many women her father had
fucked since the morning she had walked in to
see him on top of some woman. A great many,
she would imagine. As for her mother's identity,
Ouyang had gathered conclusive proof only several months ago. She was certain that, on the other
side of the world, he was wondering if she was going to see Constanza Camargo. After all, her house
was just on the other side of the park, at the corner
of Alejandro Dumas and Luis G Urbina.

Entering the room, she skirted the bed and stood

by the window, gazing out at the trees of Lincoln Park. She thought she could see that house on the corner of Alejandro Dumas and Luis G Urbina, but possibly it was only her imagination. She conjured an image of her father, but almost immediately it vanished like a stone drowned in a lake. Unconsciously, through the shantung silk of her handbag, she touched a small jade box, precious as a Burmese pigeon-blood ruby. A gift from Ouyang, it contained a sheet of paper, folded twice into a small square. Written on the paper was the name and current address of Constanza, Maricruz's mother, who, Ouyang assured her, was still alive. She carried the box with her, touching it periodically as if it were a talisman.

Turning from the window, she went through her father's bedroom, opening closets and drawers, peering in, touching nothing, drifting from one intimate item to another like a wraith. And indeed, she felt like a ghost as she descended the stairs, silent as a breeze, returning to the living room where Wendell Marsh sat drinking strong black espresso, waiting patiently for her.

"The house seems odd, doesn't it," he said, "without him in it?"

Maricruz did not think so, not really. To her way of thinking, the house was always something of a museum; now it was fulfilling its purpose.

"Sit," Marsh said, indicating a chair beside the cocktail table. "Would you like an espresso, a beer, something stronger?"

Maricruz declined everything. Perversely, she resented the fact that Marsh was more familiar with the house than she was. It wasn't his house, she thought. It would never be his house.

"Let's get on with it, Wendell."

He inclined his head. "As you wish." He set out three copies of half a dozen documents and produced a pen from his inside breast pocket.

"You seem pale, Wendell. Are you feeling ill?"

He looked up and smiled wanly, obliged to wipe his forehead and the back of his neck with a linen handkerchief. "You know me, Maricruz. I never was a big fan of Mexico. And especially these days when the gutters are running red with blood and people are being separated from their heads—" He broke off, shuddering. "My apologies. This is your country."

"Well, it was." She took up the first set of papers but did not look at it. "Where is my father's cook, Maria-Elena?"

"Murdered, it would seem. Poisoned."

These people, Maricruz thought. *The last vestige of civilization has been ground into Mexico's bloodstained earth.* "And her daughter?" she said. "She did have a daughter?"

"Yes. The girl seems to have fallen off the face of the earth."

"No one can do that these days."

"Nevertheless..." Marsh spread his hands in a gesture of helplessness.

"Have you spent any time or resources in looking for her?"

He gestured at the papers spread out on the table. "I've had more important matters to attend to."

Maricruz nodded absently, at last glanced down at the sheaf she was holding. "Shall we begin?" She shuffled some pages, then paused to look up at Marsh, who waited patiently for, it seemed to her, the objections she was sure to voice.

"Who the hell is Gavin Royce?"

"He's the new CEO of SteelTrap."

"Not until I give my approval."

"He's your father's handpicked successor."

"I don't know him. I've never even met him."

"For the last eight years, he's been running SteelTrap's highly lucrative European operations. He knows the business inside and out, and he's successful."

"Even so, he's been based in London. Europeans do business differently than my father did."

"As I said, Gavin had your father's trust."

"Am I or am I not the executrix of Maceo Encarnación's estate?"

"Indeed you are," Marsh acknowledged. "But you've been in China for some time. In this, as in many matters of the estate, you must trust me, Maricruz."

She stared at Marsh—his open face, his thick body, his immaculately tailored suit. "You had my father's trust," she said at length. "Now you must earn mine."

Something hard entered Marsh's amiable expression; his eyes grew dark. "What would you have me do?" These words seemed forced out of him, as if by a punch to the solar plexus.

"I'll talk to Royce myself. If I think he's right for the job, offer him an eighteen-month contract."

For a moment Marsh seemed bewildered. "Eighteen months? He'll never go for that."

"He will," she said, "if he wants the job."

"But he's—For God's sake, Maricruz, be reasonable, the man is doing mammoth—He's been working twenty-hour days ever since your father's death."

"Then offer him incremental overrides tied to the success of the business. Use your powers of persuasion. Incentivize him, Wendell."

"I'll do my best."

"I trust you'll do better than that." She frowned. "I assume Royce doesn't know about the other part of my father's affairs."

"God, no. Your father was meticulous in keeping SteelTrap separate."

"Good enough." Her eyes flicked down to the next document, scanning the dense paragraphs of legalese. "Now, what about these SteelTrap annual reports? Tell me what they're really saying."

6

As HE CROSSED the arrivals hall, after passing through immigration as Lawrence Davidoff, Bourne paused at a kiosk to buy a pack of gum. It was a Chinese brand, a mix of obscure herbs that, according to the print on the pack, was guaranteed to clear the liver of impurities. Taking out a stick, Bourne began to chew, the bitter, acrid taste like burnt peat moss. When he threw away the wrapper, he also tossed out Davidoff's passport.

Outside in the heat and humidity, he joined a queue of people waiting for taxis. As he passed close to one, he dropped his pack of gum. Bending down to retrieve it, he removed the wad of gum from his mouth, pressed the Mossad tracking device into it, then affixed the wad to the undercarriage of the taxi.

Rising, he resumed his spot in the queue and, soon enough, was on his way into the city.

Bourne remembered Shanghai as if from a dream. Walking its streets, packed and teeming with riotous color and exotic smells, he could feel amnesiac memories shifting like frightening unseen beasts sunk in the depths of his unconscious, as if reacting to a sight or a smell.

The air was densely perfumed with shouted Shanghainese, a language wholly different from either the broader, almost languid Cantonese or the spiky, more formal Mandarin. A dialect of Northern Wu Chinese, it used to be largely unintelligible to inhabitants of Beijing and its surrounds. Nowadays, however, the younger entrepreneurial inhabitants of Shanghai often peppered their speech with Mandarin terms. In this largest of China's cities, the dialect among its over twenty-three million inhabitants had thus become the lingua franca of commerce, of quick wit, of youthful spirit, of the future.

Once English and Dutch trading houses lined the Bund, the city's famed harborside. Now beyond the promenade rose architectural marvels that formed the futuristic skyline of a post-modern city straight out of a science-fiction film. Bourne took public transportation to the edge of the old French Concession, then walked to Yu Yuan Road. The restaurant, a beautifully restored three-story villa, had been set for his rendezvous with Wei-Wei, the Director's agent in place.

Bourne was shown to the table reserved for Wei-Wei. It was on the second-floor veranda, which ran the entire length of the villa. From there he overlooked the tiny, immaculate garden, gently shaded by its central persimmon tree, and could see everyone who entered or exited the restaurant.

While he waited, he ordered smoked carp and slices of pork belly in a Shanghainese sauce that promised to be both pungent and slightly sweet.

He was almost finished with his meal when the hostess arrived, apologized profusely for interrupting his lunch, and with an elegant bow handed him a small, square envelope. Bourne looked around, noted nothing untoward, and slit open the envelope. On a small sheet of paper, folded in half, was a hastily written note.

Detained unavoidably by business. Please come to my apartment. There followed an address telling Bourne that Wei-Wei lived in an area of the large Huangpu district, a warren of tumbledown buildings, across the river from the Bund, whose shoulders seemed the only thing keeping their neighbors from crumbling into rubble.

Finished with his meal, Bourne threw some bills onto the table and left. On his way down the narrow wooden stairs to the garden entrance, he spotted a sleek-looking Shanghainese man in a gray suit, polished loafers, and an unnatural interest in him. The Shanghainese had been in the garden, a pot of tea on the small octagonal table at which he sat. Bourne had noticed him because he never took a sip of the tea the waitress had poured for him. When he wasn't looking at Bourne out of the corner of his eye, he was contemplating his nails, which were shining as if lacquered.

The man rose just after Bourne walked past and went languorously after him as if he had all the time in the world. Bourne headed east, toward the rustling treetops of Zhongshan Park. He passed by the brilliant flower displays and under the ornate triple arches. When he entered the park the modern city seemed to fade away, replaced by graceful tree-lined walks, where couples and the elderly strolled; playful fountains, filled with giant colored fish spouting water, and human-size bubbles, surrounded by happy children; and dynastic pavilions, rising like storks from placid lakes.

Bourne headed toward the largest of the pavilions, drifting into the crowds of tour groups. Attaching himself to a group of Swedes, he began talking to two sisters, pointing out the peculiarities of the families who had once lived in pavilions like these. The girls were soon giggling and asking for more stories. By this time, Bourne had come to the attention of the girls' parents. He introduced himself as a visiting professor of comparative linguistics, and proceeded to enchant the family by speaking in Shanghainese and then translating what he had said into Swedish and then English.

When the father asked Bourne to join the family for lunch, he thanked him but said he had an important appointment to get to.

"But," he went on, "you could do me a small favor."

"Of course," the father said.

"You see that suit over there with the slicked-back hair?" Bourne said. "He's been following me all morning. He's my girlfriend's brother. He doesn't want me dating his sister simply because I'm a Westerner, and I'm concerned he plans to do me some harm."

The father nodded sagely. "I've read about the ultra-conservative faction here."

"The Public Security Bureau."

"Right. Total xenophobes, aren't they?"

"Exactly," Bourne said. "Now I wonder if you'd help me lose him so I can meet with my girlfriend in peace."

"Ah!" The father's face broke out into a wide

grin. "Your important appointment." He tapped his thick forefinger against the side of his nose. "I understand a thousand percent." His eyes twinkled. "You have a plan, yes?"

"I do," Bourne said. "It involves all of you."

"Oh, Father, can we, can we?" the girls pleaded.

Their father, chuckling, pulled affectionately at their ears. "Helping true love is always a pleasure." He turned to Bourne. "Tell us what we have to do."

From a discreet distance, Wu Lin watched Bourne talking to the Swedish family. The fact that they were all laughing confused him. Surely this wasn't a professional rendezvous, not with children present. At one point, he wondered whether he was following the right foreigner, since they so often looked disconcertingly alike, but checking the photo sent to him on his mobile confirmed he did, indeed, have the right man.

Now Bourne had taken the hands of the two girls, who were leading him deeper into the pavilion. The mother and father trailed behind, blocking Wu Lin's view of his quarry. Spurred by a twinge of anxiety, he hurried forward, slipping into the current of tourists swirling through the myriad rooms and verandas, which branched and rebranched like the limbs of an ancient tree.

Within moments he caught up with the mother and father, who were still laughing, no doubt at something their daughters said. Relieved to have picked them up so quickly, Wu Lin strolled after them, in no hurry now that he had the family in view.

But ten minutes later, in another section of the pavilion, having realized that he hadn't actually seen Bourne or the girls during that time, he pushed ahead. Coming up on the left flank of the mother and father, he discovered, to his dismay, that neither the girls nor Bourne were anywhere in sight.

Rushing past them, he glimpsed the girls through a forest of legs, sitting cross-legged, side by side on the edge of one of the far verandas. There was no sign of Bourne. The mother and father joined their children, crouched down, speaking in a language Wu Lin could not understand.

With a string of curses, Wu Lin broke away from the family, making his way through the previously unexplored sections of the pavilion. His progress was slow, constantly impeded by the press of people, shuffling like cattle through the endless rooms.

Bourne watched his Shanghainese tail searching in vain for him. He could have exited the pavilion, and the park itself, leaving him lost and bewildered, but he had another goal in mind. The quarry had decided to become the hunter, tailing the man back to the people who had sent him. This was essential, because someone had latched onto him almost as soon as he had arrived in Shanghai. What made this tail even more disturbing was that only the Director, Ophir, and a select number of operatives in the Mossad legends department knew he had been sent here.

For the next thirty minutes Bourne tailed the Shanghainese around the pavilion, and then in concentric circles radiating out through the park, moving farther and farther away from the pavilion. This methodical search pattern proved the man was a professional, which in China meant, more than likely, a federal agency.

This was not a promising start to his mission, and Bourne had to stifle the urge to bring the man in off the street and interrogate him about his identity and that of his employer. In another country he might have done just that. But this was China. Here, a low profile meant no profile at all. Anything that would draw attention to himself was out of the question.

The Shanghainese stopped at a crosswalk and checked his watch. Abruptly, he hurried off to the southwest. Bourne followed him for another fif-

teen or twenty minutes. The traffic was almost at a
standstill; at this time of the day traveling on foot
was the best way to get across town.

Bourne watched from across the street as the
Shanghainese paused in front of a school, went up
the steps just as a spate of kids, all dressed iden-
tically, came trooping out the doors. One of them,
obviously the man's son, came up to him. He was
accompanied by a teacher or an administrator—
it was impossible to tell which. Bourne's tail dismissed his son to play with his friends while he and
the official spoke briefly. The official's serious
face grew darker the longer Bourne's tail spoke.
Then he nodded curtly, in obvious dismissal.
Bourne's tail called to his son and, together, the
two went down the steps and walked away.

In preparation for the official returning inside the
school, Bourne crossed the street in time to see
a gleaming white Mercedes sedan pull up to the
curb. As if jabbed with a live electrical wire, the
official hurried down the steps.

From his angle, Bourne could see the smoked
glass of the rear window slide down. The official
bent down to speak to the car's inhabitant. Bourne,
changing his angle of view, peered into the interior. He recognized the man the school official was
talking with, and a shock went through him. It was
Colonel Sun.

* * *

Colonel Sun was not, at the moment, a happy man.

"Get in the car," he snapped at Go Han. "Bent over like that you're impersonating a street urchin."

The middle school teacher opened the door and dutifully slid in beside Colonel Sun.

"How did Wu Lin lose Bourne?"

"I don't know, Colonel." Go Han hung his head. "Bourne somehow ingratiated himself with a family of tourists. They shielded him as he made his escape."

Colonel Sun grunted as he sat back in the plush seat. "That means Bourne knew he was being followed."

"He might have simply been taking basic precautions." Go Han immediately wilted beneath Colonel Sun's withering gaze.

"You don't know this man," Colonel Sun said. "You have no idea what he's capable of, the lengths to which he'll go to kill someone, the depravity of his actions." He flicked a hand. "Get out! You're of no further use to me."

It was when Colonel Sun reached over to close the door that he caught a glimpse of Bourne out of the corner of his eye. Briefly, he considered

whether this was deliberate, but quickly determined that it didn't matter.

Ordering the driver to start the car, Colonel Sun
had him drive around the block. When the car, nosing slowly in the traffic, reached the place where
he had seen Bourne, the foreign agent was no
longer there. Naturally, Colonel Sun hadn't expected him to be, but he also knew Bourne
wouldn't be far away. After their encounter in
Rome, Bourne was not about to let Colonel Sun
out of his sight. Colonel Sun used the car's direct
line to order his men to cordon off the area.

"Begin with a six-block square, using my car's
position as the center," he told his adjutant, "then
on my order slowly move in. I want a house-to-
house search. Make certain all the men have the
same photo of Bourne I have." Thinking about
how Minister Ouyang had promised to reward
him, he felt a hot surge of purpose grip him. "No
mistakes, hear me?" he barked into the phone before hanging up.

Over his driver's objection, Colonel Sun exited
the car while it was still moving. It was imperative
now that Bourne not only see him but follow him.
He had set himself as the bait in a trap that was
about to close on his nemesis.

And he thought, *This time, I'll have him.*

7

WHEN BOURNE SAW Colonel Sun emerge from the still-moving car, he knew Sun had taken the bait.

Once he had identified Sun, his first objective was to lure him out of the car. He felt this would be best accomplished by allowing Sun to catch a glimpse of him. Then he had melted back into a place of temporary concealment to determine if his ruse would work.

It amused him to see Colonel Sun looking around like a tourist while he, Bourne, stood still amid the shadows, and watched. Months ago, before Rebeka was murdered, Bourne had been with her in Rome. She had been abducted—not an easy thing to do to a Mossad agent, especially Rebeka. She had been taken to the Roman crypts below the

Appian Way, the ancient highway to the imperial city.

Following her down, Bourne had almost been killed by Colonel Sun in the eternal dimness of the crypts. And then, after Rebeka and her handler, Ophir, had left, Sun had tried again, resulting in the deaths of two of his men.

Now Colonel Sun looked at his watch. It was a furtive glance, and Bourne, on the lookout for even the smallest anomaly, began to sense what was happening. While he was going after Sun, the colonel was coming after him with his superior manpower. As Bourne watched him from the shadows, Sun's men were no doubt drawing a cordon around the area.

In any other country, simple escape would suffice, but not here in China. An extra dimension was called for. Humiliation was the name of the game: Colonel Sun needed to lose face in front of his men.

Bourne turned, for the moment no longer interested in Sun's movements. He moved through the crowded streets. Stopping at a men's store, he bought a dress shirt and tie, donned them, then picked out a Chinese-style cap and slammed it on his head, pulling the front down over his forehead. When he exited the store it was with a pronounced limp.

Thus disguised, he proceeded directly away from where he and Sun had seen each other, which he considered ground zero. Soon enough he came upon a police officer, one of several, he could see, advancing in what could only be a tightening cordon.

Bourne brushed against the officer as they were passing each other. The officer stopped, grabbed Bourne by the arm.

"What d'you think you're doing?" he said gruffly.

"Have I offended you by walking down the street?" Bourne replied in the exact same tone of voice.

"I don't like your attitude," the cop said.

Bourne jerked his arm free. "And I don't like yours."

"We'll see about that." The cop pulled his gun and shoved Bourne into the shadows of a doorway.

The instant they were out of sight of the other officers, Bourne slammed the heel of his hand into the cop's nose, then punched him hard in the throat. As the officer collapsed, Bourne dragged him inside the building. The entryway was narrow, dim, and smelled of stale frying oil.

Past the steep flight of stairs was a small space that led out to a rear door. Bourne went to work and, moments later, was dressed in the officer's uniform, the cop's ID safely tucked in his breast pocket. Nothing fit quite right, as the cop was somewhat shorter than Bourne, but it would have to do. As for the officer himself, Bourne stuffed him into the musty space behind the stairs where it was so dark no one was likely to notice him.

Back out in the street, he hurried along to take up his officer's place in the cordon. A block later, as he approached ground zero, he broke off, heading directly for Colonel Sun's immaculate white Mercedes. Approaching on the driver's side, he rapped his knuckles on the driver's smoked window. As the window slid down, Bourne leaned in, delivering three short, sharp blows that rendered the driver unconscious.

Popping open the door lock, he kicked the driver into the passenger's foot well and slid behind the wheel. Behind him was a thick glass partition that separated him from passengers in the backseat, which was, at the moment, empty.

Firing up the engine, Bourne waited for a slot in the sluggish traffic, pulled out, and then started a U-turn. Startled shouts and a cacophony of blaring horns were instantaneous. However, drivers, perhaps intimidated by the big Mercedes sedan, braked to allow him to head in the direction of Colonel Sun.

By this time the cordon commander had appeared and was talking with Sun. If Bourne had been on the sidewalk, they would have been dead ahead. A heartbeat later, having turned the wheel sharply, he drove the Mercedes up over the curb and onto the sidewalk, scattering pedestrians like the bow wave of a battleship.

The cordon commander was the first to see the car hurtling toward him and his boss. In a flash, he drew his sidearm and fired. The windshield should have shattered, but this was Colonel Sun's car, and it was specially reinforced. The bullet pinged off the glass. The commander's eyes opened wide. He had just enough time to shove Colonel Sun aside before the Mercedes struck him full-on, hurling his broken body three feet into the air.

Immediately Bourne roared away, half on, half off the sidewalk. When the masses of pedestrians became untenable, he crossed the lanes and went up onto the median, mowing down flower beds and small ornamental evergreen bushes as he went.

He was heading for the Dapu Tunnel that would take him across the river, out of the glittering high-rises and into the old district of ancient red-lacquered buildings, narrow streets, charcoal-cooked-food vendors, and traffic-free pedestrian malls. He chose this route because the Elevated Inner Ring Road and its attendant bridges were too exposed.

Just as he entered the tunnel, sirens rose up behind him. Glancing in the rearview mirror, he saw three police motorcycles screaming down the road in pursuit. He could imagine a thoroughly chagrined Colonel Sun frantically phoning police commanders in all quarters of the city in an effort to run down his own white Mercedes. In fact, turning on the communications system embedded in the front panel display he actually heard Sun's voice, raised in anger and, if Bourne was any judge of tone, humiliation, spraying orders just as Bourne had figured. He gave off a hard bark of laughter, then settled in earnest to deal with both the traffic ahead of him and the pursuing motorcycles.

His brain instantaneously vectored the information his eyes took in. Like a chess game on a massive scale, he saw his next three or four moves as gaps in the traffic opened and closed like trapdoors. In addition, he was supremely protected within the steel-and-titanium–reinforced panels of the Mercedes.

Swerving into the left-hand lane, he stepped on the accelerator and, blaring his horn, tapped the car ahead of him. He could see a band of the terrified driver's face in his rearview mirror, as he frantically tried to get out of the Mercedes's way.

The motorcycles, with more maneuverability, were gaining on him. That was quite all right with him; in fact, it was what he was counting on. The car in front of him veered to the right, clipping the rear fender of another vehicle in the process.

Bourne put on another burst of speed, obliging the lead motorcycle to do the same in order to run up behind him. Checking his off-side mirror, Bourne's brain again factored vectors of speed and distance converging on a single point.

The instant the lead motorcycle reached that point, Bourne trod hard on the brakes. The Mercedes's tires screeched in protest as its forward momentum was stalled. The lead motorcycle was too close for the driver to have time to react. Instead, he drove the motorcycle into the rear of the Mercedes with such force that he was launched into the air as if shot from a cannon. While his motorcycle crumpled beneath the impact with the massive Mercedes, he cartwheeled head-over-heels, struck the hood of the car in front of Bourne, then slid off.

Whether the Mercedes was the first to strike him or one of the cars slewing every which way as their drivers panicked, Bourne never knew. He was off and running, taking advantage of the growing chaos to worm his way through the gaps in the traffic flow.

The traffic was now lighter as the vehicles behind him at the crash site were at a complete standstill, but he also had two more motorcycles to handle. Their drivers, having witnessed the rude demise of their comrade, had their pistols out and were not being shy about firing at the Mercedes. They might as well have been shooting at a Sherman tank for all the effect the bullets had on the bodywork.

Bourne swerved again, but now there was a vexing knot of traffic just in front of him with no discernible gaps for him to maneuver through. He was forced to slow down and, in so doing, allowed one of the remaining motorcycles to come up alongside.

The cop, lips drawn back from ivory teeth, grinned fiercely and tried to hammer out the side window with the butt of his pistol. Bourne jerked the wheel to the left, sandwiching the motorcycle between the Mercedes and the tunnel wall. Sparks flew at the grinding of metal against concrete as a line of ceramic tiles burst apart, flinging themselves like shrapnel.

The cop instinctively put his arm up to shield his face, and Bourne took advantage by pressing the side of the Mercedes harder against the motorcycle. The shrapnel kept exploding, but now the cop pressed the muzzle of his pistol against the glass of the side window.

The resulting percussion shattered the glass, but

also flung the cop against the tunnel wall. He lost his balance, fell over, his left leg instantly crushed against the wall, skin and sinew flayed off.

Somehow he regained his balance and, grimacing against the pain, aimed the gun at Bourne's head. Bourne slammed open the Mercedes's door. It hit the cop like a thrown brick. As he rocked back his head smashed against the wall then, as he slid down, the rear wheel of his motorcycle.

Two down, one to go, Bourne thought.

As it had farther back, the interaction between Mercedes and motorcycle dispersed the knot of traffic ahead of him, with vehicles either pulling as far away from the incipient crash as they could or speeding up and out the far end of the tunnel.

Bourne heard the deep thrumming of the third motorcycle even before it came into view, snaking its way through the snarl of idled vehicles he'd left in his wake. People were out of their cars, staring in disbelief at the mangled motorcycle and its bloody, shredded driver.

He was reminded that he hadn't heard Colonel Sun's voice since he had entered the tunnel. He turned up the volume on the police radio, but heard only the occasional lightning-like crackle of static. He felt a warmth crawling down the left side of his face. Leaning to his right he glanced at his reflection in the rearview mirror, saw the rivulets of blood caused by the force of the glass shards striking him.

Hearing the roar of the last motorcycle, he shifted back, saw its head-on silhouette growing in the mirror. He swerved to the right; the motorcycle followed. This driver was smart enough not to get too close; he was merely shadowing Bourne move for move, making sure he stayed with him, no matter what.

The far end of the tunnel was rapidly approaching. Something seemed to be wrong; the opening was far too bright, as if all the traffic ahead of him had been magically swept away by an immense hand.

Then the Mercedes was through the tunnel. In an instant Bourne saw the last motorcycle break off and swerve to the side. Mind racing, he understood why there had been no chatter on the police band, why the final motorcycle had shadowed him until the last moment, why there were no vehicles ahead of him.

Three minutes later, the missile fired from a shoulder-mounted launcher sped toward the Mercedes, impacting it moments later. The resulting explosion could be seen for miles.

8

JIDAN WAS POSSESSED of an amphibian calm,
Maricruz thought, as she lay back in her father's
large and opulent bathtub. The taps and faucets
were made of jade and lapis, the surround of
an enormous solid slab of jasper. Far too gaudy
for her tastes, but typical of Maceo Encarnación,
who had done everything with breathtaking ex-
cess.

This was why, she thought now, as she arched
her back, her heavy breasts crowned with dark
nipples rising out of the water like questing sea
creatures, she had once been in love with Jidan.
He was the precise polar opposite of all the hot-
blooded males, who acted first, considered afterward, among whom she had grown up.

At first, calmness was something Maricruz came

to respect. Amid the incessant clamor of her cities—Mexico City and Beijing—the interior spaces Jidan designed and provided were oases of reverential silence to be cherished, only broken, now and again, by her shouts and cries of ecstasy. Those days seemed long gone.

Her large, coffee-colored eyes finally lit upon the small jade box Jidan had given her before she had left Beijing. That Jidan had discovered the identity of her mother, a mother she had never known, a mother from whose arms her father had taken her, to be raised as he alone saw fit, was miracle enough, Maricruz thought, but that she was still alive was beyond her imagining. Though she had opened the box, she had yet to unfold the paper inside and read the name of her mother. She wondered if she ever would.

Her heart was torn by complex emotions: a desire to be held by the woman who had borne her, anger at her for allowing her baby girl to be taken away, curiosity as to why, all these years, she had made no attempt to contact her daughter.

The jade box gleamed, its engraved pair of dragons seeming to mock her. Of course, her rational mind knew that no man and certainly no woman could stand against her father once he had made up his mind. Her mother had had no choice but to acquiesce to his wishes. But still . . .

She heard a sudden rustling in the bedroom suite beyond the closed bathroom door.

"Wendell," she called, "is that you?"

"Yes, Maricruz, I'm sorry to disturb you. I was looking for certain papers of your father's."

"Perhaps I can help you."

"Perhaps. When you're finished with your bath."

"I'm finished now, Wendell," she said.

"I don't under—"

"No reason to be shy. Come in."

"I don't think that would be a good idea, Maricruz."

She could hear by the sound of his voice that he was just outside the door now. "But I do, Wendell."

The doorknob turned, slowly at first, then more rapidly as he pushed the door open. He stood on the threshold, his eyes drinking in her lush, firm body.

His mouth opened. "Oh, God," he said softly.

"Wendell, it occurs to me," Maricruz said, ignoring his gaping mouth, "I know nothing about you personally. I've read your CV, of course, but there's more to a man than his academic achievements, don't you think?"

Marsh said nothing. Having gazed upon the goddess Medusa, he looked as if he had been turned to stone.

"I see the cat's got your tongue," she said with a knowing smile. "No matter. I fancy myself an excellent judge of character. I'll tell you what you're like. You only have to answer yes or no." She cocked her head, her full lips in a moue. "Surely you're up to the task."

He coughed drily, tried to say something, failed.

Maricruz looked him up and down before settling her eyes again on his face. "Let's see, either you're divorced or you've never married. Either way, you've no children."

"Divorced," Marsh managed to croak. "No children."

"No girlfriend, either," Maricruz said. "At least, not for some time."

Marsh swallowed, nodded mechanically. His eyes never left the glistening hemispheres of her naked breasts.

"Hmmm. So how do you get your rocks off, Wendell?" She stared pointedly at the bulge in his trousers. "You're not asexual, I can see that." She sat up suddenly, her breasts bobbing provocatively. "Whores, prostitutes, call girls, escorts. They're your sort of thing, aren't they?"

Marsh did not reply, but his reddened face revealed the truth of her statement.

"No need to be embarrassed, Wendell. Sex is a natural human desire." She rose out of the bath and, without toweling off, back arched, shoulders squared, powerful thighs propelling her forward, crossed the tile floor and pressed her gleaming naked body against his.

He gave a strangled cry but did not recoil. With a languid smile, Maricruz snaked her right arm between them and squeezed the growing lump between his thighs.

"Nice and thick, Wendell," she whispered in his ear. "I like that."

She pushed forward and Marsh took a step back. They continued this way, stuck together, his clothes now sopping wet, as she maneuvered him across her father's vast bedroom. When the back of Marsh's legs came up against the bed, Maricruz leaned her upper torso forward, applying enough pressure that he tumbled backward.

Sitting astride him, she began to pluck off his clothes. Water dripped from her hair, off the erect tips of her breasts. Slowly, his trembling hands rose up to cup her breasts.

"Do you like that, Wendell?" She stripped off his sodden shirt. "I'll just bet you do."

He squeezed her nipples and her eyes closed briefly.

Her hands worked faster, then, pulling down his zipper, unbuckling his belt, peeling his trousers away. She unfolded him like an origami sculpture.

She leaned into him, her flat belly fluttering. "Here's what I like, Wendell."

The percussion blast wave that burst outward when the missile impacted with Colonel Sun's white Mercedes slammed into Bourne as he rolled across the pavement, shoved him off the road entirely and into a drainage ditch, where he was protected from the terrible effects of the shredded car, bits like shrapnel, like miniature missiles themselves, radiating out from the point of impact.

Numb and temporarily deaf, Bourne lay in the ditch unmoving. He watched the sky turn from orange to yellow to smoky gray, and then to the clear blue it had been in the first moments he had exited the tunnel.

He tried to shake off the numbness, felt only a rumble deep in his bones. Then all of a sudden his hearing returned with an unpleasant *pop* and, looking up, he saw the approaching police helo.

Scrambling out of the ditch, he ran toward the red-lacquered buildings, gilt signs, and narrow streets of Huangpu.

What was left of the white Mercedes was still burning hotly when the helo landed a safe distance away. The moment it alit, Colonel Sun pushed open the door and leapt out. He was followed closely by another man in army uniform.

"Who's responsible for this?" he cried, pointing to the fire. "Give me a name!"

An officer appeared, saluted, and pointed to the soldier who had fired the missile. Colonel Sun stalked over to the man, who seemed to turn to water as Sun closed on him.

"What did you think you were doing?"

"Following orders, sir," the soldier said fearfully.

Colonel Sun's black eyes bored into the man with a terrible intensity. "Your orders were to aim *in front* of the vehicle, not *at* it."

He lashed the man across the face, leaving a trail of fresh blood and ripped flesh. Thinking of what he was going to tell Ouyang, he hit the man again and again until he slid to his knees. Bourne wasn't meant to die, not here, not now. Not yet. Colonel Sun kicked the man so hard he fell over backward.

"Get this dog out of my sight," Sun snapped at the officer.

After the man was hustled away, Colonel Sun turned to the man who had been in the helo with him. "Captain Lim, as soon as the fire has burned itself out, get a forensics team in there. I want a definitive ID on the driver as quickly as possible."

* * *

Wow." Wendell Marsh, lying sweat-slick on his late boss's bed, stared at Maricruz's flawless back as she sat up. "When can we do that again?"

Maricruz laughed. "Don't mistake me for one of your call girls, Wendell."

"I'm just asking—"

"I do the asking, Wendell. You would do well to remember that."

He watched her, a little frightened now. He was in a foreign country that gave him the willies, in a situation suddenly beyond his understanding. He waited, listening to his own breath sough in and out of his half-open mouth, until the silence weighed too heavily on him.

"I meant no disrespect, Maricruz."

"Of course you did. That's just your way. You never learned how to treat a woman."

Certainly not a woman like you, he thought, but wisely kept his own counsel.

Maricruz sighed deeply. "You know, Wendell, you've been a bad, bad boy."

His heart skipped a beat, forcing him to sit up, pushing the pillow behind him. "What d'you mean?"

"Do you really think I'd meet with you without gathering all the information on you I could? And what you did, Wendell, was embezzle money from my father."

Marsh's blood pressure went sky-high; he felt an unpleasant heat traveling through his body like an invisible serpent. "I mean to pay it back, Maricruz. Every cent of it. In fact, I've already started to—"

"Why did you do it?" She turned on him now, and he quailed to see the force and determination on her face. "My father trusted you."

Marsh hung his head. "The money wasn't for me, it was for my sister. She married a very rich, very abusive man. She thought she loved him, thought she could change him but..." He shrugged. "I finally convinced her to leave him. In retaliation, he came down on her with a legal team that threatened her, tried to strip her of all her rights. I had no choice but to find her the best defense money could buy. The problem was, that team of lawyers and private investigators was way beyond even my means."

Maricruz considered this for a moment. She already knew he was telling the truth, but the mess he had made had to be cleaned up before they could go forward. "Why didn't you ask my father for the money?"

"You mean a loan?"

"To fight such a man, he would have given it to you."

Marsh looked away. "I was ashamed."

"So instead you just took the money."

"I was sure I could pay it back before anyone discovered it, but the divorce proceedings went on longer, and then I needed more money, and it was too late." He looked back at her. "Is it too late with you?"

She studied him for a moment. "Wendell, do you know what *aliyah* means?"

He shook his head.

"I'm not surprised. *Aliyah* is a Hebrew word. It means 'penance' or 'atonement.' You will perform an *aliyah* for me, Wendell."

He felt a cooling wave of relief flush through him that obliterated the serpent of fire. "Yes, Maricruz. Of course I will."

"The *aliyah* will be difficult, Wendell, and not without a considerable amount of danger. However, when you have completed it, I will know that I can trust you again."

Wei-Wei, the Mossad agent in place whose mysterious pressing business had caused him to postpone the meet with Bourne, lived on Jiujiaochang Road, just down the block from the gaudy facade of the China Citic Bank and Fanghua pearl shop. In the distance, a clutch of ugly pastel-colored high-rises marred the skyline like chewed nails on a dowager's scented hand.

Wei-Wei's apartment was on the second floor, above the China Beauty shop, where women were trying on all manner of patterned silk scarves. Bourne was still slightly numb, his digits tingly, not totally at his command. On the way he stopped at another clothes shop and, for the second time, bought a new wardrobe, dropping his burned and torn jacket, shirt, and trousers into the trash bin next to the sink in the filthy toilet. He was sorry to see his military uniform go, but he had no choice; it smelled like singed hair and roasted metal.

Continuing his walk, he paused at a street vendor's stall to eat cubes of roast pork belly on a bamboo stick, washing the protein down with two bottles of Coke so chilled, shards of ice were floating in them. By the time he was finished consuming the food, his fingers had stopped tingling and his head had cleared.

On reaching Jiujiaochang Road, he spent the next several minutes checking the immediate vicinity. While he watched the passersby, he listened to snatches of their conversations. He neither saw nor heard anything out of the ordinary. When a siren sounded, it was far away, headed in other directions. At length, he ducked through the front door to Wei-Wei's building. It was narrow, as was the entryway, which smelled of hot oil and sizzling Sichuan peppercorns. The stairs rose steeply ahead of him, creaking with every step he took.

On the second-floor landing the cooking smells were stronger. Even out here, the oil from the burst peppercorns stung his eyes. Wei-Wei's apartment was at the far end of the landing, in the back. As he passed a grime-coated window, he peered out, could see a narrow alley abutted by the over-lapping tiles of steeply pitched rooftops on the neighboring buildings.

Wei-Wei's doorbell was out of order, so he knocked on the door, then harder. There was no response. He put his ear against the door. At first he could hear nothing but what sounded like the wind soughing through the apartment, as if Wei-Wei had left the window open. Then, following his third knock, a brief rustling came to him, as of stiff clothes rubbing against flesh. Still, Wei-Wei didn't answer.

Standing back, Bourne kicked the door in, and was immediately confronted by a Shanghainese police office pointing a gun at him.

"Who are you?" he said in an affected and offi-cious voice. "What are you doing breaking into a private citizen's home?"

"Wei-Wei is a friend of mine," Bourne said. He

showed the cop his Carl Halliday passport. "From time to time, we do a little business."

The cop's eyes narrowed. "What sort of business?" The muzzle of his service pistol never wavered from Bourne's chest.

"Nothing major," Bourne said. "Just, from time to time, shipments of gum."

"Gum?"

"Chewing gum." Bourne produced the pack he had purchased at the airport and held it out. "Chinese herbs. See? Canadians are nuts for Chinese herbs."

Then Bourne frowned as he put away the pack of gum. "Where is my friend? Where's Wei-Wei?"

The cop beckoned with his free hand and he and Bourne went into the tiny bedroom, where the man known as Wei-Wei was hanging from a rope looped over a wooden rafter.

"Seems a competitor got to him," the cop said. He gestured with his gun. "I'll have to ask you to leave. The forensics team is on its way. I can question you in the hallway."

Bourne was about to protest when he heard a sound like that of a small box closing. The cop's eyes opened wide, his lips pulled back from his nicotine-stained teeth, and he pitched forward into Bourne's arms.

A tiny dart stuck out the side of his neck.

9

DANI AMIT, head of Collections, entered Director Yadin's office with a grim look on his face. Across from Yadin sat Amir Ophir.

"We've lost Davidoff," Amit said.

The Director frowned. "What d'you mean? He's not in Shanghai?"

"He may be," Amit said, "or he may not."

"I think you'd better explain yourself," Ophir said.

Amit gave Ophir merely a glance. Using a tablet computer, he pulled up a short video on the Director's large monitor, which took up most of the wall opposite the desk. In it, the three men saw Bourne going through passport control.

"This comes from the Shanghai airport," Amit said. "Bourne boarded the flight on the ticket we provided for him, deplaned, and, as you can see, arrived safely in Shanghai as Lawrence Davidoff, the legend we concocted for him."

Yadin spread his hands. "So what's the problem?"

Amit passed a hand across his forehead. "Ever since then, he's been going around the city, stopping here and there, in what seems to be a completely random pattern."

"You have a printout of the stops?" Ophir said.

Amit touched the tablet's screen and the video vanished, supplanted by a list of street addresses.

"Maybe he's trying to shake a tail," Ophir said.

Amit shook his head. "It's been going on for hours now."

Director Yadin's frown deepened. "Our agent in place hasn't checked in yet." He glanced at his watch. "He and Bourne should be meeting anytime now." He looked away from the screen to the faces of the two other men in the room. "I want to give Bourne his lead. Let's give him some more time."

"What if Bourne has gone off the grid?" Amit said. "It would mean he's repeating a dangerous pattern he was known for with the Americans."

"He knows too much of our plans, Director." Ophir's tone, if not his words, was a subtle rebuke of Yadin's faith in the foreigner. "As I've said before, he's not one of us."

The Director absorbed everything that had been said. Abruptly, his expression changed. He had made up his mind.

"Amit, this is a surveillance matter. I think we ought to let Collections take charge."

Ophir did not want to let this happen. "Sir, Retzach is an hour's flight from Shanghai."

"Retzach is an assassin," Amit said.

"He's much more," Ophir said, pressing hard to keep the assignment. "And he has a great deal of experience in China."

The Director pondered for some time. "For the moment, do nothing, Amir. Understand?"

"*Elef Ahuz*," a thousand percent, Ophir said as, behind his back, he punched in Retzach's number on his mobile.

There was a time, Maricruz thought, sitting next to Wendell Marsh in the backseat of a heavily defended armored vehicle, when she would have relished this kind of confrontation. When she would have, in fact, demanded that her father take her along instead of her brother, who had never been a great military mind. Now it was just business. Now her life was far away, on the Pacific Rim. Now she lived and worked and schemed with grown-ups.

These perpetual adolescents with their guns and

knives and machetes were tin soldiers, preying on the weak, the cowed, the defenseless. It enraged her that they murdered women. In Ciudad Juárez alone, thousands of women and girls had either disappeared or been killed from 2008 to the present. And while it was true that some of them had been killed in family disputes, the truth was a vast majority fell easy victims to the drug cartels.

So what did the cartel leaders know of the world beyond Mexico's bloodied borders? They would only act—and react—one way. That she could predict their moves and decisions did not necessarily make them any less deadly. Their guns were always loaded, their rage constantly at hair-trigger level. She knew they would not hesitate to kill anyone, at any time. Not only were they lawless, they were uncivilized. They simply did not give a shit.

She stared out the small, square window as she thought these thoughts. The bulletproof glass was so thick, so encoded with titanium filaments, that the world of her childhood bore no resemblance to her memories as it slid by.

She fingered the hand-hewn grips of the Bersa Thunder .380 holstered at her waist. A smaller pistol—a .25—was strapped to her leg at the top of her right boot. In fact, she carried more weapons than a Roman centurion marching onto the battlefield.

A battlefield was precisely where she was headed now. She had called Felipe Matamoros on her mobile. Matamoros was the head of Los Zetas, the one drug lord she needed to see. The Gulf cartel had been decimated by Los Zetas to the point that they were merely vestigial, and as for the Sinaloa—still the largest cartel in numbers—Los Zetas had for some months now been eating away at their traditional territory. It was only a matter of time before Raul Giron, head of the Sinaloa, would lose what control he had left. The strategies devised by the paramilitary minds at the core of Los Zetas were too much for the old-school peasant drug overlords. After she briefed Marsh, they had been met outside her father's house by a contingent of fifteen heavily armed men, who led them to the waiting armored vehicle, and they had set off for the place Matamoros had indicated.

Marsh, stirring beside her, brought her back.

"Why did you do it?" he said.

"Do what?" Her mind was still on today's strategies.

"Seduce me."

She glanced over at him and shrugged. "How else was I to know what kind of man you are?"

"You mean it was a test?"

"To keep you or to send you packing, yes."

He shook his head in disbelief. "I don't see what you could—"

"In the throes of sex, men reveal parts of themselves even they are not aware of. There's something in you, Wendell, something I don't want to let go of."

"You mean I can be of use to you."

"That's a poor and inaccurate way of putting it. I sensed I could trust you, that you might have learned from your transgression."

"That I have."

"Well then, our coupling was a success"—she smiled in that way that could shrivel another woman and send shivers down a man's back—"for both of us."

Marsh stared at the metal floor between his feet. She sensed him brooding and, before the fear set in, she said, "You're perfect for your role in this little play of ours."

"Play?" Marsh said. "Is that what you call a meeting with the most feared man in Mexico?"

She put a hand on his forearm. "*Cálmate, Juanito, por favor*." She smiled in that winning way of hers. "This is all foreordained. My father's power protects us better than these armed men."

"Then why are they here?"

Her smile widened. "*Machismo*, Wendell, is the watchword by which I have lived my life. I had no choice. This is why I chose to leave Mexico, which still today is no place for a common woman. But now I come back to Mexico as a citizen of the world. This is an unknown to men like Matamoros. The world beyond Mexico is a mystery to men like him. They know what they know, and that's all. Their knowledge of their world is complete, it's what makes them secure. But it also limits them."

"But Matamoros is different," Marsh said. "He was trained by the Mexican military."

"And you think the military is any different from the cartels?" She shook her head. "Only in how it wages war. But you see, Wendell, for all of the military's superiority in weapons, helicopters, manpower, it is no match for the cartels, whose fervor of purpose makes them stronger. They bend the Mexican state to their will. Everything else is extraneous and of no interest to them.

"But I bring them a means to their end—drugs and money. Here in Mexico, these are the only two things that must be respected."

By this time they had reached the northern precincts of the Distrito Federal. They made a right, then another, and finally a left. At the end of the street, they turned into a curving driveway that led to an enormous house of pale pink stucco, in the Mexican hacienda style. The instant their vehicle began to crunch over the crushed-shell drive, men appeared from the feathered palm-frond shadows around the house. They were grim-faced and clearly armed, but they made no threatening move. It was as if they were statues strewn about the property, but Maricruz was under no illusions. At the drop of a hat they could turn into land mines.

The vehicle ground to a stop in front of a country-style portico. Her men emerged first but, following her orders, stayed within a handbreadth of the vehicle.

"Come," Maricruz said to Marsh as she stepped out onto cartel soil. The front door was painted the particular shade of blue the Mexicans referred to as *azul*. It swung inward, and a massive human being stepped across the lintel. *This must be Juan Ruiz*, she thought, one of Matamoros's right-hand men. He was as big as a sumo wrestler and, according to her information, as deadly as a puff adder.

Any hesitation would be perceived as a sign of weakness, she knew, so she strode purposely forward. She had not been exaggerating her father's power and influence with these people to Marsh, but she had perhaps underplayed the innate disadvantage of being a female in this world of primal crime and animal mayhem. She had her father's reputation to uphold, something she had vowed to do from the moment news of his death had reached her in Beijing.

"Juan Ruiz?" Maricruz said.

Juan Ruiz nodded almost imperceptibly as Maricruz stepped up to his level. Then his dead-stone eyes refocused on Wendell Marsh.

"Who?" he said. "Why?"

Language was not his forte. That, she knew, would be left to Diego de la Luna, Matamoros's other right-hand man.

"Juan Ruiz, I am pleased to introduce Wendell Marsh."

"Señor Matamoros said one person. Here are two."

"Señor Marsh was my father's longtime adviser, and now mine. Where I go, he goes."

Juan Ruiz's eyes seemed to close as if he were about to fall asleep on his feet. In fact, Maricruz could see that behind those lowered lids, the big man was scrutinizing Marsh. At length, he gave another scarcely perceptible nod, then stood aside, an invitation for them to enter.

When they did so, it was as if they had entered a modern-day emperor's palace. There was such a dazzling array of cut-crystal chandeliers, jasper-topped side tables, marble statues, porcelain pots, Aztec jade masks, ivory utensils, Olmec stone heads, scrimshawed whales' teeth, and ormolu clocks in just the vast two-story entryway, as well as the hallway that yawned beyond, she soon stopped counting. A majestic mahogany staircase spiraled up to a second floor guarded by an ornate balustrade that would not have been out of place in Versailles.

"Weapons," Juan Ruiz said in his peculiar monosyllabic style.

Maricruz handed over both her guns.

Juan Ruiz motioned with a jut of his monumental chin. "Him?"

"Wendell isn't armed," she said.

Juan Ruiz set her guns on the jasper-topped table.

"Arms up."

Juan Ruiz frisked them both with rapid, expert pats and slides of his hands. Finding no other weapons, he led them down the hall, through a drawing room, a formal library, and the living room, each space larger and more ornately decorated than the last, as if from the hidden coffers of the world's finest museums. By the time they reached the study, she was exhausted with a surfeit of visible wonders, which was undoubtedly the point. Felipe Matamoros wanted to lay out his power and wealth for her to see in the most tangible way.

The man himself stood with his back to the doorway, facing out to the vista of long sloping emerald lawn that led to a sparkling pool. A waterfall cascaded at one end and a bevy of startlingly young, bikini-clad women with bronzed, well-oiled flesh lounged at the other. His hands were behind his back. One held an oversize old-fashioned glass containing, Maricruz guessed, aged tequila.

A moment after Juan Ruiz escorted them into the study, a slender, almost willowy man detached himself from the shadows on the right side of the room and stepped across what appeared to be an heirloom Tabriz carpet to confront them. He, too, held an old-fashioned glass of liquor.

"Señorita Encarnación," he said, "may I get you and your guest a drink?"

"It's *señora* now," she said in a perfectly neutral tone.

"Ah, yes," the man said, "Señora Ouyang, isn't it?"

"Agave," Maricruz said with an unaffected smile, "for both of us."

"Of course."

The willowy man crossed to a sideboard. Through this all, Matamoros hadn't stirred. In fact, he seemed not even to have drawn a breath.

As the willowy man was pouring their drinks, Maricruz said, "I am still my father's daughter. Still an Encarnación."

At this, Matamoros turned to look at her. He was darkly handsome in a brutish sort of way.

His eyes were clear, dark, and intelligent. He had a hawk's nose and a jaguar's mouth. His cheeks were pocked or scarred, in the low light, Maricruz could not tell which.

"This is good." He had a deep, rolling voice like thunder through mountain valleys. "Your skin hasn't turned yellow, your eyes haven't become slanted."

"What a relief!" Maricruz cried.

Matamoros's thin, blue jaguar lips twitched in what might have been the semblance of a smile. It could just as easily be a smirk, Maricruz decided, but turned her mind in a different direction. Matamoros might be baiting her, testing her to gauge her toughness, the quality of her strength.

The willowy man brought them their agave. As he was about to hand her the drink, Maricruz said, "I've met your brother, Señor de la Luna."

The slight tremble of the glass as it was passed from his hand to hers told her that she had scored bonus points.

"My brother," de la Luna said, vamping for time to recover.

"Elizondo de la Luna." She took a sip of the agave, keeping her gaze on him over the rim of the glass. "He *is* your brother, is he not?"

De la Luna stared at her as if he had found a deadly insect in his bed. "Where did you meet?"

"Manila." Maricruz wondered what Manila was like, never having set foot in the Philippines. Advance intel was invaluable, she thought. Never more so than at this moment. "You and Elizondo haven't seen each other in some time, I gather." She savored the flavors of the aged agave on the back of her tongue. "Nor have you spoken."

"Señora Encarnación," Matamoros intervened, smiling cat-like, "I agreed to fly in from Nuevo Laredo to meet with you. We have important business to discuss."

Maricruz nodded without taking her eyes off de la Luna. He seemed to have gone pale beneath his glossy Mexican skin.

"Manila," she repeated, "where Elizondo and his Interpol team were in the process of shutting down an illegal pharmaceutical factory." Her eyes at last turned to the head of Los Zetas. "Lucky for you, Señor Matamoros, that your business interests lie strictly within Mexican borders."

Now Matamoros did smile, an unpleasant sight by any measure. "I get by." He gestured to a pair of large tobacco-colored leather chairs. "Please."

Maricruz chose the chair with its back to the French doors that overlooked the pool and sat. The afternoon light streamed in from behind her. Matamoros seated himself opposite. Marsh and Juan

Ruiz stood side by side, as if guarding the two, while de la Luna retreated into the shadows.

"Your father was a good man," he said. "I respected him. My heartfelt condolences. It's a great pity he's gone."

"You never met my father."

"I dealt with him through an intermediary."

"Tulio Vistoso. The Aztec."

Matamoros inclined his head. "This was by his request."

"Vistoso is dead, too," Maricruz said. "And you have appropriated his organization."

"Well…" Matamoros spread his hands. "What would you have had me do? Without the Aztec and your father's guiding hands, the men were rudderless. Giron had his eye on them. I couldn't let them fall into the lap of the Sinaloa." He finished off his drink and put the glass aside. "However, awkwardly that leaves the Encarnación family without a presence in the world of cartels."

Maricruz, having known this moment would come, said, "Awkwardly, that leaves you without our lines of supply."

"I have my own lines of supply."

"Not direct from China, you don't. You have to deal with a succession of middlemen, all of whom dip their beak into your stew, diminishing it significantly."

"Not significantly."

Maricruz knew he was lying, but then she hadn't expected anything like the truth from him. Not at this point, anyway.

"I wonder," she said, "what your costs are for your meth business." She looked at Matamoros. "Meth is the future, so I hope that segment is growing exponentially."

Matamoros was silent for several moments, apparently deciding which way to play her new foray.

She did not wait for a reply. "Meth would be more profitable if it weren't such a low-margin business, isn't that right?" She sipped her drink. "I have direct access to all the required chemicals—a virtually unlimited supply."

"Your husband."

"Is a member of the Chinese Politburo. You can see how advantageous that is."

"In fact, Señora Encarnación, I do see. Very clearly." Matamoros nodded.

De la Luna emerged from the shadows holding a 9 mm handgun. He was aiming it at Wendell Marsh.

"It is good that you brought the *abogado*," Matamoros said. "Good for me, but not for you. Now you will provide me with everything I require— every advantage your cartel had—or this man dies."

10

TOSSING THE CORPSE aside, Bourne glimpsed a retreating figure through the open window. Instantly he climbed onto the sill, then down onto the sloping roof. The curved tiles were treacherously smooth, and he skidded, sliding close to the edge of the eaves. Ahead of him was a narrow gap between houses; below, the shadowed alley he had seen through the window in the hallway.

Gathering his energy, he leapt across the space, grabbing onto a cluster of antennas as he hit the roof of the adjoining building to keep from sliding off. Gaining his footing, he set off after the figure, which was already over the peak of this side of the roof, vanishing from his view.

Moments later, on the peak, he saw the figure, which way it was headed, and thought he saw a way to cut it off before it got too far ahead of him. Leaving the peak behind, he sprinted at an acute angle, leaping to another rooftop that more or less paralleled the route the hastening figure was taking. Clearly, the murderer had a specific destination in mind.

Bourne found that keeping his center of gravity low made running over the slippery tiles easier. Still, the figure ahead of him continued to hasten, clearly more knowledgeable when it came to the rooftops peculiar to Shanghai's old quarter.

Half running, half sliding, Bourne negotiated the steep rises and falls of the narrow rooftops, the leaps across alleys stinking of garbage and animal remains, using a quartering action to keep pace with the murderer. The figure he was chasing seemed fueled with inexhaustible energy.

Once a slim blur of face glanced back and, seeing him in pursuit, the figure slid across the tiles, vanishing over the edge. Bourne followed down into a cramped street market overcrowded with makeshift stalls selling fruits, vegetables, and bootleg DVDs of American films.

The figure flitted through the tiny spaces between the merchants, squeezing through the crowds of shoppers like a cockroach. Bourne was closing in when the figure turned a corner. When he followed, the murderer was gone. He looked up to see a small figure climbing up a drainpipe like a monkey.

Seeing that the pipe would never hold them both, he ducked into the building's doorway, taking the crumbling stairs three at a time. Reaching the top floor, he crashed through a door on the drainpipe side of the building, crossed the floor, and, amid screams and panicked residents, smashed through the window, climbed through, and reached up for the tiles on the eaves.

Swinging his legs up, he gained the roof in time to see the figure already two rooftops away. At the far edge, he leapt, grabbed onto a metal exhaust pipe on the neighboring building, and, using it as a fulcrum, swung his body around, flinging himself across the width of the rooftop, landing on the one beyond—the same one the retreating figure was on. Another blur of a face as the figure saw him coming hard. Then, abruptly, the figure went rigid, a small cry bursting forth. It began to tremble violently.

Putting on a burst of speed, Bourne caught up to the figure just past the peak, grabbing it around the curiously slim waist. Swiveling, he saw that the figure he had been pursuing was a young woman, small as a preteen, who could not be more than twenty years old.

Her face was drawn into a rictus of pain, and

looking down, he saw that her right foot was caught between the vicious steel jaws of a bear trap.

Really?" Maricruz said. "This is the route you want to take?"

"Is there another?" Matamoros said. "The tried and true always works, Señora Encarnación. What was true yesterday is just as true today."

Without another word, Maricruz rose and stepped in front of Marsh.

"They have no business threatening me, do they, Wendell?"

"No," he said, "they don't."

With a quick, contemptuous glance at de la Luna, she slammed the heavy old-fashioned glass into Marsh's face. As he swayed, stunned and confused, she withdrew a small dagger from between her breasts and buried it in his throat.

She stepped away, though there was scarcely any blood. Marsh collapsed onto the rug. For the next several moments, the only sound in the room was the terrible aquatic gurgle of him trying to suck air into his lungs. Maricruz gazed down at him impassively. Once betrayed, always betrayed, she thought. No matter his protestations to the contrary, he could never be trusted. But now he had fulfilled his purpose, he had given his *aliyah*.

Finally, as his convulsions slowed, then stilled altogether, Maricruz looked up at Matamoros, who had leapt out of the chair and now stood with shoulders hunched forward, feet at shoulder width, in the classic street fighter's stance.

"Step up," Maricruz said, beckoning him on with her cupped fingers. "It's what you've wanted from the moment I walked in the room."

My name is Yue," the young woman said breathlessly.

"What is a bear trap doing up here?"

Bourne could see how much pain she was in; the teeth had penetrated skin and flesh down to the bone.

"They're used to trap sun bears." Yue was taking long, deep breaths in an attempt to lessen the pain. "It's illegal now, so sometimes the trappers keep the jaws up on the roofs of their apartment buildings."

On one knee, Bourne ripped off a loose tile. Pressing an end against one side of the trap's teeth, he jammed his heel between the two jaws and, using his bent leg as leverage, slowly, agonizingly, pulled apart the bloody jaws enough for Yue to pull her leg free. A moment later the tile cracked and Bourne just missed having his foot injured as the jaws snapped shut again.

Yue tried to put her weight on the bleeding ankle.

"Fuck!"

Bourne caught her as she toppled. She was almost weightless. With her in his arms, he stepped to the edge of the roof. Below, a narrow alleyway was filled with enormous plastic bags of garbage.

"Hold tight," Bourne said as he launched them over the side.

Down they fell, with him cradling her protectively. They hit the bags, and Bourne rolled, using their momentum across his left shoulder to help break the fall.

Her gun slid out. As she snatched at it, he wrestled it away from her. It was an odd-looking weapon, and he soon realized this was what she had used to launch the poison dart into the cop's neck.

"Where did you get this?"

Yue, sitting atop the garbage pile, crossed her arms over her bony chest and stared at him with a belligerence that belied her age.

Bourne tried another tack. "Why did you kill that cop?"

She threw her head back and laughed at him. It

was a true laugh, coming from deep down in her belly.

When she started to curse him, he gripped her tiny wrist more tightly and pulled her to him. "I speak fluently," he said in idiomatic Shanghainese. "Don't fuck around with me."

The only reply he received was the emergence of her bottom lip. She was only a slip of a thing, but she was lightning-quick on her feet, and now Bourne wondered whether the same was true for her mind.

"Why were you at Wei-Wei's?" she said finally.

"He asked me to meet him there."

"Why would he do that?"

Bourne studied her for a moment. "He had something he wanted to tell me."

"I don't believe you. Wei-Wei would never ask you to meet him at home."

"Why not?"

"His home was sacred space," Yue said. "He never conducted business there."

Bourne thought about the note he had been given at the restaurant, then he gestured with his head. "Let's get out of this alley. Do you know someone who can fix you up?"

"My mother taught me not to talk to strangers," Yue said.

Bourne sighed, pulled out the slip of paper with

Wei-Wei's message, and held it out to her. "Is this Wei-Wei's handwriting?"

She snatched the paper from him and opened it. "Wei-Wei didn't write this," she said, handing it back. "Not that I'm surprised."

"What do you mean?"

"That man I killed was no cop. He was an assassin sent to kill Wei-Wei. You interrupted him before he could get out of the apartment. I followed him to Wei-Wei's, but he got ahead of me. I was too late to stop him. Then you showed up."

"In fact, I distracted him long enough for you to get a clear shot at him," Bourne said.

She looked away.

"Who d'you work for?"

She gave him that poisoned look again. "You said you were meant to meet with Wei-Wei."

"That's right. At a teahouse." He gave her the name and address.

Her look seemed slightly less skeptical. "What were you to say to him when you met?"

Bourne hesitated only slightly, then gave her the recognition code provided by the Director.

Something dark and dangerous vanished from behind her eyes.

"Okay, then." Her voice was brisk, all business. "Take me to Tak Sin. He's just around the corner."

*   *   *

Put that weapon away," Matamoros said to de la Luna while he watched Maricruz warily. "You and Juan Ruiz make yourselves useful." He waved vaguely at the pool. "Go talk to the girls; they're looking bored." He snorted. "And take this piece of human excrement with you before he ruins my rug."

When the room had cleared, Matamoros broke his fighter's stance and, sighing, crossed in front of Maricruz, kicked her fallen glass into a corner, then went to the sideboard and poured them both a generous portion of tequila.

"Your father brought you up right," he said as he turned to her.

Maricruz wiped down the blade, then put the push-dagger away. "My father had nothing to do with it."

"*¡Ay de mí!*" He handed her the drink. "*Cálmate, mi princesa guerrera. Usted ha ganado la batalla.*" Calm yourself, my warrior princess. You have won the battle.

He held his sparkling glass aloft and they clinked rims. Both drank deeply. Matamoros sighed. "To be honest, I am grateful to find you as you are— a soldier as fierce as any of my men, and far more resourceful."

"I don't believe you."

He chuckled, shaking his head. "*Mujer*, I have never met a female like you. I want what you're selling. Can I be any more frank?"

"I am most concerned with my father's legacy."

Matamoros frowned, for the first time looking disconcerted. "Money doesn't enter the equation?"

"You don't understand."

"Please." He lifted his glass again. "Enlighten me."

When she said nothing, his frown deepened, and then, as if a veil had been lifted, he nodded. "I see. You think your words will be wasted on me."

He stepped away and sat back down in the chair she had been sitting in. Now the sunlight was coming in over his shoulder, wreathing his head in a curious brilliance. "You have erred in assuming my ignorance."

She sat opposite him. "Enlighten me. Please."

He grinned his strange jaguar grin, which, following their face-off, now seemed more compelling than dangerous. "When I was a child, I fell ill. In those days, my family lived in the mountains, in a tiny village, in a dirt-floor hut. My father worked twelve hours a day. When he died, his lungs were as black as the coal he hacked out of the mines.

"That was the day I fell ill. I was ten, burning

up with a fever that refused to break. No one knew what was wrong with me, not the village doctor, who prescribed herbs, not the old women, who cast spells of enchantment. No one.

"By the second week, the fever had started to waste me. It was my older sister, Marissa, who took me down to the river, took me in her arms as she waded in. There was a spot she particularly liked, an almost circular pool, out of the main current. Soft eddies buoyed me as she bathed me in the cold, clear water.

"She held me in her arms for hours. I remember the clouds passing by overhead—they looked like mythical beasts keeping watch over me. I heard the calls of birds, but they came to me distantly and distorted, as if in a dream.

"The sun went down and still she held me, rocking me gently. In the darkness, she sang to me. The moon came out and I stared up into her face, and confused it with the moon. I must have slept then; the next thing I knew dawn was spreading over the sky and Marissa said to me, '*Look at you,* joven. *You're smiling.*'

"Later that day or maybe it was the day after, I don't remember, while I was enjoying my first real meal in two weeks, Marissa put her head close to mine and said, 'Joven, *you almost died because of ignorance. Remember now and always, ignorance is a form of death.*' I never forgot what she said, *mujer*. Never, because, you see, my sister is a goddess. From that moment on, every chance I got, I educated myself."

Matamoros finished off his drink and said, "Now, come. Let us eat a great fucking meal together and talk about how together we will keep Maceo Encarnación's legacy alive."

11

RETZACH ARRIVED IN Shanghai and hit the
ground running. He had been recruited to Mossad
when he was seventeen. Three years later he was
chosen for induction into Metsada. Retzach's
climb to notoriety within Kidon began when he
killed Muhammad, head of Syria's nuclear program, by firing from a boat while the target relaxed
on a beach in Tartus. It was cemented when he
infiltrated into Damascus and killed Imad Mughniyah, a senior leader of Hezbollah complicit in
the notorious 1983 bombing of the American embassy, by planting a small square of C-4 in the
headrest of Mughniyah's car, setting it off via his
mobile phone.

The Mughniyah assignment was of particular interest to Retzach, which was why he fought so

hard to get it. His younger brother had been a liaison officer assigned to the American embassy in Damascus, and was one of the victims. Payback was a matter of family honor, which was one of the reasons Amir Ophir, then the newly minted head of Metsada, granted Retzach's request. The other reason was to irrevocably bind Retzach to him. Retzach knew this, if not at the time, then soon afterward when Ophir assigned him an off-the-books assassination. Retzach didn't mind—frankly, he was pleased. Mossad was like a family—never more so than inside Metsada. For Ophir to consider him a kind of son was high honor indeed.

Traveling in from the airport, Retzach got on his mobile and started calling his local contacts. He had them in every major city. None of them was aware he was Israeli, let alone Mossad. The money he paid them came from his own pocket; he didn't want even Ophir to know of their existence. Retzach cared little about money except for the information it could buy him. He had no use for material objects, the inevitable accumulations of an adult life. He'd had a wife once, and a strange child, whom he saw once a year.

He himself had been a strange child. Later, after much reading and research, he came to understand that he lacked empathy. That this was one definition of a psychopath concerned him not at all. After all, academics lived in a different world than he inhabited, a world as protected from life on the street as a pharaoh's had been. What did they know of the exigencies of his life?

Having received as much intel as he was going to on his first go-round, he exited the taxi along densely packed Shanxi Nan Road, in Huangpu, and walked to Dongbei Ren, a teeming, cacophonous restaurant beloved by locals and tourists alike. He pointed to one of the large round tables and found a place open for him between a Chinese family of six and a fat local, wattles loaded with grease. The place, with its eye-bleeding gold-and-red decor, and uniformed waiters with pigtails, looked as if it were still mired in Mao's Revolution.

"What to order, what to order?" Retzach said as he scanned the huge menu.

"Try the drunken shrimp," the fat Shanghainese said.

"I'm allergic to shrimp," Retzach said without turning his head.

"Pity," the fat man replied. "They're so fresh they're still wriggling when you pop them in your mouth."

Retzach ordered jade dumplings, a lamb shank,

and a pot of chrysanthemum tea. Then he put the menu aside and said to the fat man, "Have you seen him?"

The fat man glanced again at the photo of Bourne that Retzach had sent him via his mobile. "I haven't," the fat man said, "but someone who has will be here shortly." He belched mightily and stood up, bits of food flying like sleet from his over-ample lap. "In the meantime, please enjoy yourself, but be careful, the food's so good here you can eat yourself into a coma."

Retzach laughed and, dumping hot sauce on the dumplings the instant they arrived, took up his chopsticks and dug in.

Tak Sin owned an apothecary, as only the Chinese understand the word. To left and right, on either wall, were wooden drawers filled with countless herbs, ground horns of rhino, tiger teeth, dried sun bear paws, and the like. The shop was long, narrow, and dark as a subway tunnel.

When Bourne entered, carrying Yue in his arms, an old woman looked up from counting out on an abacus, cursed mightily in rapid Shanghainese, and ran into the back. Moments later a thin man with a potbelly, stringy white beard, and rheumy eyes shuffled out in slippers.

He peered closely through thick round lenses at Yue's wound, then glanced up at Bourne with a disapproving look. He made a face and, gesturing, turned on his heel. The shop's rear was a warren of rooms as antiseptic and immaculate as the front was dusty and odor-laden. They were also brilliantly lighted.

Again, Tak Sin gestured, and Bourne put Yue onto a long table.

"This man saved me, Uncle," she said. "He speaks Shanghainese."

"Does he now?" Tak Sin said. He didn't bother to look at Bourne, busy as he was cleaning and disinfecting Yue's bloody ankle. "What have you gotten yourself into, little sister?"

She laughed, then grimaced as a bolt of pain shot up her leg.

Tak Sin shook his head. "I knew I shouldn't have given you the *Passiflora caerulea* liquid."

"Cyanide," Bourne said.

Tak Sin nodded. "You see, I have a soft spot for this little sister." Finished with the cleaning, he began to wrap her ankle securely in swaths of gauze impregnated with an herbal antibiotic. He shrugged and smiled a secret smile. "What can you do?"

Bourne took hold of Yue's hand and pulled her up to a sitting position. "The man you shot."

"The one dressed as a cop? He's a professional assassin."

"Who hired him?"

"A man from Beijing, though for the last week he's been here. Colonel Sun."

Bourne started.

"You know Sun?"

"He and I have a history," Bourne said thoughtfully. "Why would he target Wei-Wei?"

"I don't know." Yue hopped off the table. The leg with the injured ankle bent under her and Bourne held her as she grabbed the table's edge. She looked at him. "But I know someone you can ask."

You have a problem," Maricruz said as she pushed back a plate filled with shrimp shells. "A serious problem."

Felipe Matamoros wiped the grease off his thick lips. "And what would that be?"

"MEL Petroservicios."

He sat back, his face as stony and enigmatic as a sphinx.

She had scored a direct hit, as she knew she would. "Simply put, the Americans have just put MEL out of business."

"And that concerns me how?"

"Don't be coy. You used the oil company—or I should say *former* oil company—to launder Los Zetas's ill-gotten gains. Now you're dead in the water."

"I see you're better informed than I had expected, *mi princesa*." He cocked his head. "But actually, we'll get by. We're used to this kind of shit from the gringo. All life is shit in Mexico. No one values life. You think it's just us in the drug trade? No, no, *mujer*. It's the police, the army, the business tycoons, and most of all, the politicians, who spout platitudes out of one side of their mouths, while eating off my plate with the other."

He spread his hands wide. "Now tell me, what are you going to do for me? Offer your father's cyber-security business to launder our money?"

"Absolutely not. SteelTrap is one hundred percent legitimate and it will stay that way."

"Then I don't see what—"

"Art, Señor Matamoros. In China the new upper class is desperate to spend money in order to feel a sense of self-worth." She looked around the opulent room with its many expensive artifacts from Mexico's storied past, before returning her gaze to Matamoros. "Pathetic though that may be, it's a fact of life in today's Middle Kingdom."

"I was born into poverty, *mujer*. From where I sit, the world has a very different look."

"That's as may be." She gestured around the room. "But do you think this is the sort of legacy a man of ambition wants to leave? Don't you think he wants to achieve something more, something greater than what has been?"

"Go on," Matamoros said after a time.

"The benefit for you is that, unlike in the rest of the civilized world, the art market in China is entirely opaque. Real works of art commingle with fakes and no one knows the difference. All are bought for exorbitant prices and are sold for exorbitantly higher prices."

"So you take Los Zetas's money, buy artwork in Beijing, sell it to newly rich Chinese businessmen, and return the laundered money to us, for a fee."

"Fifteen percent," Maricruz said. "Plus fifty percent of the profit made from each sale—and believe me when I tell you we will make a tidy profit on each sale." She smiled, her eyes shining. "It's foolproof. And best of all, the Americans can't touch you or your money."

Matamoros rose and walked around the room, touching each piece of Aztec and Olmec sculpture as if they might speak to him, guiding his decision. At length, he turned back to her. "If I say yes, there are still five others who have to agree."

"A hive mind. I understand a thousand percent."

His expression remained somber. "First and foremost, *mi princesa*, we are commandos, the elite of the Mexican Army, which, I admit, is something of a joke. But nevertheless, we who make up the core of Los Zetas were well trained, because we set our minds to learning the art of war. Better still, when we defected we took both our advanced weapons and our contacts with us. There are six of us. We operate as a cadre. This is what makes us so strong; this is what makes us invulnerable."

"Then take me to meet the rest of the cadre. I'll convince them as I've convinced you."

He smiled as he extracted a cigar from an elaborately carved humidor, offered it to her, stuck it in his mouth when she declined, and took his time lighting up. Puffing out blue clouds of smoke like an iron locomotive, he said, "With the untimely death of your father, liaising with the cartels has fallen on your shoulders, I understand that completely. But at the same time I understand it must be difficult for you. After all, this is not your business—you rub shoulders with the elite businessmen, politicians, and entertainers on the opposite side of the world. Every day you spend here is dangerous, I suppose I don't have to remind you of that."

"I very much doubt you can frighten me, Señor Matamoros."

"Felipe, *por favor, mujer.*" He tilted his head

back, blew smoke at the coffered ceiling of his vast, cluttered dining room. "Of course you're right. And it was not my intention to frighten you." He gestured. "But I must warn you my *compadres* are blunt, brutal men. They might not find you as charming as I do, they might not see the intelligence I do."

"Let me worry about that."

"Now you insult me, *mujer*. You are my guest here. If we embark on this trip, you are under my protection. I am responsible for your well-being."

This commitment was what she had been waiting for. Now to drop the other shoe and see how he reacted. "I appreciate that, Felipe. But as long as we're going to meet the cadre, I'm thinking we should meet with the head of the Sinaloa as well."

Matamoros stood stock-still. "*¡Mujer, por favor!*"

"I am perfectly serious, Felipe."

"You speak of us getting together with our mortal enemies. This is insane. We are winning the war against them. Eventually—"

"Eventually. How many of your men will be killed before *eventually* rolls around?" Maricruz kept her smile in place, but a cold, dark place was forming in her heart. She had no friends here; she never would. But she would make her mark in Mexico, of that she was certain. She leaned forward. "Listen to me. Consider the damage, the deaths you and the Sinaloa inflict on each other. Then there's the time the war you're slowly winning takes away from earning money."

Her eyes searched his, looking for the effects her words were having. "Why do you think *el presidente* does the minimum against you? Because, as you say, you're invincible? Perhaps, but I don't think so. *El presidente* is sitting back in his golden chair, patiently waiting, knowing it's just a matter of time before you and the Sinaloa decimate each other. Then he'll swoop in with his tanks, armored cars, and helicopters, and take credit for cleaning up crime, for destroying the severely weakened cartels.

"But if you and the Sinaloa join forces, think of the strength, the power the one cartel will have. You will have the run of Mexico without fear of reprisal or damage. I want you to leave the bloodshed behind. I want to take you into the twenty-first century. Think of the glory that can be yours, Felipe."

For a long time there was silence in the room. Then, all at once, Matamoros laughed long and hard, the sound coming from deep down in his lower belly. At last, he wiped his eyes. "*¡Ay de mí!* You have a golden tongue, *mujer*; you could sell wool to sheepherders. *Es la verdad.*"

"Nevertheless, it's for you to decide."

"Allow me to make some calls." He gestured. "Help yourself to some coffee—anything you want."

"You know what I want."

He smiled and left the room, an aroma of Cuban tobacco trailing after him. Maricruz thought of calling Jidan, but her acute sense that nothing was secure here gave her pause. There was nowhere in this vast villa or even on its grounds where she could be certain of not being overheard. Instead she amused herself with imagining outrageous erotic scenarios.

Twenty minutes later, Matamoros returned. He said nothing, only nodded to her.

Maricruz felt relief and also excitement surging through her. This was why she had come; this was what she was born to do: forging new ties, new alliances that would outstrip anything her father had ever dared attempt.

"We'll go forward, Felipe." Reaching across the table, she took his hard, callused hand in hers. "The future will be ours."

Yue led Bourne through the narrow, impossibly teeming streets of Huangpu, limping less and less heavily, batting away his offers of help. They had been traveling for nearly half an hour, but she hadn't paused for even a moment.

Taking him beneath the sign announcing THE CHINA SEAS PEARL, she entered the small but elegant store that seemed more suited to the upscale Pudong district across the river. But perhaps that was its secret, for it was packed with tourists eager to pay less for first-rate pearls than at the sky-high–priced shops along the Bund. The shop was the brainchild of Sam Zhang, who, when he heaved his bulk through the front door shortly after Yue asked for him, was slightly out of breath from his walk from Dongbei Ren, where he had left Retzach eating his steamed dumplings.

Zhang led a complicated life, one that was, at times, enervatingly difficult. He had stolen the idea of playing both sides against the other when, in a darkened movie theater, he had watched Clint Eastwood rid a town of its two warring bandit clans by doing just that. After that, he watched *A Fistful of Dollars* almost every week until he knew each scene by heart and could quote every line of dialogue.

The lessons of the film's plot had stood him in good stead for close to two decades. While treading a path as narrow as a balance beam, and far more perilous, would have made most men quail, Zhang thrived on the adrenaline rush. Or at least he had. Lately, sleep deserting him, he found himself dreaming of a less complicated existence, somewhere far from jam-packed China.

By its very capitalist nature, Shanghai had become the nexus point for the clandestine affairs of both East and West. Zhang was simply taking advantage of the benefits derived from both the business and geography of the city of his birth.

Zhang greeted Yue warmly; he had a genuine affection for her, unusual for him. In his line of duplicity, it was often fatal to get emotionally involved with his clients; however, her history as she had related it to him had affected him deeply. He had been a child of the streets, like her, and like her he was an orphan, dependent on his own wits as well as the occasional kindness of strangers for his survival. This years-long trial by fire had made him tougher, smarter, more self-reliant—all qualities he recognized in Yue. If not by blood, then spiritually, she was like the daughter he'd never had.

He was doubly dismayed, however, when he became aware of her injury, and how she had gotten hurt. Then he spotted the man with her. Having been shown Bourne's photo by Retzach, Zhang, of course, recognized him instantly. When she told him that this man had saved her life, he knew he had erred in agreeing to help Retzach find him.

Wondering how he could call off the man who even now was heading toward his rendezvous at Dongbei Ren without causing Retzach to become suspicious, he led the two into his office at the rear of the shop.

The walls, painted a pale green, were covered with black-and-white photos of slim pearl divers swimming powerfully underwater, surfacing in glittering stop-motion sprays of water, grinning as they displayed their finds, as they dug pearls out of the tender, meaty flesh. Behind his simple desk was a wall safe and a filing cabinet. His swivel chair groaned as he lowered himself.

He waved them to jute-seated chairs and, smiling, though his racing heart was increasingly troubled, said, "How can I help you, little sister?"

"This afternoon Wei-Wei was killed, but I imagine you know this because you know everything that goes on in Shanghai."

Zhang did not contradict her with false modesty. He *did* know everything that went on in his city—everything of import. Instead he said, "Go on."

"Three days ago, Wei-Wei hired me to keep him safe."

Zhang nodded, studying her carefully.

"I failed," Yue said miserably. "He was killed by Amma. You know Amma."

"I do." There was no point in denying the obvious.

"You knew him," Bourne corrected. "Yue shot him with a dart dipped in a cyanide derivative."

Zhang pressed his thumb and forefinger into his eyes, massaging a headache that was forming behind them.

"Why did Colonel Sun send Amma to kill Wei-Wei?" Bourne asked.

Zhang hesitated a moment. "You know who Sun works for?" he asked Bourne.

"Ouyang Jidan."

Zhang nodded appreciatively. "So you know the players."

"Not all, I think."

"Allow me, then, to describe them to you." The big man shifted his bulk. "Ouyang is in a battle to the death with his nemesis, Cho Xilan. Both men are in the Politburo, but that's where any similarity ends. Cho is the secretary of the powerful Chongqing Party—stocked with reactionaries ready to set China back three decades or more. On the other hand, Ouyang is a progressive."

"He's also up to his eyeballs in the drug trade out of Mexico," Bourne said.

Zhang raised a porky forefinger. "And therein lies the rub. For years now, Cho has been trying to catch Ouyang in this game, but Ouyang has always succeeded in outsmarting him. Now, however, because of the imminent Party Congress that will set new leaders in the Politburo and determine the direction of the country for the next decade, their feud is coming to a head.

"Cho will do anything to uncover Ouyang's illegitimate dealings with the Mexican cartels, and now, perhaps, he's found the crack in Ouyang's armor. Maceo Encarnación's recent death has changed everything. Up until that point, Encarnación was acting as Ouyang's shield; he made Ouyang invulnerable. Now he's gone and, sensing victory, Cho is closing in for the kill. On the other hand, Cho is so desperate to get Ouyang he may have left himself open to an attack."

Yue shook her head. "How does this have anything to do with Wei-Wei's murder?"

"Ah, well," Zhang said, "the largest of battles always begins at the margins, out of sight of the principals. It's the way the principals want it."

He took out a bottle of whiskey and three glasses, pouring out dollops and handing over the glasses. He downed his drink in one gulp, then poured himself a double. "Wei-Wei is Ouyang's creature."

"Wait a minute," Bourne said. "He's a Mossad asset."

Zhang smiled. "Welcome to Shanghai, dear sir."

He swallowed more whiskey, smacking his lips.
"So now we have the first foray in the war's
endgame: Amma is controlled by Captain Lim,
who reports to Colonel Sun. And you know who
Colonel Sun reports to."

"Ouyang," Bourne said. "But if what you say
is correct, Ouyang ordered his own asset killed.
Which means that Wei-Wei had become a liability."

At that moment the woman they had seen in
the front of the shop entered the office, so clearly
shaken that she did not even knock first. Hurrying
around the side of the desk, she bent to whisper in
Zhang's ear.

His eyes widened before he dismissed her. When
they were alone again, he rolled his chair to one
side and beckoned them. "Speaking of Captain
Lim has summoned him from the precincts of
hell."

"He's here?" Bourne said.

Zhang nodded. "With enough men to surround
the shop." He beckoned again. "Come, come!
There's no time to waste."

He pointed down to the small rug on which his
chair had sat. Pulling it back on itself, Bourne discovered a cunningly fitted trapdoor.

"It leads to the basement," Zhang said as Bourne
opened the door by pulling on a brass ring. "You'll

find a kerosene lamp and a box of wooden matches in a niche on the wall as you go down the ladder. An exit from the basement will lead you through a tunnel with many branchings. Keep always to the left. Just beyond the fourth branching you'll find your way out." He lifted a forefinger. "But have a care, the tunnels are old and crumbling."

They could hear a commotion from the front of the store—the insistent snap of Captain Lim's voice and the answering wail of the woman who had delivered the news of his imminent arrival.

"Quickly, now," Zhang said. "Go, go! I'll take care of our army friend."

Bourne went down a vertical wooden ladder, then, reaching up, took Yue in his arms. As they slowly descended, she pulled a cord that closed the door after them. A moment later they heard Captain Lim's voice raised in anger and frustration seeping through the floorboards directly over their heads, then the sharp report of a handgun's discharge.

12

SAM ZHANG DID NOT know that Retzach was Israeli, let alone a Kidon operative. He knew him as Jesse Long, and although he assumed that was a legend name he was not interested in his real one. He was not in the habit of digging into his clients' private lives; any hint to them that he was snooping around would have caused his business to tank overnight.

As a result, Captain Lim knew less about Retzach than Zhang did. Zhang did, however, know that Sun, through Lim, was looking for Bourne, which is why Zhang had contacted Lim and told him to meet "Jesse Long" at Dongbei Ren. There was a level of instant mutual dislike between the men, which only deepened for Lim when he discovered that Long was after the same man he had been tasked to capture.

Long was properly vague when Lim asked him why he was trying to find Bourne, which led the captain to make the assumption—false though it was—that the Western operative was from the American Central Intelligence Agency.

Lim, who had his men tracking Bourne since the incident in the Huangpu tunnel, had no intention of divulging to Long anything pertaining to Bourne. He feigned ignorance, but he was unsure whether or not Long believed him. His skepticism proved well founded when he discovered Long was shadowing him. Unluckily for him, he didn't find this out until he had deployed his men around Sam Zhang's pearl shop.

Lim caught a glimpse of him in the crowd that was forming in the street along which The China Seas Pearl was located. Briefly, he thought about dispatching one of his men to detain Long, but decided that any hesitation on his part would give Bourne the chance he needed to escape.

Striding into the shop, he ordered his men to clear out the customers in an orderly fashion, which proved more difficult than he had foreseen. The Western women who bought pearls from Zhang were all wealthy, their husbands powerful in business and politics. They weren't used to being rounded up by cops—and Chinese ones, at that—and frog-marched out onto the street, there to be ogled like apes in a cage.

Shouting matches arose. Then one woman shoved a cop who had gotten too close, and began to beat on him. A cry rose up from the surrounding crowd. As they began to surge forward, Lim knew the trouble was about to escalate. He sent his trusted lieutenant out the front door to deal with the crisis while he rushed through the now nearly deserted shop, pulled open the door to Zhang's office, and roughly pushed his way through the opening.

What he saw was this: Sam Zhang, massive as a whale, sitting behind his desk, drinking whiskey from a glass. A second glass sat beside the bottle, and when Lim rushed in, Zhang leaned his bulk forward, chair loudly creaking in protest, filled a third of the glass, and pushed it across the desktop.

"Welcome, Captain. This is a surprise."

"I'll bet it is," Lim said caustically.

Zhang smiled. "Sit down. Have a drink. You look like you need to calm your nerves."

"Where is he?" Lim said, hands on hips.

"Where's who?"

Lim stepped forward menacingly. "Don't give me that." He reached for his holstered sidearm. "Jason Bourne."

"That name is unfamiliar to me," Zhang said truthfully.

"He was seen going in here."

Zhang shrugged. "Then he left. I've only been visited by my little sister, Yue."

"Listen, now—"

"She was hurt, you know. She—"

Lim raised his pistol and fired at the ceiling. Plaster rained down across Sam Zhang's desk. He was just able to save his glass of whiskey, but the one he'd poured for Lim was now filled with shards and dust.

"You've wasted a glass of fine whiskey, Captain." Zhang shook his head. "Unforgivable behavior."

Lim lowered his pistol. "The next one will go through your heart."

"And where will that get you, Captain? I'm telling the truth. The man you're seeking isn't here."

"Where is he, then?"

"How should I know?"

Lim clicked his tongue against the roof of his mouth. "I *will* find him, Zhang. This I promise you."

"Captain, it really makes no difference to me what you do," he said to Lim's back as he disappeared through the open doorway.

When the police had gone and the shop was his again, Zhang pulled out an oversize handkerchief and wiped his face.

Gods and demons, he thought. *I'm getting too damn old for this.*

In pitch darkness Bourne grabbed the lantern and box of matches he had glimpsed before Yue closed the trapdoor. Lighting the lantern, Yue, in his arms, held it high so that they could get as much light into the basement as possible.

At the bottom of the ladder, they found themselves in cramped quarters. The ceiling was so low it was impossible for Bourne to stand up straight.

"Let me down," Yue whispered.

As soon as her feet hit the floor, she tested her ankle. She nodded to him and mouthed, "I'm okay."

But as they picked their way toward the tunnel's aperture, he could see her grimace every time she put weight on her wounded ankle. Surely she wouldn't be able to walk far, let alone run, if the situation called for it.

The basement was like a warehouse, filled with crates nailed shut and cartons bound with heavy twine. They maneuvered through a narrow aisle between two walls of stacks that rose to the ceiling.

Once, Yue's leg faltered and she put a hand on a dusty box to steady herself. She shook off Bourne's offer to help.

"I'm not going to be a burden to anyone," she whispered fiercely.

The mouth of the tunnel was clear enough. Once, it had been closed off and later boarded up. They saw remnants of rotten boards bound by iron no one had bothered to throw out. Gripping two of the boards, Bourne paused a moment to work one of the iron bands free. It was about eight inches long and still solid.

They reached the opening of the tunnel. Even Yue had to bend somewhat in order to enter it. It reeked of filth, metallic water, decay, and centuries of human squalor. Bourne took the lantern from her and led the way. The tunnel initially sloped steeply downward before leveling off. It appeared hand dug out of the earth, supported at intervals by thick wooden beams. Above their heads were the floorboards of adjacent basements. A trickle of water had runneled the center of the tunnel's packed-dirt floor, making even the simple act of walking difficult. Occasionally he heard tiny scrabbling sounds and saw pairs of red eyes. A flash of light revealed rats, large and active.

Suddenly Bourne heard a different kind of sound behind him, turned to see Yue stumble again. Despite her protestations, he took her again in his arms and began to move forward.

"Damn you," she sighed. "I'm not helpless."

"But you're in pain."

"You don't know anything about pain."

They came to the first branching, and, as Zhang had directed, Bourne headed left.

"No?" Anything to keep her from dwelling on her physical pain. "Please tell me."

Yue was silent for a moment. Then she said softly, falteringly, "My father was a writer, a dissident. He wrote about the corruption inside the Politburo—the special farms its members got their food from, while everyone else was eating food contaminated with heavy metals, adulterated with melamine.

"You can imagine what happened. He was arrested on trumped-up charges and sentenced to twenty years at hard labor. My mother began her protests the day he was convicted. Two weeks later, they came for her, tried her on charges of sedition, and took her away, God alone knows where.

"I was seven at the time they took her. I admire what my parents did, but they had no regard for me or my life. I was given over to my mother's brother. He hated my father for what he had done to my mother. Having no one else to take out his hatred on, he beat me, starved me, locked me in a closet. One day, I escaped and never went back. I was eleven. Four years with him; four years in hell."

Bourne heard her breathing hard, as if she had just finished a sprint. He came to the second fork and again went left. He thought about his own years in hell—the hell of not knowing who he was, where he was from, anything about his parents. Into his mind swam the many people who had been close to him, now all dead. But most of all, he thought of Rebeka, of their time together, of her bravery and her determination. He thought of dragging her through a drainpipe in Mexico City—so eerily similar to these moments with Yue—unable to stanch the bleeding of the knife wound in her side. He thought of her bleeding out in the back of a taxi as he sped toward help that would come too late. He felt the small star of David he had taken from her, which he could not give up at her memorial service in Tel Aviv, which he kept with him because he could not let go of her.

He had wondered about this, ruminated on it during his time of convalescence on the beach at Caesarea, but could come to no good conclusion. So much of himself was still unknown. Apart from the skills ingrained in him during his time in the original Treadstone program, he did not know who he was or what motivated him beyond an overrid-

ing sense of justice and deep-seated anger, a sadness, almost a kind of despair. There were times
when he'd wondered if he suffered from a lack
of empathy—a sure sign of psychosis. But then
Rebeka—or someone like her—would come along
and for a time he'd feel deeply and completely,
and his fear would be assuaged. Then, inevitably,
the person would die, and he would be left alone
again, vowing never to allow himself to feel again.
His life had resolved itself into a kind of seesawing
back and forth between these two volatile points,
depriving him of a sense of balance and serenity.
He was a man adrift on a half-wrecked ship, so
far out to sea no land was visible, in a perpetual
fog-bound night that made any course correction
impossible.

A sound from behind them brought him back to
the tunnel. It sounded like someone kicking a small
stone.

"There's someone following us," Yue whispered.

He was at a third branching; one more to go.
Instead of going left this time, he went into the
right-hand fork. He kicked at a couple of rats,
sending them skittering away. Setting Yue carefully down in front of the lantern, so the light could
not be seen by anyone behind them, he turned to
face the way they had come.

* * *

Retzach had waited until Captain Lim and his police contingent had begun their quartering of the area around The China Seas Pearl, leaving the shop to return to its business. Then he went inside, mingling with the Western women in their expensive outfits who were determined to get their bargains, despite their having been treated like cattle by the Shanghai police. In fact, it was for that very reason—to show their contempt for the civil authorities—that they crowded inside.

Retzach slipped in with them. Immediately he saw that the two saleswomen were so overtaxed, it would be child's play to slip past them without being seen or challenged.

He didn't bother to knock on the office door, but instead shoved it open and went inside. Zhang looked up, startled to see someone else in his office. For a moment he didn't recognize Retzach, then he sighed.

"What is it, Mr. Long? I've been having a trying day."

"So I understand." Retzach stepped across the room. "Well, I won't keep you but a moment."

As he came around the side of the desk, Zhang said, "What are you doing?"

"Do you know the meaning of blunt-force

trauma?" Retzach said as he slammed the side of his snub-nosed Beretta Px4 Storm against the top of the fat man's head.

Zhang rocked so far back in his chair, Retzach was forced to grab him to keep him from falling out. As Zhang's bloodshot eyes cleared, Retzach leaned over and placed the muzzle of the 9 mm against his temple and, finger on the trigger, said, "Bourne came into this shop, but he didn't come out. Where the fuck is he hiding?"

Zhang looked up at him. "Like I told Captain Lim—"

"I'm not Captain Lim. I will fucking spatter your brains all over the walls of this office and then I'll tear the place apart."

Zhang tried to take a breath, failed. "I don't want Yue hurt."

"Who's Yue?"

"She's like my daughter. She's with this man."

"I don't give a shit about her."

"She can't get hurt."

"This isn't a negotiation."

"Yes, but it is," Zhang said. "I would gladly give my life for her."

Retzach studied the fat man's face, looking deep into his eyes for any hint of prevarication. He found none. "I will make sure Yue isn't hurt, okay?"

In his turn, Zhang studied the man in whose hands his life lay. "How do I know I can trust you?"

"How do we know either of us can trust the other? Sometimes we have to rely on faith." This was, of course, a lie. Lacking empathy, Retzach had no faith in anything or anyone. However, he would do his best to keep the girl out of it.

"Push me back," Zhang said, having made up his mind.

"What?"

"The chair. I can't move it with that thing to my head."

Retzach removed the muzzle of the Beretta, and the fat man rolled his chair away.

"Underneath the rug, and keep to the left," he said with a despairing sigh.

"Flashlight," Retzach said, staring down at the blackness.

Zhang had no recourse but to give it to him.

Bourne, crouched down, remained absolutely still. After that first sound, he'd heard nothing more, beyond the doleful drip of water somewhere nearby and the incessant scurrying of rats. But there was now a subtle shift in the flow of air along the tunnel, indicative of a moving body blocking a section of it. A moment later he saw the silverfish brilliance of a flashlight beam advancing toward them. He had positioned himself far enough back in the right-hand fork to remain invisible in the periphery of the circle of light trained on the left-hand fork.

As the light, bobbing slightly with each footstep, came ever closer, Bourne prepared himself. At the last moment, the beam swung away to illuminate the left-hand turning, and Bourne could just make out the silhouette of the human form behind the dazzling light.

Whoever was following them proceeded down the adjacent tunnel at a steady pace. Bourne counted to fifteen, then rose, silently returned to the branching, and followed to the left. He was going by scent now, but there was none. Not a hint of a human scent—just the mineral rock, the seeping water, the black earth.

It's not possible, Bourne thought. *He must be here; he must be close at hand.*

At that moment something metallic swung into the side of his head and a shot went off.

13

MARICRUZ AND FELIPE Matamoros were traveling in his private plane. Three of her men and three of his, plus the pilot, made up the others on board. The plane, which had taken off from a private, hidden airstrip a mile from his villa in Malacates, was headed north to San Luis Potosí.

"This place we fly into," Matamoros was saying, "is the site of the worst of our turf wars with Raul Giron and the Sinaloa cartel."

"So now," Maricruz said, "it will be the last battleground and the first area of the new alliance."

He stared out the Perspex window at the shell-like sky and, below, the rolling geography of the land north of the Distrito Federal. Maricruz wondered whether he felt like a god—the Aztec winged serpent Quetzalcoatl.

"For so many years the Sinaloa were the kings of Mexico," he mused. "The cartel was riding high with no one to mount a serious challenge. Then the Gulf cartel made a group of us an offer we didn't want to refuse and we defected from the elite forces of the army. Right idea, wrong result.

"For a time we worked for them, killing Sinaloa soldiers and gobbling up territories, until we had a complete picture of the lay of the land. Then we broke away and formed our own cartel and turned on our former bosses. Now the Gulf is a shadow of its former self. We have taken over their territory and an increasing amount of the Sinaloa's as well. But the Sinaloa are stronger, better established, their leadership smarter, hooked into the right politicos. They know how to resist us. Still, slowly but surely, we keep pushing them back, gaining more and more territory." He turned back to her. "But you're right, now that you have given us an alternative, the price we have been paying is too high. Now we have you, your foolproof method of money laundering, and your pipeline to unlimited drugs direct from the source. My *compadres* agree with me absolutely.

"We're with you now, *mi princesa*. No longer do we have to make deals with the disgusting pigs who call themselves politicians, with police leaders so greedy they all but drool when I seal my pacts with them. Now we can fuck all of them, as we've been longing to do for years."

The main thing about greed, Maricruz thought now, was that it made you stupid. Even worse, it made you careless. The gloss on Matamoros's eyes was pure greed. Again, he had given himself away without knowing it. Maricruz was grateful, but she knew better than to gloat. She was still in extreme peril; she'd need all her wits and guile to navigate through the next several hours.

At that point, she could feel the change in air pressure as the plane began its descent into the San Luis Potosí area. Peering out the window, she could already see a contingent of armed men standing around enormous black SUVs, their heads raised to stare at the plane as it came in for a landing on the isolated airstrip.

Matamoros turned to her as the wheels made contact with the tarmac. "My *compadres* have chosen to allow me to negotiate for them, *mujer*. There is no need for you to meet them."

With that enigmatic instruction, Matamoros released his seat belt and, though they were still taxiing, rose and stepped past her men and his to the cockpit where, bending over, he spoke at length to the pilot in a low voice that was not audible to her or to anyone else inside the plane.

Behind him, his men were reaching for assault rifles. When they were armed, they handed out more to Maricruz's men in a show of solidarity. Matamoros strode back through the plane, grinning at the six armed men.

"Is this necessary?" she asked.

"Protection must be put in place," he said, "until such time as the alliance is consummated."

The plane had come to a stop at the far end of the runway, but Maricruz noticed that the pilot had not shut down the engines. Still, one of Matamoros's men twisted the lock bar, opened the door, and unfolded the metal staircase to the tarmac. He went down first, fitting his sunglasses in place. The other two men descended close behind, followed by Maricruz's men.

It was almost sunset, the western sky aflame with streaks of red and orange. The oval of the sun, free of the terrible brown haze gripping Mexico City, was clear and strong and hot, even as night was on its way. Maricruz and Felipe Matamoros stood at the top of the steps, surveying the tableau before them—their men at the ready, the Sinaloa contingent smoking with their assault rifles slung across their broad chests. Some of them carried machetes. They glowered at the couple just emerged from the plane.

"You see that man there, second from the left,"

Matamoros said without pointing or moving his head.

Maricruz saw a portly man, shorter than she had imagined, with a great Zapata mustache that might have been comical on someone else. It wasn't on him. He had small, round ears, like a monkey, a hawk-like nose, and black eyes like shiny buttons, sunk deep in his flesh. "I do."

"Raul Giron," Matamoros said. "He wears his personality on his face."

"You don't respect him," Maricruz said.

"Respect, don't respect. I want to crush his fucking head like a beetle underfoot."

Maricruz recognized the tiny quaver in Matamoros's voice. "That emotion belongs in the past, Felipe. From this moment on, you must keep the vision of the future firmly planted in your mind."

"Time to confront that fucker Giron," Matamoros said.

"Just take it easy and let me do the talking. That's all I ask."

"Yes, of course," he said, smiling pleasantly as they began to descend to earth.

Then, when they were almost at the bottom of the stairs, a rear door to one of the black SUVs swung open, and out stepped a man as handsome as any telenovela actor. Tall and stately, with slicked-back silver hair and an immaculate mustache, he wore an impeccably tailored suit, expensive lizard-skin boots, and a telegenic smile. He looked as if he had just come from a film's makeup wagon.

Maricruz felt a slight tremor go through Matamoros. A kind of electric charge lit him up.

"Carlos Danda Carlos," he said under his breath. "Chief of Mexico's anti-drug enforcement agency."

"What in the hell is he doing here?"

Matamoros ignored her question. "In many circles, he is known as Tezcatlipoca, the Aztec god of judgment, night, deceit, and sorcery."

At last, they were on the ground. Men shifted, tense, vigilant, waiting with an almost terminal degree of impatience.

"Raul Giron is boss of the Sinaloa, but in a sense he is also a figurehead," Matamoros said, picking his way at a deliberate pace toward the meet. "He takes his orders from Carlos Danda Carlos, the real power behind the Sinaloa cartel."

Yue, creeping up behind Bourne, had barreled into Retzach's legs so that when he pulled the trigger, the shot flew harmlessly into the tunnel's ceiling. In reflex he kicked out, by chance connecting with her wounded ankle. She cried out, rolled to one side, and crumpled up into a fetal position.

Bourne, head throbbing from the blow Retzach had delivered, reacted in a blur of motion, delivering three kites in rapid succession to Retzach's ribs. Retzach brought his gun down, but Bourne was ready for that. He grabbed the wrist with one hand, chopped down on it with the edge of the other. Retzach grunted, and, leaning in, jammed his shoulder into Bourne's chest, using his weight to drive him back against the wall.

As they both struck the side, a shower of dirt and debris rained down on them. Retzach slammed Bourne back against the wall again, causing a heavier shower, which included bits of rotten wood chips. Something groaned above them. Retzach drove Bourne into the wall once again, and now the boards above their head sagged, the most rotten of them cracking as if made of balsa wood.

As Bourne staggered, Retzach whipped him around in front of him, wrapped his arm around his throat, and put the heel of his left hand under Bourne's left ear. This was one of the killing holds taught to Kidon recruits; it was meant to break your victim's neck in one short movement.

Bourne, at once recognizing Retzach's intent, drove the heel of his shoe so hard into Retzach's instep he shattered it. For a split second Retzach's left hand wavered as the shock slapped him like an ocean wave. That was all the time Bourne needed. Grabbing Retzach's left hand, he slammed it against the wall, then bent the thumb back until it snapped.

Retzach, more debris showering him, grimaced, but made no sound. Unwinding his arm from around Bourne's neck, he absorbed blow after blow while he snapped his thumb back into place, then curled it inside his fingers as he made a fist.

As Bourne continued to pound him, Retzach drew out a knife with a wicked serrated blade and a fishhook claw near the tip that would cause tremendous damage as it ripped into sinew, muscle, and nerves when he pulled the knife out of a stab wound.

He feinted with the knife, then aimed his left fist at Bourne's right ear. As Bourne moved to counter the blow, he stabbed inward, aiming for a spot between Bourne's third and fourth ribs. Bourne saw the maneuver at the last instant, shifting sufficiently, striking the knife blade with the edge of his hand to deflect it to one side.

Seemingly oblivious to the pain, Retzach clubbed Bourne with his injured left hand, then redirected the knife to cut open Bourne's side. Bourne grabbed Retzach's wrist, wrenched it hard over, but no matter what Bourne did, Retzach would not let go of the knife. His attention had narrowed to the weapon, concentrated on the amount of momentum needed to drive the knife forward. Bourne turned Retzach's momentum—impaired and slowed by the awkwardness of having to keep his weight off his fractured foot—against him. Using elbows and knees, he swung Retzach around, rocking him back against the side of the tunnel.

That impact was one too many. The boards above their heads cracked through with a thunderous noise, causing the ceiling of the tunnel and the floor of the basement of the building above it to come crashing down on all three of them, burying them in wooden beams, tamped-down earth, and floorboards, along with crates, boxes, cans, and bottles.

14

OUYANG JIDAN WAS in the midst of a business meeting high up in one of the glittering mixed-use skyrises overlooking the Bund when Colonel Sun entered the conference room. Since Ouyang had left orders that he be disturbed for only the highest-priority situation, he broke off his negotiations with the farmers and chemical manufacturers he had agglomerated into a federation that supplied him with the raw materials required to fabricate the drugs inside Mexico.

Giving his apologies, he rose and stepped away from the highly polished paulownia table, strewn with teapots and cups, as well as half-empty bottles of whiskey and squat old-fashioned glasses.

"What?" he said brusquely to Colonel Sun. The negotiations had reached a fever pitch and he was none too happy to be dragged away at this crucial moment.

Colonel Sun gave silent indication that they should step out into the hallway. When the heavy conference room door had sighed shut behind them, Sun said in a very low voice, "An emissary of Cho Xilan's is here in Shanghai."

Ouyang started. *Emissary* was their private code word for "assassin."

"Is his mission to disrupt my negotiations?"

"Unknown," Colonel Sun said.

"How much of our business does Cho Xilan know?"

Colonel Sun shrugged. "Difficult to say, but just from the hard evidence I'd say he knows that Bourne is here, though whether he knows what we're up to is a mystery."

"How would he know anything, Sun?"

The question hung between them, filling the air with its toxic implications.

Sun took a breath, let it out slowly. "On the face of it, it seems we have a leak."

"On the face of it?" Ouyang said hotly. Then, remembering where they were, he lowered his voice to its previous level. "The moment I wrap up the negotiations I'll fly back to Beijing and dig around until I unearth the culprit."

"And what about the emissary?"

"What information do you have on him?"

"He's traveling with a woman posing as his wife."

"Quite the elaborate cover Cho Xilan manufactured for him." Ouyang tossed his head. "Take care of the emissary, don't let him get anywhere near Bourne. I'll plug the leak."

Turning on his heel, he pulled open the door, and went back into the conference room to nail down the next ten years of his prosperity.

Maricruz watched Carlos Danda Carlos's eyes spark like miniature suns as he studied her approach across the runway tarmac. At once, even before he extended his hand, before he bent over to kiss the back of hers, or opened his mouth to welcome her like a member of the tourist board to sunny San Luis Potosí, she could see how they all wanted a piece of her—Wendell Marsh, Matamoros, Carlos Danda Carlos. That included Ouyang Jidan. He wanted to possess her body, and she had given it to him, freely, wantonly. Whatever he needed her to be during their coupling she could be. And in return, she was using him to get what she wanted: independence, of course, but also the power and wealth to outdo her father, whom she both loved and hated.

Jidan knew better than anyone just how lucrative she had made the pipeline, and with her father gone, he needed her more than ever—as the shield her father had provided, behind which he could continue to operate covertly. He had no contact with anyone in the Mexican cartels; he never had. Keeping his hands immaculately clean was essential to his political aspirations. In that respect, he had put himself in her hands. In the end, she had no love for him, only need.

"I am most curious as to why you called this meeting, Señora Ouyang," Carlos Danda Carlos said as he raised his moist lips from her hand.

As for these Mexicans, she thought, they all wanted to take advantage of the pipeline her father had put in place, the pipeline she had expanded and perfected during her time in Beijing.

"You surprise me with your presence, señor," Maricruz said drily. "I had no idea—"

"A summons from the daughter of Maceo Encarnación, and all the way from China," Raul Giron interrupted. "How could any of us refuse?"

Maricruz saw the naked hostility in his eyes, the utter contempt for her. He resented what he had called her *summons*.

But now Carlos was smiling easily as he shook Felipe Matamoros's hand, murmuring, "A pleasure," as if they were at a cocktail party. Then he turned to Maricruz and, with a sharp look at Giron, said, "Please excuse this soldier. He has obviously been so long in the wilderness he has forgotten his manners." Turning slightly, he addressed Giron again. "Raul, please step back and see to your men. Have them stand down. We are among friends here, is that not right, Señora Ouyang?"

"It is," she said, nodding. "This I guarantee."

"You see, Raul?" Carlos gestured grandly. "We are in the presence of civilized people. Please remember that the next time you address the señora."

Giron mumbled something no one could hear, busy as he was instructing his soldiers.

"You must have patience here, Señora Ouyang," Carlos said in a confidential tone. "These men see only enemies, and react instinctively—it's a survival technique they've perfected. And who can blame them? The endless brutality and bloodshed between the Sinaloa and Los Zetas is a matter of public record."

"No longer endless, Señor Carlos," Maricruz said. "This is why I'm here. I am proposing a permanent truce. More, I am proposing a merging of cartels."

"Why should we consider this?"

"In the short term," Maricruz said, "it will end the needless killing of your men and Señor Matamoros's."

Carlos shook his head. "I doubt I can convince either Giron or the rank and file to give up—"

"You're speaking of power," Matamoros interrupted. "Los Zetas, who have been pushing you back for the past year, have more to lose in this merger than the Sinaloa."

"In the long run"—Maricruz picked up where she left off—"the combination of the Sinaloa and Los Zetas will put all of Mexico in the hands of the new cartel. Plus, it will have the benefit of the pipeline of raw materials I and my husband control that's vital to your business interests."

Carlos appeared to consider her words. "Tell me, who will lead your proposed combined cartel?"

"That is why we are here," Maricruz said, "to work out the details."

"Where the devil resides," Carlos replied.

"This is bullshit!" Giron stepped forward, his pugnacious face thrust forward like a club. "This is a ploy. They're trying to take advantage of us."

"You're wrong," Maricruz told him. "But I understand. This is your view because the history of the cartels is steeped in blood."

Giron's curdled smile made her cringe inside. "It's no more bloody than any other history. Man is a war-like creature. Men adore battle, we enjoy lording it over others. Territory is a vital imperative."

"And women?" she asked as they slowly closed the gap that had formed between them. "What about us?"

"Your blood is different," Giron said in a matter-of-fact voice. "It brings life. As it should be. Women have no place on the battlefield. This is a known fact, it's simply part of your makeup." He shrugged. "God decreed it, and for good reason. Who else would tend to the wounded, bury the dead, and mourn their passing?"

It took all of Maricruz's considerable will not to rip his eyes from his head. What satisfaction that would give her! she thought. But, this being the real world, she put the thought away for another time, another place.

As if divining her thoughts, Carlos inserted himself between her and Giron. "If we stand here any longer we'll all die of thirst." Night had swept across the plain on which they were standing, extinguishing all but the last dusky glow of the sunset. "I propose we continue this discussion at—"

"A cantina of my choosing," Matamoros said.

Without hesitation Carlos replied, "As you wish, señor." Smiling genially, he gestured with one hand. "Where you lead, we will follow."

15

THE MOMENT BOURNE stirred, an avalanche of debris cascaded away from him. He remained buried. Scarcely able to breathe, he wormed his right arm upward, fingers scrabbling, until he felt the coolness of air against his skin. Then he pushed away as much of the ruins as he could before using his shoulders to rise through the murk into the compromised tunnel.

A modest amount of light filtered down through the beams from the basement above. The air was thick with columns of dust that had yet to settle. Looking around, he could just make out his attacker's legs and feet in the gloom. Nothing else was visible. But Bourne was most concerned with Yue, who, though lying curled against the opposite wall, must have been buried by the cave-in.

Bourne climbed out of the grave, which had closed over him in the span of a heartbeat, and stumbled across the mounds of debris. Using the brass hinge holder, he scraped aside the piled-up wreckage that had dropped into the tunnel near the far wall. He could detect no sign of Yue, though he called out to her repeatedly.

His anxiety escalating, he dug faster, pushing aside slabs of wood, pyramids of earth, and a jumble of small rocks. At length, he reached a cross of two pieces of a beam, the wood showing signs of advanced dry rot. He needed to be careful now so as not to cause the wood to disintegrate as he moved it. Setting the pieces aside, he peered into the hole he had made and was rewarded with a view of Yue's right shoulder. She was still curled up in the fetal position. He called to her again, first softly, then more forcefully, but she neither replied nor moved. He could not tell whether she was breathing.

Hurrying now, he pushed away more rubble until there was enough room for him to reach under her, scoop her up, and bring her into the air, which he fanned to keep the dust off her face. He put two fingers against her carotid artery, and was relieved to find a pulse, faint though it was. Opening her mouth, he tilted her head back to open her airway and, bending over her, began to force air into her lungs.

Every so often he pulled back long enough to check her pulse and to see if her chest was rising and falling in a normal manner. Her pulse was a bit stronger, but her chest was still barely moving. He went back to work with a renewed vigor, creating the bellows that rhythmically filled her lungs with air.

All at once she twitched, her eyes flew open, and, pushing on his chest with the palms of her hands, she said in a thin, raspy voice, "What are you doing?"

Bourne sat back on his heels, grinning down at her. "We had a cave-in."

"So it would seem," she said, craning her neck to look around her. "Where's the dirtbag?"

"Under it all." Bourne pointed at the man's feet. "Dead."

"I should fucking well hope so."

Bourne laughed. "Now I know you'll be okay." Standing up, he held out his hand and pulled her to her feet. "How's the ankle?"

"Fine."

"I'm guessing it hurts like fire."

"Go to hell." She grinned hugely.

"Already been there." Bourne grinned back.

"Think we can get out of this shithole now?" She glanced up over her head. "The cops should be here any minute."

"First I need to find out who was following us and why."

"You think you'll get that from a dead man?" she said as she painfully scrambled over the mounds of debris, following him to where the man was half buried.

Bourne began the digging-out process. "Often," he said, "I've found that dead men speak most eloquently. Sometimes better than when they were alive."

Bracing herself against a sloping wall of rubble, she began to help him, so that within minutes Bourne was able to drag the man out from under. Streaks of blood followed in his wake, like a snail's glistening trail.

Quickly Bourne went through his pockets. He found a roll of money, a driver's license in the name of Jesse Long—obviously fictitious—but no wallet, passport, or anything that might accurately identify him. Bourne was just digging out his knife and mobile phone, which had been lodged underneath him, when he cocked his head, hearing the sound of sirens, barely audible, still far away.

He stuffed the items into his pocket, then scooped Yue off her feet and, with her cradled in his arms, mounted the highest pile of debris, climbing into the basement of the building above their heads.

* * *

The cantina Matamoros had chosen was long, low-slung, and dimly lit, redolent of agave, tortillas, refried beans, and stale beer. Multicolored party lights in the form of tiny lanterns were strung from the ceiling. A young woman was dancing by herself in front of a jukebox playing Shakira's "Addicted to You."

The long plank tables were nearly empty, and whatever bar business the cantina was doing was huddled at the front, in a poignant example of the cliché *Misery loves company*.

The various bodyguards took up positions near the front door, while Matamoros led his small contingent to an empty table in the rear. At once the owner popped out of the kitchen as if launched from a cannon, hovering over them to distribute menus and take their drinks orders.

In due course, the beers were served and the four of them were alone again. Matamoros and Giron eyed each other like two wolves circling a carcass.

Carlos said, "Señora, perhaps you'll join me out on the terrace where we can drink our *cerveza* in comparative peace."

As the two of them rose, Matamoros said, "No you don't. I'm not letting her go outside where she could be easy pickings for one of your snipers."

"Señor Matamoros," Carlos said blandly, "this is your territory. You hold all the cards. We are the invited guests—at the behest of this lovely lady. Do me the courtesy—"

"It's all right," Maricruz said as she took her beer. "I'll be perfectly safe."

However, she felt anything but safe as she and Carlos walked out onto the broad terrace in the rear. It was filled with rough-hewn wood tables and chairs. A striped awning, faded by the blinding sun, flapped disconsolately overhead. The northern edge of town, which the cantina overlooked, was dusty and gray.

"You're not one of those women who smokes cigars, are you?"

She glared at him stonily.

"I thought not." He lit up with the great fanfare due a man of his rank. "I want to tell you a story."

"Is this really necessary?"

"Indulge me." He let smoke drift out of his open mouth. "Giron's grandfather had a business partner. He was a gringo. This gringo made all manner of promises to Giron's grandfather and, over the course of time, they were fulfilled. The two men grew rich, until one day the gringo vanished and Giron's grandfather discovered he was left with nothing. His partner had absconded with everything."

Maricruz's stony stare did not let up. "There's no gringo here."

Carlos nodded vigorously. "True, true, as you and I see it. But for Giron it's a different story. He sees you as being worse than a gringo. You're a Mexicana who abandoned her country. To him, you're an outsider, no longer one of us—an apostate, if you will."

"Do you see me that way?"

"I told you, no." He sighed. "But the fact is I have to deal with Giron."

"That's your problem," Maricruz said shortly.

"Well, but when we merge, it will be your problem, as well, señora."

There was silence for a time. Inside the cantina, the jukebox was playing a poignant *ranchera*. In her mind's eye, Maricruz saw the young woman swaying her hips to the beat, her arms around an imaginary lover. How sad her life must be!

Maricruz cleared her mind. "I suppose you brought me out here to propose a solution."

Carlos stared out into the distance, the twinkling lights of town tiny and insignificant against the night. "You know, Maricruz—may I call you Maricruz?"

"By all means."

He nodded, clearly pleased. "While it's true everyone envies me, being engaged in a double life is most difficult."

"Are you going to cry on my shoulder now?"

He smiled, though his gaze was still fixed on dim constellations of light steeping the town in a ghost-like aura. "You may laugh, but when there's no one to talk with, there comes a moment when one thinks to oneself, *What am I doing, what's it all for?*"

"You have no family?"

"My wife is home with the children. Do you imagine I whisper in her ear the things I do here?"

"I'm not certain you go home at all."

He looked at her then, a long, penetrating stare. "I tell my mistress less than I tell my wife, which is nothing at all."

"A wise choice."

He threw her a jaundiced look.

"So there's no one."

"Absolutely so. The people I work with are id-iots."

"Yet here you are confiding to me. A total stranger."

"Hardly a total stranger."

"But a stranger nonetheless."

"Sometimes it's easier to talk with an outsider."

"So you do see me that way."

"I see you as someone who has no ax to grind. Your interests are purely monetary."

Maricruz's heart skipped a beat or two. "Are you trying to recruit me?"

"I'm trying to cut a path through the animus between Giron and Matamoros."

"We can—"

But he was already shaking his head. "There has been too much blood spilled, too many family members plowed under, too much hatred and bloodlust. These cannot be erased or forgotten, no matter what Matamoros has told you."

"What are you saying?"

Carlos stepped closer to her, lowering his voice further. "Giron and Matamoros are the same in one basic respect: They're part of the past. Their time is over and done with." His voice, though low, gained a certain intensity. "You and I, Maricruz, belong to the future. This is our time—we need only reach out and grasp it."

When Captain Lim received the radio message concerning the cave-in at the silk shop, he consulted his detailed neighborhood map, saw the shop was only six blocks from Sam Zhang's pearl establishment, and acted on the stirring in his gut.

Mobilizing his men via wireless network, he instructed them to converge on the address of the silk shop, surrounding it and cordoning it off.

"Detain everyone who comes in or out of the building," he ordered. "But under no circumstances is anyone to set foot inside until I get there."

Then he got into his car and, directing his driver, cut a swath through the dense traffic of the Shanghai streets.

"Faster," he said, leaning forward.

As they rounded a corner and the shop came into view, he drew his gun.

16

FLICKERING LIGHT FROM a pair of nearly defunct fluorescent tubes threw crazy shadows across the ruined basement. The sirens were so loud now Bourne had to believe the police were already on the scene. Bypassing the staircase up to the shop above, he headed toward the rear right corner, where he had caught a glimpse of another set of stairs, less steep. Taking them two at a time, he leapt up to the landing, put his shoulder to the door. It flew open and he went through.

Yue, trying valiantly to fight the pain, had at last succumbed. She lay unconscious in his arms, her head lolling with every move he made. He turned toward the building's rear door, but through the translucent glass panel he could see shadows moving, hear police commands. Turning, he sprinted

back down the stairs and leapt down into the basement instants before the rear door banged open and
heavy boots could be heard tramping across the
floorboards.

Sliding down a pile of debris, he returned to the
tunnel, where he set Yue down and began to dig
through the fall of packed earth until he found his
way to the other side of the cave-in. Returning for
Yue, he headed back the way they had come, away
from the opening he had made, leaving the ruins of
the cave-in behind. His progress was slowed by the
lack of light, the uneven floor, and the small falls
of rock and stone that had occured over the years
since the tunnel had been dug by unknown hands.
Still, he made steady progress.

A sound came to him. He stopped, held his
breath, and listened. Sure enough, he heard the reg-
ular sound of footfalls. And then the cone of a
flashlight's beam swung briefly across the tunnel
behind them.

Captain Lim instructed his men to comb every
floor, every apartment, every closet and hiding
place imaginable, looking for Bourne, but he himself did not join them. Instead he headed down the
staircase to the basement.

At once, in the illumination thrown off by the

buzzing fluorescents, he saw the enormity of the cave-in. Picking his way over to it, he peered over the edge of a fall of debris. As the beam of his flashlight penetrated the darkness, he saw the body of a man, lying facedown. From the streaks of blood, now congealed, he knew the man must have been dragged. Moving the beam of light illuminated the hole from which he had been dragged.

Was the dead man Bourne? There was only one way to find out. Gripping his flashlight between his teeth, he half scrambled, half slid down the sloping side of the cave-in. Using the beam of light to orient himself, he discovered that he was in a tunnel. From the look of it, it ran all the way back to Zhang's pearl shop.

So that's how you eluded me, he thought.

Turning now to the dead man, he squatted down and heaved him over onto his back. It was Long. Lim cursed under his breath. How in the name of heaven had Long gotten ahead of him? Then a wave of relief swept over him: The dead man wasn't Bourne. Colonel Sun's orders were to detain Bourne. If, instead, he had brought back Bourne's corpse, all hell would have broken loose, and he would have been in the center of it. He shuddered at the thought. No one in their right mind wanted to get on the wrong side of Colonel Sun.

Rising, he shone his light ahead. Immediately he saw the hole Bourne had made in the debris to continue on. He picked his way through the rent in the cave-in, heading down the tunnel the way he surmised Bourne had gone.

Bourne, with Yue asleep in his arms, arrived back beneath Sam Zhang's shop, but as he was seeking to ascend the ladder to Zhang's office, he heard voices. Cops! Captain Lim had been clever enough to leave two of his men behind to guard against Bourne's return. Immediately he stopped, listening to the two cops speaking desultorily to each other.

"What did I ever do to Captain Lim to be given this dogshit assignment?"

"You're alive. That's all you need to have done."

"But this is crazy. The *gwai lo* isn't coming back here; he's probably a hundred miles away by now."

"You know it and I know it. Too bad Lim doesn't give a shit."

"Lim's a prick. Anyway, he's army; he's not even from around here."

"Like all of them in Beijing, he's a political animal."

"All he cares about is wiping Colonel Sun's ass."

"That's what you've got to do to become captain in the army."

"Fuck that. Count me out."

A short silence. Then:

"How much longer?"

"A little over an hour. Then we can go home and forget all about that fuck Lim."

Bourne hunkered down in the basement, propped Yue against one wall. She was sleeping peacefully. Then he rose and, silently, went back to the short ladder up to Zhang's office. He couldn't afford to wait an hour, or even fifteen minutes. Any moment Lim would realize that he had lost Bourne or, worse, that he hadn't in fact kept on down the tunnel, but had retraced his steps.

Launching himself up the ladder, he put his left shoulder against the bottom of the trapdoor, sprang it open, and leapt up out of the vertical shaft. Slamming his elbow into one of the cops, he slashed the other with the knife he had picked up in the tunnel. One cop went down, bleeding, the other drew his gun, and Bourne, chopping down on his wrist, got him to drop it. He struck him in the throat and the cop collapsed, unconscious. Turning back, Bourne kicked the mobile out of the bleeding cop's fist then, as he, too, drew his sidearm, rendered him unconscious with a blow to his ear.

When Bourne looked up, he saw Sam Zhang, looking big and terrified, gagged, bound to his chair, which had been rolled into the far corner.

His eyes darted madly from Bourne to the downed cops and back to Bourne again.

As soon as Bourne removed his gag, he said in a hushed voice, "What are you doing back here? Where is Yue?"

Bourne, using his knife to slit open the ties with which Zhang had been affixed to his chair, said, "I doubled back. I figured this would be the last place Lim would look for me now."

Zhang nodded and, somewhat unsteadily, held his arm out until Bourne poured him a glass of whiskey. Zhang grabbed it out of his hand, downed it in one fiery gulp. He gasped, shook his head like a wet dog, and held out the glass for more.

As Bourne was pouring it, he gasped out, "Yue?"

"Asleep in the basement."

Zhang sipped at the whiskey. "How is she?"

"I'll bring her up," Bourne said, reluctant to tell Zhang that his "little sister" had been caught in a cave-in.

For the first time, noticing Bourne's dust-strewn, disheveled appearance, he said, "Wait a minute. What happened down there?"

Ducking away from the question, Bourne returned to the basement, scooped up Yue, and, without waking her, climbed back, depositing her into an office chair.

"Mother!" Zhang cried, struggling out of his

chair on legs made wobbly by his confinement. "She looks worse than you do!"

"She's fine," Bourne assured him. "There was a cave-in." Before the fat man could comment, he added, "The man following me was caught in it and killed."

Still, Zhang knelt in front of her chair, swaying precariously, holding on to the arms. "Little sister," he whispered. "Little sister."

"Who was the man who came after us?"

Zhang, scrutinizing Yue's face, did not reply.

"Zhang," Bourne said more forcefully. "It was the man who caused the cave-in."

The fat man started as if Bourne had whipped him. "He promised to keep her safe!" It was almost a wail.

He was holding Yue's tiny hand between his. "I don't know," he said tenderly, as if he was talking to her. "I never saw him before. I asked, but he was too busy putting a gun to my head." He shook his head sadly. "I never should have given in; I never should have told him where you had gone."

"You had no choice."

"Cowards never have a choice, do they?"

Bourne put a hand on his meaty shoulder. "Think how much pain you saved Yue by staying alive."

He tried to laugh, but it presented itself as more like blubbering. Bourne dragged the two cops out the back, dumping them in a putrid alley. When he returned Zhang was scrubbing the blood off the floor.

After he was finished, Bourne said, "C'mon." He gathered Yue into his arms. "Why don't we find someplace more private to talk while you care for little sister?"

Zhang nodded, lumbered out into the alley, and, opening his mobile, called for his car and driver.

Amir Ophir was working on the last-minute logistics of a rescue mission in the Sinai. Three Israelis hiking up Mount Sinai had been mistaken by a Hamas group for Mossad agents and taken prisoner. As he began the last modifications on the sitrep the call came in on his private mobile. He rose from his desk, strode down the hall as he answered.

"A moment."

Banging into the men's restroom, he checked the stalls, which were empty, then, putting his back to the door to keep anyone from entering, said, "What?"

He listened for some time, his expression becoming more and more clouded. "Retzach is dead? Are you absolutely certain?" He rolled his eyes, his tongue unconsciously clucking against the roof of his mouth. The situation had progressed from dangerous to untenable. How was he to explain this lapse to the Director? Yadin was not known for his lenience in the face of failure, and Ophir had no intention of placing himself on that sacrificial platter. He knew full well the fate of those who did because they had no choice.

He had a choice, though it was unpalatable. There had seemed little or no possibility that he would have to activate the backup plan, but Retzach's death—probably at Bourne's hands—had forced his hand. It was either that or face the music with the Director.

No choice. No choice at all.

Returning to his office, he picked up the phone and made a call.

17

THE DIRECTOR WAS standing in front of a painting by Alighiero Boetti composed of letters, mainly in English, but also in Arabic. In that context, the letters took on another, more artful meaning that lent them a beautiful impressionistic dimension, shockingly and thrillingly at odds with the usual concreteness of language. He did not turn when Ophir came up beside him. At this hour of the day the Tel Aviv Museum of Art, housed in its severe post-modern building, was nearly empty. Here and there, the Director's bodyguards could be seen strolling nonchalantly as they pretended to study the paintings on the walls.

"Have we ever sent any of our cryptographers here?" the Director said. "I've always harbored the suspicion there was a hidden message in this."

Ophir did not bother to answer; he knew the Director was as interested in Boetti's painting as he was, which meant not at all.

"Update," the Director said with such frost in his voice that Ophir felt himself shudder.

"Bourne has definitely slipped his leash," Ophir said. He was sick to death of not knowing what mission the Director was running. "I warned you. The Americans couldn't control Bourne; I can't imagine why you thought you could." When the Director made no reply, Ophir continued. "He discovered the bug in the passport we gave him. Apparently, the moment he set foot in Shanghai, he affixed it to the underside of a taxi, leading us on a wild goose chase until we figured out what had happened."

"Clever chap, that Bourne."

"What are you saying? His actions are indefensible."

Director Yadin finally turned to look at Ophir. "Bourne did precisely what I expected him to do."

Ophir stared at him with a dumbfounded expression. "I . . . I don't understand."

The Director shrugged. "Amir, my friend, it's just as you say. Bourne is ungovernable. He will not work leashed. This is what the Americans never understood about him. They continually tried to tame him, to fit him into the mold they made for him. But when he escaped that mold he was absolutely determined never to go back."

"Then how can he help us, Memune?"

The Director, hands behind his back, began to stroll with Ophir at his side. "Though Bourne can't be leashed, Amir, he can be guided. Bourne is a bullet. Aim the gun and the bullet finds its mark. That's precisely what I've done: I've guided him onto the proper path. How he finds his way along that path is of no interest to me." He nodded his shaggy head. "From here, I will take my boat out for a sail, to grieve and to help clear my head."

"And I?"

"Finish up this Sinai business before it gets more messy than it already is. I want our citizens out of our enemies' hands and safely back on home soil by midnight. Is that clear?"

"Perfectly, Memune."

"Forget Bourne, Amir. You have had your say. Now leave him to me."

Ophir watched the Director and his retinue of bodyguards leave the museum, then started out himself. On the plaza in front of the museum, he saw the three cars pull out, and was surprised to see the entourage separate. The two cars housing the bodyguards peeled away, while the Director's car went in another direction—and it wasn't toward the waterfront where his boat was rocking at its slip.

Curious, Ophir slid behind the wheel of his car and followed the Director as his car slid in and out of traffic. He had been pleased when Yadin had told him that he was going for a sail. The Director had looked pale and haggard—and was it his imagination or had he lost weight?

In front of him, the Director's car had turned onto Weizmann Street, then parked in front of the Sourasky Medical Center.

What in the world? thought Ophir as he watched Yadin stride up the ramp and enter the medical center itself. Pulling his car into a space, Ophir got out and hurried up the ramp, into the cool, quiet interior.

Heading over to the information desk, he asked for Eli Yadin, an outpatient at the center. The man behind the granite banc directed him to another banc on the right side of the immense glass-paneled entrance hall.

The woman behind this counter was young, fit, with that certain confident air only a stint in the Israeli Army could give her.

"How may I help you?" she said with a practiced smile.

"I'm looking for Eli Yadin," Ophir said. "I believe he's an outpatient here."

"In what specialty?"

"I don't know."

The young woman wrinkled up her freckled nose, frowning at him. "Sir, we have sixteen separate outpatient clinics."

Ophir considered for a moment. "Try oncology."

She input the Director's name. "Sorry, sir. I don't find his name listed."

"Surely you can cross-reference all of them."

She looked both dubious and suspicious. "I can, but..."

Ophir flipped open his official ID. He hadn't wanted to identify himself, but she had left him no choice.

The young woman, looking hard and long at the ID, finally said, "I'll see what I can do."

Her fingers flew over her terminal keyboard, the end result of which was a firm shake of her head. "I'm sorry, sir, there's no one in any of the outpatient clinics by that name."

"But there must be," Ophir said, baffled.

"I've done everything I can for you, sir," the young woman said, and turned away to take a phone call.

Of course, Ophir thought as he retraced his steps and exited onto the ramp leading to Weizmann

Street, if the Director had registered under an alias he'd never find him. But by the time he was back behind the wheel and driving away, the small mystery was far from his thoughts. His mind was already overtaken by the last crucial steps he needed to take in order to assure the safe return of the three Israelis held prisoner in the Sinai.

Carlos is on board," Maricruz said when she and Matamoros had retired to the Los Zetas compound.

They stood on the long veranda, sipping mescal *viejo*, staring out at the palm fronds clacking in the wind.

"You were with him a long time."

"Jealous?"

Matamoros snorted.

It was past midnight. A horned moon appeared and disappeared behind scudding clouds that brought a humid wind presaging heavy rain. Around them, armed guards patrolled the periphery, just beyond the eight-foot stucco walls that enclosed the compound. Other guards paced through the gardens and oasis-like fistfuls of palms. Save for the cicadas, tree frogs, and the occasional harsh bark of a street dog, the night was blanketed with a velvety silence, as if they were at a resort on the Mayan coast. All that was missing was the soft splash of the waves onto the beach.

"It was a pleasure dealing with Carlos," she went on. "He's a businessman; he understood the benefits of my proposition without my having to go into a dog-and-pony show."

"Giron wasn't involved?"

"He wasn't even mentioned." Maricruz finished off her mescal. "The three of us will meet tomorrow morning at nine to finalize the alliance."

Matamoros nodded. He seemed distracted. They went inside. He pointed out her room, then went down the wood-paneled corridor into his bedroom and shut the door behind him.

The bedroom designated for Maricruz was also wood-paneled, generously proportioned, with a king-size bed, oversize furniture, an odd combination of bullfight etchings and photos of exotic dancers on the walls. The en suite bathroom was luxurious—marble-clad, with separate shower and soaking tub from which the occupant could gaze at the floodlit gardens.

Stripping off her clothes, she stepped into the shower, let the needles of water sluice the dust and sweat off her skin, while she threw her head back, closed her eyes, and thought of nothing at all.

Toweled off and in bed between the soft sheets, she half expected Matamoros to knock on her door.

When he didn't, she was unsure whether she was relieved or disappointed.

That night she dreamed she was swimming in blood, a suffocating dream that not so much frightened her as left her feeling enervated. She opened her eyes, slowly surfacing, and thought she heard gunshots. But when she started fully awake, sitting up in bed, the early morning held only cocks' crows and, again, the barking of dogs, foraging the streets of San Luis Potosí.

Swinging her long legs out of bed, she relieved herself, dressed quickly, and went out of the bedroom. Down the hallway and into the living room, which she found deserted, she looked around, and then proceeded to the kitchen. Also deserted. Turning back, and now with a mounting sense of urgency, she returned to the bedroom hallway, pushed open the door to Matamoros's room. It was empty; the bed hadn't been slept in.

Returning to her bedroom, she pulled out her Bersa Thunder .380, checked that it was fully loaded, then headed immediately to the entrance, where she pulled open the front door and stepped out into the courtyard. There were no guards, no one at all. The compound was blanketed by a deathly stillness, and she was reminded of her suffocating dream.

Hurrying through the gardens, past the clumps of

palm trees, she hauled open the gate to the compound. A large black SUV was parked a hundred
yards away. The rising sunlight spun off its windshield, turning it opaque.

Scanning the immediate vicinity, Maricruz approached the SUV with a measure of caution. She
moved around to the left side of the vehicle, bending slightly to look in the windows, but they were
smoked and she couldn't see a thing.

She looked around again, hoping to see Matamoros or one of his men, but there was no one.
Resisting an urge to run, she approached the SUV,
reached out, and opened the passenger's-side door.

A gasp escaped her half-parted lips. Crammed
into the interior of the SUV were fourteen men. All
had been beheaded. She jumped back as something
came bouncing out, hit the SUV's running board,
then dropped to the ground.

Staring up at her with gray, glazed eyes and a
terrified expression was the severed head of Raul
Giron.

You need somewhere safe," Sam Zhang said. "A
place where neither Captain Lim nor anyone else
can find you." He tapped his driver on the shoulder
and spoke to him in a voice that didn't carry back
to Bourne and Yue. Then he sat back, his bulk

squeezing his two passengers together. "I know such a place. We're going there now."

Yue was slung across the seat, her head and shoulders against Bourne's chest.

"Lim cut our conversation short," Bourne said to Zhang.

"Is that so? What were we talking about?"

"Ouyang Jidan."

Zhang pursed his thick lips. "I don't remember that."

"I had heard he had come here from Beijing."

"Why does that concern you?"

"He and I have a reckoning. He's responsible for the murder of someone I knew."

Zhang turned his head. "That sounds properly lacking in details." He shrugged. "Minister Ouyang has been responsible for many deaths."

"I only care about this one," Bourne said.

They went across the bridge, heading back to Pudong, Shanghai's glittering modern half. The car turned down the Bund, then rolled to a stop in front of the glass-and-steel facade of one of the city's finest hotels.

Zhang asked for a wheelchair when the door was opened by one of the uniformed attendants. Moments later Bourne placed Yue in the wheelchair and, with the man who brought it pushing it, the four of them went through the doors, past gleaming

polished marble and Maw-Sit-Sit—a green stone
mined in Burma—to the bank of elevators. They
rose in silence until they reached the twenty-first
floor.

"I'll take it from here," Zhang said, slipping a
bill to the man and replacing his hands on the
wheelchair's handlebars.

They left the attendant in the elevator. Bourne
followed Zhang down the lushly carpeted hallway,
past the shell-shaped sconces emitting mellow
light, to the double doors of a suite. Zhang used
an electronic key-card to enter the room, then
wheeled Yue in.

As Bourne stepped across the threshold, he felt
the quick jab of a needle in the side of his neck. He
tried to whirl, but whatever had been injected into
him had already slowed his reflexes. He was in
midturn when his knees buckled. Someone caught
him from behind. His balance failed, his vision
blurred, and his thoughts swam away from him
like a school of fish.

The last thing he saw was Yue rising from the
wheelchair, a wolfish smile on her face. She kissed
him on the lips, then struck him hard across the
face, plunging him into oblivion.

Book Two

18

Jin put his foot between the elevator doors, preventing them from closing. When the doors retracted, he hit the EMERGENCY STOP button. By straining, he could hear the soft click of the wheelchair as it progressed down the carpeted hallway.

Bending down, he removed the 5.8 mm QSZ-92 pistol from the holster affixed to his ankle and called in via wireless.

"Captain," he whispered, barely able to contain his excitement, "we've caught two birds with one stone. Cho Xilan's emissary and Jason Bourne."

"Proceed with caution," Captain Lim's voice buzzed in his ear. "Backup is on site and will be on your floor within minutes."

"Apart from clearing the surrounding rooms,

which should be done in conjunction with the hotel
manager, too many people are going to be a hin-
drance, rather than a help." Jin stepped out into the
hallway, which was now deserted.

"I don't want you unprotected," Lim said.

"With all due respect, Captain, you don't know
me well enough to have that worry." Jin grinned to
himself. "I do better on my own."

"There's no room for error," Lim said.

"I don't make errors, Captain."

"You understand the directive regarding Jason
Bourne."

" 'Detain, do not harm.' Got it, Captain."

"All right." There was a short pause. "See you on
the other side."

Cutting the connection, Jin crept down the hall
on the outsides of his soles. He held the QSZ-92
tilted slightly upward, at the ready. When he
reached the double doors to the suite, he stopped,
remained motionless for a space of twenty seconds, then put his ear to the polished wood.

Go back into the bedroom and close the door,"
Yue ordered the man who had accompanied her
from Beijing as her husband. He nodded and complied.

When she was alone with Sam Zhang, she

glanced down at Bourne's inert body lying at her feet, and said to Zhang, "You have been playing a dangerous game."

With a sigh, the fat man lowered himself into a Mandarin chair. "Does this warning come from you or from Cho Xilan?"

Her lips twitched in the semblance of a smile. "Pulling both ends against the middle can get you killed. Just look at Wei-Wei."

"Did you have to kill him?"

"By definition, Sam, everything I do, I have to do."

"And Sergeant Amma?"

"An honest cop is a dangerous cop, Sam. You know that."

Zhang shook his head. "The trouble with you, little sister, is that you have no ethics."

"I have plenty of ethics," Yue said. "What I lack is remorse, and thank the gods for that."

The fat man tilted his head back and spoke to the ceiling. "What have I done to deserve this morass of immorality?"

"Don't kid yourself, Sam," Yue said as she kicked Bourne to make certain he was still unconscious. "Like me, you've done everything humanly possible to survive in this cesspit of a city."

Her eyes lowered to Bourne. "I kind of like this fellow. He's got something of value burning inside him. I envy him that." When Zhang grunted, she glanced up at him. "He did save my life, Sam."

"What does it matter now? We have to turn him over to Colonel Sun, as instructed."

"Not yet." Yue squatted down beside Bourne, put a hand on his head. "He intrigues me."

"Come on, little sister, no one intrigues you."

"Oh, but he does, Sam. Truly. He has a history not only with Sun, but with Minister Ouyang." She smiled. "Now, that *is* intriguing." She caressed Bourne's head. "I'm not letting him go until I find out what that history is and whether it can benefit me."

Zhang licked his lips. "Now who's playing a dangerous game?"

Yue chuckled softly. "The difference is I can handle it, Sam. You, I'm not so sure about."

"It's true I'm getting older," Zhang said ruefully.

"That's not the same as getting old," Yue pointed out.

He smiled at her. "Sometimes, you do surprise me."

"Sometimes I'm convinced I was hatched out of an egg."

"I have observed your reptilian brain is highly developed."

For a moment, Yue sat back on her heels and

watched him thoughtfully. "You're the only one who knows me, Sam."

"As much as one can know a Komodo dragon."

Yue smirked, prodding Bourne between the ribs. Then she slapped his face. "Time to get down to business."

Zhang leaned forward, his massive belly compressed. "How are you going to handle him?"

"How d'you think." Yue held up the knife Bourne had taken in the tunnel.

For the first time, Zhang looked alarmed. "Colonel Sun was quite clear. Bourne is not to be harmed in any way. Minister Ouyang wishes to interrogate Bourne himself."

"Minister Ouyang has returned to Beijing to root out the double agent in his inner circle."

"You know that?"

"I keep learning from you, Sam. My network of contacts has broadened exponentially."

Zhang, sighing, said, "Little sister, it occurs to me, not for the first time, that this—intrigue, this mayhem—may not be what *we* want."

She gave him a curious look. "It's what we've always wanted." She shrugged. "Besides, our lives are not our own."

"So we have been told. A lie becomes the truth when it is repeated often enough. Tell me, is this acceptable to you?"

Yue eyed him speculatively. "You talk as if we have a choice."

"Well, actually we do."

She shook her head. "An illusion, Sam."

"We can get out."

Yue's expression turned quizzical. "Get out?"

"Yes. Leave. Go somewhere else. We have the means."

"We have money, yes. But where in China would we go? We'd be found even in the most remote corner of the country, where, frankly, I'd rather slit my wrists than live anyway."

"There's an immense world outside China, little sister. It's so vast we could get lost in it in no time."

"You think so. Cho Xilan's reach is long, his influence great."

"Here in China, yes, that's true enough. But beyond the Middle Kingdom is a world he knows very little about. This is where Minister Ouyang has a great strategic advantage. Cho is a tactician, which means he's involved in the finer details of maneuvering within the Politburo. This is his concentration. He and his Chongqing reactionaries are hidebound, myopic. The Middle Kingdom is their sole focus. Their influence outside China is negligible."

Yue rocked back on her heels. "You're serious."

"Perfectly." Zhang passed a hand across his broad face. "It isn't simply that I'm getting old, little sister. I'm tired of this life, doing other people's bidding, making them rich, receiving only the crumbs from their table. It has occurred to me recently that I have never paid any attention to myself. I've never had the time. I'm guessing neither have you."

He looked down at Bourne. "Let's begin by giving this man back his freedom."

Yue considered. "Bourne knows things about Sun and Ouyang—information we can use as leverage should there be a need. Bourne's our insurance policy."

"Then you're with me?"

At that moment a bullet blew out the lock on the suite door.

What have you done?" Maricruz said as she saw Felipe Matamoros walking toward her through the watery dawn light. "What the fuck have you done?"

"I?" Matamoros pointed at his chest. "I've done nothing. However, my *compadres*, lacking your faith that Raul Giron was ready to let go of the Sinaloa's independence, decided to take action."

Maricruz glanced again at the severed head between her feet. "The decision was out of Giron's hands. It was agreed to by Carlos. I told you that."

"Carlos flew back to Mexico City the moment dinner was over. I imagine he's already plotting your demise."

"*My* demise?"

"You're now more dangerous than Los Zetas. Us he can deal with, but you—you're another story altogether. You're threatening to overturn the balance of power in Mexico. That he cannot abide."

Maricruz looked at the abattoir of the SUVs interior. "This is a fuck-up of another order, Felipe."

"*Mujer, por favor.* Since this is my territory, let me explain the vicissitudes of the situation. First, my good friend Giron wasn't going to roll over for anyone, least of all you. If you believed that fairy tale, you were living in an alternate universe."

He kicked Giron's head as if it were a soccer ball. It flew through the air, struck the trunk of a palm, and spun away onto the ground. The eyes had grown as opaque as those of a dead fish.

"Second, Carlos comes from money; he never bloodied his hands, he never lived in the muck like me and our friend here. He has no real knowledge of us and our motives. Third, Carlos is a prick, a liar, and a thief. Worst of all, he's a coward. Cowards never move forward; they cling to the status quo. To ensure the status quo they hide behind their mothers' skirts—in Carlos's case, the federal government. *El presidente* is who gave him his job, it's *el presidente* who protects him. He's the only one who can. Carlos was happy to take his skim off the Sinaloa top line, but when things threaten to get complicated you can count on him to cut and run."

"If that's the case, why the hell didn't you tell me this last night?"

"Would you have believed me, after you played kissy-face with him out on the veranda?" He studied her face. "So now here we are faced with a new reality—change, but not precisely the change you envisioned."

"Since your *compadres* have taken care of Giron and his lieutenants it seems to me Los Zetas will have little difficulty overcoming the Sinaloa now."

"I can't disagree, *mi princesa*."

But he did not look happy, and Maricruz knew why.

"Carlos has become the problem, which is both good and bad," he said. "Instead of going to war with a rival cartel, the war has been reduced to one man. But because Carlos cannot tolerate change, he will surely bring to bear on you, me, and Los

Zetas the considerable resources of the Mexican government. And though in the past we have fairly easily fended off the *Federales*, for Carlos this war has become personal. The most perilous times lie ahead."

"Then there's only one thing to do," Maricruz said. "We have to kill him before he kills us."

Felipe Matamoros threw his head back and laughed. "I see I was right in trusting you."

He thrust up one hand, signaling. Maricruz, turning, saw his *compadres*, the rest of the ruling Los Zetas cadre, appear, striding toward her, dressed in camo fatigues, as heavily jawed as they were armed, glowering darkly, broad shoulder to broad shoulder, as if they were part of the Magnificent Seven.

When Jin slammed the door open and rushed into the hotel suite, he aimed his handgun at Zhang and Yue. He ignored the figure lying inert on the floor between them. That was a mistake.

Erupting into violent motion, Bourne twisted the knife out of Yue's hand and threw it the short distance to where Jin stood in the classic shooter's stance, finger about to squeeze the trigger. The knife blade buried itself to the hilt in Jin's chest.

He looked down, staring in disbelief at the first spurt of blood, and he began to keel over. As he did so, Bourne snatched the gun out of his hand, rolled over, and aimed it at Yue.

"Now we've reached the heart of the matter," he said. "Where are Colonel Sun and Minister Ouyang?"

Yue looked at him blandly. If she was impressed by his maneuvers, she refused to show it. "Sun and his toady Lim, along with a fistful of heavily armed soldiers, are most likely on their way up as we speak." She plastered an enigmatic smile on her face. "We should leave now."

"I'm not going anywhere with you," Bourne said.

"If you want to find Ouyang," she insisted, her smile turning wolfish, "you will."

When she reached over to help Bourne up, he slapped her hand away. "You've already done enough."

Zhang heaved his bulk out of the Mandarin chair. "You might find it in your heart to forgive her. She has a reptilian brain and a feral heart."

Bourne, shaking off the last effects of the drug, directed them out into the hallway, which was eerily quiet.

"They've evacuated the floor," Bourne said.

Hue nodded. "See? What did I tell you?"

As he headed for the elevator bank, she said, "What are you doing? They'll already have had the elevators under their control."

Shooting her a murderous look, Bourne went past the farthest elevator in the bank and stopped in front of a narrow door set flush with the wall. He picked the lock, then swung open the door. Beyond, the four elevator shafts loomed.

"You're joking," Zhang said, peering into the gloom. He was sweating like a faulty generator. "We can't go in there."

"Do you have a better idea?" Bourne said.

"Sam," Yue said urgently, "all the elevator cars are frozen, except one, which is full of police. In a moment, it's going to open on this floor."

Bourne stepped into the interior, picking his way to a concrete ledge on one side of the right-most shaft.

"Come on, Sam." Yue, standing behind Zhang, fairly pushed him sideways through the narrow opening.

He screamed softly as he tottered, until Bourne caught him, hauled him onto the ledge beside him. Zhang wobbled like Humpty Dumpty on the wall. Behind him, Yue entered the shafts, shut the door behind her. Bourne pulled Zhang along to make room for her on the ledge.

"Sam," Yue warned, "don't look down."

But it was already too late. Zhang's gaze was drawn down the shaft as if watching a multi-car accident. He seemed powerless to look away until Bourne slapped his face.

"Look at me, Zhang," he said. "Keep your eyes on me and you'll be okay."

"Why shouldn't I be okay?" Zhang asked shakily.

"Because we're going down the ladder."

Seeing he was about to howl, Bourne clapped a hand over his mouth.

"Shut the fuck up, Sam!" Yue hissed. "Unless you want to be interrogated by Colonel Sun."

Zhang shuddered, but seemed to calm down somewhat. Bourne took his hand away.

"What ladder?" Zhang whispered. He was clearly terrified.

"The one the maintenance workers use to move from floor to floor. Yue will go first. You follow, then me. Don't worry. We'll guide you onto the rungs. Once you're on, stare straight ahead at the wall and keep descending until I tell you to stop. That's all there is to it."

Zhang gave a stifled sob. "Listen," he said. "I'm not going to make it. Just leave me here and go on. I'll take care of myself."

"Like hell you will," Yue said as she and Bourne manhandled him to the iron bars of the vertical ladder that paralleled the shaft they were in. "How will you take care of yourself in here?"

Zhang didn't bother to answer her. Instead he mournfully watched Yue start down the ladder. They all stopped as the elevator car closest to them rose into view and stopped at the floor they were attempting to leave. They could hear the doors open, a man's muffled voice, probably giving orders to regroup around the doors to the suite.

"All they're going to find is that idiot I came with," Yue said under her breath. "He almost got us flagged at the airport. Whatever they're going to do with him, he deserves it."

"Let's go," Bourne said to Zhang, now that the car was stationary.

Yue descended while Bourne placed the fat man's hands onto the rungs of the ladder, swung him onto it. Zhang clung there, paralyzed, until Bourne crowded on, forcing him to descend.

"Remember what I told you," Bourne said. He despised having to deal with other people, and this was one of the reasons why. He operated best on his own, but there were exigencies in the field that could be neither anticipated nor avoided. Unfortunately, this was one of them. On the other hand, he was convinced that both Zhang and Yue would prove invaluable sources. If he could keep them alive.

The next moment rapid-fire shooting broke out on the floor they had left behind, and Zhang, his nerves already shredded, lost his hold on the rung and began to topple into the space between the ladder and the elevator car.

19

REACHING UP, YUE slammed the flat of her hand against the center of Zhang's back, preventing him from falling backward. An instant later Bourne grabbed Zhang, righted him fully, and pulled him inch by inch back to his perch on the ladder.

"Everything's fine, Sam," Yue said soothingly. "We're away from the guns. You're safe now."

Zhang, whose breathing had mirrored his too-rapid heartbeat, swallowed hard and, resting his forehead against the cool iron of a rung, closed his eyes, regulating his breathing to a more normal rhythm.

"Gods," he breathed, "if I survive this I'm going to change my ways."

"We're witnesses," Bourne said, looking past him to where Yue stared up at him.

Yue gave him a brief nod, which, Bourne suspected, was as close as she would come to an apology. He returned her nod, and the exchange became that of two soldiers on opposite sides, each one acknowledging the accomplishments of the other. A grudging truce had been called, though whether it was permanent or temporary was still to be determined.

They continued down, past the hanging car, and now the open shaft yawned below them. Then Bourne held up his hand and, as one, they all paused.

"Do you have any idea how to get out of here?" Yue asked. "Sun has undoubtedly got the hotel surrounded."

"First stop, the kitchens," Bourne said.

Zhang groaned.

"I have to agree," Yue said. "That's a long way down."

"That depends on how we get there." He pointed. "Climb."

"What?" Zhang said. "Up?"

"That's right. Yue, let's go. We have no time to lose."

They went up now, faster than they had descended. When Bourne came level with the car's roof, he climbed onto it. Crouching down, he held out his hands while Yue held the fat man's hips in place. Bourne lugged him onto the roof, settling him onto his haunches. Shortly thereafter, Yue joined them.

"These new elevators are controlled electronically through a wireless network." Bourne opened a small panel in the rooftop. Inside was a miniature computer keyboard. He took out his mobile phone, accessed the proper screen. "The phone has already ID'd the network. The next step is to hack into it so we can use the maintenance controls."

Yue held out her hand. "Let me take a stab at it," she said.

Bourne handed over his mobile, watched her fingers flying over the virtual keys. Her expression darkened in concentration, and the tiny tip of her tongue appeared between her lips.

"There," she said, offering him the phone. "We're in."

Bourne took it, marveling at her handiwork. He input the hacked passcode into the panel's keyboard.

"Hold on." He punched a key, and, with a small shudder, the elevator began its smooth descent of the shaft.

They were all headed back to the villa when the sound of helos could be heard chopping up the early-morning calm. Then four silhouettes began to darken the sky, and all of them began to run.

Matamoros took hold of Maricruz's elbow, directing her to the armored vehicle in which she had arrived from the airstrip. "There's a forest a quarter mile to the northwest," he said as he settled in beside her. "Once we're hidden by the trees, we'll be safe." His mouth gave a twitch. "If the helos even make it that far."

Maricruz had no idea what he was talking about, but as the armored vehicle coughed into life, moving out of the compound at a pace that astonished her, she saw through the thick bulletproof window on her side that Matamoros's *compadres* were not following them. Instead two of them brought out ground-to-air missile launchers while the others loaded them.

As the armored vehicle left the area behind, she was afforded a glimpse of a pair of percussions as two white streaks took to the air. Explosions shook the vehicle, but the driver kept to his course. *Two helos down*, Maricruz thought.

She had no view forward, so she could not know what was ahead of them. But just after a third explosion shattered the atmosphere, the vehicle began to bump along, continually jarring her, which meant they had exchanged the paved road for a dirt track. Moments later her window was filled with thick greenery, and she sighed in relief. They had reached the forest; they were safe.

At that moment, there came a great whooshing sound and the green outside her window turned red. One of the helos had gotten past the missiles. Swooping low over the forest, its soldiers were using flamethrowers to set the trees alight. All around them came cracking and great thudding as huge trees came falling down. The flames licked higher.

The armored vehicle was trapped in what once had been a safe haven, but was now a massive conflagration.

They rode the elevator all the way down to the spa level. On the way, Yue described the hotel's layout. When the car settled, Bourne reached out for the ladder, clambered off the elevator, and climbed up a short way to the narrow door that led out onto the restaurants-and-kitchens level.

Now that he was near the ground, Zhang's bravado returned, and he was able to transfer himself onto the ladder and follow Bourne up. Yue took up the rear. Within moments the three of them were back inside the hotel proper.

"I still don't see how we're going to get out of

here without Sun's soldiers shooting us dead," Yue said.

Bourne ignored her, headed down a utility corridor that separated the hotel's several restaurants from the kitchens that served them, and entered an employees' washroom, where all of them cleaned themselves up as best they could.

Then they exited, went through the kitchens, bustling, steam-laden, into a second corridor at the end of which was a double door that seemed to lead out to the street. A uniformed hotel guard stood to one side, looking vacant as he picked his teeth.

Around the corner from him were a number of large rolling carts, two of which were piled high with soiled linens from the meal services. Quickly Bourne mashed Zhang into one of them, rearranging the linens over him while the fat man crouched down as best he could. Yue was climbing into the next one when they heard footsteps approaching.

A harsh male voice said, "If this wasn't the last pickup—"

"You'd what? Quit?" A second voice laughed. "Big talk."

Bourne leapt into the cart with Yue, burrowing them both down, drawing the linens over the tops of their heads. Not a moment later they heard the

wheels of the cart holding Zhang squealing away
from them, then their own cart was moving along
the corridor, around the corner. A bump and then,
even through the mountain of soiled linen, Bourne
could feel the humidity and temperature rise as if
they were on a griddle.

They heard more voices as they were being
wheeled across what must have been a loading
dock. Then another bump as the carts were loaded
into a large truck. Doors were slammed shut, and
whatever vague light that had come to them was
abruptly cut off.

Darkness. Then the grinding of gears as the truck
started up. The cart started to rock back and forth
as they left the hotel behind.

Out!" Matamoros shouted. "Out, out, out!"

The interior of the armored vehicle was almost
as hot as an oven. One of his men broke open
the door and they slipped out. The forest was an
inferno, but his men led them along a corridor between trees that had not yet been consumed by
flames.

Above them, over the roar of the conflagration,
they could hear the rhythmic *thwop-thwop-thwop*
of the helo's rotors. The aircraft seemed like it was
just above them. The severe downdraft fanned the

flames, spreading the fire into the corridor down which they raced. Flames licked the trees right behind them; they could feel the heat rising greedily at their backs, seemingly determined to sear the clothes off their backs.

Maricruz and Matamoros followed the soldiers as they veered to the right, trying to reach the periphery of the fire, trying to outrun the flames the personnel aboard the *Federales'* helo were doing their best to spread.

"Our nemesis has wasted no time closing for the kill," Maricruz said over the intense racket as they crashed through the dry underbrush.

"He won't stop, either." Matamoros had a Heckler & Koch MP5 assault rifle, handed him by one of his men. He was now looking up as they ran, trying to find a gap in the treetops through which he could fire at the low-hovering helo.

"It's as I said," Maricruz said. "We have to find a way to kill him before he kills us."

Up ahead, a gap in the trees let in a beam of light that seemed harshly blue compared with the fire-red of their immediate world. Looking up, Maricruz could see the glint of metal, then the body of the helo came into view, glinting blue-green like the body of a gigantic insect.

Matamoros lifted the assault rifle and was taking aim when the blue of a missile caught the tail of the helo, blasting it into smithereens. The helo bucked with the impact, then spun around madly and plummeted straight down toward the small glade in which Maricruz and Matamoros now stood.

20

WE HAVE A proposal to make you." Sam Zhang looked across the table to where Yue sat, hands clasped around a cup of jasmine tea, eyes cast down, staring into the limpid depths.

"You're joking." Bourne pointedly rubbed the side of his neck where he had been injected. "The both of you have used up any goodwill you might have accrued."

"I understand that," Zhang said. "And until this moment we have neglected to thank you for saving our lives back there."

Bourne's gaze shifted. "Why don't we let Yue speak for herself."

At the mention of her name, Yue flinched, but her eyes remained pinned to her cup of tea.

The trio sat at an interior table of a tumbledown

tea shop on a dusty, ancient lane in Zhujiajiao, a suburb of Shanghai. Pearl Stream, as it was known by its inhabitants, was a fan-shaped village, crisscrossed by glimmering waterways spanned by innumerable bridges made variously of wood, stone, and marble, some topped with coiled dragons or fierce lions with pearls caught between their open jaws. Outside, a bruise-toned sunset glowered, reflected on the water. The heat of the long afternoon wavered, vanquished by a freshening breeze. They had arrived here after leaping off the laundry van just before it entered its facility. From there Zhang made a call using Bourne's mobile and, some time later, a trishaw picked them up.

Zhang cocked his head. "Little sister?"

"What is it you wish to say?" Bourne asked her. "Or maybe it's nothing at all."

Still, Yue said nothing. She had not moved in minutes; she scarcely seemed to breathe.

Bourne looked meaningfully at Zhang, who said, "Excuse me. This tea has gone right through me."

After he had left, Bourne reached out and gently unfolded Yue's fingers from around the teacup. Only after he slid it away did she look up.

"I trusted someone once," she said at length. "I took a vow never to trust anyone again."

"What about Zhang?"

"Sam's an opportunist. For him, Sam comes first, last, and always."

Bourne said nothing. The afternoon rushed away from them and, with it, the terror and hustle of their harrowing escape. Surrounded by the slow pace and utter serenity here, it was difficult to imagine the frantic metropolis that had threatened to swallow them whole just hours before.

Yue said, "I ask myself over and over, what is it this man wants from you?"

"What do you imagine I want?"

"That's just it, I don't know."

"But I've already told you: I'm tracking down Colonel Sun and Minister Ouyang." He watched her for a moment. "I see. You don't believe me."

Yue put her hands flat on the table as if she was about to lever herself up and run away. "Why should I?"

It was a valid question for which Bourne had no answer. A small boat, fragrant with tea and spices, glided past, trailing an indigo wake. He continued to watch her, considering how to proceed. "Having faith in nothing at all is a terrible burden for anyone to carry," he said at last, "especially someone as young as you."

A tear leaked out of her eye before she turned away. Brusquely, almost angrily, she brushed it off her cheek.

"Sun and Ouyang are responsible for the death of someone I cared a great deal about," Bourne continued. "I can't go on until my debt to her is paid."

"You've put yourself in jeopardy for her; not even for her—her memory."

"My memory of her is all I have."

She looked away for a moment, as she often did when she was considering revealing a hidden part of herself. "It must be so painful to care about another person that deeply."

Bourne was filled with sadness for her. "Sometimes there's a satisfaction, if not pleasure, in pain."

Yue watched the female waiters gliding to and fro, balancing their trays of fragrant teas and steaming dim sum in wicker baskets like dancers in a ballet. For some time she seemed lost in thought. Finally, her gaze returned to Bourne.

"Love is a form of faith, is that it?"

"I never thought of it that way, but maybe it is."

She filled her cup with fresh tea, but did not touch it. "Living in China makes it easy to lose faith," she said in a whisper. "If you're born with any at all, it slowly squeezes the life out of it."

"Were you born with any?"

"It's too long ago to remember," she said shortly.

"I don't believe you."

When she turned back to him, her expression

was as fierce as that of the carved stone lions on the village's bridges. "I choose not to remember, all right?"

"No," he said, "it's not all right." Ignoring the glare she gave him, he continued. "I consider memory a privilege, a precious thing. I have almost none. I'm an amnesiac."

Yue's expression underwent a fundamental shift. "You don't know who your parents are or where you came from?"

"That's right."

She snorted. "I'd say that's a fucking gift."

"I doubt you'd say that if your memory vanished in an instant."

Yue looked away for a moment, then her gaze swung back to Bourne. "Maybe you're right—but I doubt it."

"At last," he said, "a break in the clouds."

She smiled. It was a shy smile, the expression of a child. Almost at once, her expression sobered, the smile beating a hasty retreat behind the clouds of her armor.

"I'm sorry," she muttered, just before Zhang returned.

He looked from one to the other. "I notice a marked lack of tension." He rubbed his hands together. "Does that mean we're cleared to continue?"

"Always the deal-maker," Yue said.

Zhang seemed pleased by her remark. "You know that film, *Glengarry Glen Ross*? My favorite character is Blake. Why? Because his mantra is *ABC: Always be closing*." He tapped his chest with a pudgy forefinger. "Blake and I, we're—what d'you call it—soul brothers."

He called for another pot of jasmine tea, along with several plates of dim sum, without asking if anyone else was hungry.

"So." He spread his hands. "Shall we get down to brass tacks? You want information on Colonel Sun and Minister Ouyang. In return, we want to get out of China. That's our quid pro quo."

"Ask for something that's not impossible," Bourne said.

Zhang leaned forward. "Listen to me. You want to get close to Colonel Sun. That's impossible now. You've got to get out of Shanghai as fast as we do. In this, we're all in the same boat. I have contacts; for me it's a snap. Getting out of the country is another matter entirely."

"And you think it will be easy for me?"

"Easier for you than for us."

The conversation ceased for a moment as a waiter brought the tea and food.

"The thing is," Zhang resumed after he had popped a *shui mai* into his mouth, chewed, and swallowed, "Ouyang is no longer here. He flew back to Beijing last night, and as long as he stays there, he's invulnerable. Neither you nor any other Westerner will be able to get to him to do him harm."

"Then what do I need you for, Zhang?"

"Ouyang has many enemies. I can find a Cho sympathizer in Beijing who will be up to the job."

"First, I very much doubt that. Second, the debt I owe must be repaid personally."

Zhang's mouth opened and closed. He picked at the remaining dim sum as an awkward silence engulfed them.

Yue piped up, "Well, but there's another way to get to Ouyang." The two men looked at her. "One I very much doubt you know about." Now Zhang goggled at her; he knew everything, didn't he?

"And what's that?" Bourne said.

Zhang gestured. "Have a *shui mai*. They're really superior specimens."

Reaching across the table, Bourne grabbed Zhang's shirtfront and jerked him forward. "I've had enough of you, Zhang. Shut up and let the lady speak."

Bourne turned his attention back to Yue to find the hint of an admiring smile on her face. He nodded at her.

"Ouyang has a wife."

Bourne nodded. "A Western woman named Maricruz, right?"

"Yes. She's Mexican."

"Little sister, what are you doing?" Zhang cut in. "You're undermining our bargaining position."

"This is no longer a negotiation," Yue said. Then, turning back to Bourne, "What isn't widely known is that Maricruz is the daughter of Maceo Encarnación."

Bourne sat stock-still, his heart beating fast. "Maceo Encarnación had one child—a son, now dead along with his father."

"No," Yue said. "He had another child by a woman named Constanza Camargo, a daughter whom he hid. Maricruz is that daughter."

"Yue, stop!" Zhang cried. "Giving out free information is madness."

Bourne's attention was concentrated solely on Yue. "And this is the Western woman married to Ouyang Jidan."

"It is."

If she was right, Bourne understood the true nature of Maceo Encarnación's involvement with Ouyang. "How does that help me?" he asked.

"Ouyang adores Maricruz; she's his weak spot." Yue now ventured a real smile, again as shy as a child's. "As it happens, she's currently not in Beijing with her husband."

"Do you know where she is?"

"I do. She's in Mexico City, dealing with the fallout from her father's death on his drug business with the cartels."

Zhang rocked back and forth in obvious agony. "Oh, little sister, such vital information and you've thrown it all away. Why?"

"Because," Yue said, finally addressing him, "I trust this man. Sometimes in life you have to have at least a little bit of faith."

The two soldiers that were accompanying them were buried within seconds of the helo crashing into the forest glade. Luckily for Matamoros and Maricruz, its trajectory took it into the trees on one side of the glade. The men were killed as it flew apart, shearing off the tops of the trees, a huge section of the fuselage striking them.

Matamoros and Maricruz were spared such a fate, as they shrank backward, away from the ring of falling debris. But as they turned to run, a shard of metal, spinning hotly, struck a tree trunk and ricocheted into Matamoros's shoulder, knocking him off his feet.

Maricruz turned, dodged more flying debris, crabbed her way back to where Matamoros lay. Blood oozed from the wound in his shoulder and his eyes were glazed with shock. Stripping off his jacket, she tore off the sleeve of his shirt, fashioned it into a makeshift bandage.

A sudden burst of flames caused her to duck down, covering him with her body. He seemed to wake from his stupor, saw her protecting him from the fire, then winced as the pain lanced through him.

"Come on!" Maricruz helped him to his feet. He was unsteady, but by force of will and by dint of leaning on her, he moved forward blindly through the flames and rising smoke toward the far edge of the forest. Several times they were forced to stop to catch their breath, the thick, piney smoke rolling over them in waves that threatened to suffocate them. At one point the smoke became so dense that Maricruz forced him down on hands and knees, and though the position filled him with agony, at least, as they crawled forward, they were able to breathe relatively clean air.

Ahead of them, she heard voices, some raised in shouts, and she took possession of Matamoros's assault rifle, aiming it at the shadows. Then, through the underbrush that had not yet been touched by the fire, she saw more of Matamoros's men—no doubt the cadre that had brought down the four government helos. They recognized her at once, which was fortunate, because when they saw one of their leaders injured they were inclined to shoot first and ask questions afterward.

Twenty minutes later, she and Matamoros were inside another armored vehicle—protected by a convoy of jeeps mounted with machine guns and soldiers bristling with weaponry.

The men tried to pull her away from their leader, but Matamoros shook his head.

"Leave her," he said, through parched lips. "Leave her alone."

Maricruz fed him water from a plastic bottle before she herself gulped greedily, until this moment unaware how thoroughly the fire had sapped them of moisture. They rolled along rough-hewn back roads. Though she had no idea where they were headed, she no longer cared as long as it was away from the disaster in the forest.

When Matamoros beckoned to her with a crooked finger, she bent over, her ear to his lips in order to hear him over the roar of the powerful engines.

"You're right. We have to kill Carlos. There's no other way. But how?" He paused as the vehicle swayed around a bend in the road. He licked his lips and continued. "None of my men has a chance now. Carlos will be on his guard."

"Leave that to me." Maricruz lifted her head a

moment to look into his eyes, which had widened in surprise.

"What d'you have in mind?"

"I'll return to Mexico City. You tried to kill me, too, but I escaped, that will be my story."

"Carlos will never believe you."

"Trust me, he'll be convinced. Why? Because he wants to believe. I'm his best and only chance of taking Los Zetas down." She gave him a meaningful look. "You will have to hurt me."

"No, *mujer*! No!"

"Felipe, you understand it must be done."

He grimaced in pain. "I forbid it."

"It's not up to you, Felipe," she said softly, put a hand against his cheek. "As you said, there's no other way."

Matamoros's eyes turned dark and glittery as he bit his lip. At length, he nodded. There was a peculiar sadness behind his eyes as he looked past and above her.

Maricruz stared deep into his eyes. Then something exploded against the back of her head. Pitching forward, she lost consciousness.

The Israeli consulate?" Zhang said, querulous as usual. "Not the American?"

"Surprises come in all shapes and sizes."

"It's just as well," Zhang mumbled. "I hear Colonel Sun has the American consulate under twenty-four-hour surveillance."

"Then you're sitting pretty. If..." Bourne pointed to a pad he had laid before the fat man. "Write down everything you and Yue know about Sun and Minister Ouyang. After I'm satisfied, I'll take you to the Israeli consulate and we'll get you two out of China."

"Is that a guarantee?"

"Sam, don't be an asshole," Yue said firmly. "Give him what he wants."

Zhang made a face, then nodded and, somewhat reluctantly, began to write. While he wrote, Bourne questioned Yue. Two hours later, as night tried to make its mark on the glittering city, they arrived in the vicinity of New Town Mansion, No. 55 Lou Shan Guan Road.

"Stay here," Bourne said, leaving the shadows in which they huddled. He spent the next forty minutes quartering the immediate vicinity, checking doorways, parked cars as well as passing traffic, and the rooftops of the buildings with sight lines to the front of the consulate.

At last, satisfied that the area was free of surveillance, he returned to Yue and Zhang and hurried them down the block and across Lou Shan Guan to the consulate's front door.

Once inside, Bourne asked for the consul general, who was at dinner at this hour. He used the code Director Yadin had included in the packet he'd given Bourne in Tel Aviv, and several moments later the trio were led into the consul general's office by the assistant on duty. The phone on the consul's desk rang a moment later. The assistant took the call, but as soon as he had ID'd his boss he handed the receiver over to Bourne.

"This is Avi Brun."

"Jason Bourne."

"*Boker tov Eliyahu!*" Brun said sourly. Nice of you to show up! He did not bother hiding his displeasure at being interrupted at dinner. "We cannot continue without—?"

Bourne gave him the second code phrase.

Brun cleared his throat. "You need an immediate exit from Shanghai."

"Correct."

"That has been prearranged."

"I'm not alone."

"Come again?" Brun said.

"I have two Chinese nationals with me. I've promised them asylum and an exit along with me."

There was a lengthy pause, during which Bourne could hear the consul general breathing like an asthmatic.

"I can't authorize that," Brun said at last.

"Director Yadin can. Call him."

"I don't think—"

"Do it," Bourne said flatly, "or I will."

"*Elize balagan!*" What a mess!

"*Avarnu et Paro, na'avor gam et zeh*," Bourne said. We overcame Pharaoh, we'll get through this, too.

"What? Now all of a sudden I'm speaking to a Jew?" But the softening of his tone proved Bourne had gotten through to him.

"Tell the Director that my guests have proprietary intelligence on two people of particular interest to him."

"Hmm. All right, all right, I'll call Eli now. Stay put and I'll get back to you."

Bourne left Yue and Zhang in the capable hands of Brun's assistant while he went out of the office, down the silent hallway, in search of the lavatory. Locking himself into a stall, he pulled out the items he had taken off the man who had pursued them down the tunnel. The knife, which Yue had given back to him, was a good one, but unhelpful since it was one used by NATO.

The other item he had taken was the man's mobile phone. Now that he was alone, he turned it on. The phone book was empty. He saw there was just enough battery life left to make a single call. He hit

REDIAL and saw the numbers come up, one by one. Country code: Israel. City code: Tel Aviv.

Bourne's blood ran cold. Mossad, he thought.

Then a man's voice answered: "Retzach, where the hell have you been? I thought you were—" The tone changed entirely. It was filled with suspicion and anxiety in equal measure. "Who is this?"

Bourne cut the connection. Retzach was a code name; it meant "murder" in Hebrew. He knew who had sent Retzach after him.

Turning off the mobile, he replaced it in his pocket, rose, and left the lavatory. Yue and Zhang watched him with no little curiosity when he returned.

"Any word?"

The assistant shook his head. "These things take time."

"No," Bourne said, "they don't." He gestured. "Get the consul general back on the line." Bourne shook his head. "Too slow." He picked up the phone, checked the readout for the last incoming call, and dialed it.

"I was just about to ring you," Brun said when he heard Bourne's voice. "I spoke to Eli." His tone indicated that it had pained him to do it. He sighed deeply. "I hope your guests like Tel Aviv. They're apt to be there a good long while."

21

AMIR OPHIR TOOK his private cell phone away
from his ear and threw it across his office as if
it were a poisonous insect. It crashed against the
wall, shattering into its basic components. One of
his assistants opened the door at once.

"Is everything all right, sir?"

"Of course it's all right," Ophir bellowed. "Why
shouldn't it be all right?" He glared at the young
man with such ferocity that, whey-faced, he turned
and retreated, closing the door after him.

"Fuck, fuck, fuck!"

Ophir felt as if he were suffocating. Rising, he
strode out of the office without giving a word of
where he was going or why to his staff. Riding
down in the elevator seemed to take a week. His
ears were burning and his throat felt inflamed.

It wasn't until he was outside, walking quickly in the direction of the harbor, that he could gather his thoughts sufficiently to inject a modicum of clarity into the swirl of panic threatening to drown him.

Bad enough that Retzach was dead. In answering his operative's mobile, Ophir had been revealed to whoever had killed Retzach. But only, he reminded himself, if the person on the other end of the line recognized his voice—the number was an untraceable Tel Aviv number.

Then the panic returned full force. On the other hand, he told himself, the person who had killed Retzach could ID the number as Israeli. It wouldn't take a genius to figure out that Retzach was Mossad. In the wrong hands, that knowledge could prove catastrophic not only to him, but to all of Mossad. If Retzach's mobile was in the hands of the Chinese authorities, and not Bourne...He shuddered at the thought.

The angry blare of a car horn caused Ophir to start back. He hadn't been looking where he was going and was almost run over. Wiping his hands down his trouser legs, he waited impatiently for the light to change, then hurried across the avenue.

The logical answer was to inform the Director immediately of the breach in security. But then Eli would ask how it was that Retzach was killed and, at the moment, Ophir had no answer. In that event, telling Eli was out of the question, at least for the moment.

If only the person on the other end of the line had said something, but he had offered not a word. Closing his eyes, Ophir wondered how he had gotten himself into this situation. At the time, it had seemed logical to send someone to find Bourne—he had even cleared it with Eli, who had agreed. But he could see now that he had made a grave miscalculation in sending in one of his Kidon assassins. He should have listened to Eli and handed the assignment over to Collections, but his hatred for Bourne had distorted his decision making.

Ophir had had no intention of keeping Bourne alive. He had intentionally disobeyed a direct order. He closed his hands into fists. Too late for recriminations now, and anyway they were counterproductive. What he needed was a solid foolproof plan. He pondered this puzzle the rest of the way to the water. It wasn't until he reached the harbor and breathed in the fresh salt air that he saw what had been in front of his face all along.

There was only one way to ensure a plan would be foolproof: He had to carry it out himself.

Maricruz awoke to pain. Every bone in her body seemed to vibrate with it, making her teeth chatter until, with a force of will, she clamped her jaws shut. Even that hurt. She opened sticky eyes to see the top of a van, which seemed to be traveling at a heart-stopping pace. She lay on a filthy blanket on the floor of the van. She would have rolled this way and that if a soldier didn't have the flat of his hand on her breastbone. She recognized him as one of Felipe's cadre *compadres*, one of the leaders of Los Zetas. He had a thick, curling beard and mustache and the cruel eyes of a wolf.

Grinning down at her, he said, "Welcome back to the land of the living, *mujer*."

"Is that what this is?" Her voice was thin as the whisper of wind through a wheat field. "I feel like I died."

"You may wish you had," the *compadre* said, "if that motherfucker Carlos gets even a hint of what you're up to."

Maricruz tried to smile, but failed. Her lips felt swollen; perhaps they were. She must look a fright, but then, that was the idea. Her idea. The van went over a bump and she tried to groan, but couldn't even get much volume in her voice.

"What was that?" the *compadre* said, leaning over her.

Maricruz tried to lick her lips, but her tongue felt swollen as well. The inside of her mouth was gluey.

"Water," she croaked.

"You'll get water from your new friend, Carlos."
He looked up at a muffled shout from the front of
the van. "Okay," he said, probably to the driver.
Then he looked down at Maricruz. "We're almost
there, *mujer*. The rest is up to you."

He winked at her just before he opened the rear
doors. "Let your body go slack." The streaking van
slowed down just long enough for him to kick her
out the back. As she went rolling across the tarmac, he shouted to the driver, who accelerated fast,
tires shrieking as he took the turn at speed.

Maricruz, covered in dust, lay as if dead. Then
the buzzing flies started to alight, swarming greedily over her blood-streaked skin and clothes.

There are three things you have to know," General
Hwang Liqun said when he met Minister Ouyang at
the VIP arrivals hall in Beijing. "First, the Chongqing conservatives have begun an all-out campaign
to elevate Cho Xilan to president-in-waiting at the
Party Congress. Second, major disagreements on
the future path of China have broken out among
the military leaders, the major state business enter-
prises, and the fistful of descendants of the remaining revolutionary families. All coalitions have been
fractured. The atmosphere has become toxic."

"Fatally?" Ouyang said as he and Hwang headed for his limousine.

"The word is the Chongqing think so."

A liveried driver opened the rear door, and the two men climbed into the cool, dim interior.

"And the third thing?" Ouyang said as he settled himself into the plush seat.

"Cho Xilan has gone missing. He hasn't been seen in public since you left for Shanghai."

"And in private?"

The general fidgeted beside him as the limousine rolled out of the airport. "My people have heard nothing."

"We have no eyes on Cho, then."

Hwang, looking straight ahead, said nothing.

"You disappoint me, General." Ouyang stared out the window. "Am I going to have to demote you?"

Hwang flinched. "There's good news—I have word that Cho is ill, perhaps gravely. That's why he hasn't made any public—"

"Bullshit!" Ouyang said. "I know Cho. He hasn't been seen at China Agricultural University to mark National Science Popularization Day or at any other nonsensical time-wasting function, because he's been too busy scurrying from faction to faction trying to cobble together a coalition large enough to stop my rise to power."

He turned to Hwang. "You have no idea how it pains me to have to tell you this, which seems as clear as the bewildered look on your face."

Abruptly, he leaned forward and said to the driver, "Stop the car."

"But, Minister, we're on the main highway into the city and there is no breakdown lane that I can—"

"Why do you tell me what I can see with my own two eyes?" Ouyang shouted. "Stop the fucking car!"

The driver complied. Traffic behind them in their lane drew to a standstill. No one honked their horn; the limousine was a clear sign of power.

"General," Ouyang said with a poisonous look, "this is where you get out."

Hwang's eyes nearly popped out of his head. "Minister?"

"Out, Hwang, you useless turd." He shoved him. "Now!"

Ouyang leaned back in his seat, closed his eyes; when he felt Hwang's weight come off the seat and, a moment later, heard the door click shut, he sighed deeply. Then he fished out his mobile and made a call. Despite what he had told Colonel Sun, his first concern was maintaining control of the all-powerful Politburo Standing Committee. Once he had these major players in his pocket it wouldn't matter what machinations Cho got up to, Ouyang would defeat him.

Cho and his party had no idea what a dangerous game they were playing. Once you unleashed nationalism within the masses you were bound to ride the back of that tiger with the dire prospect of not being able to get off even when you wanted to.

"We have a problem that needs solving," he said to the voice at the other end of the line.

"Does this problem have a name?"

"General Hwang Liqun."

"A shame."

"No, not a shame," Ouyang said. "A relief. I imagine the general has been working for Cho Xilan for some time."

"Purges are a vital part of our history. Like an enema, they flush the shit down the toilet."

Ouyang laughed, the first time he had done that since before Maricruz had left for Mexico City. How he missed her! No one understood him like she did. His world was like a shark tank. She was the only one he could really trust.

"How's the old Patriarch?" he asked now.

"Still full of piss and vinegar."

"He's my next port of call." The old Patriarch controlled more than half the vote that would reform the Politburo Standing Committee at the Party Congress. "I just dropped Hwang off. I'm sending the coordinates now. Use the white SUV. Meet me at the tower when you've solved the problem."

The voice at the other end of the line chuckled. "I can already hear the flush of the toilet."

Maricruz, far from dead, lay dazed but hardly confused. She knew exactly what she needed to do and when she needed to do it. Her plan formed in exquisite detail in her mind. It had the precision of a military campaign.

For some minutes all she heard was the whir of traffic, the brief staccato of querulous voices. A dog barked, approaching, and at his noisome snuffling the cloud of flies lifted off her. Then she heard steps clacking over marble steps, voices raised, chasing off both the dogs and the flies.

Someone said, "*Dios mio*, call the paramedics!"

Another said, "For the love of God, get her off the street!"

Two pairs of strong hands lifted her off the tarmac, carried her gently up the marble steps, through the open doorway, past the massive carved oak and olivewood door to the ministry, out of the stifling heat.

She passed through an octagonal entryway, sparkling with light drifting down from a massive crystal chandelier. Briefly, she smelled fresh flowers. Then she was being taken down a long, wood-paneled hallway and into a carpeted room with leaded-glass windows. A sheet was spread over a plush sofa onto which she was carefully laid.

She sighed when she sank into the soft cushions.

"My God, look at her!" a voice said.

"Shush!" another admonished. "She'll hear you."

She felt a great lassitude suffuse her, pressing her down, down into the delicious depths of the cushions. Her increasingly heavy eyelids fell closed, and she felt herself whirled away into the depths of a vertiginous slumber from which she did not want to wake.

22

THE FIRST THING Maricruz saw when she opened her eyes was a blindingly white wall. The nauseatingly sweet stink of antiseptic filled her nostrils, making her want to gag. She heard the measured beeping of a heart rate and blood pressure monitor. Shifting her gaze, she saw a needle stuck into the inside of her elbow. A thin tube was attached to the needle. A clear fluid dripped into her vein.

"Don't worry," a familiar male voice said, "it's only to keep you hydrated."

Her gaze shifted yet again and she saw Carlos Danda Carlos, dressed neatly in a summer-weight suit, sitting by her bedside.

"Where?" The words stuck in her throat and she licked her dry, chapped lips. She stared again. "Where am I?"

"Hospital Ángeles Pedregal," Carlos said. "You've been severely beaten." He cocked his head. "Do you remember that?"

A nurse bustled in, shooing Carlos away for the moment.

"How are we feeling?" she said with a smile as she began to change several dressings on Maricruz's shoulder, chest, and right hip. Clearly, she wasn't interested in eliciting an answer, which was just as well. Maricruz was in no mood to make small talk.

"You," she said officiously to Carlos, "don't stay too long. She needs her rest."

"*Niñera*," Carlos said, "do you know who I am?"

"I don't care if you're God himself," she said stiffly. "This is my house, this is my patient, and these are my rules."

With a twitch of his lips, Carlos inclined his head, forgetting about her the instant the door closed behind her. He returned his attention to Maricruz, but instead of sitting back down he chose to stand over her, clearly reestablishing the pecking order in the room.

"Has your memory improved?"

In her current state, she couldn't tell whether he was being hostile or solicitous, and this lack of clarity concerned her greatly. She knew she would need all her analytical faculties at their cutting edge in order to accomplish her goal. Outwitting Carlos would be no easy task in the best of times, and right now she was far from that longed-for state.

"I'm tired," she said, and it was no lie. "Please let me sleep."

For a terrifying moment, Carlos studied her with the critical eye of a collector. Then his lips twitched again and he nodded.

"One of my men will be right outside at all times. When you're feeling up to it, let him know and we'll speak again, at length this time." At the door, he turned back to her and bared his teeth. "I wish you only sweet dreams, señora."

Sometime during the flight to Tel Aviv, Bourne sank into a dream. He stood on a sun-washed shore. Behind him rose the gap-toothed ruins of a Roman town. Seagulls called. The sun had barely risen in the eastern sky, and a fresh wind was blowing in from the endless plain of the sea.

He heard her coming up behind him, though she was barefoot in the sand.

"Did you miss me?" Rebeka said.

Bourne felt the words of his reply stick in his throat.

She put her arms around him and he felt her body

press against him as warmly as the morning sunlight on his face.

"I missed you."

"You've been gone a long time," he managed to say.

"I've been very far away."

He wanted to turn around, but something prevented him.

"What was it like, where you were?"

"A land of shadows. That's all I remember."

He felt a constriction around his heart. "You're back. That's what's important."

He turned around, then, within the curve of her arms, only to find that he was being embraced by Maricruz Encarnación. She was grinning wolfishly.

"Soon enough," she said, "you will miss me."

He pushed her violently away. She tumbled, and immediately the sand embraced her, covering her as if she had never existed. He turned to find himself alone on the deserted beach, the endless sea lapping at his toes, drawing the wet sand from under his feet. He was miles from nowhere...

He awoke to find Yue sitting next to him.

"I came over to see if you were all right."

"Why wouldn't I be all right?" He was annoyed at her for engaging him at this moment, while he was still entangled in the last strands of his curious dream.

"You were talking in your sleep," she said.

"What did I say?"

"You were calling her name."

"What name?" Bourne asked. Had it been Rebeka?

Yue looked at him. "Maricruz."

Bourne turned away to stare out the window, but there was nothing to see except Rebeka's face.

When he turned back to Yue, she said, "Thank you for saving us. I hope our information helps you." She paused for a moment, something unpleasant clearly on her mind. "These Israelis—we don't know them. They're aliens to us. We don't know their motivations. We can't trust them."

"Speak plainly, Yue."

"We'll talk to you, not to them."

"They're the ones who brought you out of China."

"They're the conduit," she said. "You brought us out."

He could tell by her expression there was no point in arguing further. He nodded. "I'll tell them."

"I mean it."

"I know." He tried to make his tone reassuring. "How do you know so much about Ouyang's wife?"

Yue smiled her sly smile. "A proprietary underground exists. Even in China, women know how to weasel out information about other women."

Bourne laughed, dissipated the last of the hangover from his dream. "Universal truths."

"Like faith," she said.

Just under eight hours later, Carlos was again standing over Maricruz. This time, however, she was sitting up, after just having finished a breakfast of soft-boiled eggs, toast, and coffee. Her room was huge, more like a hotel suite than a hospital room. She supposed that came with being a VIP championed by Carlos himself.

"The cobwebs are gone from my head," she said in her normal voice. And it was true. The sleep had done wonders; her mind was clear and working at its usual full speed.

"Wonderful news," Carlos said, in a tone of voice that reminded her of the undertaker who had seen to her father's repatriated corpse. "May we speak candidly?"

"Always," Maricruz said, thinking, *Here we go*.

"Beautiful. Now, can you remember what happened?"

"Like it just happened," she said with a genuine shudder. She was acutely aware of Carlos's suspicion, and had determined the best way to deal with it. She manufactured a defiant expression, the opposite of what he would be expecting. "It's damn difficult making friends in this country."

Carlos grunted. "Outsiders always make the same complaint."

"Just an observation."

"You seem to have forgotten our conversation outside the cantina." He could not keep the edge of anger out of his voice. "What happened to you?"

"They beat me," she said. "As you can plainly see."

"My eyesight is twenty-twenty. The question before us is *who* beat you, señora?"

She turned her face away from him. Giving up the information he was seeking that easily was not in the cards. She had to make him sweat, otherwise his suspicions would grow.

"You do not want to say?" He stepped closer, so that he was right beside her. "Why would that be?" Crossing his arms over his chest, he tapped his foot like an impatient schoolmaster. "Come, come, señora. Surely the time for reticence is past. Why won't you tell me?"

"Because," she said with just the right note of bruise in her voice, "I refuse to be humiliated."

Her words—the ones he must have been longing to hear—acted as a trigger. He put a hand lightly on her knee. "In this room, Maricruz, in front of me, you cannot be humiliated."

His switch to her Christian name was the key that unlocked the first door. Now she walked through, heading directly into the heart of him. She had succeeded in making him complicit in her emotion; she had set up a powerful bond on which the next phase of the conversation would be based.

"When a friend betrays you," she said slowly, "you cannot help but feel humiliated."

"Violated, perhaps—yes, I can understand that." He smiled thinly. "But you see, Maricruz, violated is how you have made me feel."

"I? How?"

"Hours after I left San Luis Potosí, Los Zetas slaughtered Raul Giron and his lieutenants, effectively destroying the Sinaloa infrastructure."

Maricruz stitched a puzzled look on her face. "But, Carlos, is that not what we spoke about that night?"

"What?"

She could see that she had taken him completely by surprise, and she smiled inside. The beating was already starting to pay dividends.

"Didn't you tell me that Giron and Matamoros were a part of the past, that you and I were the future?"

"Yes, but—"

"Well, I had to start somewhere. Now Giron is dead."

He stared at her wide-eyed. "And you were beaten—"

"Because Matamoros was convinced that I had conspired with you to bring the government helos down on him and his cadre. He was certain that you had left prematurely because of a deal you and I had made." The stricken expression on his face inspired her to continue. "In that he wasn't wrong." She shrugged. "As a practical lesson to both of us, he had me beaten and dumped on your doorstep."

"Then we must create our own lesson. We must make certain he knows that he cannot punish us." He put his hand on her again. "But now you must rest. We will see each other again, when you are stronger." He smiled back at her, his hand on the knob of the door. "You continue to surprise me, Maricruz. That is a good thing."

In Tel Aviv, Bourne met with Director Yadin and Amir Ophir. This was not what he wanted, but it was what he had to endure. Ophir had sent Retzach to kill him, either with or without Yadin's consent. Either way, he could not trust either man. Once again, as so often in his life, he seemed to be treading in quicksand. Once again, he had only himself to trust in—only his own instincts to keep the treacherous wolves at bay.

"I should throw you the hell out of here," the Director thundered as soon as Bourne arrived, "considering the stunt you pulled."

"After I found the tracker in the passport, you gave me no choice," Bourne replied.

"We always protect our assets," Ophir said. "Standard operating procedure."

"I'm not one of your assets," Bourne shot back.

"Then what are you doing here? You asked us to get you out of Shanghai—with a couple of nationals of dubious value in tow."

"They know far more than you do about Ouyang and Sun, but they won't speak to you, only to me."

"You see?" Ophir said with open disgust. "I told you using him was a mistake from the get-go."

"Now we know where we stand," Bourne said.

"Your Chinese *pals* are now ours. We do with them what we want."

"They're human beings, not chattel."

"They are what we say they are!"

"That's enough!" Yadin was fuming. "Stand down, Amir."

"But, Director—"

"No buts," Yadin said, cutting him off. "I'll have the room."

After a small hesitation, Ophir stalked out, but not before shooting Bourne a venomous look. Was it Bourne's imagination or had there been a hint of fear in that glance?

When the door closed behind him, the Director sighed. "In the old days," he said as he went around behind his desk, "one never had to endure bad manners." He sat down wearily. "In fact, there was none at all. It wasn't tolerated."

"What's changed?"

"Everything." The Director waved him to a seat. "The Arabs, us, the world. Nothing is what it used to be. Old alliances crumble, friends slink away in the night, and the shadows gather around us with ever-increasing evil intent."

Elbows on desk, he steepled his fingers. His eyes were pale, his expression bleak. "I imagine you're wondering why I keep Amir on."

"When it comes to clandestine organizations," Bourne said, "nothing is what it seems and there is no room for rationality."

The Director nodded his shaggy head. "Too true. Well, I'll tell you anyway. He's the best I have." His hands spread, spatulate. "That's the worst indictment of what has become of all of us—the long, inevitable slide into the darkness of incivility."

When Bourne made no reply, he nodded. "All right, mistakes were made on both sides."

"I couldn't afford for you to have eyes on me in Shanghai."

"There was a man," the Director said, almost distractedly, "but I had Amir pull him."

This was the moment, Bourne thought, to tell Yadin about Ophir's treachery. But no, there was another, better way, and he said nothing.

Yadin drummed his fingers on the desktop. "About the Chinese nationals."

"Keep them away from Ophir, tend them as you would a garden," Bourne said, "and they will bear fruit."

"I can't have you talking to them," Yadin said. "You understand."

"It doesn't matter. Tomorrow I'll be gone."

The Director raised his eyebrows. "Where are you going?"

Bourne smiled.

23

DENG TSU LIVED in the clouds—literally and figuratively. His palatial residence sprawled across the top floor—eight hundred feet above street level—of the Fortune Plaza Office Building. The offices of his many interconnected businesses resided ten floors below this residence, making it possible for him to shuttle between the two without ever having to walk outside into Beijing's often near-toxic atmosphere.

Approaching his eighty-seventh year of existence, Deng Tsu, Patriarch of the most influential revolutionary family in a constellation that had never lacked for influence, was still as vital as he had been in his fifty-fifth year. He swam daily in his private saltwater pool, practiced both tai chi and aikido with handpicked masters, and meditated for an hour each morning and evening without fail. He was never ill, an exalted state he attributed to his rigorous routine, his staying current on every nuance of his businesses as well as the business of China itself, and taking to bed a different woman three times a week.

Of course, diet was important—he was religious about what he ingested—but where would he be without his ground rhino horn and freeze-dried tiger paw to keep him as virile as a teenager?

Deng Tsu received Minister Ouyang in traditional Mandarin dress, which he always wore when he was home. Ten floors down he was never seen without a smart Huntsman bespoke suit, John Lobb brogues, and a Hilditch & Key Sea Island cotton shirt.

"Tea and cakes have been prepared," Deng said without preamble as he led Ouyang to what was commonly known as the sunroom—a glass-enclosed solarium in which were planted a profusion of prizewinning roses and orchids in beds set all around the sides.

In the center of the room were cushions on either side of an antique paulownia-wood scholar's table meticulously set with a lacquer tea service and small plates of what Deng had termed *cakes* but were actually rounds of baked seaweed. Deng ingested no sugar.

The two men sat. Deng poured tea in the ritualistic manner of the old Mandarins. They shared the first cup in companionable silence. Amid the soft, humid air, perfumed by the roses, their velvet petals outstretched like welcoming arms, the cacophony, sandy grit, and pollution of the teeming city seemed a thousand miles away.

"Now, younger brother," Deng said as he refilled their cups, "what brings you to my eyrie?" In Deng's world, the second cup of tea was for questions, the third cup for discussion, the fourth for answers.

"I imagine you think it's Cho and his conservatives," Ouyang said, "but they're only part of the problem."

"Explain."

"I am speaking now of Ling's son's death."

"Yes, a terrible tragedy—but those Italian cars—a Ferrari, wasn't it?—are notoriously difficult to control."

"Especially when the driver had consumed a great quantity of alcohol. Especially when the driver is partying with two girls in the car with him."

"Your point, Ouyang?"

"Those girls are still in critical condition."

"They're not my concern."

"Oh, but they are, Patriarch. Just as the horribly botched cover-up of the crash is your concern."

Deng turned away, stared out the window at the tops of buildings, lost in a mist as dense as a Gobi sandstorm.

Ouyang sipped at his tea, which was so exquisitely delicious that in other circumstances it might have been distracting. "The stain of this incident, pointing up the profligacy of the elite, has traveled all the way up to the president."

Deng drew his liver-colored lips together. "It's true that Ling is the president's protégé and political fixer."

"This incident has already begun to weaken the president's position. It has made him look corrupt, if not outright foolish."

Deng turned back, his face livid. "You have no right to make these outrageous accusations!"

"I am only echoing the news," Ouyang said.

"You are not the first one to bring it to my attention."

"Ignore it at your peril, Patriarch."

Deng stared at Ouyang, blinking slowly as an owl. At length, he sighed. "I suppose you have an answer to the problem."

"Your forebear made a compact with the people."

Deng inclined his head. "What has come to be known as the Grand Bargain."

"That's right. He—and now we—promised to raise the people's standard of living, to modernize the economy, in exchange for keeping us in power, no questions asked."

"It was a good bargain," Deng said. "It was the right one—the only one—to make."

"It's impossible to disagree, of course it is." Ouyang put down his empty cup, which Deng immediately refilled. "However, current events are leading me to the conclusion that the Grand Bargain is unraveling. The old ways that have served us well for decades are now making us the enemy in the eyes of the people. Today they are wealthier, better educated, more aware of the world outside the Middle Kingdom than ever before. More important, their exposure to the Internet has made them politically savvy. It has given them a belief in their individual rights we are powerless to fight."

Deng poured himself more tea. "Why is that?"

"Because once the cat is out of the bag the only way to stuff it back in is to kill it."

Deng stared out the window at the non-weather, sipping his tea contemplatively. At length, he turned back to Ouyang.

"So, younger brother, what do you suggest?"

"You're not going to like it."

"I already don't like what's happening outside my residence, younger brother. Please continue."

Time for their fourth cup of tea.

"Your forebear's Grand Bargain was, as you

rightly say, the right one at the right time. But times have changed. I no longer believe that turning the economy toward capitalism while keeping the old political system intact is working. There is growing unrest among the populace. We have had an alarming rise in the number of scandals among the elite, which have caused the governed's anger to escalate."

"All this is known," Deng said. "Again, I ask you for your solution."

"We have to get out in front of this. We have to make moves that will not only forestall the anger before it spills over and completely engulfs us, we have to extinguish it once and for all. In my opinion, the only way to do this is to come out of next week's Party Congress with sweeping changes. We must present a government that is transparent, that openly works for the populace."

"I know your heart is in the right place, younger brother, but what you're asking is simply impossible. The Congress would never agree to so sweeping a change. There are too many who treasure their elite status above the law. Old habits die hard—or not at all."

"The economic changes instituted by your forebear have borne fruit," Ouyang said. "We must embrace the fruit, both the bitter and the sweet."

"Speak plainly, younger brother."

"There have been consequences, perhaps unforeseen, from the institution of capitalism. We cannot go back; nor can we turn a blind eye to what is happening to both the increasingly restless populace and the members of our own political elite, many of whom live well beyond their means and take what they want whenever they want it. This practice can no longer be tolerated."

"No one will listen. The twin forces of entitlement and inertia will defeat you."

"Then the people themselves will take it away. Listen, Patriarch, whether we like it or not, the Grand Bargain with the people is about to expire. Either we find our way to a new bargain that will satisfy the populace or we will face open rebellion. This I can guarantee."

Deng put down his cup. "Your endgame?"

"First, Cho and his Chongqing Party must be defanged. Second, I must be installed as president at the Congress. With your help, I will forge an unshakable coalition that can withstand the tremors of the changes that need to be made in order to ensure our continuing rule of China."

Deng shook his head. His eyes held an infinite sadness. "It will never happen that way. It can't. We're like a train; our tracks run straight ahead."

Ouyang rose. "Listen to me, Patriarch. In the nineteen seventies the Soviet Union was the Evil

Empire." He was shaking. He had never spoken to Deng this way. "If we do not change course, soon it will be our turn."

"But don't you see, younger brother, that is just what Cho and the Chongqing fervently hope for. They want us isolated from the world. They see it as contagion, a spreading stain upon the face of the Middle Kingdom. They want to wash China clean, to make it as it once was."

"Nothing can be as it once was, Patriarch. You, of all people, know that. And just look at where the Party Congress is being held this year—the seaside town of Beidaihe. Up until now, it's always been held in Beijing. The story goes that the Congress hall's renovations have not been completed, but you and I know that the story's bullshit. We're all afraid of demonstrations filling the streets of the capital. Five years ago such a concern would not have even existed."

"Jidan, Jidan," the old man said, "we are but two leaves blown by the wind."

Ouyang stared down at Deng, for the first time seeing him for what he was, not what Ouyang wanted him to be. *If Deng is too old*, Ouyang thought, *if he no longer has the will, I must be it for him*. He marshaled his thoughts for one last stand.

"All our lives," he said, "we have made history, just as our fathers did before us. That's an extraordinary—a singular—power. We still can, but the ability is fast slipping through our hands. If we do not alter our course now, that singular ability to make history will be stripped from us; it will be given to the people of China. Then we are finished.

"So this is what we must do, Patriarch. We must harness the wind."

Bourne found Amir Ophir in his office, partially shielded by three computer screens. He did not look up when Bourne walked in, but Bourne could see his shoulders tense as if he were bracing for a street brawl.

"You killed him." There was no emotion in Ophir's voice, only bitter accusation.

"You sent him to kill me."

"That's a lie. He was sent—with the approval of Director Yadin—to keep tabs on you after you broke your promise to the Director and went off the grid."

"I don't do well with leashes," Bourne said. "And you would have no knowledge whether or not I made such a promise. Here's what really matters: I find it suspect sending a Kidon operative to do surveillance work."

"First, Kidon is not an assembly of assassins. We do surveillance and rescue work all the time. In fact, my department is in the process of acting on a complex and highly sensitive rescue of three Israeli citizens held in the Sinai."

"Citizens?" Bourne said. "Or your agents?"

Ophir pointedly ignored him. "Second, the man I sent in was both close to hand and possessed a comprehensive knowledge of China, Shanghai in particular."

"First, his code name means 'murder,'" Bourne said. "Second, he attacked me and Yue, the young woman with me. His intent was clear."

"Then he exceeded his mandate. Why would he do that?" Ophir said without taking his eyes off his pixeled screens.

"Because you ordered him to kill me."

At last, Ophir raised his eyes to Bourne's. "You have no proof—"

Bourne produced Retzach's mobile. "Retzach called you minutes before he entered the tunnel to track me down and kill me."

"That's not—"

Bourne tossed Retzach's knife onto Ophir's desk. "Here's how he tried to kill me."

Ophir, staring at the knife as if it were a viper suddenly come alive, licked his lips.

Bourne scooped up the knife, held it up with Retzach's mobile. "Shall I give these to Director Yadin or will you invite me to sit down?"

With a wave of his hand and a poisonous look, Ophir said, "Be my guest."

Bourne gave a steely laugh as he sat down opposite Ophir. "I need an armorer."

Ophir looked relieved, as if he was thinking, *Is that all?* "No problem. We have several excellent ones in the basement labs."

"I don't need one here," Bourne said. "I'm speaking of Mexico City."

For a moment there was only silence between them. The soft chatter of assistants and secretaries somewhere beyond the four walls rose and fell like ocean waves. Someone dropped a glass, which shattered against the floor tiles. A brief string of curses, then silence.

At length, Ophir cleared his throat and said, "Director Yadin will never sanction it."

"Which is why I've come to you with my request."

"It's not a request."

Bourne stared at him, unblinking.

Ophir shook himself like a dog trying to shed muddy water. "I assume you require a handgun."

"Everything from a handgun to a grenade launcher, plus ammunition for them all."

"I don't—"

"And it needs to be *be'shu'shu*." It has to be done secretly.

"*Gilita et America.*" Tell me something I don't know. "Anything else I can provide?" he added with a deliberate smirk. "A tank? A fighter jet, perhaps?"

"Another time."

Ophir waved a hand as if in surrender. "All right, all right. Let's see." He checked his computer screen. "I have a good man in Mexico City. His code name is J. J. Hale. Here's what he looks like. That's all you need to know about him." He drew a scratch pad toward him, scribbled a couple of lines on it, tore off the sheet, and handed it across to Bourne. "Starting tomorrow, he'll be at this café precisely at eight o'clock in the evening every day for five days. The second line is the code words to introduce yourself and his response."

He smiled. "Anything else I can do for you?"

"I'll let you know." Bourne rose and left the office.

The moment he was alone, Ophir contacted Hale and gave him his instructions via coded email, then added the line, *Stand by for a pkg via the usual method.*

After he sent the email, he used a key he kept around his neck to open the lowest drawer on the right side of his desk. He took out a black folder and opened it. Inside was the transfer tape that his man had used to pick Bourne's fingerprint off the glass in his hotel room in Caesarea.

Ophir stared at it for a moment, a thin smile playing across his lips. It was a good thing Bourne didn't know enough about how Mossad worked. Those two items he assumed were so incriminating, weren't. Their presence could be explained—though perhaps not easily—to Eli. Ophir had nothing to fear from Bourne on that score, but rather than inform him he had come to a better conclusion. One that would lead to Bourne's undoing.

He packed the tape carefully in a small envelope, which he sealed with wax. He put this into a larger envelope then hand-wrote instructions to Hale, put these in the larger envelope with the fingerprint, sealed the larger envelope with wax, placed it in the proprietary secure packing Mossad used.

Then he called for an immediate overseas courier.

24

MINISTER OUYANG, exiting the Patriarch's building, found his white SUV waiting at the curb, its huge motor thrumming. The rear door opened as he approached and, ducking inside, he slammed the door behind him. The instant he sat, the SUV nosed out into the incessant traffic.

"All went as planned," said the tall, thin man who sat beside him. His face bespoke his Manchu blood lineage. He had the delicate long-fingered hands of a surgeon or a pianist.

Why not? Ouyang thought. The man was an artist.

"And how did you make out at the summit of the Middle Kingdom?" From anyone else's mouth the question would have had a sardonic edge, but not this man.

"Kai," Ouyang began, "the Patriarch may indeed come around to our way of thinking, but for the moment he remains lost in the clouds."

"Pity," Kai said with a sigh. "The old man used to be a visionary of extraordinary usefulness."

"His time may not yet be past," Ouyang said a touch too sharply.

"Time," Kai said, clearly not taking offense, "is what we have the least of. In less than a week the Party Congress will convene to elect a new Politburo, which will map out the next ten years of China's future. If we do not act now—and act decisively—we will not be offered a second chance."

Ouyang shifted uneasily in his seat. He knew he was being forced into the one dangerous position he had labored so hard to avoid.

"I hope you're wrong, Kai, but it's becoming increasingly clear that we must act now."

Bourne arrived in Mexico City on a teary morning, gray with mist and pollutants. The air stank from the human excrement used as fertilizer for fruits and vegetables.

He knew the city well. Though he was, in a way, closer to Rebeka, to the place where she had died, this knowledge brought him no solace. He experienced Mexico City as a necropolis throbbing with shadows, nightmarish memories, and an eternal sense of peril and foreboding.

By the time his taxi had reached the city streets, the sun—an ugly tannish ball—had fought its way through the mist, but had been defeated by the smog, which hung over the city like a translucent mask.

Bourne had given the driver an address in Coyoacán, a neighborhood five miles from Colonia Centro. The district name was derived from the Náhuatl Coyohuacán, an Aztec word meaning "place of coyotes," possibly because the native people, the Tecpanecas, hated their Aztec conquerors to such a degree they welcomed in Hernán Cortés, hastening the demise of the Aztecs and their history and culture.

Bourne got out at Francisco Sosa, not far from where Frida Kahlo and Diego Rivera had lived, a cobblestone thoroughfare, the neighborhood's main artery. He walked to 23 Caballo Calco, a two-story apartment building of whitewashed cement, trimmed in terra-cotta and faced with intricate white wrought-iron fencing.

He rang the bell for apartment 11, which had no name on it, and was at once buzzed in. Apartment 11 was on the second floor, facing the street. Almost directly across rose the Iglesia de Coyoacán, looking much the worse for wear, weeds and tumbledown bricks covering its feet, rude graffiti defacing its flanks.

When 808Azul opened the door, Bourne at first didn't recognize her. She seemed a galaxy away from the girl, confused and enraged, who, with his help, had escaped Maceo Encarnación's house in Colonia Polanco last year.

He had suggested that she run far away, over the Mexican border, but instead she had chosen to remain in her homeland, changing her name, becoming a first-rate computer hacker, as much feared as respected.

Online she was known as 808Azul, but Bourne knew her as Anunciata. Her mother had been Maceo Encarnación's cook for many years until he had had her poisoned. That was when Bourne had helped Anunciata escape.

She was a beautiful young woman now, with an open, smiling face, wide-apart chocolate eyes, and a mane of black hair that glimmered in the lamplight of her large, airy apartment. Photos of her mother adorned shelves, as well as the shrine-like area surrounding her computers—a mix of the most powerful laptops, smartphones, and tablets. To his right, a row of wooden jalousies partially hid a long, narrow balcony that overlooked Caballo Calco.

"Jason, I was so happy to get your call," she exclaimed, embracing him. "I never thought I'd see you again."

"You stayed in touch."

She laughed. "Good friends are rare as hen's teeth." She gestured. "You must be hungry, they don't feed you well on flights. I made enchiladas and rice and black beans."

She led him into the large kitchen where the meal was spread out on a scarred wooden table.

"You have your mother's touch," he said as he began to eat. She had brought a clutch of cold beers from the refrigerator.

"You're well, Jason?"

"Well enough."

"You look sad, but then I think that's the way you always look."

There was a small silence when only their eyes spoke.

"I never thanked you for killing my father." She said these supercharged words in a matter-of-fact tone.

"No need."

"I disagree."

Bourne inclined his head, understanding only too well. Anunciata's parents had conspired to hide the identity of her father. But when her mother discovered that her father had seduced her and was taking her to bed, she threatened her employer. A brave but foolish gesture.

Anunciata put down her knife and fork. "So what brings you back?"

"Something serious."

"How could it be otherwise?"

"I'm looking for Maceo Encarnación's daughter."

"His daughter." Anunciata laughed nervously. "You're looking at her."

"He had another one. Maricruz."

"Ah, the one he had with Constanza Camargo."

Bourne nodded. "You know her?"

"We never had the pleasure," Anunciata said through bared teeth. "However, I've heard stories. She's become sort of a legend."

"She's here," Bourne said. "I need to find her."

Anunciata thought for a moment. "Hold on," she said as she rose.

She went to her workstation. Sitting down, she twisted on her headset, began typing on one of the laptops. Several moments later, she started asking questions, nodding at the answers as she continued to type.

Bourne got up and followed her in when he heard her say, "No shit. Really?"

Her eyes tracked him, her eyebrows raised for an instant, until she returned her attention to the call.

"I need someone inside...no, no, *really* inside... and reliable...of course for money." She glanced up at Bourne again, and he nodded. "I understand. The amount's not an issue," she continued, "but reliability is...your assurances aside, if my client walks into an ambush I'll hunt you down and pull your balls up into your throat...Go on, but I assure you it's no laughing matter to suffocate on your own testicles." She winked at Bourne. "Okay, got it. Be seeing you."

After jotting a couple of lines on a scratch pad, she ripped off the sheet, rose, and handed it to Bourne. Then she took a picture of him with one of her phones and sent it off to her contact.

"You're in luck. It seems my half sister got herself into a huge pile of shit," she said. "Apparently, she came back to deal with Maceo's cartel business and inserted herself into the war between Los Zetas and the Sinaloa. She can't be that stupid so she must have had a plan in mind, insane as that sounds."

Aware of Ouyang's partnership with Maceo Encarnación to keep the raw materials for his drug pipeline coming into Mexico, Bourne didn't think Maricruz's plan was in the least bit insane—it was more like a necessity.

Anunciata shrugged. "I don't know what happened but she's been roughed up pretty badly. Currently, she's recuperating at Hospital Ángeles Pedregal. I wrote down the address for you. Anyway, it seems that along the way she's made some powerful friends. Her room is guarded by *Federales* and her only visitor has been Carlos Danda Carlos, the head of the anti-drug enforcement agency."

She cocked her head at Bourne's silent laugh. "This isn't a joke. What's so damn funny?"

Maricruz was up and walking to physical therapy twice a day on her own, ignoring the wheelchair her nurse wheeled just behind her. Her legs were covered in bruises but it was her arms that needed the most help, specifically the shoulder that had been most badly damaged in the beat-down. It had needed arthroscopic surgery.

There were times when she hated Matamoros, certain that he had had his men expend their full fury on her, pounding her far more than necessary. But then would come the visits from Carlos and she would see on his face the genuine sorrow and guilt at his complicity in her terrible drubbing, and she knew that anything less severe would not have erased the suspicions crowding his mind.

No, she finally concluded, Matamoros had been a maestro at directing his men to beat her just enough to fool Carlos without doing anything to damage her permanently. And then there was the fact that apart from several scrapes and bruises, they had left her face unscathed. She had to be grateful for that.

In fact, she was grateful for it all. Matamoros was proving far more intelligent than she had given him credit for. Even better, he was desperate to defeat Carlos—almost as desperate as Carlos was to finish him off once and for all.

She was in the best possible position—directly between the two, trusted by both, with her own agenda completely uncompromised. When she reminded herself of that, she smiled to herself. She had never been naive enough to think this process would be easy, but she never could have imagined the shape it would take or the physical pain she would suffer.

These thoughts occupied her during the morning exercises her therapist put her through, which were both difficult and painful. Still, she had to admit that, though sore, she felt better afterward. Several minutes after she had started her afternoon session, an orderly wheeled in a girl of no more than seven. She looked beat up, malnourished, but worst of all her expression was a complete blank. Her cheeks were sunken, her huge eyes black and depthless. She stared into the middle distance at something no one in the room could see. Maricruz watched her clandestinely all through her own workout. Occasionally, a therapist would crouch in front of the girl, try to talk to her, even, once, taking her hand, all without receiving even the minutest response.

An hour later, when Maricruz was done, the girl still had not moved a muscle or altered her gaze. It was eerie, unsettling. Nevertheless, something about the girl stuck in Maricruz's consciousness like a hook in a fish's mouth and would not let go.

"That girl," Maricruz said to her therapist, "why isn't anyone taking care of her?"

"We've tried—many of us," the woman said, wiping massage cream off her hands, "but nothing gets through to her. She's catatonic. She was down in psychiatric, but since they can't do anything with her, she's been moved up to your floor."

"What happened to her?"

The therapist sighed. "The story is her father was a drug mule. You know these people—they see an easy way to make money and they take it instead of getting a decent nine-to-five job like the rest of us. Anyway, something must have gone wrong, as it almost always does. Who knows what? It could have been a million things." The therapist folded the cloth and put it away. "Her parents and two older brothers were killed in front of her—beheaded with machetes."

The breath caught in Maricruz's throat. "Who?"

"Los Zetas, Sinaloa, some local drug dealer in their employ, who knows?" The therapist turned away in disgust. "What does it matter?" She shook her head. "These people—you can't talk to them, you can't reason with them. Their greed outweighs everything—even their responsibility to their family."

"How can you be so coldhearted? Whatever the sins of her father, surely you can't take it out on the child."

"Señora, do you know how many of these children we see each year? Please. It's beyond counting. If I got involved with them I'd be burned out within a year and no good to my own family."

Maricruz kept her gaze on the girl, as if willing her to magically emerge from her catatonic state. "What happens to them when they leave here?"

"They're picked up by an aunt or uncle, a cousin, if they'll have them. Otherwise they become wards of the state."

"What about this girl?"

"How should I know?"

When she returned from her afternoon session, Tigger put down his newspaper, stood up, and smiled at her through his grizzly face.

"How'd it go, señora?"

"Satisfactorily," she said dully. Her mind was still on the girl.

She paused as he opened the door to her room.
Carlos had assigned three shifts to guard her while
she was in the hospital. Tigger was part of the
second shift. His name wasn't actually Tigger, of
course, but like the animal drawn by A. A. Milne
he looked uncannily like a stuffed animal—both
fierce and amusing. How he managed this no one
could say, least of all Tigger himself.

"You should be gettin' outta here soon, huh?"

"Not soon enough to suit me." Then seeing the
look on his face, she pursed her lips in an almost
comical moue and stroked his rough cheek. "Oh,
but Tigger, I'm sure we'll still see each other when
I leave the hospital. In fact, I'll request that you escort me out. How's that?"

Tigger's eyes lit up, and now he really did look
like a stuffed tiger, happy and eager.

"*Muchas gracias*, señora." Ignoring the nurse
and her useless wheelchair, he ushered her inside.
"Estefan's just arrived. Is there anything I can get
you before I take a break?"

"No, Tigger. Thank you." Maricruz awkwardly
climbed into bed, trying not to wince at the pain in
her shoulder. "Run along now and play."

He laughed as he left her. The nurse bustled officiously around the bed, neatening the bedclothes,
refilling the plastic water jug from the store of bottled water Carlos had his men bring in for her.

"Enough!" Maricruz cried at last. "For the love of Christ, leave me in peace!"

The nurse didn't bat an eyelash, but she made her exit as quickly and discreetly as possible. Apparently, she had had enough experience with her VIP patient's violent fits of anger and frustration to know when to get out of the way.

Maricruz lay back on the pillows, furious that she was out of breath, furious that her shoulder hurt like a bitch, furious that she was stuck in this hospital room. Furious at the thought of that little girl who had lost her childhood if not her life.

One of the things she had learned from her husband was the importance of patience. Still, Latin blood coursed through her veins; patience had never been in her vocabulary, let alone one of her virtues. But now, as she lay back, she thought of what he had taught her, thought of the long hours of sitting za-zen trying to empty her mind of thought, emotion, and consequence.

Slowly, painstakingly, she forced herself to let go of her fury, let go of her frustration—most important, most difficult, let go of her intent. Her mind emptied like an hourglass of sand, and she felt the utter peace of nothingness engulf her, lift her up, take her to another plane of existence.

Then the door opened and the spell was abruptly broken.

25

BOURNE MET TIGGER on the grounds of Hospital Ángeles Pedregal. The exhausted sun had retired prematurely, shouldered aside by a drizzle that darkened the sidewalks and roadbed. Thunder rolled in the distance, harbinger of a hard rain soon to come.

Bourne handed him a thick envelope, which Tigger opened. Running his callused thumb across the tops of the bills, he grinned, showing brown teeth like tombstones. "American dollars."

"Put it away," Bourne said.

Pocketing the bribe, Tigger gestured for Bourne to follow him. They went through the ER, where everyone was too frantic to notice them or to care where they went. In a storeroom, Tigger picked out a doctor's coat and Bourne put it on.

"You have the ID?"

Tigger nodded. "She's never seen you before?"

"Never," Bourne said, "but Carlos has. Install yourself in the lobby. Text me the moment you see him coming."

"*Bueno*." Tigger clipped a hospital ID tag to the pocket of Bourne's coat. As far as the hospital personnel were concerned Bourne was now Dr. Francisco Javier.

"You're good to go," Tigger said, then recited a room number. "Estefan won't be any problem," he added with an even wider grin. "He's terrified of doctors."

Bourne took the elevator up to the second floor, strode to the nurses' station, and asked for Maricruz's chart. The duty nurse gave him only the most cursory of glances before plucking out the requested chart and handing it over.

As he went down the corridor toward Maricruz's room, he scanned the pages. Anunciata's contact had been right: Whatever else had happened, Maricruz had been really and truly battered.

He looked up to find Estefan sipping a cup of vending-machine coffee and making faces into his mobile as he texted someone. He noticed Bourne coming and, checking that the ID photo matched the face he saw in front of him, gave a shudder as he stepped aside to let Bourne into the room.

Maricruz seemed dazed, her eyes glazed when Bourne stepped in. She blinked several times, then frowned when she saw him.

"Another fucking doctor? I've never seen you before."

"I peeked in several times while you were unconscious," Bourne said, closing her chart with a snap. "I assisted in the procedure to secure the tendons to your shoulder."

"Is that medical terminology?"

Bourne laughed as he had observed doctors laughing. "I prefer using everyday language with my patients."

"How refreshing. Doctors are always trying to prove their superiority, possibly because they're aware of how little they really know." She tilted her head. "What does my chart say?"

"Since I don't know much, my opinion probably won't mean anything to you."

"Very funny. Go on."

"You're mending well," he said in a more serious tone. "In fact, you're healing quite a bit faster than normal. We're very pleased with your progress."

"When can I get the hell out of here?"

"Okay if I sit down?" He pulled a chair over and sat down.

"You might as well please yourself," Maricruz said. "There's no one else here to please."

"Well, I always hope I can please my patients."
Bourne crossed one leg over the other and, el-
bows on the chart in his lap, leaned toward her.
"Maricruz—may I?"

"You already have." But there was a slight lift to
the corner of her mouth, and her tone had lost its
steely edge.

"Maricruz, can you tell me what happened to
you?"

She seemed taken aback by the question. "How
is that relevant?"

He shrugged. "I like to get to know my patients."

"My, you really *are* a different kind of doctor."

"Will you indulge me?"

Her frown deepened. "I'm not the subject of
some kind of psychological experiment or something, am I?"

He laughed again. "Not at all."

"I fell off a bike."

"And got run over by a car?"

"I beg your pardon."

"The nature of your bruising is inconsistent with
a fall off a bike."

"After my bike hit a pothole I tumbled down an
embankment."

Bourne decided to study her chart in more detail.
"I notice there's a police report attached here. A

witness claims someone threw you out of a vehicle and sped away." He looked up. "Friends of yours?"

Her eyes grew large before she turned away.

"I see here there was no follow-up to the initial police report."

"The entire matter is being handled by Carlos Danda Carlos," she said shortly.

Bourne closed her chart. "Ah, I see. Friends in high places."

She smiled thinly. "Something like that."

"Tell me, how do you find Señor Carlos Danda Carlos?"

Now she laughed, a soft, musical sound like bells echoing through a mountain pass.

"Define *find*."

"It's only that I've heard so many stories about him. I don't know what to believe. For instance, is he a good man, do you think?"

There was that frown again. "Are you really a doctor?"

"What do you mean?"

"I'm beginning to think Carlos sent you in here to interrogate me."

Bourne, knowing he had to redirect her, stood up. "A thousand pardons, señora. I didn't mean to give you the impression—"

"Do you work for him?"

"I've met him once, briefly," Bourne said truthfully. "That's all."

She studied him a moment more. "Sit down, Doctor."

He hesitated just the right amount of time before resuming his seat, but this time he sat on the edge, his back stiff, his shoulders slightly hunched.

"Oh, relax. I won't bite."

"You certainly won't bite me if you call me Javvy—all my friends do."

Maricruz arched an eyebrow. "Now we're friends? I thought I was your patient."

"I misspoke before. You *were* my patient when you were in the OR. Dr. Fernandez is your attending physician."

"But you came to see me anyway."

"I told you. I feel a connection with all my patients."

"That must be exhausting."

"Better than treating them like slabs of meat. That kind of assembly line deadens the heart as well as the soul."

For the first time since he entered, she seemed to regard him with different eyes, as if a curtain had parted, revealing something that had always been there but had remained hidden from her.

At that moment the nurse bustled in carrying a tray of food, which she placed on the bedside rolling table. Swiveling it over the bed, she smiled her vaguely wicked smile and stalked out.

Bourne stood up. "I'll leave you to it then."

Maricruz looked at Bourne over the tray. "My food is provided by Carlos's chef. It's invariably delicious, but there's always more than I can eat."

"Are you asking me to join you for lunch?"

"Don't get any ideas."

"I have rounds." Bourne lifted the metal cover off the steaming-hot main course, inhaled the delicious aromas. "But on the other hand, maybe I can spare a couple of minutes."

What we're contemplating is insane, you know that," Ouyang said.

"I suppose that depends on your definition of *insane*." Kai stared out the window for a moment, but he seemed utterly disinterested in the passing cityscape. "My definition is cutting the Politburo Standing Committee from nine members to seven." He regarded Ouyang severely. "I take it the Patriarch neglected to inform you."

Ouyang felt a certain tension inform his frame. "You know this for a fact?"

"I do." Kai sighed. "The old guard may be stepping down next week, but they're determined to have their influence carry on. By dictating that the Standing Committee members be reduced they ensure the younger, more progressive candidates will not get enough votes."

"And so great decisions will fall by the wayside."

"The committee will remain more to their liking."

Ouyang shook his head. "You're quite right, Kai. This is the true meaning of insanity."

"Jidan, my friend, I've had enough depressing talk for one day. I propose we head for a small club I own where we can dive into a swimming pool of naked Japanese girls. What do you say?"

"You go if you want, Kai. I'm married."

"Married," Kai scoffed. "Your wife is thousands of miles away."

"What difference does that make?"

"I would think every difference," Kai said with a salacious wink.

"I love my wife."

"I don't get how you could live with a Western woman, let alone love her. I mean, the ones I've been with are plagued with an offensive body odor."

"I have no idea what you're talking about."

Kai sat back, sighing. "The trouble with you,

Ouyang, is you have a stick up your ass. You've got to learn how to relax, let your hair down, forget who you are for a couple of hours."

"I can't forget," Ouyang said. "I'm not made that way."

"What the hell does that mean?"

"It means that every moment Maricruz is away from me is agony." He crossed his arms over his chest. "You have no idea what I'm talking about, do you?"

Kai shrugged. "I find women the most disposable of commodities. Now and again my penis becomes inordinately interested in them, and then I follow its lead. But when the act is over, I forget all about them. Why wouldn't I? There's nothing of interest in an act that's part mechanical, part chemical."

"Nothing interesting about the other participant?"

"The women are the least memorable part of it," Kai said. "One body blends into the next, and as for their faces, frankly, I can't recall a single one."

Ouyang laughed. "You know, Kai, I think a sojourn to your club would do you a world of good. Who knows, maybe this time you'll find someone memorable."

"I doubt it." Kai put his head back and closed

his eyes. "Spending too much time with you has sapped me of my desire for fun."

"Outstanding!" Ouyang, piqued despite himself, gestured at the driver. "The car will drop us both at the office and we can get back to work plotting Cho's imminent demise."

As they rode along, invulnerable to any interference, either human or atmospheric, Kai took out a small folding pocketknife and gently inserted the point of the blade beneath one nail.

"Kai, what are you doing?"

"Excising the last of General Hwang Liqun."

Looking closer, Ouyang could see thin crescents of dried blood that had become lodged beneath Kai's well-manicured nails.

"See that you put that into the ashtray on the door," Ouyang said. "I don't want it soiling the carpet."

"You bet." Kai started on the second nail.

"What did you do to him?" Ouyang asked idly.

"You don't want to know." Kai flipped a thin dark red crescent into the open ashtray. "I didn't want to make it look like an execution, so it got rather...messy."

He looked over at Ouyang, smiling. "You know, the product of a—how shall I characterize it?—a disordered mind."

And Ouyang thought, with an unpleasant start: *Is*

it my imagination or is that smile more than a bit mad?

Another shaving of blood, curling like a living thing about to be born, was transferred from the tip of Kai's knife to Ouyang's ashtray.

26

"YOU'RE A LONG WAY from home," Bourne said when they had finished the meal.

"I'm a long way from my husband. It's not the same thing."

Bourne considered this, knowing her husband the way he did. "Why did you leave Mexico?"

"I could no longer tolerate the constant drumbeat of *machismo*." She smiled. "I'm a very modern woman."

"So I've noticed."

Maricruz wiped her lips on a paper napkin, pushed the tray table away. "Tell me, Javvy, do you have someone to love?"

"I don't."

"It's sad to be alone, isn't it? I've spent a lot of time alone and I know."

"It's sadder to lose someone you love."

She scrutinized him a moment more than was necessary. "I'm so sorry. Your wife must have been special."

"She died here in Mexico City." Why did he tell her that? Abruptly, he found himself on dangerous ground that was of his own making.

"Did she fall ill?"

"She was stabbed to death."

"How terrible."

Bourne could see that Maricruz was genuinely horrified, and this produced a gush of strange, strangled pleasure inside him, in a way that brought Rebeka back from the dead, made her seem close to him again.

"She called me, but she bled out before I could get to her."

"You were the one who found her."

"I was." He stared down at his hands. "All my knowledge and I wasn't able to save her."

"At least you were there," Maricruz said. "I was on the other side of the world when my father was killed."

Bourne looked up, stared into her eyes. "How did it happen?"

"I could never find out. The circumstances were murky. All I know is, he stepped into chaos and never got out."

"That's a shame."

"Not really. My father knew what he was doing and where he was going. He was aware of the dangers as well as the rewards. In that respect, he died on his own terms. I wonder how many people can say that at the end of their lives?"

"I imagine not many," Bourne said.

He was starting to get the measure of her. She was not at all as he had imagined her, and this worried him. It was dangerous to make assumptions about anyone, especially someone like Maricruz. What a pedigree this woman had: daughter of Maceo Encarnación, married to Ouyang Jidan. In every sense of the phrase she was a precious commodity, and Bourne was determined to treat her as such. As long as she remained ignorant of his true identity he knew he'd be all right.

"It seems to me," she said now, "grief is the loneliest emotion. You get locked into it and it becomes something of a prison to which you've forgotten the key. Sometimes, I think you deliberately hide the key from yourself because you don't want to be set free."

Bourne looked at her. "Is that how you feel?"

All she offered was a thin smile.

"I think I ought to go."

"Of course." As he rose and crossed to the door,

she added in a steely voice, "I pity you, Javvy. You can't outrun your sorrow. Your wife is gone. You loved her, but now she's just a memory."

He stopped, but did not turn around to face her.

"It's time to let it go."

For the first time since he had left Tel Aviv, Bourne realized that he was sinking, realized that something had been left unsettled by Rebeka's death, something fundamental, something beyond mere revenge.

"I have to go. I'll look in on you tomorrow."

"I know you can't. Men are weak this way." Maricruz turned her face to the wall.

Do you trust her?" Diego Salazar said.

Felipe Matamoros lit a cigar and began the process of obtaining just the right burn. "Why should I trust her?"

"There's a cure for that," Salazar said.

The two men, sitting at a table in El Ángel, on Venustiano Carranza, had just finished lunch. Dotted around them, no less than six tables were occupied by their Los Zetas soldiers, on the lookout for more intervention from the *Federales*.

Matamoros, crossing his legs, sat back and blew a plume of smoke upward into air redolent of blackened peppers and beer. "There's a cure for everything, Diego. But unlike you, I know it doesn't always involve murder. I have someone keeping an eye on her."

"The Special Forces trained us both, *compadre*. Who voted early and often to defect when the Gulf cartel elders contacted us? Our future and our fortunes were made by that decision."

"Now Maricruz Encarnación holds the key to our future and our continued fortunes."

"Ouyang," Salazar said. He was as thin and deadly as a rapier, with a long face, sunken cheeks scarred by a virulent bout with childhood smallpox, and dark and burning eyes, watchful as a crow's. "She's Señora Ouyang now."

"Blood is blood," Matamoros said. "She's an Encarnación. She never would have returned to Mexico otherwise."

"She has her husband's interests to think of now."

"As well as her father's legacy." Matamoros looked out at the wide street, with its median planted with palm trees. "As long as her husband's interests are aligned with her late father's she will follow them. But I have a feeling that if or when they deviate, she will choose the Encarnación path."

Salazar frowned. "You think they will deviate?"

"Possibly not." Matamoros turned back to his *compadre*. "Not without our intervention."

Salazar grinned, lit a cigarette, and filled his lungs with calming nicotine. "I see you have formed a plan."

Matamoros nodded. "But first, I would like an explanation as to why the *Federales'* helo was struck while it was hovering above us in the forest."

Salazar shook his head. "I don't understand you, *compadre*. The soldiers in the helo were raining fire down on you. Of course I gave the order to fire the missile."

"When the helo came down, it killed our men. It almost killed Maricruz and myself."

"What was I to do? I was caught between two conflicting poles."

Matamoros uncrossed his legs, leaned forward so that his abdomen pressed against the edge of the table. He took the cigar out of his mouth, saw Salazar's eyes follow it, so that when he pulled the trigger on the noise-suppressed handgun he gripped under the table, his *compadre* was so surprised a stunned expression paralyzed his face in the instant before he keeled over.

"You could have resolved not to try to kill me under the cover of chaos," Matamoros said, as his soldiers left their tables and, gathering around, hauled Salazar up and dragged him away with such alacrity and precision not a single diner harbored an inkling of what had actually happened, assuming drunkenness or a sudden illness.

Octavio Luz, another of the Los Zetas *compadres*, sat down in the chair previously occupied by Salazar, but not before wiping the blood off the seat.

"You know, Felipe, we keep this up, we'll be doing Carlos's job for him."

"Not if we stick together." Matamoros continued to smoke his cigar as if nothing untoward had transpired. "The danger comes when someone in the cadre decides to be an individual. But, examining your point from another angle, it occurs to me that Carlos may be deliberately trying to divide in order to conquer us."

"Explain."

"I have a suspicion that he's using Maricruz like a fox in the henhouse. I have hardly to tell you that some of us have been dead set against her involvement from the moment she showed up on our doorstep."

"Salazar was one of those who was certain she was Carlos's agent, sent in to cause this dissension."

"Though I very much doubt that the daughter of Maceo Encarnación—a highly intelligent creature—would allow herself to become Carlos's pawn, nevertheless she has caused dissension. But trying to get rid of me in order to keep her at arm's distance was the decision of a madman. I only have the best interests of Los Zetas at heart."

"You have a believer in me." Octavio Luz hitched his chair forward. "*Pero, dígame, compadre*, there are others in our cadre who harbor a suspicion that the Encarnación woman has gotten under your skin."

Matamoros spat sideways, onto the ground. "What are you saying?"

"They believe that you are infatuated with this woman, that you are—how shall I put it?—under her spell."

"What? They think she's some kind of *bruja*—a sorceress?"

"I'm merely the messenger, Felipe. I come to you as a friend."

"No, no, *compadre*. You are carrying their water—these cowards who are too craven to speak of her to my face."

Luz drew back as if struck. "Irrespective of the truth or falsehood of their belief, you see how she is affecting us. One of us is already dead. We're at each other's throats."

"If we fall out, I tell you it's not because of Maricruz," Matamoros said emphatically. "It's because there is an essential flaw in us—in the cadre."

Luz, who was as solidly built as a professional wrestler and as muscular, gestured. "Do you still have that weapon aimed at me under the table?"

Matamoros placed the gun on the table amid the plates, where only the two of them could see it. "*Ay, compadre*, what d'you take me for?"

"I tell you, Felipe, sometimes it's hard to tell."

Matamoros laughed. "Please." He handed a cigar to Luz, who bit off the end, stuck it in his mouth, and lit it slowly, running the flame back and forth close to the blunt end. "We were schoolboys together, we chased girls together, we fought off bullies together."

"Yes, brothers under the skin, is that it? You're preaching to the choir, *compadre*. I hold no suspicion, though there are many reasons not to trust the woman."

"Just as many reasons to consider otherwise. Her truth is compelling—it's good business for all of us. I believe her when she says she wants to keep her father's legacy alive. If you were Maceo Encarnación's child you would want the same."

"But, Felipe, she ran away from him, from her homeland. Now she's back, offering us precisely what we want and need."

"My friend, I think you're giving Carlos Danda Carlos too much credit. He's not Niccolò Machiavelli."

"Agreed," Luz said, shifting on his chair. "But what about the woman? What about Maricruz?"

27

MARICRUZ LAY BACK on her pillows after the man she knew as Javvy left her room. She fumbled for the bed's controls but could not find the buttons. Annoyed more than she should have been by so small a frustration, she pressed the button for the nurse, who entered with her usual official stride.

"I want to lie down."

Maricruz watched the nurse as she crossed the room and lowered the bed. She hated asking this nurse to do anything for her. At least the first couple of days, when she had to lean on her to get to the lavatory, were behind her. She shuddered at the thought; she had been as weak and helpless as a baby.

"Anything else I can do for you, señora?"

Was that a sneer on the nurse's face? At another time, another place, Maricruz would have been incensed. Now she simply couldn't be bothered.

"That will be all."

She closed her eyes as the door sighed shut behind the nurse. She wanted to think about her last visit with Carlos, but instead her mind slipped its normally tight leash and kept drifting toward Javvy. He seemed a curious mixture of power and sorrow, a compelling combination in any man, but especially so in the surgeon who had restored her to health.

While she was with him she had felt a curious sense of being sexually possessed, as if she were submitting to him. That was not a feeling she had experienced before. She was used to dominating, something Jidan liked far too much, she realized with a start. This new feeling put her in terra incognita, harking back to the darkest days of her adolescence, when a potent combination of rage and raging hormones made her mutinous, barbaric, obsessed with sex. In those half-buried days and nights she had been eager to try anything and everything for the sake of needing to feel something—anything—real, that hadn't been manufactured by her father.

As far as she was concerned, her marriage to Jidan had been something of a business transaction, though she knew full well he adored her. And yet that was part of the attraction for her—being married to a man who worshipped her, whose demeanor negated Mexican *machismo*, which, so far as she was concerned, was just another form of misogyny. On the other hand, China had once been ruled by the female emperor Wu Zetian, whose social, religious, and historical reforms outlived her. Not that there wasn't a bias against females in China—there was, to varying degrees, outright or hidden, in all male-dominated societies the world over—but there was an undeniable history of females ruling from behind the bedchamber curtains, even when they didn't rule outright.

All this brought her back to Javvy. He did not display the Mexican *machismo*, which, unlike her, many women inexplicably found attractive, but neither was he burdened with Jidan's perverse form of ambiguity, which at times bordered on the androgynous.

The truth was, she had felt magnetized to him when he was near her, as if her inner sense of True North had been stripped from her, and this caused a certain fear to rise inside her like mist obscuring the ground on which she walked.

She had closed her eyes and was just falling asleep when the bustling silence of the floor was pierced by an unearthly shriek. She sat bolt-upright. The shriek came again, echoing through the corridors.

Sliding out of bed, she made her way into the corridor. The nurses' station was deserted and, apart from Julio, one of her night guards, who was on his feet nervously shuffling from one foot to the other, so was the corridor.

"What's happening?" she asked him.

He shrugged.

A third shriek, high-pitched, fueled by terror, seemed to emanate from a room not more than a hundred feet from hers.

"Where the hell are the nurses?"

Again, Julio shrugged. "This often happens at night," he said. "One of the reasons the boss has us here."

One of the reasons, she thought as she headed down the corridor toward the room.

"Where are you going?" Julio called. "Señora, *por favor*! You'll get me fired!"

Ignoring him, Maricruz reached the room. The door was shut. The shrieks had stopped, but now she heard deep, heart-wrenching cries, as if pulled directly from a bloody chest. Steeling herself, she pushed open the door.

Inside the room, she saw the girl from physical therapy. She was sitting up in bed, the sheets rucked around her. The stench of fresh feces filled

Maricruz's nostrils, and as she approached, she
saw that the girl was sitting in her own shit. Her
head was thrown back, her neck exposed. She
stared at the ceiling and, as Maricruz stepped toward her, she let out another unworldly howl that
spoke of an anguish beyond imagining.

In the silence between those dreadful wails,
Maricruz called for her guard. When he stuck his
head in the door, she said, "For the love of God,
where are the nurses?"

"I don't know, señora. Truly."

"Christ on a crutch," she murmured to herself.

"Señora?"

"Come here, Julio, and pick this girl up."

"What are you doing, señora?" He held one hand
over his nose and mouth. "How can you stand that
stink?"

"Are you serious? Oh, for God's sake!"

Leaning over the bed, she picked up the girl, who
felt as cold and stiff as a marble statue. Ignoring
the searing pain in her shoulder, she carried the
girl into the bathroom, stripped off her gown, and
spent the next ten minutes cleaning her up, holding her all the time, murmuring soothingly to her.
The girl's weight against her shoulder was agony,
but as in physical therapy, it was a good pain, it
meant something beyond the aftermath of Maricruz's beating. It brought her out of herself.

As she worked, she felt a shift in the girl. It was so gradual that at first Maricruz, busy with the physical work, scarcely noticed. But by the time she had dried the girl off, Maricruz became aware that the girl's death-like stiffness had softened, that her head now rested normally against the hollow of her shoulder. She had long since ceased her shrieking, but she wasn't silent, either. Words and phrases burst from between her lips like air bubbles escaping someone drowning. Maricruz listened closely, but even so the words sounded like nonsense to her, the kind of babble that comes out of a toddler's mouth before it learns to speak.

She could find no other gown, so she wrapped the child in a bath towel and took her out of the room. True to form, Julio backed up when he saw the two of them coming. Maricruz wished for Tigger, who surely would have helped her.

The corridor was still deserted, but by the time she reached her own room a nurse finally appeared.

"Señora, what are you doing?"

"What does it look like?" Maricruz said, elbowing Julio out of the doorway and stepping into her room.

The nurse hurried toward her. "Is that another patient? Señora, stop! You cannot—"

"The fuck I can't!" Maricruz said even more vehemently than she had intended.

The nurse went immediately to the station and picked up the phone. "If you don't stop, I'll be forced to call security to take the girl back to her room. It's against hospital policy—"

"Is it hospital policy," Maricruz said, "to leave an entire floor unmanned? Is it hospital policy to leave a child howling like a wolf, sitting in her own shit and piss? Is it hospital policy to leave a pitiful, severely traumatized creature alone at night?" She glared at the nurse. "So go ahead, call security. I'll have Julio here call Señor Carlos and we'll see who prevails."

The nurse held on to the phone just long enough so as not to lose maximum face. As soon as she put the receiver down, Maricruz told her to get an orderly to clean up the girl's bed. "Better still, do it yourself. Then find a bed and put it in my room."

"That I can't do until tomorrow," the nurse said icily. "The storeroom is in the basement and it's locked for the night."

"Then get me a fresh gown for her," Maricruz said, taking the girl into her room and laying her on her own bed.

When the nurse came in with the gown and attempted to put it on the girl, Maricruz stopped her.

"I'll do that," she said, taking the gown from her and unfolding it. "Go clean the room."

When she hesitated, Julio came into the room. "Do as the señora tells you," he said gruffly, "or it will be your job."

Making a sound deep in her throat, the nurse turned on her heel and left. Maricruz heard the soles of her shoes squeaking against the linoleum as she went down the corridor to the girl's room.

Julio took another step into the room. "How can I help?"

Maricruz gave him a look that set him back on his heels, and he retreated to his usual position on the folding chair outside her door. Turning back to the girl, Maricruz unwrapped her and put on the fresh gown. The girl lay passively in her bed, staring up at her.

"You're safe now," Maricruz whispered, bent low over her. Her lips brushed the girl's cool, damp forehead. "Warm and safe."

When she climbed into the bed and pulled the covers up, the girl froze, trembling like a dry leaf in a storm.

"It's all right," Maricruz whispered. "You're safe now, you're safe now."

Gradually, the terrible tension gripping the girl's narrow frame began to lose its grip, until, eventually, she curled her little body into Maricruz, as a dog or cat would. She was so thin, Maricruz could feel each knob of her spine as it pressed into her. She curled forward, kissed the top of the girl's head.

Much later, Maricruz could swear she heard the child purring.

Hale received the packet from Amir Ophir via the courier at his chicly appointed apartment in Roma, just south of the Zona Rosa. When he was alone, he slit open the arcane packaging. He smiled when he saw the sealing wax, thinking, *That's Amir for you.*

For a long time he stared at the tape with its fingerprint, then he opened Ophir's instructions and read it twice through, committing it to memory. Drawing an ashtray to him, he struck a match, held the flame to one corner of the paper, watched as it was consumed by the fire. He rose, then, and flushed the ashes down the toilet.

Then he got to work. First, he went to his large oak cabinet, which contained thirteen long and narrow drawers of the kind artists and art dealers use to store prints. Each drawer was labeled with two letters of the alphabet. He opened the second drawer, labeled C–D, and pulled out the architectural blueprints for Carlos Danda Carlos's palatial villa. Bringing them over to the table, he spread them out under a goosenecked lamp and devoted his complete attention to them for a solid thirty minutes. When he was certain of what needed to be done, he returned them to their drawer. Next, he crossed to his workshop and gathered the parts he needed, fitting them together beneath a strong light, a jeweler's loupe over one eye.

Before he was finished, he took the tape Ophir had sent him and applied the fingerprint to the inside of the item he had made.

Finishing assembling it, he packed it and everything else he needed into a plumber's tool bag, then set out. Night had fallen several hours before. The sky was roiled with low, menacing clouds, off which the lights of the city bounced, creating eerie patterns and lurid colors. Every few seconds thunder boomed, and once or twice lightning split the sky and rattled windowpanes. The air was heavy with rageful electricity.

Hale took a bus that ran alongside Chapultepec Park. Past the statue of Diana, he got off. The rain began to fall first as steaming mist then, abruptly, in sheets that bounced off the sidewalk like sleet. He traveled down Avenida Presidente Masaryk all the way to Rubén Darío. Turning down a quiet, tree-lined street, he immediately saw the plain-clothes security detail staked out around Carlos

Danda Carlos's SUV and residence. *Good*, Hale thought, *Carlos is at home*. The villa rose like a spiked medieval castle behind a high stucco wall, festooned with purple bougainvillea and wicked razor wire.

Backtracking to Rubén Darío, he went along to the next street, the trees of the park across the avenue dark and forbidding in the storm. Passing cars threw up bow waves of water as they passed, headlights rearing up, then veering away.

Hale entered the street parallel to the one he'd been on. He was now nearing the rear of Carlos's villa. In the heavily shadowed alleyway, he found the electrical box, half hidden by thick foliage, precisely where the architectural blueprints showed it would be.

Completely sheltered from both the rain and the prying eyes of the security contingent, he set down his plumber's bag, donned rubber gloves, and wiped the bag free of prints. Then he dug out the tools he needed and went to work. Seven minutes later, the lights winked out in the villa as the power lines were cut. At once, he heard the shouts of the security team as they called to one another. Leaving the open bag where it lay, he raced back around the way he had come.

As anticipated, the security team had been drawn to the electrical box, and must even now be poring over the plumber's bag. One man stood guard on the sidewalk in front of the villa, but even he was peering back along the alleyway in a vain attempt to see what was going on. Hale could hear him ask urgently for an update, and while he was listening via his wireless earpiece, Hale went down the street.

When he was parallel to Carlos's SUV, he saw a large truck turn onto the street. As if that were a signal, he bent, affixing the small box he had prepared, bearing the incriminating print, to the underside of the vehicle. He pulled out his mobile as he stepped out into the street almost directly in front of the truck. The truck's horn blared, the guard whirled, briefly catching sight of his back in the headlights as he sprinted out of the way and across the street.

"Hey, you!" the guard called. "Stop!"

Two other guards came running down the alleyway toward their comrade's shouts.

Then, protected by the steel bulk of the truck, Hale pressed a button on his mobile, detonating the bomb. The car went up, blowing to pieces that shot outward from the epicenter. The guard who had shouted was immediately incinerated. The lead running guard had his face and chest ripped away. The third remaining man was thrown backward against a light pole with such force his spine shattered.

As for Hale, he was lost in the shadows between two buildings. He heard more shouts raised, but he had worked out his escape route and, of course, the heavy rain helped conceal him. Not ten minutes later, he had boarded a bus, which carried him back past the statue of Diana and into Colonia Roma.

28

WHEN, AT LENGTH, Maricruz fell asleep, she dreamed of Jidan—a restless dream, in which she was running, only to come upon abrupt dead ends inside a labyrinth she had lost the power to navigate. But when she awoke, she could recall only shadowy bits and pieces, filling her with a strange dread that lasted through the early-morning hours and made her temper repeatedly boil over.

What do you want from Maricruz?" Anunciata asked.

Bourne shook his head. "Better not to know."

Rain rattled the long windows in Anunciata's apartment, thunder crashed, and the church across the street was fitfully illuminated by the fleeting glare of lightning, cold as moonlight.

Anunciata gave him a look, shrugged. "You hate being here, don't you?"

"I wouldn't call it hate, exactly."

"Because Mexico City is where she died, the woman you loved."

Bourne lay back on the sofa. "Am I to pay you for this session?"

Anunciata laughed. "You're under no obligation to tell me anything."

"I'm here because there's a job to do."

She went over to the refrigerator, took out two bottles of beer, and handed one to Bourne. She sat down opposite him. "You don't have a job. You do what you want."

"I do what I need to do." He put aside the beer. "Isn't it the same for you?"

She thought about this while she drank. Then she rose and stood in front of him, kicked off her shoes. She sat, straddling him.

"Anunciata, what are you doing?"

"What I want to do." She raised her arms. "Take off my shirt."

"This is not a good idea."

Putting aside her beer, she crossed her arms, shrugged off her shirt. She had no need of a bra. Her bare breasts gleamed in the copper lamplight, nipples hard and dark. As she leaned in to kiss him, he stopped her with the heels of his hands on her creamy shoulders.

"Don't you find me attractive?"

"You know I do."

"Then what's the problem?" Her smoky gaze held his for what seemed a long time. "Oh, I see. I'm sorry."

"Don't be."

She put her shirt back on, but stayed where she was. "You're the only man who ever helped me, who ever showed me kindness and never expected payment." She leaned in, but this time put her head in the crook of his shoulder. When he felt her shoulders shaking, he put one arm around her and stroked the back of her head. Her hot tears burned the side of his neck.

"You've made a good life for yourself," Bourne said.

She pulled away to look into his eyes. "I've learned how to survive, that's not the same thing. Sometimes, rattling around in these rooms, I feel as if my brain is about to explode. And when I can't stand it anymore, I go out to a bar or a club. Sometimes I meet someone, sometimes not. Once in a while I actually like him and I realize I've told him my name is Lolita and Lolita doesn't exist except in one of my favorite novels and I'm about to invite him home and then I think, *What if he's one of my father's people, what if he's been looking for me ever since I left the villa on Castelar Street, what if I'll wind up dead in some back alley with my throat cut open?* What it comes down to is that I have no family, no identity except my hacker handle."

"Lolita."

"That name's a sick joke."

He resettled her beside him. "Isn't it easier now that your father's dead?"

"Not really. His people still crisscross the city; his influence never dies. And everything is made more impossible because this is Mexico. I'm not a lady like Maricruz. I come from a humble background, peasant stock. I could never move in the circles she moves in."

"I don't think you'd want to."

"You only say that because, like her, you can."

"And you really want that?"

"I don't know what I want," she said with a deep sigh. "I only know something vital's missing from my life and I can't stand being without it."

They were quiet for a time, listening to the petty arguments running down the street, along with the barking dogs. The rain continued to pelt down.

After some thought, he said, "It's exhausting being tough as nails."

As if he had given her permission, she curled up against him. "Tell me a story," she whispered. "Tell me a story about her—a happy story. I want to know about Rebeka."

The man had attached the bomb to the underside of your SUV when he was spotted," Sergeant Rivera said.

"Did you get a good look at him?" Carlos Danda Carlos, clad in a maroon silk dressing gown, stood in the grand marble entryway of his villa. His men had tried to hustle him to another location, but he had brushed their pleas aside, refusing to be displaced by any form of threat. He would not be seen as a coward, running for cover.

"Unfortunately, no," Rivera said. "He was fleeing the scene and was only in the truck's headlight beam for a split second. I wanted to pursue him, but there was the utter chaos in the aftermath of the bomb, I had three comrades dead, and your safety came first. Besides, as you know, the weather was very bad. I would never have been able to find him."

"The sonofabitch bombed my car. He killed three of my men," Carlos said, thinking the bombing had to be in retaliation for what had happened in San Luis Potosí.

Rivera shifted from one foot to the other. "The good news, however, is that we discovered a fingerprint on a fragment of the interior of the bomb."

"How is that possible?"

"There was shielding inside the bomb. Forensics says it's very sophisticated."

"Find Lieutenant Rios," Carlos ordered. "Bring him to me."

"At once."

Power had been restored, the lights were back on, but he could not shake the sense of foreboding that had electrified him like a lightning bolt when the power was cut. He had immediately pulled out of the girl beneath him, fearing the worst. He had been fearing the worst ever since Los Zetas had executed Raul Giron and his cartel lieutenants, ever since he had received official word that the four military helos he had ordered launched had been shot down, all soldiers lost. The cartel war that had been ripping the country to shreds had now taken on a new and malevolent urgency. Further, there was no doubt in his mind that Maricruz Encarnación Ouyang was the catalyst not only for the ratcheting up of the mayhem but for the radical altering of the playing field.

When Lieutenant Rios, a dapper, mustachioed man whom Carlos both trusted and relied upon, arrived, Carlos said, "About the bomb. Follow it to forensics. I want that fingerprint run through the American systems—they're always barking about how they can help us in the drug war. Take advantage of their eagerness." He gripped Rios's shoulder. "I want that fingerprint identified by sunup. I want to know who set that bomb."

What have we here?" Bourne said when at last he appeared in Maricruz's room at more or less the same time as the day before.

"So you have the courage to return. Good. Angél, meet Dr. Javvy," Maricruz said. She kept one arm around the girl.

"*Hola.*" Bourne smiled. Then to Maricruz in English, "Where did she come from?"

"Keep smiling."

"My pleasure."

"And don't direct any questions at her."

"As you wish."

Maricruz briefly told him why the girl was in the hospital.

"Is she all right? I should examine her."

"She's already been examined God alone knows how many times. I don't think she'll react well to another one, especially by a man."

Bourne nodded. "Does she have family left?"

"So far no one's claimed her."

"And if no one does?"

"I'll deal with that then."

He nodded again, then, squatting down so they were on eye level, said to the girl, "Angél, do you know why bees have sticky hair?"

The girl stared at him for a moment, then slowly shook her head.

Bourne grinned. "Because they use honeycombs."

Angél giggled, Bourne laughed, and Maricruz gave him a curious look.

"Would you like to hear another? Maybe you'll know the answer."

Angél nodded shyly.

"Okay, let's see." Bourne pretended to ponder. "Why do cows wear bells?"

The girl's brow wrinkled. "I...I don't know."

"Because their horns don't work."

Now Angél laughed. It came from deep inside her, and Maricruz gave both of them a wondering look.

As Bourne rose, the girl begged to hear another one.

"Okay, one more," Bourne said. "I really don't know that many. Let's see. Where do books like to sleep?"

Angél thought a moment, then grinned broadly.

"I know this one! Books like to sleep under their covers!"

"That's right." Bourne reached out and tousled her hair.

"Don't!" Maricruz warned.

But the child didn't flinch. In fact, she held out a hand, which Bourne took. "I like you," she said softly. "You're funny."

Bourne smiled again as he stood up.

"Thank you for making time for Angél," Maricruz said. "So few have."

"So it seems." The girl was still holding his hand. "You don't have to tell me how she ended up in your room," he said to Maricruz in English.

Handled correctly, telling people they didn't have to do something, Bourne thought, often led them to do precisely what you wanted them to do.

"I found her shrieking in a pool of her own excrement." Maricruz stroked the girl's hair. "It was the middle of the night. The nurses' station was deserted. It was a terrible thing."

"Yes," Bourne said. "Terrible." He could sense they were speaking now of two separate incidents.

Their gazes met for a moment, then Maricruz's eyes slid away.

"You were right," she said at last, "there was no bicycle accident. In fact, there was no accident at all." Her eyes found his again, and this time there was a determination in them that would not be denied. "I was in San Luis Potosí, the guest, I suppose you could put it, of someone I had no business being with."

That would be either Felipe Matamoros or Raul Giron, Bourne thought. His money was on Matamoros, by far the more powerful of the cartel bosses.

"A difficult man."

She looked at him curiously. "*Abusive* would be a more accurate adjective."

"He beat you?"

"There was a misunderstanding, you might say, and this is the result."

"Some result."

"Some misunderstanding."

Looking into her eyes, it seemed to him that she knew he didn't believe her. But she was not yet ready to tell him the truth. He could understand that.

He filled a plastic cup from the jug on the rolling tray and handed it to her. Angél was still between them, a kind of bridge, the first green shoots of trust emerging between them.

"*Gracias*, Javvy," she said. She drank deeply, then put the empty cup aside.

She smiled, the first sign of true warmth he had seen in her. It seemed clear to him that slowly but surely she was letting her defenses down.

"Maricruz, are you in some kind of trouble?"

At once, something in her retracted. "I told you. It was a misunderstanding, that's all."

But the flicker of anxiety that crossed her face told Bourne she was lying.

29

SEVEN MINUTES AFTER Carlos arrived at his office, Lieutenant Rios entered with a slim file, which he placed in his boss's hand.

"According to our forensics, the bomb was sophisticated, C-4—a professional job, for certain, and nothing like the cartels would cook up."

"Not even Los Zetas?"

"It's nothing we've ever seen before from them."

A worm of dread crawled through Carlos's belly. "A foreign import," he said.

"That's the only logical conclusion," Rios said, nodding. "Which fits with the hit we got on the fingerprint. Our own files had nothing, but we struck gold through the American database."

"Excellent."

Outside, the streets and rooftops had been

scrubbed clean by the night's storm. The sky was a clear, piercing blue, the city's perpetual haze being kept at bay at least until the sun rose high enough to raise the temperature and resurrect the smog.

"It wasn't easy," Rios continued. "Initially, we came up against increasingly higher-level security clearances."

"But you got through."

"Our friends at the CIA eventually provided access," Rios said. "They seemed keen on helping once I told them the circumstances that led to the inquiry."

Carlos opened the folder, which contained a single sheet of computer printout, including a grainy head shot taken with a surveillance telephoto lens.

"Bourne," he said. "The bomb was made and set by Jason Bourne."

No wonder it was sophisticated, Carlos thought.

"He seems to terrify them," Rios continued. "They want him dead."

"So do I." Carlos handed the folder back to his lieutenant. "Get this photo out to everyone—all branches of the police and military. I want it in the hands of all airport, train and bus station, taxi depot, and rental car personnel within the hour. Find this fucker, Lieutenant. And when you do, shoot to kill."

* * *

When Lieutenant Rios left his boss's office, he went down the hall, called to Sergeant Rivera. When he poked his head out of his cubicle, Rios handed him the photo of Bourne. "See that this is distributed to everyone—and I mean everyone." He detailed the order as Carlos had recited to him. "The boss wants this in their hands within the hour."

"Right on it, sir."

Rios watched Rivera hustle off, then he went into the stairwell, trotting down the stairs to the lobby. Outside, he crossed the street, went into a vest-pocket park. The only inhabitants around this early were a couple of vagrants, whom he kicked out, and a flock of pigeons, which followed him around, believing he was about to feed them.

Taking out a burner mobile—he bought a new one three times a week—he pressed a SPEED DIAL button and waited for the familiar voice to answer.

"News?"

"Big news. Jason Bourne's fingerprint was found inside a bomb he affixed to Carlos's SUV last night."

"I don't believe it," Felipe Matamoros said. "Bourne wouldn't be that careless."

Rios was curious as to why Matamoros wasn't surprised that Bourne was in Mexico City, but he stifled his curiosity, which was a dangerous thing when dealing with Matamoros. "Still," he said, "this is the evidence we have. The boss has us handing out his photo to everyone—"

"How the hell did you get a photo of him?"

"CIA."

"Of course. The CIA has wanted him dead for years. Now they're letting Carlos do their wet work for them."

Rios looked around furtively, always on guard during his short phone sessions with the man paying him a small fortune to inform on Carlos. "Any instructions?"

"Just keep me informed on your progress with Bourne."

Maricruz worried her lower lip. "I want to trust you, but I don't think I can."

"Then you *are* in trouble."

Her expression told Bourne she was.

"I would help you if you asked."

She eyed him skeptically. "Why? I'm only a patient, one of many—"

"But Angél isn't," Bourne said.

That seemed to give her pause.

"She needs an advocate here," Bourne went on. "She's formed an attachment to you, true enough. But you're a foreigner now; there's only so much you can do on Mexican soil."

Maricruz drew the girl to her, wrapped her arms around her. "I can't let anything happen to her. I won't."

"Who understands that better than me?"

She studied him long and hard.

"What is it?"

"I'm trying to figure out what your angle might be."

He laughed. "I live in a different world than you, Maricruz. I calculate rates of survival, not angles."

Maricruz put her head alongside Angél's. "What d'you think, *guapa*?" she whispered in the girl's ear.

Angél grinned at Bourne. He grinned back. Silently, they spoke to each other.

Maricruz lifted her head, nodded in a kind of surrender. "The beating I received," she said slowly, almost painfully, "was deliberate."

"Of course it was deliberate. This man in San Luis Potosí was a pro. He knew what he was doing."

She offered him a bleak smile. "I'm afraid I ordered it done."

Bourne wasn't easily surprised, but this revelation rocked him. "Why would you have such a terrible thing done to yourself?"

"To gain someone's trust—someone who had reason to be suspicious of me."

Bourne stood up. "I think you should stop before you say something you'll regret."

"Javvy, you said I could trust you."

"Of course you can trust me, Maricruz. I'd not reveal a word of our conversations, but it seems to me we're heading in a direction I don't feel comfortable—"

"Javvy, sit down." She gestured. "Please."

Bourne remained standing. She needed more incentive to keep coming toward him. "Back to the subject at hand, perhaps you're wise not to be more specific about the source of your beating."

"You don't really believe that," she said.

"I'm going to go now."

As he turned to leave, she said with some force, "It's Carlos I need to get close to."

He turned back. "Why are you telling me this?"

"I don't know."

He regarded her critically. "I think you do. By confessing you're making me complicit."

"Yes."

"That's what you wanted all along."

She hesitated a moment. "It would seem so, yes."

"Why?"

She had thought about this ever since waking with the sense, if not the form, of her dream hanging ripely in her mind. "Do you want the truth?"

"Always."

"Because you seem fearless," she said. "Because as I said, I need help."

"Help with what?"

"Not what," Maricruz said. "Who."

"Carlos."

"Yes," she said. "Carlos."

"Maricruz, since you've opened us up to sedition, why did you return to Mexico?"

"I needed to speak with Felipe Matamoros and Raul Giron."

"Drug business. How do you know I won't report you to the *Federales*?"

She smiled sweetly. "What would you tell them?"

"What, indeed?" He laughed, and in that laugh was the certain knowledge that he had won her over.

She likes winning, Bourne thought. *No, she loves it. She lives for it.* And therein lay the weakness embedded in her strength.

"What do you know about Carlos Danda Carlos?"

Bourne shrugged. "Only what I read in the papers. He's a hero, according to *el presidente*."

"*El presidente* appointed Carlos. What else is he going to say?"

"Political expediency, okay."

"That's all?"

"There's more?"

"Under the guise of ridding Mexico of the cartels, Carlos benefits from their profits," Maricruz said.

"You have proof of this?"

"When I met with Matamoros and Giron in San Luis Potosí a few days ago, Carlos was with Giron. In fact, it was he, not Giron, who acted as the Sinaloa mouthpiece."

"I read that Giron and his lieutenants have been found executed in San Luis Potosí," Bourne said. "But I don't believe everything I read in the papers."

"This story's true," Maricruz said. "I was there. Los Zetas had had enough of their double dealing."

"But they didn't touch Carlos."

"Carlos was clever enough to fly back here to the capital during the night," she said ruefully.

"Fled the scene."

Maricruz nodded in accord. "Like the coward he is."

"And then you had Matamoros's people beat you up," Bourne said.

"I am a Trojan horse."

"And now what?"

"Now," Maricruz said, "you help me kill Carlos Danda Carlos."

30

"YOU CAN'T BE SERIOUS," Bourne said, after the
nurse had taken away the breakfast tray. Despite
Maricruz's urging, Angél had eaten very little,
though it was more than she had consumed the day
before. "I'm a doctor. What makes you think I'd
help you kill anyone?"

Angél whispered something in Maricruz's ear.

"*Claro, sí, guapa,*" Maricruz said, kissing her
cheek.

The girl hopped off the bed and, with one backward look at Maricruz, crossed to the toilet and
went in.

"Believe it or not," Maricruz said, "that's a big
advance for her."

"I see you had a second bed put in for her."

"Yes, but so far she refuses to use it. It's all right, I like the company."

There was a small silence, cut finally by Maricruz. "As to what you said, Carlos Danda Carlos isn't just anyone."

"Granted, but I've taken an oath to save life, not take it."

Maricruz shot him a speculative look. "Extreme circumstances call for extreme measures."

"Okay," he said, "what am I missing?"

"Someone has to expose Carlos for what he is and what he's done. Would you be against doing that?"

"Of course not."

"That's fine, but this is Mexico, Javvy. Neither you nor I nor anyone else, for that matter, will ever be able to successfully expose Carlos. And even if by some miracle we managed to gather enough hard evidence against him, that evidence would be incinerated before it got out, and we'd be killed." She cocked her head. "Am I wrong?"

"No."

"Nevertheless, you agree that Carlos must be stopped masquerading as a champion of the Mexican people while he stuffs his pockets with cartel blood money."

"Of course. Nothing could be clearer."

"Well then, the only path open to us is to kill him, isn't that right?"

"Come on, Maricruz. People like us don't just go around killing other people."

She crossed her arms over her breasts. "Then please provide an alternative."

Bourne had to admire her powers of reasoning. He could imagine a real surgeon—the one who had actually worked on her shoulder—being persuaded by her argument. Of course, he had been ready to jump right in, but in order to maintain his cover he'd had to rely on her to provide a compelling argument. She had not disappointed him.

"I can't, but that doesn't mean—"

"Are you a coward, like Carlos Danda Carlos?"

"I think you know the answer to that."

She swung her legs out of bed, held out her hand, which he took, though it didn't seem as if she required help to stand. "Let's walk around the suite. I need the exercise."

Angél emerged to find her with her arm slung through Bourne's. She stared at them both, blinking hard. At that moment, Tigger poked his head inside the room, and the girl scampered back into the bed, pulling the covers over her.

"*Perdóname,* señora. I've just now heard from Señor Carlos. He sends his regrets, but pressing business has kept him from visiting you today." He smiled. "But tomorrow's another day, eh?"

"Thank you, Tigger," she said, but Bourne, catching the guard's eye, knew this piece of information was as much for him as it was for her.

They began their circumnavigation of the suite, skirting the second bed.

"How are your legs feeling?" Bourne asked.

"Like tree trunks." She laughed softly, and Angél poked her head out from the covers. Maricruz laughed again for her benefit. The girl responded with the ghost of a smile.

Bourne didn't believe Maricruz. Her gait was sure and strong.

Maricruz waited until they were as far away from the door as they could get. "You know, Javvy, I've put a lot of faith in you—telling you all these things."

"Your secrets are safe with me, Maricruz."

"I'm glad of that because you've seen me at my worst."

"Surely your husband has seen you—"

"Not like this. Not bruised and in pain. Not without makeup and my hair unwashed for days."

"Not even in the morning when you wake up?"

"He's up at four in the morning, working. By the time we see each other I'm as I always appear to him. As far as he's concerned I'm perfect."

"And what would he think if he saw you like this?"

"Weak and vulnerable? It'd be a fatal loss of face. He thinks of me in a certain way. I work very hard to keep it that way."

"That can't be fun."

"Who says marriage is fun?"

"I know it's work, but—"

"Believe it or not, sometimes it's just a job," she said.

"Don't let Angél hear you say that."

Maricruz snorted. "Right."

At that moment his mobile vibrated. It couldn't be Tigger warning about Carlos; he would have popped his head in as he had done before.

"Excuse me, I have to take this."

"Of course," Maricruz said, turning back to Angél while Bourne went out of the room.

He strode down the corridor to the public toilet, locked himself inside. The call was from Anunciata.

"Trouble," she said without preamble. "An urgent BOLO has gone out from Carlos's office to all police and public transportation personnel including rental car companies."

Bourne frowned. "What about?"

"A bomb went off last night outside Carlos's residence, destroying his SUV and killing three of his men. You didn't—"

"Of course not."

"Well, the BOLO claims you did. The entire city's looking for you. You're wanted for terrorism and murder."

Bourne was surprised that the *Federales* knew he was in-country. "Why are they fingering me?"

"Apparently, your fingerprint was found on a bomb fragment," she said. "It was a sophisticated bomb, Jason, not anything the cartels use."

"Even Los Zetas?"

"Even the deserters don't have that expertise." She took a breath. "You're going to need help now, more than ever."

"Not from you."

"What? Why?"

"I'm not going to involve you any more than you are. As of this moment I'm toxic to be around. I don't want you anywhere near me."

"But no one knows who I really am or where I live."

"And it's going to stay that way. I'll be fine. I know how to deal with these people."

"But—"

"Stop!"

"Okay, okay. How are things going with Maricruz?"

"She's not what I had imagined."

"I know she hasn't gotten under your skin. In your current state, you won't allow it."

Bourne knew she was speaking of his rejection of her physical advances. "She isn't flirting," he said. "She's too busy plotting Carlos's murder."

"That sounds like her."

"Does she know she has a half sister?" Bourne asked.

"Who would've told her? Not our father, and certainly not my mother. Apart from you, no one else knows."

"There's something else," Bourne said.

"*Dígame.*"

He told her about Angél.

"I wouldn't have believed it of her," Anunciata said. "The child really has no family?"

"No one's come to claim her, and Maricruz isn't one to adopt her."

There was a slight hesitation before Anunciata said, "You know, when it comes to children you never can tell with women. I had a friend—a hard, fierce girl—who claimed she'd never have kids. '*I'm just not cut out to be a mother*,' she told me more than once. Then she got pregnant, and when the baby was born she melted like butter in the sun."

Bourne knew Anunciata wasn't talking about either her half sister or her friend; she was talking about herself.

31

COLONEL SUN ARRIVED in Mexico City, under diplomatic cover. As he exited the arrivals building he was immediately hit with a foul taste in the back of his throat. The embassy limo took him into the city. Forty minutes later he dropped his single small suitcase in the modern hotel room one of Ouyang's many obedient minions had booked for him high above the city.

It was Sun's first time in Mexico, his first time in the Americas altogether. He'd been here less than an hour and already he despised everything about it, especially the alien smells, which made his stomach heave and left the slick remains of acid in his mouth. He could not stop washing his mouth out with bottled water from the mini-fridge. He ran the shower, wishing he could bathe in bottled water instead of the filth that came out of the showerhead. Maybe this trip would prove short enough that he wouldn't bathe, but he doubted it.

He was on a private mission for Ouyang—completely dark, off the books. Having heard she was in the hospital and adhering to their strict protocol not to contact each other while she was in Mexico, the Minister was concerned about the state of his wife's health. *This is what I've been reduced to*, Sun thought sourly, *checking up on his wife like a fucking private detective*. He'd even been provided with a special mobile with a twelve-megapixel camera to record Maricruz's physical state. Ouyang's paranoia surrounding his wife was already legendary among his inner circle. On the other hand, Sun felt for his boss. He could not even call the hospital to inquire after her health. With the Party Congress so close and Cho Xilan eager to pounce on any hint of impropriety, Ouyang needed to sit tight, something he was ill equipped to do when it came to his wife.

Not that Sun had any love for Maricruz—how could he? She was an alien—but he did not for one moment envy her job here. He shuddered. These people were animals.

To that end, he took himself to the address of an underground dealer in Iztapalapa whom Ouyang's ministry had unearthed. The greasy owner stank of badly fried food. Holding his breath as best he could, he bought a tactical knife, a couple of hand-guns, along with several clips of ammunition for each. Sun was sure the owner sneered at him as he left.

Back at the hotel, he climbed into the waiting limousine. Once, as he had emerged from the dealer's filthy den, he was certain he was being followed. Drawing one of the guns he had just purchased, he whirled around. If there had been anyone behind him, they had melted into the store-front shadows.

Still, he was grateful for the diplomatic protection of the embassy vehicle. Ouyang had traced Maricruz's whereabouts from Mexico City to San Luis Potosí and back here again. He had remained in the embassy just long enough to fulfill the necessary protocol, a complete waste of time, so far as he was concerned. On the other hand, he had picked up a curious bit of intel: A bomb had been detonated outside the residence of Carlos Danda Carlos, chief of Mexico's anti-drug enforcement agency. Three of Carlos's men had died in the blast. The city was on high alert. They passed a number of army jeeps crammed with heavily armed soldiers.

"Even though you are officially part of the am-bassador's diplomatic staff," the ambassador had told him, "keep your head down. These people are trigger-happy in the best of circumstances, and today is far from the best of anything."

Now, well armed, Colonel Sun was heading straight for Hospital Ángeles Pedregal, where he would see for himself what had happened to Maricruz and what shape she was in. The problem here, Sun brooded, was he was on alien ground. Apart from what mileage he could get from being on the ambassadorial staff, he had no leverage at all. Plus, he stood out like a sore thumb, though some of the Mexicans he saw with Indian blood had nearly the same epicanthic folds to their eyelids as he did. Much as he hated to admit it, the adjutant was right: He needed to step carefully and keep his head down. In a state of high alert the last thing Ouyang would need was for him to get into trouble with the *Federales*.

At length, they had crossed the city and the limo drew to a stop in front of the busy hospital. Telling the driver to wait for him, Sun emerged onto the sidewalk and went through the front doors. Inside, he went to the information booth and joined the short line. When it came his turn, he produced his false diplomatic credentials and asked the female attendant for Maricruz Ouyang.

"I'm afraid I have no information on that patient." She had scarcely looked at his official ID.

"What do you mean, you have no information?" Sun said in his painfully accented Spanish. "You didn't even bother looking her up. I know she's a patient here."

The woman shrugged. She was middle-aged, with a face like a lion's cage, lined and confined. "Absolutely no visitors. Orders from the anti-drug enforcement agency," she said with no little obstinacy.

"This is outrageous."

She shrugged. "Take your outrage to the ADEA. I can't help you." She peered around him. "Next?"

Colonel Sun retreated. Even though he was unused to being treated like a peon, he knew enough about the Western world to keep his own counsel and bury his sense of outrage and shame. Though he had made several journeys outside the Middle Kingdom, he had yet to catch the harsh and jolting rhythm of Western civilization, which, he thought now, was something of an oxymoron.

His last trip to the West had been more than a year ago, when he'd traveled to Rome, following the Mossad agent Rebeka, in whom Minister Ouyang was intensely and mysteriously interested. Coming upon her, he had discovered Jason Bourne in her company. Following them down into the catacombs off Rome's Appian Way had not turned out well for him, and he was not about to forget the humiliating defeat he had suffered at Bourne's hands.

Now, standing against a pillar in the hospital lobby, he was at a loss as to how to proceed when he saw a young man stride through the front doors. He was not in uniform, but he might as well have been. Colonel Sun recognized the type immediately—a soldier, like him, in civilian attire. As he passed the two guards in front he smiled and waved at them—a half salute, which they returned in kind.

Pushing himself away from the column, Colonel Sun followed the man into an elevator, riding up with him to the second floor. He let the soldier exit before following him down the corridor, past door after door, until up ahead he saw another soldier in civilian dress, sitting on a folding chair just to the right of the entrance to a room. The man was reading *Contralinea*, which he put aside as soon as he saw the man Colonel Sun had been following. They exchanged greetings, then the guard took his newspaper and left, while his replacement—the soldier Colonel Sun had been following—sat down in the chair and began to text someone on his mobile.

Colonel Sun was certain he was guarding Maricruz's room. He strode past the nurses' station. The soldier guarding the door to the room must have seen him out of the corner of his eye, because he immediately stuck his mobile in his pocket and rose, assuming the classic defensive stance as he sought to bar Sun's way.

"Back up," the soldier said in Spanish, then English. "Turn around and leave."

"I'm here to see Maricruz Ouyang," Colonel Sun said in English.

The soldier shook his head. "You've lost your way, señor." One hand slipped ominously inside his jacket. "You won't be warned again."

"You don't understand," Colonel Sun said. "I'm from the Chinese embassy." He showed the soldier his ID. "Minister Ouyang Jidan, Maricruz's husband, is concerned about her health."

"The señora's health is fine."

"And yet, she's still in here." Colonel Sun stitched a smile to his face he did not feel. "Minister Ouyang sent me from Beijing to see her and talk with her."

The soldier continued to eye Sun as if he were a scorpion who had just crawled out from beneath a rock. "A moment," he said as he pulled out his mobile and poked at a SPEED DIAL key. "Boss," he said into the phone, "there's someone here who claims Minister Ouyang sent him all the way from Beijing to see the señora." He listened for a moment, then said, "He showed me his credentials.

They look legit...Okay." He looked at Sun. "My boss is calling the embassy. We'll see...Yeah, boss, right here...Okay, right, right. I'll tell him."

The soldier disconnected. "You have five minutes."

"That's not even time to—"

"If what you said is true, that's all the time you'll need to assure Minister Ouyang that his wife is on the mend."

I'll take it, Colonel Sun thought. *But what can happen in five minutes?*

When Maricruz saw Colonel Sun walk into her room, her heart turned black and seemed to sink into her belly.

"What are you doing here?" she said in Mandarin. "You know the ground rules Jidan and I laid out. No contact whatsoever."

"That was before you landed in the hospital. He became concerned. What happened?" Though Colonel Sun said this to her, he was looking directly at Angél, who seemed to shrivel up like a matchbook on fire as she crawled into the crook of Maricruz's arm. "And what's this?"

"I fell in San Luis Potosí—a sinkhole—and I injured my shoulder."

Colonel Sun frowned. "It looks like you injured

more than your shoulder. Were you beaten?" He took out the phone.

"What are you doing?" Maricruz said, alarmed.

"I'm going to take photos of you."

"The hell you are," Maricruz snapped. She lunged for the phone, but Sun kept it away from her.

"Give that to me."

"Not a chance."

"Don't talk to me in that insolent tone of voice."

Beside her, Angél bared her little teeth, snapped her jaws together.

Sun put the phone up to his face. "Get that monkey out of the way. I don't want her in the photos."

The statement was not only highly insulting, Maricruz thought, but a clear indication that, despite his claim, he had no real interest in her physical condition.

"Get out," she said. "The longer you stay, the better chance you have of fucking things up."

"From what I can see, you've already fucked things up."

"How dare you speak to me that way! I said, get out!"

Colonel Sun grinned like a jackal. He seemed to be enjoying himself immensely. "Listen to me. You have no idea how protected you are in

Beijing—how completely Ouyang coddles you. But you're here now—a long way from the Middle Kingdom, so I'm going to give you some advice I otherwise wouldn't. In Beijing, you are despised. The other Ministers smile to your face, but behind your back they call you *chùsheng*—an animal. They say you're *bùyàoliǎn de dōngx*—a thing without shame, completely without face.

"In China you're nothing without Ouyang's chop; you are what he made you, nothing more. But I know the truth: You're a liability to him. He's constantly preoccupied with protecting you while he should be advancing his position within the Party. But how can he with you around his neck?" He leered at the child. "And now you harbor *this*—a *Mexican* child? What, you think you'll take it back to the Middle Kingdom with you, this stinking piece of shit?" He lunged at Angél. "I'll kill it first, do you hear me? I'll fucking slit its throat."

Who's in there with my patient?" Bourne said to Tigger as he came down the corridor. "Señor Carlos?"

"No, Doctor." Tigger was already on his feet, agitated. "A man from the Chinese embassy. He claims he came all the way from Beijing to find out the señora's health. I told him he had five minutes, that's all."

"Stay out here," Bourne said as he pushed the door open.

Tigger shook his head emphatically. "It sounds like they're already arguing. This is my job, Doc. I want you out of harm's way."

He brushed by Bourne, his right hand already on the grips of his handgun, ready to pull it, should the need arise. Colonel Sun turned, saw Tigger, who blocked his view of Bourne. Maricruz had put herself between Sun and the child.

"Get back to your station," Colonel Sun warned. "This is official diplomatic business. Get out or I'll report you to the ambassador."

"I don't think so," Tigger said. His voice was quiet, almost like velvet. "If this was an official visit it would have been set up by the ambassador and I'd know about it." He indicated Maricruz with his head. "My orders are to protect the señora— and the girl."

"This woman and I still have matters to discuss." Colonel Sun's voice was every bit as velvety, but beneath cords of steel were rapidly forming.

"Get away from her," Tigger said, with a bit more force.

"Not until I'm finished."

"Your five minutes are up."

"They'll be up when I say they're up, *shăbī*."

Tigger's eyes narrowed and his body tensed. "What did you call me?" He turned slightly to Maricruz. "What did this *maricón* call me?"

"*Te llamó una chucha estúpida*," Maricruz said. He called you a stupid cunt.

Now everything happened very fast: Tigger pulled his handgun as he took a threatening step toward Sun. In a blur Sun's left hand dipped, drawing Tigger's attention while his right hand went to his waist, then suddenly flicked upward. The tactical knife buried itself to the hilt in Tigger's chest.

Tigger's eyes opened wide in shock, then he keeled over, his head at Colonel Sun's feet. Maricruz turned the girl's head away, placing her body between Angél and the violence.

Bourne was already on the move.

"Javvy," Maricruz cried. "Call security!"

Ignoring her, Bourne kept coming, not too fast for Sun to be able to draw one of his guns, but, looking up, he recognized the face of the man about to run into him, and for a split second shock paralyzed him.

Then Bourne's forearm slammed into his throat, and he reeled back against the wide windowsill. Bourne fought the gun out of his hand, and it went skittering under the bed. Sun clamped his fingers onto the nerve bundle in the hollow between

Bourne's right shoulder and neck. Bourne's right side went slack, numbness racing from shoulder to fingertips. Sun, seeing his advantage, hammered Bourne's rib cage, staggering him.

"I *will* get my revenge," Sun said.

But Bourne kept on coming, used the edge of his left hand in three quick, vicious kites. A heel thrust to Sun's mouth brought out a violent burst of blood. Bourne vaguely heard Angél give a tiny scream, half muffled in the meat of Maricruz's shoulder.

Grinning, Sun drove his fist toward Bourne's heart to deliver a killing blow. Bourne slashed down against the outmost carpal bone in Sun's wrist, shattering it. Now they were both one-handed, but just as feeling in Bourne's right hand and arm was returning, Sun tripped him.

Bourne went down, Sun on top of him, banging on him with his good hand. Bourne caught movement out of the corner of his eye—Maricruz sliding off the bed, the girl scrambling after her, over her, getting ahead of her. Angél was on all fours, disappearing, hiding within the mechanism under the bed.

Sun slammed Bourne's head against the floor, then drove his fist into Bourne's throat. Bourne gagged, then retched. He grabbed Sun's crotch, squeezed so hard Sun's eyes watered, seeming ready to pop out of his head. He began to choke on his own blood.

In Bourne's peripheral vision Angél reappeared. She was holding Sun's gun in both hands. Her arms were outstretched as she braced her back against the side of the bed.

"Maricruz!" he cried, "stop her!"

But Maricruz did nothing of the sort. Instead she rose slowly, almost magisterially. Even in her bare feet, she took on the appearance of an empress. She was staring fixedly at Colonel Sun, as if her eyes contained the bullet that would be fired, that would kill him.

In Angél's expression could be seen many things: She knew what she held was not a toy; she knew the serious consequences of pulling the trigger; she knew there was no retreating from the decision to fire; and there was no doubt that she knew firsthand the power inherent in the gun.

Who was she aiming at, Sun, Bourne, both of the men? It was impossible to tell.

Closing one eye, she squeezed the trigger as slowly and steadily as Maricruz had risen, just as, time and again, she must have seen her father and her brothers do. The gun went off, the recoil slammed her backward.

All hell broke loose.

32

O PHIR HAS LEFT ISRAEL," Dani Amit, head of Collections Directorate, said.

Director Yadin nodded. "I know."

"You know everything, Memune."

"Don't flatter me, Dani. It's as cheap as a paste diamond."

The two men sat opposite each other at a café along Tel Aviv's harbor. They were in sight of the Director's sailboat. Someone on board was putting in stores, moving in that slow, calm, considered way of all boaters, whether amateur or professional. The two men, dressed similarly in white cotton short-sleeved shirts, lightweight slacks, and colored espadrilles, looked like family. Father and son, perhaps. And, as members of Mossad, they were family, a close-knit group, one relying on the brain power and expertise of the other.

Amit toyed with the small dish of olives. "Do you know where he's going?"

"Wherever Bourne is."

"But do you know?"

"It doesn't matter."

"You trust Bourne that much?"

The Director took a sip of iced tea. "I trust Bourne with my life."

"Ophir's going to kill him," Amit said in his matter-of-fact manner.

"Well, he's going to try." The Director bit into a chicken sandwich and chewed reflectively. "Yes, he's going to try."

Amit eyed his boss judiciously. "By which you mean you believe he's going to fail."

Yadin sat back, stared up at the blue sky, the white, puffball clouds scudding by on the considerable breeze.

"It's a good day for a sail. Of course, you always think that when you set out, but how can you really know? An unexpected storm might be lurking just over the horizon, for the moment out of sight, but moving in so quickly it catches you unawares, vigilant though you might be, as accomplished a sailor as you are."

The Director returned to his sandwich, dredging

the corner of it in the shallow bowl of hummus that sat between them. "You're not eating, Dani. Have you no appetite?"

"I have no appetite for the secrets—"

"Find another occupation, Dani."

"—for the secrets you withhold from me."

"We all have secrets that have no business seeing the light of day," the Director said, "let alone being shared, even among colleagues."

Amit paused a moment, gathering his thoughts. At last, trying not to make a hash of the conversation, he said, "Everything seemed to change when Rebeka was killed." He waited a moment, hoping for a reply, even a word of encouragement, but when none was forthcoming he plowed on, thinking, *In for a penny*... "Then everything changed again when Bourne showed up on our doorstep."

"Can you blame him?" The Director took another swig of iced tea. "He was with Rebeka when she died."

"I never figured him as a sentimentalist."

"He's not—so far as I can tell. But he is human. It was a very human reaction for him to come here, to attend her funeral, to mourn her passing."

"And then, even while the funeral was in progress, you figured out a way to use him."

"You make me out to be so cold."

"Well, how would you characterize your thought process, Director?"

"Is that a rebuke, Dani? Because my job, as I understand it, is to safeguard the State of Israel. That's the job we've all undertaken—it's why we've committed ourselves—our lives—to Mossad. Am I wrong?"

"No, Director."

"Then let us proceed accordingly."

"Well, that's the problem," Amit said. "In this instance, there is no *we*. There is only *you*." He spread his hands. "I simply want to help, Memune. We've been like brothers."

Yadin's gaze drifted to his boat, to the broad, round-shouldered back of the man who was methodically sluicing the deck.

"Ophir and I have been like brothers also, Dani. Should I tell him all my secrets?" His eyes slid back, gripped Amit's. "Do you think that wise?"

"To be truthful, I've never gotten along with Ophir. You know that, Director."

"Of course. As you say, I know everything." He sighed, pushing his plate away. "In fact, I did, once upon a time. But the world changes. Every day brings new puzzles to be solved, but now the complications are of such a magnitude that I often feel lost inside the forest of enemies that seek to rip from us their pound of flesh."

Amit leaned forward. "All the more reason to accept my offer of help, Memune."

"I made the mistake of confiding in Eden," the Director mused, "and now he's dead."

"I'm not afraid of death, Memune."

"Nor are any of us." The Director finished off his tea, then he nodded. "Perhaps you're right, after all, Dani."

For the next ten minutes, he spoke in a soft, low voice. Not once did Amit think to stop him or ask a question. He was far too dumbfounded to utter a word.

Later, after Amit had left to return to the office, Eli Yadin paid the check. Then, baseball cap on his head, hands in the pockets of his trousers, he strolled down to the harbor and went out onto the dock where his sailboat was berthed. The afternoon had turned hot. Despite the breeze, the sun burned down from the top of the vault of heaven. Clouds seemed to flee from it, as if terrified.

The man who had been preparing the boat turned the moment Yadin stepped aboard.

"It's done?" he said.

"It's done, *abi*."

Yadin's father was a bear of a man, his barrel

chest a mat of white hair. In his mideighties, he had the energy of a man twenty years younger. He had a wide face, with large ears and open features. He looked like a Greek sailor. Yadin often imagined him as Odysseus, setting sail for a life at sea, defeating every challenge the jealous, resentful, covetous gods threw at him. He also thought of him as the unnamed fisherman in Hemingway's *The Old Man and the Sea*.

Though his father was more than a decade removed from his retirement as Mossad Director, he had not let the years get the better of him. He was as up-to-date as any of Yadin's people. He was also the only human being Yadin confided in, despite his false confession to Dani Amit.

"You're sure it was the right move to make?" the old man said as, together, they made ready to cast off.

"It was the only move to make."

Yadin's father nodded, and the Director started the engine.

"Truly, I don't envy you," his father said. "When I was Director I had friends inside Mossad."

"Another time," Yadin said, "another place."

The old man came up and put his hand across his son's shoulders. "You'll beat them, Eli. You'll beat all of them."

"*Im Yirtzeh Hashem,*" the Director said, guiding the boat out into open water. If God wills it.

His father expertly let the sails full out to get the boat running before the wind. "God has nothing to do with it," he said. "Jason Bourne does."

But his words were lost to the quickening wind.

Book Three

33

THE GUN WENT OFF, the recoil jolting Angél's arms and shoulder, even though she was prepared for it. Colonel Sun arched up, blood, bone, and brain matter sprayed from the side of his head, and he fell back, cold-fish eyes staring into whatever lay beyond life.

Leaping up, Bourne crossed the room. He was sliding the bed toward the closed door when the clamor being raised in the corridor outside rose to a fever pitch. The door burst open and Estefan, Tigger's partner, bulled his way through, gun drawn.

In the split second before it happened, Bourne shouted to Angél, but it was already too late. The child, traumatized both by threats and by the death of her family, swung the muzzle around and squeezed the trigger.

The resulting shot tore through Estefan's chest, took him off his feet, and launched him backward into the corridor. Bourne slammed the door shut, then finished sliding the bed against it as a make-shift barrier against more intruders.

By this time Maricruz had taken the weapon from the child's hand. Angél was shivering and sobbing with great gasps of breath. Picking her off her feet, Maricruz pressed the girl against her breast.

In the bathroom Bourne grabbed a towel and, wrapping it around his right hand, went back across the room, smashed the window, and quickly picked out the remaining shards of glass.

"Okay," he said to Maricruz and Angél, "let's go."

"I'm not going anywhere."

"Three men are dead," Bourne said.

"Carlos will protect me."

"Angél shot two of the men—one of them a foreign national with diplomatic credentials."

"I'll tell the authorities you shot them."

"Multiple witnesses saw me in the corridor when the first shot went off. It's more than likely you'll be blamed for the murders. Even Carlos won't be able to protect you from that." There came more shouts and a pounding on the door. "You're out of options." He gestured with his head. "Now let's go."

"Through the window?" Maricruz said.

"Can you think of another way to get out of here?"

"Who are you?" she said as she picked her way to the open window. "Sun said something about getting his revenge. How could he possibly know you?"

Someone on the other side of the door was shouting questions.

"You in there! The police have been called! They're on their way!"

Then the hammering started up again, more urgently this time, precluding any more talk. Bourne grabbed Angél from Maricruz, climbed up on the sill, and leapt to the lawn below. The child opened her mouth in a silent howl. Tears streamed down her cheeks. She shook like a victim of malaria. Setting her down beyond the ring of glass shards, he looked up and, seeing Maricruz balanced on the sill, held out his arms.

"Jump!" he called. "Jump now!"

But just as she was poised to leap, Bourne caught a glimpse of two *Federal* soldiers running full-tilt toward them. As the soldiers approached, they drew handguns. Bourne scooped up a dagger-shaped shard of glass, and, in the same motion, flung it at the leading soldier. It slashed through his uniform, pierced his chest like a fist to the sternum.

He fell to his knees, then toppled face-first onto the ground.

The second soldier fired a shot, but he was running so fast it went wide, the bullet burying itself in the side of the hospital. Bourne launched himself at the soldier. The soldier took a swipe at him with his gun, but Bourne was already prone, rolling hard into the soldier's lower legs. As the soldier fell forward, Bourne twisted, slammed his fist into the man's spine. The soldier hit the ground hard, and Bourne delivered a blow to the back of his head.

Stripping him of weapons, he turned to see that Maricruz had made the jump. Her bare feet were already bleeding from landing on the glass shards. Striding toward her, Bourne lifted her up, depositing her alongside Angél outside the glittering periphery of strewn glass.

The mayhem had driven the child's personality inward again. She was curled into a fetal position, and when Maricruz picked her up, she was all but unresponsive. Maricruz began to rock her, crooning softly into her ear.

The gunshot had rendered the area around the hospital devoid of people. The citizens of Mexico City knew all too well when to seek shelter from the crime-ridden streets. Therefore, Bourne found no witnesses, let alone resistance, as he rushed

Maricruz and Angél to the empty police cruiser the soldiers had commandeered. Its front doors hung open in its occupants' haste to race to the scene of the supposed crime.

Bourne herded the two in, got behind the wheel, and fired the ignition. But when they were a dozen blocks away, Maricruz, sitting beside him, said, "Pull over."

Ignoring her, Bourne continued to drive, intent on putting as much real estate between them and the hospital as possible.

She pressed the muzzle of the handgun she had taken from Angél against the side of his head. "I said, pull over."

When Bourne had complied, she said, "You're not Dr. Francisco Javier. You're not even a doctor. Now who the fuck are you?"

"The man who got you out of an increasingly difficult situation."

"And into another one. So don't expect a thank-you." Maricruz tapped the muzzle against his temple. "Tell me who you are."

In a blur of motion Bourne took the weapon away from her. "Next time, don't get so close to your target," he said as he laid the gun aside. "My name varies, depending on who you ask. Carlos Danda Carlos knows me as Jason Bourne."

At the sound of his name, the color dropped out of Maricruz's face.

"That's how my father knew you."

"Yes."

"You were his downfall."

"And not the life he chose?"

"Rationalize it any way you want."

"It's not a rationalization, Maricruz. Who better than you to understand that?"

"Nothing matters except that he's dead."

"And did you mourn? I knew him better than you did."

Lunging at him, she tried to scratch his eyes out. But he was prepared for her and grabbed her wrists, pinioning them together as she raged at him.

"No one could help your father, Maricruz," he said. "Least of all you, parking yourself on the other side of the world. How could you mourn a man you ran all the way to China to get away from?"

"Whatever else he was," she said, "he was my father."

"A man totally unequipped to be one."

"And you would know."

"Anyone who met him would understand that, you didn't even have to know him well."

She didn't want to cry, Bourne could see that.

Still, several tears squeezed out, forced themselves down her cheeks because she was unable to wipe them away. Seeing how humiliated she was, he released her wrists.

In the backseat, the girl, Angél, had absorbed all of the sometimes confusing conversation. But tears she understood absolutely, and now she poured herself over the seat back and into Maricruz's arms.

"Don't cry," she said into Maricruz's hair. "Don't cry."

Maricruz, who had roughly wiped her cheeks, now laughed. "Listen to this child." She sat back against the seat and closed her eyes. "God in heaven."

"We need to get you both some clothes," Bourne said, putting the cruiser in gear.

Maricruz opened her eyes and looked down at her bare feet as if seeing them for the first time.

"Jesus," she said, "I'm bleeding like a stuck pig."

It was Amir Ophir who met J. J. Hale at the appointed café he had designated for Bourne.

Hale was seated at an outdoor table, beneath a white umbrella. He was sipping a cup of espresso and reading the current *La Jornada* newspaper on his tablet. He looked up when Ophir slipped onto a chair facing him. Ophir set a small nylon carry-bag down beside him.

"To say I'm surprised would be an understatement," Hale said.

"Has Bourne made contact?"

Hale put his cup onto its saucer. "I'm trying to remember the last time you were in Mexico City, let alone graced me with your exalted presence."

"Cut the antics." Ophir raised a hand, snapped his fingers to gain the attention of a passing waiter. "Triple espresso," he said to the man, who nodded and went off into the bowels of the café's interior.

Ophir occupied himself with examining the patrons at the surrounding tables until his triple arrived. He downed it in one shot, then shoved the cup and saucer away.

"I'm looking for Bourne," he said.

"So I gather."

"What did I just tell you?"

Hale shrugged his shoulders, spreading his hands in a helpless gesture. "He hasn't made contact. My ass is getting sore. What else can I tell you?"

"Something I can use."

Hale tapped the electronic newspaper. "There's a BOLO out on Bourne for the bomb he planted under Carlos's car."

"Isn't that a shame."

Hale gave him a crooked grin. "Sure is. But that means he's gone to ground. He'll be hard to find."

"On the contrary. Now more than ever he's going to need your services."

Hale's grin expanded. "Said the spider to the fly." He tapped his tablet. "Another bit of news you'll enjoy. Our friend Carlos Danda Carlos has been relieved of all official duties."

This did surprise Ophir. It also filled him with a fierce joy. "What happened?"

"The Chinese happened." Hale briefly recounted the incident at the hospital where Maricruz had been recuperating. "Colonel Sun's murder has set off countless reverberations that have *el presidente* tearing his hair out. I can tell you Minister Ouyang is no one to piss off. The Chinese government, in the person of Ouyang himself, has called for a criminal investigation of Carlos's conduct, since it was he who put himself in charge of Ouyang's wife's safety."

"And where is Maricruz Ouyang, at this moment?"

Hale shrugged again.

"Well, she's no concern of mine," Ophir said. "Let's concentrate on Bourne." He studied the café again, gauging sight lines. He pointed to an empty table lost in the shadows of the interior. "I'll be over there. Just make sure he sits where I'm sitting now." Leaning over, he unzipped the carry-bag, briefly pulled out a Ruger .22 Charger rimfire and an NC silencer. "I'm not going near the fucker. I'll take him down with one shot to the head. At this range it won't be a problem, and with the silencer on the noise won't be more than a pellet gun would make."

Hale appeared nettled. "Are you reduced to telling me my business now?"

"Just do as you're told and don't fidget." Ophir grinned. "I wouldn't want to take your ear off."

Bourne drove toward Coyoacán. He kept an eye out for passing military vehicles. The two-way radio in their stolen cruiser kept crackling, staticky voices raised, calling out the stolen cruiser's license plate number, along with the repeated BOLO. He knew he'd have to switch vehicles sooner rather than later.

Spotting a pharmacy, he pulled over. It was an ancient place with a coyote lovingly painted above the doorway. The coyote, its long, thirsty tongue out, was the official symbol of Coyoacán. To the right of the pharmacy, a vacant lot filled with debris and old, rotting furniture looked like the gap between teeth in an old man's mouth.

"Stay put," he told Maricruz as he climbed out. "I'll be right back."

Inside, he bought an anti-bacterial spray, a box of cotton pads, rolls of gauze, and surgical tape. Returning to the cruiser, he saw that the passenger's door was open. Maricruz's legs and feet were sticking out. Angél, crouched on the pavement, was pulling out shards of glass from the soles of Maricruz's feet with the meticulousness of a nurse.

Bourne kicked the small pile of glass into the gutter, then crouched beside the child. He let her finish plucking the last pieces of glass from Maricruz's flesh, then began to spray her soles and wipe clean the tiny dozen or so incisions with the cotton balls.

When he started to bind her feet with the gauze, Angél stood up and whispered in Maricruz's ear.

"In the lot over there," she said.

As the child crossed the sidewalk, Bourne looked up at her.

Maricruz shrugged. "She has to pee. I couldn't think of a better place." She kept her eye on Angél as the child entered the lot.

"Maricruz, have you thought about Angél?"

"She's all I've thought about for the last twenty-four hours."

"You can't keep her," he said. "You can't take her with you."

She gave him a penetrating look. "She has no family, no one volunteered to pick her up."

"That doesn't mean it's you who—"

"It doesn't mean I'm not."

Finished with her right foot, he started on her left one. He lowered his voice. "Sun was right about one thing: If you intend to return to China it won't be with her. Ouyang won't permit it."

"Jidan will permit me anything."

"Anything that won't poleax his political career; you've already jeopardized it. Sun was right about that, too."

"I can't just leave her," Maricruz said. "I won't."

Finished, he packed up the leftover items and stowed them in the cruiser. "I'm not arguing for that."

"Out of the question."

"Maricruz, be reasonable."

Angél was returning, her large, dark eyes on Maricruz.

"I can't let her go," Maricruz said. "No, no, no."

Bourne drove to the Centro de Coyoacán shopping mall, where he parked at one end of the outdoor lot. Maricruz recited her sizes and, between them, they estimated Angél's.

"Keep an eye out for more soldiers," he said. "The city's crawling with them today."

He spent twenty minutes or so in and out of four or five shops, making purchases. When he returned to the lot, he was dressed in new clothes from head to foot. He immediately saw that the cruiser they had appropriated was surrounded by a pair of jeeps and half a dozen soldiers. He could see nothing of Maricruz and the child, however.

Cursing under his breath, he started to make a circuit of the lot's perimeter in the hope of spotting them, but within moments a white SUV pulled up in front of him. The front passenger's door popped open and Maricruz said, "Get in! Quickly!"

She stepped on the accelerator even before Bourne had pulled the door closed behind him.

"Where do you think you're going?" he said as she exited the lot.

Behind them, the soldiers were beginning to fan out in a tight grid-search pattern.

"No idea."

"Then stop and let me drive. You and Angél can change in the backseat."

After several moments of consideration, she turned down a side street and pulled the SUV over to the curb.

Bourne got out, came around, and stopped her before she could get back in the car.

"You see how this can't go on, Maricruz. You're putting the child in harm's way."

Maricruz's eyes slid away for a moment. Unconsciously, she gnawed at her lower lip. "I don't know, I don't know."

"Of course you know," Bourne said. "It's in everyone's best interests—especially hers."

Her gaze returned to him. "But who—?"

"There's someone I know—her name is Lolita. She's young, single, lonely, and loving. We should take Angél to see her."

Maricruz's eyes got hard. "Why the hell are you involved in this, anyway?"

"Carlos," Bourne said, which wasn't, strictly speaking, a lie. It wasn't the whole truth, either. But he wasn't going to tell her he was after her husband.

"Carlos," she repeated. "Shit."

"Maricruz, you haven't answered my question."

"There's no good answer."

"Of course there is. I just gave you one."

Silence.

"The two of you were almost caught back there. What d'you think the *Federales* will do to her if they catch her?"

Maricruz shifted her gaze to Angél, sitting patiently in the backseat. "She's been damaged, Bourne."

"You had to learn that. Lolita can, as well. She's got an enormous heart."

"Really?"

"Really."

Maricruz took a deep breath, let it out. "What if I don't like her?"

"You will like her."

"But what if I don't?"

"You won't leave the child with someone you don't like or trust, will you?"

"No," she said. "I won't."

"I wouldn't ask you to."

Silence again.

Bourne took out his mobile. "I'm going to tell Lolita we're coming, and why."

"A call? I don't know—"

"You don't want to spring Angél on her. It wouldn't be fair to her or to the child."

Maricruz hesitated, looked at Angél again, an uncertain figure through the smoked glass. Then she nodded.

Bourne called Anunciata.

34

WHAT HAPPENED?" Felipe Matamoros said into his mobile phone. He was in his San Luis Potosí hacienda, the urgent call taking time out from working with his cadre of *compadres* to integrate the local Sinaloa into Los Zetas.

"It's still such chaos here, five men dead, the police and the *Federales* swarming like ants," the female voice on the other end of the call said. "I— I don't really know."

"What d'you mean you don't know?" he shouted. "You were her nurse—I'm paying you to know everything that happens to her in the hospital."

"I told you everything, Señor Matamoros. First a man named Colonel Sun claiming to be from the Chinese embassy got through your guards—"

"Colonel Sun. You're certain that was his name?"

"Absolutely, señor."

That means Minister Ouyang has seen fit to stick his piss-yellow nose into my business, Matamoros thought sourly.

"All right. Then what?"

"Then the chaos started," the nurse said. "Your guard, Tigger, yes? There was shouting from the room, the señora and Colonel Sun were having sharp words, and he rushed in. There was a shot. Then the doctor who had been coming to see the señora entered the room. The other guard—Tigger's partner—came running down the corridor, gun drawn, and went in. Another shot, then the sound of glass shattering. More shots from outside."

"And this doctor, you said he went with her?"

"With her and the child, yes."

"This is what I don't understand."

"Well, I'm afraid it gets stranger, señor." There followed a brief hesitation. "The doctor—Francisco Javier—he doesn't exist."

"You mean he's from another hospital."

"No. I mean, yes. I found a doctor of that name, but he's a pediatric surgeon. He was in surgery when I called. He'd been there all day."

"What?" By this time, Matamoros wanted to

punch his way through a wall. "What are you saying?"

"I don't know who *this* Francisco Javier is, that's what I'm saying. I think he may have abducted the señora and the child."

"I don't give a shit about a child," Matamoros said, massaging his temples beneath which a vicious pain had begun to form. "The woman—the señora—"

"Is gone," the nurse said, clearly off her even-keeled game.

"Gone," Matamoros repeated, as if it were an incantation. "Gone where?"

"No one knows, señor. Just...gone."

"And Carlos's two men dead."

"Yes, señor."

"Well, that's something."

"Plus the Chinese man from the embassy. And outside two soldiers—"

"Stop! My only concern is the woman. She was your charge—in your care."

"Señor?"

"Expect a visitor." Matamoros abruptly disconnected.

Turning, he shouted to Juan Ruiz and Diego de la Luna. "Get the plane ready! We need to be in Mexico City as soon as possible."

* * *

Carlos Danda Carlos had awakened that morning from a nightmare of indescribable horror. He could no longer conjure up the details, which only made the lingering emotions all the more anxiety producing. Then the nightmare extended its long black arms into his waking world with the call informing him that two of his guards had been shot dead, two soldiers had also died under more mysterious circumstances, and Maricruz was missing. As if that weren't enough, a Chinese foreign national—an army colonel, for the love of God!—had also been shot to death in Maricruz's hospital room.

After fielding an exceptionally unpleasant call from *el presidente* while he was still in his pajamas—an old habit he refused to let go of—he showered, shaved, dressed, and had his driver take him to the hospital.

He arrived amid a shitstorm of uniformed men, all running around like chickens with their heads cut off. The hospital administration was in an uproar, as was the Chinese ambassador, who was threatening to decamp from Mexico with his entire staff after delivering a guardedly threatening statement to the worldwide press. Within twenty minutes Carlos understood that the international conflagration dwarfed his own concerns regarding Maricruz. He met with the ambassador, who made it clear in no uncertain terms that he needed to find the perpetrator of the colonel's death, a man who was closely connected with Minister Ouyang Jidan.

Inwardly, Carlos shuddered at the name. He needed Minister Ouyang—and his wife—if he was to continue to line his pockets with the proceeds of the cartels' drug sales. He needed to find out what Sun had said to Maricruz to make her kill him and his men, for surely she was the one who had pulled the trigger. Who else? He needed to find out where she was and who was with her. After canvassing the floor staff, it seemed clear that she had been in the company of a seven-year-old girl patient and a mysterious man who had palmed himself off as a hospital doctor assigned to her case. Could he have shot Sun?

None of the facts—or partial facts, since the scene was still in chaos—made much sense to him. The only person he knew who had all the answers was Maricruz herself. Where had she gone?

One line of inquiry seemed promising. It appeared the trio had fled the scene in an official cruiser, which had subsequently been discovered abandoned near the shopping mall in Coyoacán.

Approximately thirty minutes later a white, late-model SUV was reported stolen out of the same lot. The owner had provided the license plate number to the police. That was less than twenty minutes ago. When Carlos followed up on this, he discovered that a dozen cop cars had been dispatched to scour the streets for the vehicle in question. He ordered the police captain in charge to triple that number.

When the captain asked how he was going to get that many vehicles in so short a time, Carlos shouted, "I don't care! Pull them out of your ass if you have to! Just get them rolling now!"

He wiped his sweating face down. Then, realizing he had done all he could at the scene, he returned to his waiting car before he had a nervous breakdown. The international element, always a potential menace lurking at the periphery of the plans he had been enacting, had now jumped front and center, threatening to completely derail his career, not to mention his very life. In Mexico people in disgrace fared about as well as prisoners.

"Sir?" his driver said. "Where can I take you?"

I have to pull myself together, Carlos thought. *This situation might be a major fuckup, but use what little you have been given to grab the tiger's tail and shake it until its teeth rattle.*

"To Coyoacán."

"Yessir!"

As the driver rolled out onto the street, Carlos made the first of many calls coordinating his people in a dragnet around the district of Coyoacán.

Bourne drove the SUV down Caballo Calco, but did not stop at No. 23. Instead he circled the block several times, checking to see if the immediate environment held any dangers. Then, two blocks away, he pulled into a parking spot, climbed out, and exchanged the SUV's plates with a vehicle's at the end of the block. As he pulled out, a cop cruiser turned the block, moving in the slow, deliberate manner of a shark approaching a reef filled with fish.

"Down!" he ordered, and Maricruz slid low in her seat while Angél crouched on the floor. For a seven-year-old, she was remarkably adept at hiding herself, possibly the only positive consequence of her terrifying experience.

"Don't worry," he said. "The cops are only coming close enough to read our plate. They'll soon see we're not who they're looking for."

Moments later, proving his comment prophetic, the cruiser peeled off, making a right as they passed an intersection. Maricruz pulled herself up to a sitting position.

"If I had any doubts about what you're proposing, they're gone now," she said in a low voice she hoped wouldn't travel to the backseat. "I can't keep putting her in danger."

Bourne nodded.

"You'll make the introductions, yes?" Maricruz seemed nervous, suddenly unsure of herself, in need of assistance, clearly an odd state for her to be in.

"There's no need," Bourne said. "My time is better served finding us a new vehicle. This white SUV is too conspicuous."

"But I don't know anything about her."

"Then you'll be on equal ground. Now, go on. She's in apartment eleven. It's on the second floor."

Maricruz, in the Mexican-style clothes he had bought for her, opened the door and slid out. She was about to take Angél in her arms, but at the last minute thought better of it. Instead, she took her hand, so that the girl, in her pale yellow dress and patent-leather Mary Janes, walked beside her. A mother and daughter like any others one might see in Coyoacán, heading down the sidewalk. They entered number 23.

Bourne watched them until they were swallowed

up by the building. Then he wiped down the interior of the SUV and exited. Unscrewing the license plates, he slid them through the bars of a nearby sewer grate and went in search of a vehicle that would better suit their needs.

35

ANUNCIATA OPENED the door and was stunned to see her father's features repurposed in a beautiful female face.

"*Hola*," the woman said with her father's smile. She held out her hand. "My name is Maricruz." When Anunciata, somewhat in a daze, took her hand, she said, "And you must be Lolita."

"That's right." Anunciata produced a smile that flickered like a candle in the wind.

Maricruz moved the child in front of her, hands lightly on her shoulders the better to steer her. "And this is Angél. Her parents are dead—murdered—and her family—"

"I understand. Would you like to come in?"

The child pushed back against Maricruz's legs as Maricruz attempted to move across the threshold.

Anunciata crouched down so that her eyes were on Angél's level. "Well, you don't have to." She spoke directly to the child. "You don't have to do anything you don't want to do." Her smile brightened, steadied, as if a light switch had been thrown. "Tell me, are you good at keeping secrets?"

After a brief hesitation, Angél nodded.

"I thought so. You have a face that can hold secrets." She cocked her head. "Did you know that?"

The girl, her growing interest beginning to overcome her shyness, shook her head.

"Well, you do. And not many people do. Because of that, I'd like to tell you a secret—if that's okay with you."

Angél responded slowly, still shy: She nodded.

"So this is a sad story, Angél, but you of all people will understand. My parents are also dead. They were also murdered. I have no family. So that makes us—I don't know—birds of a feather. And if you like, we can flock together."

Perhaps it was the rhyme, or it might have been the image of herself as a bird. In any event, the child began to laugh.

"I like birds, but I *really* like coyotes," she said softly.

"Then coyotes we will be," Anunciata said

As Angél clapped her hands, Maricruz pushed

her gently forward. Anunciata rose and stepped back, allowing them to enter her apartment.

Outside, Bourne was trolling for an old, beat-up vehicle to snatch when he became aware of two patrol cars rolling toward him from either side. He was one street over from Caballo Calco, moving in and out of the shadows thrown by the building facades. He needed to be mindful of being spotted, knowing that every cop car must have a photo of him taped to its dashboard.

As the cruisers moved closer, he turned into a building entrance, opened the door, and stepped into the darkened vestibule. A young boy was squatting by the bottom of the staircase, bouncing a filthy rubber ball off the lowest tread, catching it, and throwing it again in a repetitive motion that was almost mesmeric.

The boy, paying him no mind, continued with his solitary game. Bourne turned, peering out the thick cut-glass panels of the front door. He could see the nose of one of the cruisers, which had pulled over and was now stopped. Soon enough, several uniforms came into view. They seemed in no hurry to get anywhere. Rather, they lit up cigarettes and began to smoke. They seemed to be taking turns telling jokes. Every once in a while, they'd break out into laughter for no good reason Bourne could discern.

Then two plainclothes cops appeared in his limited field of view. They approached the uniforms who were smoking and the senior of the two spoke sharply to the beat cops. The uniforms stiffened, threw their cigarette butts into the gutter. The detectives gesticulated, the uniforms nodded and hustled across the street. They split up, out of Bourne's sight.

The detectives consulted for a moment and then, clearly having decided on a course of action, also split up. One of them came directly toward the building Bourne was in. Bourne retreated up the stairs, stopping on the second-floor landing.

He heard the inner door open and sigh shut, then the sounds of the detective's shoes ringing against the worn stone tiles, echoing up the stairwell.

Voices came to him and he leaned forward, listening as the detective spoke to the little boy.

"*Niño*, have you seen anyone come in you didn't recognize?"

There was a long pause, then the boy answered: "I saw a man who doesn't belong in the building."

"When?"

"Just now."

"Did you see where he went?"

"Up," the boy said.

Without another word to his small witness, the detective began to climb the stairs. Bourne saw the flash of a handgun.

Being in the presence of her half sister unnerved Anunciata. Maricruz intimidated her, both by her elite pedigree and by her hauteur, which chilled Anunciata to the bone. The sole saving grace was the child. Angél's presence was like a ray of bright light in the apartment. Everything she touched seemed to glow, as if the child were able to bring out the inner warmth of polished wood, spun silk, and thrown ceramic.

"You have a beautiful home," Maricruz said as she strolled slowly around the living room.

"I don't know about that," Anunciata said. "It's rather poor."

"Poor?" Maricruz turned to her. "No, no. It feels comfortable, lived in. There are roots here."

The comment struck Anunciata as curious, since she herself had been lamenting the lack of roots, a place she could come home to. She glanced at Angél. Maybe it wasn't the things in the apartment that lacked the feeling she was looking for, because now that the child was here she could see that Maricruz was right. This *was* home.

From a shelf, she took down a wood carving of

a coyote she had purchased in New Laredo, its head raised as if howling at the moon. Bringing it over to Angél, she crouched down, holding it out to her.

"You know, this coyote has been waiting a long time for a name," she said. "Do you think you could give it one?"

The girl took the carving.

"Is the coyote a boy or a girl?" Anunciata asked.

With a serious expression, Angél turned the coyote around between her hands.

"A boy," she said. "His name is Javvy."

Maricruz looked at her for a moment, the ghost of a smile on her lips.

"Now that you've named him," Anunciata said, "I think he wants to stay with you."

The child hugged the coyote to her breast.

"Who is this beautiful woman?" Maricruz said.

Anunciata looked across the room to see her half sister holding a photo in a Oaxacan silver frame.

"Is she your mother?"

Anunciata stood up. All at once her heart was in her throat. It beat like a trip-hammer. "Yes, she is."

"You're a lucky woman." Maricruz put the photo back on the shelf almost reverently. "To know your mother." She seemed to say this last to herself, rather than to anyone else in the room. "You said she was murdered?"

"Poisoned."

"Really? Who would want to do that to this beauty?"

"Shall I make tea?" Anunciata asked.

"Angél doesn't like tea." Maricruz turned, she had continued to stare at the woman in the photo. "You look just like her—your mother."

"Thank you. She was a special woman—"

"But I suppose everyone tells you that."

"—inside as well as out."

Maricruz produced a smile that almost cracked her face. "Angél prefers coffee. And she likes it black, don't you, *guapa*?"

The child, sitting on the sofa, legs straight out in front of her, hands clasped around Javvy the coyote, nodded. "With sugar."

Maricruz laughed. "Yes. *Lots* of sugar."

She followed Anunciata into the kitchen, watching her from the open doorway as she measured out the coffee and set a pot of water to boil.

"So many photos of your mother," she said. "But not one of your father."

Anunciata's heart began to beat so hard it hurt. "My parents divorced when I was young. My father abandoned us." Her hand was shaking so hard the cup rattled against its saucer before she had a chance to set them down.

"You don't see him?"

"It was a long time ago." Anunciata poured the coffee into the filter. "For all I know he's dead."

Maricruz continued her study of Anunciata's back. "And you have no brothers—no sisters?"

Anunciata shook her head, not trusting herself to speak. She felt like she had let an enemy into her home, a venomous serpent who, loyal to their father, could destroy her if she found out who she really was. Why had Bourne done this to her? But she knew. It was the child. A child she longed for. He should have brought her himself. But again, she thought she understood why this was impossible. Maricruz—and Angél herself—might not have allowed it.

Finished making the coffee, she poured it into the cup. "Do you want to add the sugar?"

"Four teaspoons." Maricruz came toward her. "You'd better get used to doing it."

"Four isn't healthy," Anunciata said. "We'll settle on two."

"That's the spirit!" Maricruz said softly.

Her voice was so close that Anunciata turned. Maricruz was a breath away, her eyes locked on Anunciata.

"Can you be trusted, I wonder?"

"There's no real way for you to know, is there?"

"To tell the truth, I mean."

At that moment, the distinctive crackle of gunfire sounded from outside.

Bourne, holding his ground on the second-floor landing, heard the detective whispering into an earbud connected to what must be a wireless network that linked him to his partners. He retreated into the shadows of the door frame just to the left of the staircase.

He held his breath, watched as the detective, 9 mm drawn and ready to fire, eased up the last few stairs to the landing. Because it curved around to the right it was natural for him to look that way first. When he did, Bourne stepped out, slashed the edge of his hand down on the detective's gun hand. When the 9 mm hit the tiles, it went off, the percussion unnaturally loud in the confined space. The bullet ricocheted and the detective flinched, his body all but doubled over.

Driving a knee into his chin, Bourne lifted him by his collar and struck him hard on the side of his neck. The detective's eyes rolled up as he plunged into unconsciousness. Stripping off his ankle-length overcoat, Bourne put it on, dropped his own jacket on top of the body, which he dragged out of sight of anyone coming up or down the stairs. He relieved the detective of his badge, earbud, and ID case. Just then one of the apartment doors cracked open. He held up the badge and said, "Official business, señora." He worked the electronic device into his ear. "Please step back into your apartment and keep your door locked until our inquiry is finished." The door slammed shut, and he heard the locks being thrown.

At that moment the front door opened and the second detective stepped into the vestibule.

"Hernan?" he called. "Did I hear a shot fired?"

"Up here," Bourne said into the wireless network. "I have subdued our target."

"Our orders are to kill on sight." Hernan's partner took the stairs two at a time. "What the fuck are you waiting for?"

"This."

Bourne strode into him as he reached the landing, kicking him hard down the stairs. The kid who had been playing at the bottom was no longer there, Bourne was gratified to see. He followed the tumbling body, stepping over it as he picked his way across the vestibule and went out the front door. When he was halfway down the block, he raised the two uniforms on the wireless network, called for help, and gave them an address five blocks away.

Then he headed straight for Anunciata's building.

36

NGÉL!"

Maricruz ran into the living room, bathroom, bedroom, then, returning to the living room, turned to Anunciata. "Where is she? She's gone!"

Anunciata stopped her as she headed for the front door. Opening the wooden jalousies, she stepped out onto the long, narrow balcony with its curling wrought-iron railing.

Maricruz, a step behind her, said, "Angél, what are you doing?"

The girl was at the edge of the balcony, her small fingers entwined with the railing as she stood on tiptoe, scanning the street below.

"Get back inside!" Maricruz cried. "It's not safe out here."

Anunciata held her back as she lunged toward the girl.

"She's taking care of herself," Anunciata whispered, "in her own way."

"What d'you mean?"

As if Maricruz were talking to her, Angél said, "He's coming."

"Who's coming?" Maricruz asked.

"Dr. Javvy."

"That's not his real name."

"It is to me," Angél said without turning around.

"Out of the mouth of babes." Anunciata looked at Maricruz. "He is who he is."

"No matter what name he uses?"

"You know the answer to that."

Following the sound of gunfire, the neighborhood had become preternaturally silent. Even the street was devoid of vehicular traffic.

"He's here," the girl said, at last turning away from her vigil of Caballo Calco. She rushed inside, slipping between the two women.

Maricruz stood stock-still. "I'll be leaving with him."

Anunciata nodded. "I know."

"Angél likes you."

"The feeling is mutual."

Maricruz nodded. As Anunciata stepped toward

the apartment's interior, Maricruz put her hand on her arm.

"It doesn't matter to me what name you use, either."

When Anunciata's eyes opened wide, Maricruz moved her hand to Anunciata's cheek. "Did you think I wouldn't recognize his face in yours?" Her smile was tentative, almost shy, if that could be believed of her. "The only difference between us is that I had the means to run far away."

"Sadly," Anunciata said so softly that Maricruz had to bend her head closer to hear clearly, "that's not the only difference."

Maricruz put her arm around Anunciata's waist in what could only be described as a sisterly embrace. "What d'you mean?"

Anunciata looked her half sister in the eye, weighing whether or not to answer. In the apartment, they heard Bourne's voice calling: "Maricruz, we have to go. Now!"

In that heated split-second Anunciata made up her mind. "I never knew he was my father until it was too late, until he coerced me into becoming his lover." She winced at the shocked expression on Maricruz's face. "What could I do? My mother's livelihood hung in the balance. When he discovered that she had finally told me, he had her poisoned."

Maricruz embraced her half sister. "Oh, Lolita!"

Anunciata gave her a rueful smile. "Now you know why I chose that name."

Inside the apartment, Bourne and Angél were speaking in low voices, so earnestly that for a moment it stopped the two women in their tracks. Both of them were slightly dazed by the tumble of revelations they had shared. Without quite being aware of it, their fingers were entwined.

Bourne, always aware of everything, noticed and nodded, as if he had expected this outcome all along. And perhaps he had, Anunciata thought with a great outpouring of affection for this man who had now saved her in so many ways.

"It's time," Bourne repeated as he rose from his crouched position in front of the girl, "to say good-bye."

Maricruz detached her hand from Anunciata's, went across the room and picked Angél up, giving her a good squeeze. She kissed her on both cheeks.

"I'll miss you," she said softly.

"I like it here," the girl said.

Laughing, Maricruz put her gently down.

"That's good, *guapa*. That's very good." She smiled knowingly. "You take care of Lolita, okay?"

"Okay," the child said gravely.

"We'll take care of each other," Anunciata said, taking the child's hand in hers.

For a moment something powerful but unspoken passed between the two women. Then Maricruz turned to Bourne, her eyes magnified by tears.

"Let's go."

You set this all up," Maricruz said, though by her tone Bourne could tell it wasn't an accusation. "You knew what would happen."

"I knew what *could* happen," he said as they crossed the street and went down the block. "Not the same thing."

A battered, rust-stained green Ford pickup truck with slatted wooden sides looked to fit the bill. It took no time to get the door open and hot-wire the ignition. The truck started up in a belch of greasy smoke.

"Perfect!" he said, putting the vehicle in gear and heading out of the immediate neighborhood.

"I'm talking about the fact that I'm still with you."

"Where are you going to go on your own?" he said. "Back to Carlos? He's hip-deep in an international incident and sinking fast."

"Maybe that's better than killing him," she said under her breath.

He shot her a quick look. "Is that what Matamoros had planned for you?"

"It was my idea." She snorted. "Don't look so surprised."

He shook his head. "Why did you come back here? Why did you insert yourself between the cartels and Carlos?"

"For my father."

"Really? I don't believe you."

"Believe what you want. You don't know a thing about me."

"I know you hated your father."

"I didn't—"

"Otherwise you never would have run away so far, so fast."

"There might be other reasons."

"There might be," he said, taking a turn to avoid a police cruiser, "but they have nothing to do with you."

She stared out the window at the cityscape passing before her like a film directed by someone she once knew. "Where are we going?"

"To see Matamoros, where else?"

She turned back to him, her eyes narrowed. "What do you want with him?"

Bourne turned down another street, avoiding the heavily trafficked avenues. They passed another row of buildings, other groups of stoop-dwellers, suspicious eyes ignoring them, the old Ford painting them as part of the run-down scenery.

"This is a time," he said, "when all debts are being repaid, when all obligations will be settled."

"Retribution," Maricruz said.

He nodded. "Retribution."

She was silent for several moments, seemingly sunk in contemplation. "You're out to wreck my father's drug business, aren't you?"

"Your father and his cohorts killed someone close to me."

Maricruz nodded. "All debts are being repaid." She stared straight ahead. "That would include my husband."

He turned the wheel, guiding the truck to the curb, where he stopped, the engine idling. "You can get out now, if you like. Your choice."

"Whether I leave or not, you'll still be coming."

"Nothing will stop me."

She pulled out the handgun she had been carrying, stuck it to his temple.

"Maricruz, you're not that crazy."

She squeezed the trigger.

37

DIRECTOR YADIN HADN'T meant to spend the night on the boat, but as his father had set in plenty of stores and with darkness coming down, he made no effort to head back to shore. Instead, he and his father reefed the sails, dropped anchor, and set about making dinner. Actually, it was Yadin's father, Reuben, who prepared the food while his son set the table he pulled up off the cabin bulkhead.

"Wine?" Eli said.

Reuben shook his head. "My gout is acting up again."

"Old age."

"Age, period." Reuben stirred the couscous as he dropped in golden raisins, chopped-up dates, and toasted almond slivers.

The Director sat against the bulkhead, facing his

father. "You've become melancholy in your retirement."

"If only you'd let me retire, Eli!"

"Ha, ha! Good one, Pop."

Reuben glanced up sharply. "You know, Eli,
sometimes I worry you've become too American."

Eli reached out, grabbed a handful of almonds.
"There's no such thing."

"You see? That's precisely what I'm talking
about!" the old man said in mock-horror.

The Director sighed deeply. "*Abi*, I fear I have
set in motion an apocalyptic confrontation."

"Try harder not to understate the case, Eli."

The Director laughed without a trace of humor.
"Ophir is going after Bourne."

"Can you blame him after the way Bourne humiliated him in Damascus?"

"Amir needed to be humiliated. His secret mission was to keep General Wadi Khalid alive.
Khalid, whom Minister Ouyang had taught to ad-
minister the most heinous torture techniques;
Khalid, whom Amir and I were sent into Damascus
to terminate. We didn't, due to Amir's treachery,
but Bourne was also in Damascus, and it was he
who killed Khalid."

Reuben began to fry up some merguez sausage.
"Ancient history."

"Not for men with long memories and an exaggerated sense of outrage. I speak now of our friends, Ouyang, and Amir Ophir, Ouyang's mole inside our family."

"Are you saying Bourne is not among them?"

"Bourne can't have a long memory, and as far as his sense of outrage is concerned, so far as I can tell, it's reserved for those imperiling the ones he loves."

Reuben looked at his son as he transferred the merguez to the couscous, and in doing so burned his hand. "Dammit!" He sucked on two fingertips.

"Butter," the Director said.

"No butter aboard."

Eli rose and went to the refrigerated larder, gabbed some ice cubes, wrapped them in a cloth, and handed it to his father. He brought the pot over to the table while his father nursed his burn.

"Bourne's particular sense of outrage is the crux of your plan." Reuben sat at the table while his son dished out the couscous.

"You know, Pop, this is just like when I was a boy. You used to make me this couscous every week."

"Scandalizing your mother. '*You boys*,' she'd say. '*How can you eat meat?*'"

"The first time, she ran out of the house."

Reuben nodded. "That she did."

The Director's mood sobered. "Ophir's run out

of our house, *abi*. My old friend, working for the enemy."

"Well, you've done the right thing, keeping him close."

"But now he's gone after Bourne himself."

"And you don't think that will be the end of him?"

Eli looked out into the darkness of the sea, which was different from any other form of darkness, rolling and thick, oversprayed with starlight, like sparks from a cold fire. He thought about the confidence he'd expressed in this afternoon's conversation with Dani Amit.

"I don't know what to think anymore."

The father put his gnarled hand briefly over his son's. "Don't lose your resolve now, Eli. The worst thing a Director can do is not fully commit to the plan he's authorized. Disaster awaits such an indecisive man."

Reuben cut a sausage in thirds with the edge of his fork, then speared a section. "Trust Bourne in the same way you trust yourself."

"I have deceived him."

"Your job, Eli, is to deceive people."

"This is different."

"Is it?" Reuben popped the merguez into his mouth and chewed thoughtfully. "All right, if that's your determination, then when this is all over you'll admit to him what you've done. That will be your *aliyah*."

The Director nodded. "Thank you, *abi*."

"I haven't told you anything you yourself didn't already know." He shoveled couscous onto the tines of his fork. "Your real worry is Dani Amit—most particularly what you've told him."

"I don't suspect him."

"You didn't suspect Ophir until he proved himself worthy of it."

"Well, I gave Dani the test."

Reuben nodded as he chewed. "You've done the right thing."

"We'll see soon enough."

"Moles are often like roaches—where there's one..."

The old man didn't have to finish the sentence, but the implications stayed with both of them all through the night, causing them troubled sleep, when they slept at all.

The dry click startled Maricruz.

"I took the liberty of emptying the gun," Bourne said. "I didn't think you'd learned your lesson."

With a disgusted sound in the back of her throat, Maricruz threw the weapon into the foot well of the truck.

"Useless piece of shit." Her eyes cut toward him. "I pulled the trigger for my father."

"An empty gesture."

"As it turned out."

"It always was, Maricruz. You didn't want to kill me. In fact, somewhere in your subconscious you knew the gun wasn't loaded."

Her eyes sparked, her lips firmly set. "What if I did?"

"A grand gesture, signifying nothing."

"I suppose you know what he did to Lolita."

"I do."

"There's no excuse." She shook her head. "My fucking father."

In silence, he kept driving. After a while, he said, "How did you get along with your sister?"

"How is it you know more about my family than I do?"

"That's the way it goes sometimes."

She gave him a penetrating look. "Do you know who my mother is?"

"I met her last year when I was here."

Maricruz stared at him, dumbfounded. "I never knew who she was. I assumed she was dead, don't ask me why—maybe because everything would be easier that way. I wouldn't have to think why she abandoned me."

"Maybe she didn't have a choice."

"People always have a choice."

"Even with your fucking father?"

She let out a sound somewhere between a cough and a dry laugh. "Several months ago, Jidan handed me a slip of paper with her name and address on it. I saw that she was living here in Mexico City."

"But you haven't gone to see her."

She shook her head. "I can't decide."

"I have no idea who my parents were, if I have brothers or sisters. My past is a blank."

Bourne wondered if there was a person in the world who knew about his family. Anyone would know more about them than he did, he thought bitterly. The anger burned in the core of him, a white-hot flame that chilled, rather than warmed. He saw the world—his life—through the lens of eternal loss, the endless wasteland of not knowing who he was or where he came from. An eternal nomad, he spent his days searching for the unfindable; his nights spent in the dark war when all debts must be repaid, when all obligations will be settled.

Retribution.

Thank you," she said at last, "for bringing me and my sister together." When Bourne made no reply, she said, "What's her real name?"

"That's for her to tell you."

"Javvy." She cocked her head. "Dr. Javvy, that's how Angél knows you."

"Does it matter?"

Maricruz rested her head against the side window. "I suppose not. But still...she is my sister."

"Almost there," Bourne said.

Maricruz sat up straight. "And where might that be?"

"A café. I'm supposed to meet an armorer."

"An armorer? What the hell do you need an armorer for?"

"I was prepared to go after Matamoros to get to you. Now, with what's happened, I have no doubt that Matamoros is going to come after you."

She shook her head. "I don't understand. What do you want with me?"

"I have a debt to settle with your husband."

"And you think I'm going to lead you to him?"

"I think you already know he's not the man you thought he was."

"I never thought he was anything," Maricruz said, "besides a means to an end."

"A way to outdo your father."

"Now Maceo is dead, I control all of his businesses."

"What surprises me is how much energy you're putting into this—his drug trade."

"It's lucrative."

"So is everything else he owned." Bourne sped up to overtake a lumbering semi. "You've been hiding out in Beijing in order to get as far away from him as possible. Now you don't have to, but Mexico isn't the place for you."

"I never said it was."

"And yet here you are, dealing with the underbelly of your father's business, the link between him and your husband." He gave her a quick look. "You see the irony, Maricruz. You fled halfway around the world to escape your father, only to meet him again in the form of Ouyang Jidan."

"Is that how you see it?"

"The way you're going, you'll never be free of either of them." He slowed for a light, then stopped. "Am I wrong in thinking you want to be your own person?"

When they passed through the intersection, she said, "Is there another way?"

"Help me do what has to be done."

Her eyes raked his face. "What do I get out of it?"

"The satisfaction of knowing you helped give a young woman her vengeance for being murdered."

"You're joking."

"Think of Angél, of someone causing her to bleed out in the back of a Mexico City taxi."

They drove in silence for some time.

At last, she said, "Was your wife really knifed to death or was that a lie, part of your cover?"

"Not my wife, but it happened. Last year."

"I'm sorry."

He made a turn. "When it's done, Maricruz, you will be free. You have the means to do and be whatever you want."

She stared out the window, her hair blowing lightly, obscuring her cheek and her expression. "This trip to the armorer is really necessary?"

"I have no intention of meeting with Felipe Matamoros with just a 9 mm in my hand."

She laughed harshly.

Bourne slowed the truck and pulled into a parking space. He pointed down the block and across the street. "That café's the meeting place."

Maricruz looked dubious. "Do you think it's safe?"

Bourne stared at the target area through the windshield speckled with mud and bird droppings. "I don't for a minute trust the man who set this in motion."

"Then why are we here?"

"I need what the armorer is selling." Bourne saw

Hale, sitting at a table in the open, sipping espresso and reading on a tablet. "Under certain circumstances he'll give me what I want."

"What circumstances?"

"At the point of death."

38

I DON'T LIKE THIS," Maricruz said. "It feels like a trap."

"It feels exactly like a trap," Bourne acknowledged.

"Let's get out of here."

"When I've finished my business."

"How can you remain so cocksure?"

"I have a plan." Bending down, Bourne picked up the gun she had thrown into the foot well, and loaded it. Then he handed it to her. "My plan involves you. Think you're up to it?"

Bourne gave the verbal passcode to J. J. Hale as he sat down across from him. Hale, glancing up from his tablet, spoke the countersign.

"Now that the formalities are behind us," he said,

"we can relax. Something to eat? How about a drink? The espresso is fantastic."

"Just weapons," Bourne said.

"A man of few words, eh?" Hale nodded. "I can appreciate that. I've been instructed to supply you with anything you need."

Bourne produced a list he had written up, passed it across the table to the armorer. Hale took it, glanced down at it, and whistled.

"Planning to start your own little war?"

"Do you really want to know?"

He raised his hands, palms outward. "God, no. I was just making small talk. But I forget, you're not one for small talk."

He tried to remain relaxed, but knowing that Ophir was behind him with a silenced gun caused his spine to stiffen, so that he sat as erect and still as a soldier on the parade ground.

Giving the list another look, he said, "Most of this stuff I can get you right away, no problem. I can even get my hands on the grenade launcher, but the flamethrower is military issue. That's another matter altogether."

"Meaning?"

"It'll take time."

"No," Bourne said, "it won't."

Hale looked up, his eyebrows raised. "D'you know something I don't?"

"I know what I need and when I need it."

"Give me twenty-four—"

"You have an hour to get everything together." Bourne's eyes held Hale's. "Everything."

Hale laughed uneasily. "Or what?"

"Or I blow your brains out."

Hale failed to keep his laugh going.

"Take a peek under the table," Bourne said. "Go on."

Hale took a breath, which, despite his best effort, shuddered out of him. He shifted slightly, bent enough to glance under the table, saw the 9 mm pointed at his groin.

"That's a sick joke," he said, returning to his former position.

"I don't make jokes."

Hale blinked. "Clearly."

"An hour, then."

Hale cursed silently. Why the hell hadn't Ophir shot this sonofabitch yet?

Amir Ophir was a man with multiple masters. This seeming contradiction had never bothered him. He was an Israeli whose views had always differed from those of the people around him. Early on in life he had learned to keep his opinions to himself. As a boy, he had been exposed to any number of terrorist incursions, one of which took his brother in a fusillade of friendly fire. Perhaps it was the circumstances of his brother's death that had made him ripe for being seduced, in the strictest sense.

In any event, the money, laundered by Minister Ouyang from a bank in the Cayman Islands and amassing quietly in a Swiss bank account, did not hurt. His treason was an unholy amalgam of payback and greed, the perfect stew for a secret turncoat.

All this passed through his mind as quickly as a flash of sunlight on water as he watched Bourne sitting opposite Hale not fifty feet from him. Without taking his eyes off Bourne, he reached into his carry-bag, brought out the silencer, which he attached to the .22. The pistol was a smaller caliber than he usually fired, but in this public setting and at this distance it was the weapon of choice.

He double-checked that the Ruger was loaded, the chamber load indicator was on, the safety off. Then, covered by his napkin, he brought it up over the table. He was sighting in on Bourne's head when he felt a cold steel gun muzzle pressed to the back of his head.

"Hey, haven't seen you in a while!"

A female voice! He could scarcely believe it.

A hearty clap on the back and an urgent whisper in his ear: "Put the pistol down."

For a hallucinatory moment, he thought it was Rebeka behind him, resurrected from the grave into which her coffin had been laid. He heard her voice reverberating in his ear and, heart racing, temples throbbing painfully, he all but cried out, *My secret's safe with you now you're dead.*

Then a hand curled over his shoulder, took the Ruger, still wrapped in the napkin, out of his right hand and removed it from his sight.

"Who are you?" he said.

"You first." Silence. "No?" She dug the muzzle into the nape of his neck. "Okay, let's go ask people who know you."

When he didn't move, she gripped his shoulder with surprising strength and whispered fiercely in his ear, "Get the fuck up!"

Ophir stood, and, recalling Bourne's admonition, Maricruz stepped back, out of range of his raised fist.

"I'm ambidextrous," she said, transferring the Ruger to her left hand.

"You're not going to shoot me in here."

"No?" She lifted the barrel of the concealed Ruger.

"A silencer. Nice touch."

She walked him out onto the café's terrace and sat him down between Bourne and the armorer.

"As promised," she said to Bourne.

Bourne eyed Ophir. "Maricruz, I'd like you to meet Amir Ophir, Mossad's head of assassinations and infiltration."

"Oh, Christ!" Hale said, one hand over his eyes.

"Nothing's turned out the way you expected," Bourne said.

"For you, either," Ophir said. "The *Federales* are ready to string you up by your balls."

"Really? Why didn't you simply tell them where I'd be?"

"Because more than likely they'd fuck up the operation."

"Just like you did," Maricruz said. She was standing behind him, both guns pressed through the rattan of the chair back.

Bourne contemplated the Mossad chief. "You've lost a great deal of your field tradecraft since Damascus. Time to retire, Amir."

Ophir grinned through gritted teeth. "Dream on, fucker."

At that moment Bourne cocked his head, heard the first faint sounds of police sirens. "You're right, Amir. They did fuck it up."

Grabbing Hale, he backed away from the table, jerked his head for Maricruz to follow him.

"See you around," Ophir said. "Count on it."

*   *   *

Squeezed into the front seat of the truck three-abreast, Bourne said to Hale, "You're taking us to your warehouse." When the armorer made no reply, he added, "We can also do this the hard way."

"Makes no difference to me," Hale said.

Without seeming to move a muscle, Bourne slammed the edge of his right hand into Hale's throat. The man made a croaking sound, bent as far double as he was able, and began to gasp for air.

Bourne, glancing over him to Maricruz, said, "Sometimes there's really no need for a gun."

Maricruz pulled the armorer's head up by his damp hair. "How are you feeling, señor? Enjoying the ride?"

He stared straight ahead, tears streaming out of his eyes. Nevertheless, he gave Bourne an address.

A pair of police cruisers, blue roof lights revolving, sped past the truck, heading for the café they had just vacated. Bourne turned right at the next intersection, handed Maricruz his mobile.

She nodded, pulled up Google Maps, entered the address Hale had recited. "Two blocks," she said, "then make a left."

Between them, Hale was still gasping for air. He winced when he tried to massage his Adam's apple. The area was red, already swollen.

"This is no line of work for you, armorer," Bourne said. "You've made the wrong friends."

* * *

Hale's warehouse was an enormous self-storage facility on the outskirts of the city. Row upon row of identical concrete structures confronted them, their enormous corrugated iron doors rolled down and securely locked. The place reminded Bourne of a cemetery.

The armorer directed the truck down the eighth aisle from the entrance. Halfway down he told Bourne to stop. Bourne took him out of the truck's cab, Maricruz following. Hale fished a key out of his pocket and, squatting, opened the lock, unhooked it, then rolled the door up.

Flicking on a light switch, he led them into the cavernous interior, which was filled with crates of varying sizes and shapes that rose on three sides.

"Look at this," Bourne said, pointing out some crates to Maricruz, "Chinese manufacture. I wonder who you bought these weapons from, Hale. Could it have been Minister Ouyang?"

The armorer coughed. "What was it you need again?"

"I gave you a list."

"It's gone right out of my head." He was sweating profusely. "After what…" His hand went to his swollen throat. "After what happened I can't put two thoughts together."

Bourne told him, and he nodded dully, went from place to place bringing out the items Bourne asked for, plus the various forms of ammo to go with the weapons.

"Don't forget the flamethrower," Bourne said, taking up the grenade launcher, feeling its weight on his right shoulder. When Hale brought out the flamethrower, Bourne added, "So much for the twenty-four-hour wait."

Hale helped him load the truck with the four hard cases that contained the weapons. Bourne told Maricruz to get back in the cab. After she had done so, Bourne turned to Hale and said in a low voice, "I don't trust that woman. I need an easily concealed handgun."

"Then we're through?" the armorer asked.

"Then we're through."

A wave of relief passed over Hale's face, and he turned back inside the storage space. "I've got just the thing."

"I'm sure you do," Bourne said, as he slid the corrugated iron door down, stooped, and affixed the lock, snapping it shut.

He thought he heard the tiny echo of Hale's voice from inside, but he couldn't be sure. He turned away, swung up behind the wheel, and put the truck in gear.

"Do you know how to get in touch with Matamoros?" Bourne said as he drove out of the storage facility.

"Of course."

"Use my mobile. Find out where he is. Set up a meet."

Maricruz nodded. She punched in a number, put the phone to her ear.

"Felipe. Yes, it's me...It's a long story, but I'm fine, which is more than I can say for Carlos. *Sí, sí*, he's done...Where are you, San Luis Potosí?...No?...Here in Mexico City. We need to—"

At that moment, a black Chevy, running a red light, slammed into the truck's side with the force of a battering ram.

39

WHEN CARLOS DANDA CARLOS was transported from the courthouse where the judge had remanded him to prison awaiting his trial, he had been stripped of his uniform. With it went his dignity, not to mention the major part of his identity.

The judge who had remanded him was one of the many formerly on Carlos's payroll. He had been to Carlos's villa for dinner numerous times, had partaken of Carlos's stock of vintage wines and cigars, had had his pick of the girls who had been bused in for the after-dinner festivities. But on this day, his voice had been as cold as his eyes. He might never have laid eyes on Carlos before. And who could blame him? Such was the pressure exerted by *el presidente*, he'd had no choice. Neither had *el presidente*. The worldwide press had descended on the courthouse, roosting in its eaves while feasting on the sight of the former chief of Mexico's anti-drug enforcement agency being led away in handcuffs. The judge had thrown Carlos to the wolves, just as any loyal civil servant would have done.

Carlos inside prison was not a pretty picture. All his bravado washed down the drain as he scrubbed the harsh lye-based soap over his naked body under the jaundiced eye of a smirking prison guard. He had heard the stories, read the reports of grisly murders taking place in prison showers, a favorite haunt of psychopaths and those seeking revenge for insults real and imagined. He had read these reports with a glacial indifference, secure in the knowledge that they belonged to another world entirely. Now, incredibly, he was part of that world. *How quickly life turns upside down!* he thought, almost reduced to tears.

As he was rinsing off, a pair of inmates entered the tiled area, taking possession of the showerheads on either side of him. Their bare bodies were thick, muscled, brutish, covered with more tattoos than hair. To Carlos, they appeared to be part of another species altogether, one that, unlike himself, belonged behind bars.

They soaped up, watching him with the same

peculiar concentration as the guard. Carlos, heart pounding in his throat, felt his scrotum contract. There was a roiling in his lower belly, as if it were filled with squirming eels. Finished with his rinse, he turned off the taps, whipped his thin towel off its wooden peg, and wrapped his nether regions, hurrying across the tiles without taking the time to dry off.

"Late for an appointment, *pendejo*?" the guard sneered. As Carlos went to pass him, he grabbed him, whispered in his ear, "*Te agarró con la mano en la masa, pendejo.*" They caught you red-handed, asshole.

Carlos tensed, but when that only brought a scowl to the guard's face, he willed his body to go slack, to paste a meek expression on his face.

"That's better," the guard said, letting him go.

Carlos scurried back to his cell, where his uniform was waiting for him, cleaned, pressed, and neatly folded. For a moment, he could scarcely believe what he was seeing. Then, in something of a daze, he dressed. Was he being released? Had his "pocket judge" come through, after the press had turned its spotlight to the next scandal?

The moment he finished straightening his tie, a guard appeared outside his cell. Unlocking the door, he beckoned Carlos out.

"Warden wants a word, señor," he said, his tone

and demeanor the polar opposite of the guards at the showers.

With each step, Carlos's heart grew lighter. His head swam with plots to enact his revenge on the people who had so humiliated him. The closer he came to the warden's office the less forbidding the corridor and the people inhabiting it looked. Carlos became more and more comfortable, feeling with each step that he was closer to being on the other side of the bars, out of this hellhole, back to the life that was his due.

The guard stopped outside a large mahogany door, engraved with a bas-relief of the eagle with a serpent in its mouth, landing on a nopal cactus— the sigil of Mexico City when it was known by its Aztec name, Tenochtitlán.

The guard rapped on the door, heard the word, "Come," and opened the door for Carlos. He stayed outside, closing the door behind the well-dressed prisoner after he had crossed the threshold.

The warden's office was square, high-ceilinged, as stately as a barrister's study. The walls were lined with books on mahogany shelves, the floor covered with an Oriental carpet. The warden himself sat behind a massive, intricately carved oak desk that looked at least a hundred years old. He glanced up at Carlos, smiled, and gestured him to a comfortable-looking oak chair facing him.

"My personal condolences for the way you have been treated, señor." He spread his hands. "You better than anyone else understand how delicate this matter is. Why, just an hour ago I received a call from *el presidente* himself. So you understand..." His smile turned rueful. "Unfortunately, there is only so much even a man in my position can do...without the proper...incentive."

"*No se puede resistir el cañonazo*," Carlos said. You can't resist an enormous bribe. "Is that it?"

"In a nutshell."

"That can be arranged."

The warden nodded. "You understand that for the moment at least release is out of the question." He clucked his tongue. "Not to worry. A week or two, you'll live like a king here. Then, when you're transferred out for the trial, an unforeseen accident will befall the vehicle transporting you. I personally guarantee you'll never see the inside of that courtroom again. How does that sound?"

"And the amount?"

The warden scribbled on a scratch pad, tore off the sheet, folded it in half, and passed it across the desktop. Carlos picked it up, opened it, and read the figure.

"This can be managed," he said.

"Please enlighten me, señor. Your accounts have been frozen."

"Only the known ones. If you give me access to your laptop a transfer can be arranged instantaneously."

The warden tapped his forefinger against his lips for a moment, thinking the idea through. "I'm reluctant to give you free rein on my computer."

"Stay here while I do it. Watch me from where you're sitting now."

"I'll have to give you my private banking information."

"Yes, you will."

"I'm extremely reluctant to do that."

Carlos thought for a moment. "Change the online passcode the moment I'm done transferring the money."

"Hmm, okay. I guess that'll secure the account." The warden gave Carlos the information, then swung the laptop around to face him and sat back. "No funny business now."

"I'll tell you what I'm doing as I'm doing it," Carlos said. "How's that?"

The warden still looked dubious. "Let's see it in action."

Hitching himself forward, Carlos began to work the laptop's keyboard, giving a running commentary as he moved from step to step.

"Okay, I'm online...I have navigated to my bank's website...I'm inputting my security code and answering three security questions…All right, I'm logged onto the site…Now I'm going to access my account…There, I'm in. I'll begin to transfer the amount you requested as soon as I input your account information."

As Carlos talked the warden through the procedure, the warden surreptitiously opened a drawer in his desk, took out a Colt .45 revolver with custom mother-of-pearl grips, a prized possession long coveted, given to him as a gift. He always kept it loaded and at the ready; inside a Mexican prison you never knew who was going to step through your door.

"I'm about to make the transfer," Carlos said.

"Señor Carlos." As Carlos lifted his head, the warden continued, "Felipe Matamoros sends his felicitations on your final journey."

Carlos barely had time to register shock before a red hole bloomed in the center of his forehead. As he rocked backward, the warden leapt deftly from his chair and grabbed his laptop before it slipped out of Carlos's nerveless fingers.

The door to the warden's office swung open, revealing the guard who had brought the prisoner from his cell. He looked at the warden, ignoring the corpse. "Another prisoner trying to escape, boss?"

"They never learn, Juan," the warden said, his

gaze fixed on the laptop's screen. "Time to take out the trash."

As Juan hoisted the body off the chair and removed it, the warden finished inputting his account information. Then he changed the funds to be transferred to the entire amount in Carlos's account, which was even more than he had imagined. It was, in fact, a staggering sum. Not to worry. His friend Felipe, who had given him the Colt as a present this past Christmas, had said he could keep whatever was in Carlos's account. Yes, indeed, the warden thought, as he pressed the ENTER key initiating the electronic transfer, Felipe Matamoros was the best friend a man could have.

Glass shattered, metal shrieked as it contorted into grotesque shapes. The immense impact caused the truck to rear up on two wheels, roll over onto its side, then come to a quivering rest upside down. Its tires spun uselessly, its engine whined. Steam vented from the cracked and rapidly overheating engine. Then all was still, as if the world were holding its breath.

The calm was shortly shattered by the sound of footsteps headed directly toward the truck. Amir Ophir trotted up to the upside-down vehicle,

Beretta in hand. Peering into the cab on the driver's side, he saw Bourne and the woman hanging upside down, caught in the frayed webbing of the seat belts like flies in a spiderweb.

The woman was clearly unconscious, but as he reached inside to take Bourne's pulse, Bourne's eyes opened and his right hand slashed out toward Ophir's face. Ophir knocked it away with a smile.

"Not this time, Bourne." He gripped Bourne's throat in an icy grip. "You have been a thorn in my side long enough."

He raised the Beretta, but got it only halfway to the window before Bourne pulled the trigger on the gun in his left hand. The bullet smashed into Ophir's forehead with such force it blew the back of his head off.

Ophir's eyes rolled up as he dropped from Bourne's sight. Bourne, still groggy from the crash, unsnapped his seat belt, then turned to Maricruz. He saw blood smeared across her face, but quickly determined she had sustained only superficial cuts from flying glass.

As he maneuvered her out of the harness, he heard police sirens approaching. His door was inoperative, so he clambered out the window. Grasping Maricruz under her arms, he dragged her out after him. Sliding her into his arms, he staggered over to the Chevy that Ophir had drove into them. He almost passed out from the effort, though the distance was less than twenty feet.

Placing her in the passenger's seat, he slid behind the wheel, and was gratified to realize that the engine was still running smoothly, though with the crumpled front end he couldn't be certain how long that would last. Back at the truck, he salvaged the suitcases with the items Hale had reluctantly provided, shoved them into the backseat of the Chevy.

Putting the car in gear, he drove off, fighting back the darkness at the periphery of his vision. Behind him, the sirens were loud enough for him to estimate the cops were only blocks away.

He turned a corner, saw traffic stalled up ahead, backed up, and took another street. The sudden movement jerked Maricruz awake. She groaned, her eyes fluttering open. Turning her head toward Bourne caused her to wince in pain and rub the back of her neck.

"What the hell happened?"

"Ophir, the Mossad agent from the café, ran into us with this car."

"I hope he broke both his legs."

"That would've made him lucky," Bourne said, making another turn. "He's got a bullet in his brain." He lifted the gun. "Sometimes a gun *is* the only way."

She laughed, then immediately held her head in her hands. "Oh, wow."

"We need a little downtime before we tackle your friend Felipe."

"Where the hell are we going to go? Lolita's?"

"I don't want to endanger her any more than I already have," Bourne said. "And there's Angél's safety to consider."

"A hotel is out."

"Too many questions, especially in the shape we're in."

"Then where?"

"You've already met one member of your family," he said. "Time to meet the other."

You're nuts if you think I'm setting foot in there," Maricruz said.

"I'm afraid you don't have a choice," Bourne told her. "Constanza Camargo is our only safe port of call."

Bourne had parked the Chevy outside a beautiful mansion inhabiting the corner of Alejandro Dumas and Luis G Urbina, in the swanky Colonia Polanco. Its limestone facade sparkled in the sunlight, but the front steps were already in shadow.

The steps had been widened to accommodate a ramp built into their center, running from the sidewalk to the front door.

Looking around, Maricruz pointed out the window. "That's Lincoln Park over there." She shook her head and groaned. "On the other side of it is Castelar Street and my father's villa."

"Your mother spent most of her adult life within spitting distance of the man she had loved."

"Love!" Maricruz snorted. "What did my father know of love? He was a satyr. And as for my mother—"

"Constanza is something of an enigma—even, I think, to herself."

"That doesn't make me want to meet her."

"Why not? In that regard, I suspect you're very much like her."

"You can't make me do it."

"I know better than to try to force you into anything." He turned to her. "But the situation is this: You and I both need food and rest. We can't stay here in the car. In fact, I need to get rid of it as quickly as possible. It stands out like a sore thumb here in Polanco. The bottom line, Maricruz, is we need a safe haven."

"How do you know you can trust her?"

"I don't, but I'm not seeing an alternative."

"I can't." Maricruz shook her head. "I won't."

Bourne got out of the Chevy, walked around, and opened her slightly crumpled door. Their eyes met for a long moment, then Maricruz said, "Shit," and slid out. As she hit the sidewalk her legs started to buckle, and Bourne scooped her up.

"Put me down," she said, "I can walk on my own." But her voice was weak and her eyes were going in and out of focus.

Bourne was now concerned that she might have a concussion. "Look at me. Maricruz, look at me!"

Hurrying across the sidewalk, he went up the steps to Constanza Camargo's house, swung Maricruz around so he could press the bell.

He had to ring twice, but eventually the door opened, revealing a hulking presence.

"*Hola*, Manny," Bourne said, addressing Constanza's driver-bodyguard-assistant.

"You're the last person I ever expected to see again."

"What a greeting." Bourne took a step forward. "Let us in, Manny."

The big man blocked their way. "I think not. The señora will not want to see you."

"Maybe not," Bourne said, "but she'll want to see her daughter."

40

MANNY STAGGERED SLIGHTLY as if he'd had a stroke, and Bourne carried Maricruz into the entryway of the house. Manny, looking white as a sheet, belatedly closed the door, then trotted after Bourne as he lay Maricruz down on one of the plush sofas in the living room.

As she sank into the downy cushions, Maricruz uttered a tiny moan and her eyes started to close. Bourne pinched her, and when her eyes flew open, he said, "Maricruz, you might have a concussion. You can't fall asleep. Do you understand?"

She nodded, then winced.

"Where is the pain?"

"Behind my eyes, at the back of my head."

Bourne slipped his hand under her head, felt the lump under her hair. The truck's bench seat lacked headrests. "You hit your head. You'll be okay, just keep awake."

She reached out for him. "Help me sit up."

He moved her slowly and evenly.

"That's better," she said with a sigh.

"Manny, we need water and some food. Also a painkiller for Maricruz."

"I don't know whether my stomach can take anything," Maricruz said.

"Try anyway." Bourne turned. "Manny!"

Manny was staring at Maricruz. "I see the señora in her face. I...I don't know what to say."

"Get us what we need instead of talking," Bourne said. "And let Constanza know we're here."

"I..." Manny stood frozen.

"What is it?" Bourne said, impatient. He stood. "If you won't tell her I will."

"Listen, listen..." Manny licked his lips, as nervous now as a cat in the rain. "The señora is ill. Very ill. She has not been out of bed for weeks now. To be honest, she should be in the hospital, but she refuses to leave here. She says the only way she'll be taken out of her home is feet-first."

"What's the matter with her?"

"No one knows." Manny shrugged. "A virus, maybe. Whatever it is, it seems to be slowly killing her."

"Let me see her."

"I don't think that's a good idea, señor. She's very weak."

"I want to see her."

Both men turned to see Maricruz struggling to get to her feet. Bourne helped her up.

"I heard what you said," Maricruz said. "I want to see her." She turned to Bourne. "No, don't carry me. I want to be on my feet when I see her. I feel enough like a child right now as it is."

Manny nodded, relenting. He was about to lead them up the stairs when Bourne said, "I'll meet you upstairs."

Bourne went swiftly back to the entry and out the front door. He got the cases out of the Chevy and brought them back inside, leaving them in the entry. Hearing a car pull up outside, he peered out one of the door's sidelights. A police cruiser had stopped beside the battered Chevy. A pair of uniforms emerged. They seemed inordinately interested in the crumpled front, which no doubt had chips of paint from the truck it had plowed into. The police here might be incompetent, Bourne thought, but they could also be relentless.

Taking out the badge he'd pulled off the detective, Bourne opened the door, trotted down the steps and across the sidewalk.

Holding up the badge, he said with a great deal of officiousness, "Can I help you fellows?"

One of the cops, a whip-thin, swarthy man with the nose of an Olmec, said, "We've been looking for a vehicle involved in a collision and shooting in Taxqueña."

"You're a long way from there. What are you doing in Polanco?"

"We go where we're needed."

This from Whip-thin's partner, rising up like a wild boar from where he had been examining the Chevy's crushed front grille. He had a wide face the color of suet, punctuated by little piggy eyes and a bow of a mouth that was almost feminine. He was older than Whip-thin and obviously the senior in rank.

"Doesn't matter," Bourne said. "This is my investigation."

Piggy came around the front of the Chevy, squinted at Bourne's badge. "*What's* your investigation?"

"The homicide."

Piggy was full of bluster and belligerence. "What d'you know about it?" He'd obviously been fucked over by suits many times before. There was only one way to handle people like him.

Bourne stepped toward him. "I know the victim's a foreign national. After the mess over the dead Chinese we're still trying to clean up, this latest shooting has been elevated to the highest level."

"Which means you, does it, suit?"

"It sure as hell doesn't mean you, Sergeant. Why don't you and your *niño* get the hell out of here before I radio in a report about you."

"Fuck you, suit." But Piggy signaled to his partner and the two of them retreated to the cruiser. "We've got bigger tacos to fry than this shit." Piggy slid behind the wheel, his partner got in beside him, and the cruiser took off.

When Bourne was certain they had gone for good, he went back out to get rid of the Chevy.

Manny led Maricruz down the richly patterned, second-floor hallway. The mahogany floorboards gleamed beneath their feet, the walls were hung with expensive artwork by Diego Rivera, Frida Kahlo, and Gabriel Orozco.

Once, when she faltered, Manny turned back, held out a steadying hand. "Are you sure you're up to this, señorita?"

Maricruz smiled through her acute trepidation. "I'm a married woman, Manny."

"*Perdóneme*, señora."

"It's all right, Manny. Let's go."

He nodded, leading her to a wide olivewood door, the center of which was carved into the shapes of birds sitting in the gently curving branches of a tree. He knocked on the door and called out, "Señora, you have a visitor."

He opened the door, though Maricruz could not discern whether or not he had received a reply. The master bedroom suite was spacious, though not as large as she had imagined during her early childhood spent in her father's extravagant villa just across the park. Also, there were no religious icons, no portraits of Jesus. The papered walls were unadorned save for a Mary Cassatt painting of a mother smiling down at an angelic child cradled in her arms, which faced the bed.

Sunlight slanted in through the large window, framed by heavy, theatrical drapes. The room was dominated by an oversize bed, its canopy supported by massive pillars of olivewood, obviously carved by the same artist who had sculpted the door. To one side of the bed was a wheelchair, folded like the wings of a bird, perched and waiting.

However, all this was peripheral. Maricruz's gaze was entirely focused on the woman sitting up in the center of the bed. Though ravaged by the mysterious disease afflicting her, she was nevertheless the most exquisite woman Maricruz had ever seen. Whatever Manny had seen in her own face that reminded him of this woman Maricruz couldn't fathom, but then that was often the way with daughters and mothers.

Manny, stepping in front of Maricruz, approached the bed. "Señora," he said. "May I present your daughter, Maricruz Encarnación."

Maricruz didn't bother to correct him.

Constanza Camargo's deep-set eyes glittered like jewels as they turned toward Maricruz.

"What?" she said in a voice soft as velvet. "Manny, what did you say?"

Manny beckoned Maricruz forward, took her hand, and led her to the foot of the bed. "Your daughter, señora. Your daughter, Maricruz, has returned to you."

"Maricruz," Constanza said, "is it you? Is it really you?"

Maricruz could not speak. She felt as if she were choking, as if at any moment her knees would give out and she would fall on the bed, to be gathered up in her mother's arms like the angelic child in Mary Cassatt's painting.

"Manny, is this my daughter," Constanza said, "or am I dreaming?"

"This is no dream, señora. Look at her face. Her face is your face. There can be no doubt."

For long moments, there was an uncanny silence

as Constanza Camargo stared at her long-lost child, her eyes half glazed, her expression still one of shock.

"It's the painting," she whispered at last. "I bought the Cassatt to have you close to me, Maricruz, wherever in the world you were." The tears glittering in her eyes began to spill out onto her cheeks. "Now it has brought you back to me."

Maricruz felt light-headed. She swayed, as if at any moment she would pass out. She could not believe this was happening. So many times she had thought of her mother, wondering who she was, why she had abandoned her, why her father adamantly refused to talk about her, wondering what she looked like, how she sounded, smelled, how she moved, whether she was dead or alive.

"I know you must hate me, Maricruz. You must, I know you must, but I can't help that, can I? He took you away from me." Her mother began to weep in earnest. "I hated him, but I loved him. God help me, I couldn't stop loving him, and I despised myself for that. He could be so loving, and so cruel. How to explain him? How to explain what happened?"

"No more," Maricruz begged. She did not want this moment spoiled by resurrecting the specter of her father. She didn't want to hear any explanation of the event she had spent her entire life believing was unexplainable. She wanted to bury it in the deepest, darkest part of her, never to be examined again. "Please."

"Will you come here, then?" Constanza held out her arms. "Will you let your mother hold you as she's ached to do for so long?" She swallowed, though it clearly pained her. "Will you call me Mama?"

Something broke like crystal inside Maricruz, and she found herself climbing onto the bed, crawling across the covers, into her mother's arms, where she lay with her head on her mother's breast, listening with the naked wonder of a child to the steady beating of her mother's heart.

Bourne returned to the house and arrived at Constanza's bedroom to find Maricruz in her mother's arms. The two of them spoke to each other so softly, their conversation was nothing more than a murmur.

"Is everything all right?" Manny said with a worried expression.

"For the moment, anyway."

Manny moved to the doorway. "I think we should leave them for a while."

Bourne followed him out into the hall and downstairs into the kitchen, where the cook was preparing what looked like an enormous meal.

As in most Mexican houses, the kitchen was large, spacious, and filled with arrays of fired clay plates, bowls, and pots. A central station held a counter and dual sink. Bourne sat at a simple carved wood refectory table while Manny brought food and drink over.

The two men ate while the cook, a heavyset Mexican woman, bustled about, preparing tacos, tamales, and their various fillings.

"Are you expecting company?" Bourne asked around a bite of refried beans.

Manny winced good-naturedly. "Hope springs eternal in Bernarda's ample breast. At any moment, she expects the señora to come down the stairs with her appetite resurrected. If you ask her, she's preparing for that moment, for which she prays to the Virgin Mary three times a day."

Bourne was struck by his expression. "But you don't believe Constanza will recover."

Manny shrugged. "The doctor who comes is of no use, but he's the only one she trusts, God knows why. Each day she seems worse. She has no appetite, as I've said, her skin is pale—sometimes, toward noon, it looks blue-gray—and lately, there are moments of confusion, when she thinks Maceo is still alive, still in love with her."

Behind him, Bernarda, finished with the tacos and tamales, was preparing a tray presumably to take up to her mistress and her daughter.

"Then she knows Maceo Encarnación is dead."

Manny nodded.

"How did she take it?"

"Difficult to say. She didn't cry, didn't even look sad. She just gazed out the window at the treetops in Lincoln Park and said, '*It all looks the same. Just the same.*'"

"She did love him, then."

"Oh, yes. In her heart of hearts she kept certain memories of him alive, like eternal flames."

"Even after all the hurt he caused her."

"Well, you know, señor, humans often carry conflicting feelings at the same time." He shrugged. "Who among us can say why?"

Bernarda crossed the kitchen with her food- and drink-laden tray, and started down the hall, heading to the stairway.

"It's a matter of what we want versus what we have." Bourne looked down at his coffee. Something was bothering him. He looked up. "Manny, you said that at times Constanza's skin has a bluish tinge?"

Manny nodded. "Odd, yes?"

"Did you tell this to the doctor?"

"Honestly, I can't remember. It's a little thing."

A little thing. Bourne thought about Anunciata, about how her mother had been murdered.

"Manny, how long has Bernarda been Constanza's cook?"

"Many years, señor. She's become part of the family."

"Where did she come from?"

"Her cousin was originally part of Señor Encarnación's staff."

Bourne was up and running down the hallway.

41

WHAT AN APPETITE you had, *guapa*!" Constanza kissed the crown of Maricruz's head. "You'd grab onto my breast and not let go until every drop was gone. And while you suckled you'd stare up at me with those eyes, and I swore you were talking to me." Constanza sighed softly. Her breath smelled of chocolate and garlic. "Those were the happiest days of my life."

"Why did he take me away from you?"

A tear slid down Constanza's pallid cheek. "Why did he do anything, *guapa*? Out of fear."

"Fear?"

"Of course. Maceo Encarnación was riddled with fear. He came from nothing, and to nothing he was certain he'd return. Oh, not dust to dust; that is the fate of every human being, great and humble alike.

He was terrified that everything he built—everything he had amassed—would be taken away from him. You were one of those things."

"He thought you'd take me away from him?"

"Not physically, perhaps. I think he was frightened I'd teach you things he didn't want you to know."

"Like what a shit he was."

"He was one of those people who ruled with absolute power. He no longer understood the world around him. He had lost touch with people."

"Even those who tried to get close to him?"

"Oh, especially those, *guapa*. He was afraid they'd betray him, take something precious from him."

"He was fucking crazy," Maricruz breathed.

"*Guapa*, I am so proud of you. You broke away from him. You left and never looked back."

"Until now."

Constanza squeezed her. "For which I'm eternally grateful."

"You won't feel that way when I tell you why I came." So Maricruz told her the story of how she had landed in Beijing, how she had ferreted out Ouyang Jidan, seduced him, married him, guided his business with her father. "And now," she said, in conclusion, "I've come back to take care of Maceo's business with Los Zetas."

Constanza shook her head, her expression grave. "I'm grateful, because you have been brought back to me, but now you must stop this nonsense. You must sever all ties with this part of his business. Your destiny will take you down another road."

"But, Mama—"

"No buts, Maricruz. In one way or another, I've lived with these criminals all my life. They took the use of my legs from me, they took you from me. I will not see that happen to you. Only tragedy can result if you continue." She tilted her daughter's head up so their eyes locked. "You've been foolish enough to marry a man too much like your father. That is a tragedy in itself. But think, *guapa*, what will happen when he impregnates you. He'll never let that child out of his sight. You'll be tied to him for the rest of your life."

Maricruz thought of what Colonel Sun had said about Angél, which had both shocked and infuriated her. She knew her mother was right. She knew Bourne was right. She realized how foolish she had been to follow in her father's footsteps. For what, for what? She knew what she had to do, what path she needed to follow. All that was required now was for her to summon the courage to change course. She had done it before; she could do it again.

Then, hearing a rustling in the hallway just out-side the door, she looked up to see a heavyset woman bustle in with a tray laden with food and drink. She swallowed the feeling of being invaded and put a smile on her face.

Bernarda was already in Constanza's room when Bourne burst in. Mother and daughter were sitting up in bed, each holding a mug of hot chocolate as Bernarda arranged the plates of food and the cut-lery on their laps.

Without a word, Bourne removed the mugs.

"You!" Constanza said. "What are you doing here?"

"He brought me to you," Maricruz said. "I don't think I would have had the courage to come with-out him."

Bourne sniffed first one mug, then the other.

Manny came up beside him. "Señor, what are you doing?"

Bourne shoved one mug under his nose. "What does this smell like?"

He sniffed. "Why, chocolate, of course."

"What is this?" Constanza demanded. "Bernarda makes me a hot chocolate twice a day. She makes it so thick and dark, lately it's the only thing I can get down."

"She makes it thick and dark for a very good reason." Bourne addressed Manny. "Chocolate and what else?"

Manny took a deeper inhale from the steaming mug. "I don't know..." His brow wrinkled. "Garlic?"

Bourne looked at Bernarda. "When heated, arsenic gives off the scent of garlic."

"Arsenic?" Constanza said. "That's ridiculous."

"The first clue was Manny telling me how your skin was turning bluish, then he told me about your bouts of confusion. Constanza, we have to get you to a hospital. You're being slowly poisoned to death."

Bernarda fell to her knees, her hands clasped before her, as if she were praying in church.

"I loved you. I treated you like one of the family," Constanza said in a slightly breathless voice. "How could you do this?"

Bernarda, moaning and sobbing uncontrollably, rocked back and forth, seemingly incapable of answering.

"I'll get it out of her." Sliding off the bed, Maricruz stepped in front of the kneeling woman and, bending slightly, gripped her throat with such force that Bernarda cried out.

"You'll confess," Maricruz said, her flinty edge reappearing with renewed vigor. "You'll tell us everything or I will end your treacherous life right here."

Bourne, who had been inclined to intervene should Bernarda try to escape, decided it would be far more informative to watch Maricruz at work. He had already witnessed the soft side of her, now it was time to further study the courageous, iron-willed woman who had crossed continents, isolating herself, to defeat the will of her father.

Manny stepped forward. "Señor, perhaps the police should be called. This isn't right."

Bourne held him back. "You know better, Manny. The police have no place here."

"That was Maceo's way," Manny said stiffly.

"In the end, it's my way, too," Constanza told him.

The two men watched as Maricruz's grip on Bernarda turned vicious. Her nails, digging into the sides of the cook's neck, drew blood. Constanza seemed mesmerized; she crawled to the foot of the bed, where her daughter had the cook pinned to her knees.

"I brought you into this house at your cousin's request," Constanza said. Despite her unnatural pallor, her eyes blazed as in the old days when she was a young woman in full flower. The presence of the beloved daughter she had been convinced she'd never see again had reinvigorated her, for the time being rallying her against the pernicious effects of the small amounts of arsenic Bernarda had been stirring into her hot chocolate. "She told me that you had been mistreated, that your stepfather beat you, that he even turned you out of the house when he was sufficiently drunk."

"All this is true, señora." Bernarda's words came out thin and half strangled. "This I swear."

"It is not possible to believe you now." Constanza crept closer to her. "Did I mistreat you in some way—any way?"

"No, señora."

"Did I not take you in, pay you a fair wage, give you presents for Christmas and your birthday?"

"You did, señora."

"Did I not carefully listen to your woes and help you to the best of my abilities?"

"You did, señora."

At last, Constanza sat on the foot of the bed. Without warning, she slapped Bernarda hard across one cheek, then the other, causing the woman to whimper and weep again.

"Then what the fuck is your explanation for poisoning me?"

Bernarda hung her head, and when she spoke her voice was just above a whisper. "Blood is thicker than water, señora."

Constanza's eyes opened wide in a combination

of shock and horror. "That's it? '*Blood is thicker than water*'? That's your explanation?"

"I was ordered to do—Maceo's family still holds power," Bernarda murmured. "People have long memories, especially in our family, where bitterness and hate are taken in with mother's milk."

With a guttural sound in the back of her throat, Maricruz switched her grip on the cook and with one swift movement broke her neck. She slumped as Bernarda fell to the floor.

In pain, Maricruz turned to her mother. "Now we take you to the hospital, Mama."

42

OPHIR IS DEAD," Dani Amit said as he strode into the Director's office. "Shot to death at the scene of a collision in Mexico City."

"That would be Bourne," Director Yadin said with no little relief. "*Magniv!*" Great!

"So now he's done your dirty work for you, you should drop him like a hot stone."

Yadin looked up at his head of Collections. "Why would I do that, Dani?"

"Bourne is dangerous. He's too dangerous to fool around with. Even this—if he found out how you manipulated him—could cause a blowback of epic proportions."

The Director swiveled around to stare out across the rooftops of Tel Aviv. "His work isn't finished, and it's too important to have him stop now."

Yadin passed a hand across his face. "And to be perfectly honest, even if I wanted to stop him, I very much doubt I could." He turned back to face Amit. "Ophir tried, and look how he ended up."

"There are others who—"

"Dammit, stay out of this, Dani!" The Director's voice was as sharp and direct as a knife blade. "That's a direct order."

Minister Ouyang arrived at Beijing Capital International Airport fifteen minutes before his plane was scheduled to take off. But when his driver opened the door to his white SUV and he stepped out, he found himself facing Kai.

"What are you doing here?" Ouyang said. "This trip is need-to-know."

There was something odd in Kai's manner, a nervousness that bordered on anxiety.

An alarm bell went off in Ouyang's head. "What's the matter?"

"Let's get a drink."

"I don't have time for a drink. My flight is minutes away from leaving."

When Ouyang made to step around Kai, his friend kept himself between Ouyang and the doors to the departures hall.

"There will be another flight," Kai said.

"Kai, you know that Maricruz has been injured. I sent Colonel Sun to find out what happened."

"You should not have done that, Jidan. Now comes word that Sun is dead."

"Why do you think I'm on my way to Mexico City?"

"To compound your mistake? You never should have allowed your wife to leave your side."

"It was a business decision," Ouyang said, somewhat stiffly.

Kai took a step toward him. "There will be no next flight, Jidan."

Ouyang bristled. "Who are you to give me ultimatums?"

"This isn't an ultimatum." Kai looked sad. "It's an order."

"What? This is my wife we're talking about. Who would dare—?"

"He's waiting for you." Kai pointed to an enormous armored limousine. "There."

"I don't have time for this, Kai."

"Make time, Jidan."

Ouyang turned to his driver, who had made no attempt to remove his luggage from the back of the SUV. Instead he stood facing away from the two men, smoking a cigarette as if he had not a care in the world. Was he in on this also? Ouyang asked himself.

Kai held out an arm. "This way, Minister."

Kai hadn't called him Minister in many years; they were too close for formalities.

Ouyang walked ahead of Kai to where the limousine sat waiting, engine purring like a great jungle cat. The rear door opened as he approached and, ducking his head, he stepped inside.

"Hello, Jidan."

Deng Tsu, dark eyes watchful, greeted him. What with the windows blacked out and the interior lights dimmed to a minimum, it was difficult to make out his expression, or to identify the second man sitting across from Deng and Ouyang.

"Patriarch," Ouyang began, "this is something of a surprise."

"Well, you see, that's part of the problem." Deng shifted slightly, his right hip clearly paining him. "By all rights, Jidan, this meeting should not be taking place."

"There would have been no need for it, if you had kept your wife—I'm sorry, your greed—in check."

Ouyang stiffened. He recognized that high, phlegmy voice, but he switched on a sidelight to make certain. His stomach contracted as he saw his nemesis, Cho Xilan, confronting him, the hint of a Cheshire Cat grin on his face.

"What's he doing here?" Ouyang could not keep the hostility out of his voice.

"We are *all* here," Deng said, "to save a situation that is about to spiral out of control."

"And it *will* spiral out of control," Cho Xilan said, "unless we work together to make it go away."

Ouyang did not for a moment believe Cho Xilan wanted to work with him to get anything done. "I was hoping to do that with this trip," he said to Deng.

The Patriarch shook his head. "Your appearance in Mexico City will make things far worse. It cannot be countenanced."

"But my wife is there—somewhere. She's hurt and she must be found."

Cho Xilan leaned forward, his cat-like face, with its long eyes and tiny ears set close to his skin, shiny as if with wax. "You see, Ouyang, this is just the attitude that has generated this mess." He shook his head. "Our comrades on the Politburo are understandably upset."

"Silence, Cho," the Patriarch said sharply. "I told you, there will be no talk of the Politburo."

"There will be plenty of talk three days from now—all of it potentially bad news for us—when we convene in Beidaihe, unless—"

Deng impatiently waved away his words. "Don't

make me regret reading you in on this meeting, Cho. You and Ouyang are passengers here; I am the driver."

The Patriarch sat back, looking from one to the other. "From this moment on, you must strive to put aside your enmity and work together for the common cause. This will be our private great leap forward.

"Jidan, there is too much discord among the elite. This Party Congress has all the earmarks of being the most contentious in recent history. Your epic battle with Cho Xilan is at the core of this strife. I cannot have it. This country is at a major cross-roads—you yourself took great pains to elucidate the growing dangers of continuing to ignore our populace.

"For us—*all* of us—to maintain our exalted status within the Middle Kingdom, sacrifices must be made on all sides." Again, he looked from one to the other. "Am I making myself clear?"

After some hesitation, both men nodded, though reluctantly.

"The two of you, honestly. Like two schoolboys trying to dominate the school yard!" Deng shook his head. "First: Cho, you must soften your hard-line stance."

"The Chongqing are adamant. They will never go along with that."

"Then I must find another to lead the party." The Patriarch took out his mobile. "Shall I make some calls, Cho? I have taken the precaution of drawing up a short list—"

"That won't be necessary, Patriarch. I'll make the party elders toe the line."

"Excellent. Because there must be reform now in order for us to survive and prosper. In this matter, Jidan's ideas are good ones. Gentlemen, the entire world will be watching. We are not so secretive as we'd like to believe we are. This Party Congress will be scrutinized by every civilized country. If we wish to emerge into the world at large we cannot be found wanting."

He turned to Ouyang. "Second: Because of the delicate tightrope along which we must now walk, your trip to Mexico City will send all the wrong messages."

"Especially your involvement in the drug trade," Cho said with no little bitterness.

"Cho," Deng cautioned.

"Your greed will be the death of us," Cho Xilan nonetheless continued.

"It is far more likely," Ouyang countered, "your hidebound notion of sticking our heads in the sands of the Gobi and going about our business as we have for centuries will cause our fall from grace and our demise."

"Let them judge us," Cho sneered. "It is they who need our raw materials, it is they who must come to us on bended knee to buy what they need."

"This is nineteenth-century thinking," Ouyang shot back. "Everything is interconnected now. We cannot return to the complete isolation of the past. This is why I've directed us to buy energy companies and fields in Australia, Canada, and Africa. *That* is our future."

"Listen to the two of you." Deng clucked his tongue like a professor addressing two malcontent students. "This argument gets buried right here, right now. From now on you will work together." He lifted a forefinger. "But before we go any farther I must make the matter of reform perfectly clear: The state will collapse if the Party does not attack corruption, but the Party will collapse if that attack is too aggressive or goes too deep."

The two men he addressed remained in sullen silence for some time, making it all too evident that neither cared for the compromise Deng had ordered.

"What about the woman?" Cho said at length.

"Thank you, Cho. This question must be addressed." The Patriarch turned to Ouyang. "This wife of yours, Ouyang, was a mistake—a terrible mistake. Merely by her presence she has put you in jeopardy. As long as she is your wife, your chances of promotion are nil."

"Patriarch—"

Deng held up a hand. "This is not open for discussion, Ouyang. Nothing I say here is. I am the law and this is the law. You say she is lost in Mexico. Good riddance! Let her stay in Mexico. If she tries to return to China, she will be denied. You will cut off all ties with her. All evidence of her will be purged. It will be as if she never existed. This includes your trade with the cartels. This will cease immediately. All this must be done if you and Cho Xilan are to reach an agreement on the amount and the scope of your reforms."

Deng's eyes were hard and bright. "This is your compromise, your sacrifice. There is no recourse. It will be done, Ouyang. From this moment on, it *is* done."

The good news is it isn't the Chinese."

"Who did Amit go running to?" the Director asked his father.

"The Americans."

The Director had met his father for dinner at an out-of-the-way restaurant where Reuben had been known for many years. The owners had happily welcomed him as a silent partner upon his retirement from Mossad.

"Another bit of good news," Director Yadin said. "The Americans will be running themselves ragged in the Sinai, far from the theater of real operations."

"On the other hand," Reuben Yadin said, "we've unearthed yet another mole, as high up as Ophir."

Eli speared a chunk of cheese with the tines of his fork, chewed on it meditatively. "Ophir is dead. We no longer have anything to fear from him."

"You have been proved right about Bourne."

The Director nodded.

"And Amit?"

"A found mole is a useful mole."

"Those Americans," his father said.

"They haven't tumbled to our mole inside CIA, so why alert them that we've discovered theirs?" The Director searched around his salad for another cube of cheese. "I'll send Amit to the Sinai to ensure the Americans don't lose their focus."

"He won't find Bourne."

"But he'll waste time trying—and time is all I need."

There was a silence between father and son. Eli looked at the lights of Tel Aviv flickering through the drizzle that had obscured the sunset, letting his thoughts wander in order to come to a conclusion. At length, he turned back.

"Speaking of which, it's time for you to come to the hospital with me."

Reuben looked somewhat taken aback. "Already?"

"I think it's necessary."

Reuben looked down at his plate of chicken, for which he suddenly had little appetite. The thought of accompanying his son to the hospital filled him with dread.

"The time has come so quickly."

"For you; no one else."

"Maybe not now," Reuben said softly.

"Of course now." Eli regarded his father with curiosity. "Pop, what's gotten into you?"

"Stop with this 'Pop' business," Reuben said, clearly in a bad humor.

"Whatever you say."

His father grunted. "That'll be the day. From the moment you were born it was never whatever I said."

"I'll try to remember that."

Reuben brushed his son's apology away. "Forget it. I'm just…." He gave Eli a bleak look from across the small table. "We never took such an enormous risk when I was Director."

"Got to move with the times, *abi*."

"But *such* a risk. If it blows up in your face..."

The Director glanced briefly over his shoulder, but there was no use calling for the check. His father never paid here, even before he became a partner. "So what d'you say? It would mean a lot to me."

Something unspoken passed between father and son.

Eli leaned across the table. "*Abi*, I know you're worried about me."

"Can you blame me?"

He took his father's hand. "It's going to be all right."

Reuben's bleak expression had never left his face. "Fuck if you can tell me that."

43

DIMERCAPROL." Dr. Hernandez, a slim, dapper man with prematurely graying hair, had about him the air of a country gentleman. "It's a heavy metal antagonist. Your mother is responding very well to the treatment."

"Thank God," Maricruz said.

"Though I must caution she's not out of the woods just yet, and we need to continue monitoring her for any sign of abnormal cardiovascular function for the duration of her treatment."

"When can I see her?"

"At the moment, she's sleeping and I don't want her disturbed. I'll instruct a nurse to fetch you when she wakes up."

"Thank you, Doctor. I'm eternally grateful."

"It was fortunate you got her here in time. Another week and it would have been too late."

After he left, Maricruz collapsed onto a chair in the waiting room.

"Javvy," she said, continuing the fiction Angél preferred. "I feel like I've spent these past few days digging myself out of a grave."

"That's not so far from the truth." Bourne sat down beside her. "You have family now, a sense of place. You need to get on with your new life."

"And leave everything I have in Beijing behind?"

"How difficult will that be?"

She shook her head. "To be honest, I don't know."

"Not until you try."

She gave him a wry smile. "That's you all over, I'm beginning to see—you move forward, like a shark, ever forward."

"A man without a past has no choice."

"It seems to me now that none of us has a choice if we want to continue living."

"There's one problem, Maricruz."

She almost laughed. "Isn't there always."

"Matamoros is coming after you. He's not going to let your change of heart conflict with the continuation of his drug trade. He needs Ouyang's pipeline, and you've made yourself the key to it."

He handed her his mobile. "Time to call him and set up a meet."

She shook her head. "No, not yet. I'm not...I need to see my mother first. I need to know she's really okay."

"Fair enough."

Bourne went to get them coffee. They had just put the empty containers aside when a nurse appeared.

"Your mother's awake," the nurse said. "She's calling for you."

Maricruz went to follow the nurse, but when she saw Bourne stay in the waiting room, she said, "I want you with me."

Nodding, he accompanied the two women down the corridor and into a semi-private room. A cotton privacy curtain had been pulled across, dividing the room, which was a far cry from the spacious deluxe quarters Carlos had arranged for Maricruz at Hospital Ángeles Pedregal. Light coming in through the blinds illuminated the figure on the other bed, as if through a translucent theatrical scrim.

Constanza, needles in her arm, lay on the bed, already looking better—the bluish metallic cast to her skin had been replaced by a rosier hue that, with any luck, would continue to gain leverage as the arsenic in her system was neutralized by the dimercaprol and pumped out by the fluids being delivered along with the drug.

Maricruz leaned over the bed to take her mother's hand. "How are you feeling?"

"Better," Constanza said. "Much better." Then her eyes cut to Bourne. "You killed Maceo, didn't you?" One hand fluttered up, then fell back onto the covers. "Don't bother answering. I knew it the moment I first set eyes on you in the airport. It was in your scent, on your face."

"You couldn't know," Bourne said.

"Oh, but I did. I tried to stop you, in my own way, but it all went wrong. Because of my involvement, Maria-Elena died, as did the woman you were with. I've never forgiven myself."

"Mama."

"No, Maricruz, this must be said. Expiation can come no other way. I am a good Catholic; I believe in confession." She gestured. "Come closer. That's right. Now I will tell you that each time I tried to help Maceo Encarnación it ended in tears. And yet I never stopped. That's a form of madness, I suppose. But that's what he engendered in me— a madness that transcended sense and reality. That was his gift—a dark gift. We're all the better for his death, that I can tell you without fear of contradiction." Her eyes burned into Bourne's. "And yet, God help me, it has left an empty place inside me. This is the essential conundrum of the human condition—to continue to love someone who caused you harm."

"Like drug addiction," Maricruz said.

Her mother nodded. "Precisely like drug addiction."

"It will take time," Bourne said.

"And now," Constanza said, "thanks to you, I'll have time." But there was no smile on her face, and her eyes were filled with sadness.

Maricruz turned to Bourne. "Let me have some time with her."

Bourne nodded, went out into the corridor, stood with his back to the wall, surveying the goings-on around him. The hall was lined with gurneys pushed up against the wall, some with patients who lay asleep or half dead. Something was bothering him, something he'd either seen or smelled, something out of place.

A harried-looking doctor appeared from a patient's room, stepped to the nurses' station and handed over the patient's chart. As he did so, Bourne picked up a wink of light from the overhead fluorescents, reflected off the chart's metallic edge.

At once, he whipped around, pushed through the door into Constanza's room, where the two women looked at him in surprise. Beyond and between them, the silhouette of the other patient in the room was moving. The wink of light came again, though dulled by the curtain, as it had the first time Bourne had been in the room.

Lunging forward, Bourne leapt over the bed, reaching through the curtain. A handgun slammed down on his wrist. He twisted, pulled the curtain around him and the person in the other bed. He wasn't a patient at all, though he had been patient enough to wait for Constanza to be assigned a room from the ER and then somehow embed himself in it when she was wheeled in.

The man smashed Bourne just above his heart, and Bourne felt an electric shock go through him. Immediately the man was on top of Bourne, trying to pinion his arms, but Bourne pressed his thumb into the nerve bundle at the side of his neck, kneed him hard in the groin, and, snatching the SIG Sauer out of his hand, dealt him a vicious blow with the butt. The man groaned and rolled off the bed onto the floor.

By this time Maricruz had joined him in the area between the second bed and the window. "I thought my father's family had sent someone else to finish the job Bernarda had started." She was staring down at the unconscious man. "But I recognize him." She looked up at Bourne. "This is one of Matamoros's men." She ran a hand through her hair. "You're right. Felipe won't rest until he's got me back."

"We've got to hide him," Bourne said.

"How the hell are we going to do that?"

"We're going to hide him in plain sight."

He went out of the room, and was soon back pushing one of the empty gurneys from the hall-way. Maricruz helped him maneuver the body onto the gurney. Bourne strapped him down, then covered him completely. Wheeling the gurney out, he pushed it down to the end of the corridor, where he left it.

"That man," Constanza said, when he had returned, "it never ends, does it?"

"It will now, Mama." Maricruz took her hand. "I swear to you it will end."

Bourne took her aside. "I have to get to Matamoros, and quickly. Both you and your mother are in danger. In another country, we could find people to protect you, but not here. No one can be trusted."

"I'll call him and—"

"No. Enough time has passed that he's sure to have become suspicious. I have to find another way. Does he have a weak link in his personnel? Someone we can contact to find out what he's planning?"

Maricruz thought a moment. "There is someone," she said. "Let me have your mobile."

* * *

Diego de la Luna, Felipe Matamoros's adviser, had had an uneasy feeling in the pit of his stomach ever since Maricruz Encarnación had told him that she had met his older brother Elizondo in Manila. Now, he sat in the Mexico City hotel room with Juan Ruiz, watching Matamoros pace back and forth like a trapped animal about to gnaw its paw off, and felt his skin begin to crawl.

After the initial call from Maricruz, they had heard nothing. Of course, Felipe had ordered him to try to trace the call, but whatever mobile device she was using not only blocked the number but refused to emit its GPS coordinates.

So here they were: deaf, dumb, and blind—a state Felipe could not long tolerate. In fact, de la Luna thought with a good degree of fear, he looked to be at the end of his very frayed rope.

"I don't trust her," Matamoros said.

"Who, *jefe*?" he said in his most obsequious voice.

"Maricruz," Matamoros snapped. "I sent Martine out to bring her back here, but we haven't heard from him and now he's not answering his mobile. The exclusive with Ouyang, laundering our money through Chinese art auctions—I knew her deal was too good to be true." He cursed. "The bitch is playing some kind of game."

"But what?"

"I don't know!" Matamoros thundered. "That's the fucking problem."

On the other side of the room Juan Ruiz was studiously paring his nails with a thin-bladed gravity knife.

Matamoros ran his hand through his hair. "But no matter what it is, she's become a liability. She has to be eliminated. The sooner the better."

At that moment de la Luna's mobile emitted a tinny tune.

"Hurry up and answer that," Matamoros said, glaring. "And change your ringtone. That one grates on my nerves."

"Yes, *jefe*." De la Luna took the call, but his blood fairly froze in his veins at the sound of Maricruz's voice.

"Hello, Diego," she said. "It's been too long."

De la Luna was at a loss for words. He heard her chuckle at the other end of the line.

"Surprised I still haven't been delivered to you, Diego?"

He coughed, unable for the moment to utter a single word.

"Are you somewhere where you can talk?"

"Not really," he managed to get out in a strangled voice. His throat felt as if he had swallowed a bucket of sand.

"Then move," she said, her voice at once steely. "Now!"

He looked at Matamoros, who had resumed his pacing. "Ruiz!" Matamoros bellowed.

Juan Ruiz looked up from his work and, seeing the storm clouds building in his boss's face, flicked away his knife. "Yes, boss."

"Go find that bitch. I don't care what you have to do. Tear this fucking city apart if you have to, I don't give a shit. Just find her."

Juan Ruiz stood up. He seemed to occupy a third of the room. "And when I do?"

"Take your gravity knife," Matamoros said. "I want her head!"

Okay," de la Luna said. "I'm outside on the terrace. But I don't understand. Why have you called me? Why aren't you here?"

"Why do you think?" Maricruz's voice seemed to rattle around in his ear.

"Matamoros was right about you? You've been playing us all along?"

"Circumstances change, Diego. Now you're the one I want to talk to."

"Oh, no," de la Luna said. "No, no, no. I'm not going to help you."

"Then I'll let your brother do it for me."

"What...what are you talking about?"

"Your brother has been looking for a way to destroy the Los Zetas drug trade for years, but has failed to do so because of the power the cartel wields inside the police, army, and government. But I'm his way in, Diego. I can give him everything he needs to bring Los Zetas down. I have his mobile number right here. Do you want me to make that call?"

De la Luna swallowed hard. "Of course...of course not."

"Then meet me."

De la Luna looked back over his shoulder. Juan Ruiz was gone. Maybe he'd get lucky and Juan would find her before...

"When?"

"Now."

"Now? I can't—"

"You can; you will." Maricruz bit off each word as if it were the head of a fish.

De la Luna passed a hand across his face. He was appalled to discover he was sweating like a farm animal. He couldn't possibly return to the hotel room in this state; Matamoros, with the senses of a hawk, would pick up his distress in an instant.

Closing his eyes, de la Luna acquiesced. "Where?"

"The Pyramid of the Sun."

Teotihuacán was more or less thirty miles northwest of the city, de la Luna calculated. "All right," he said. "I'll be there in an hour."

"Forty-five minutes," Maricruz said. "Don't be late."

The moment the connection was severed, de la Luna punched a SPEED DIAL button. When Juan Ruiz answered, he said, "Any luck?"

"Too soon," Juan Ruiz said in his usual terse style.

"No, it's not," de la Luna said. His skin felt prickly as the sweat dried on it. "I know where she is."

44

*T*EOTIHUACÁN TRANSLATED as "the place where man met the gods." It was a gargantuan archaeological site of Mesoamerican culture, containing the Pyramid of the Sun—the largest such structure in the pre-Columbian Americas—but also enormous residential structures, the wide, central Avenue of the Dead, and the Pyramid of the Moon. The city was established around 100 BCE. Its burgeoning inhabitants continued its expansion through 250 CE until eventually it became, with a population of 125,000, one of the largest cities in the world.

This history was very much in evidence as Bourne and Maricruz went down the Avenue of the Dead toward the massive Pyramid of the Sun.

Everything about Teotihuacán was on a mammoth scale, including the residences with apartments built one atop the other to accommodate the swiftly increasing population.

"Do you think he'll come?" Maricruz said.

"I do." Bourne was automatically scrutinizing the faces of every tourist and tour leader they passed. The place was packed with groups huddled around their guides or walking in clouds like gnats as they were led from structure to structure. "But he won't come alone."

"He can't afford to let anyone know what he's doing."

"He doesn't have to," Bourne said. "All he has to do is tell someone he knows where you'll be."

Maricruz looked alarmed. "Then why did you tell me to set this up?"

"Matamoros can't bring his crew here—too many foreign tourists. He can't afford any undue attention now. No, he won't send a crew and he won't come himself. He'll send someone he trusts, someone in his inner circle."

"Juan Ruiz," Maricruz said. "He's Matamoros's personal bodyguard."

"All the better," Bourne said as they approached the Pyramid of the Sun.

"He's a huge man." She described Juan Ruiz in detail. "You won't be able to miss him."

Bourne stopped in the middle of a gaggle of tourists, where they could stand and talk in as much protection as Teotihuacán was going to afford them.

"It's time for you to go on alone," Bourne said. "You understand how it will work?"

She nodded.

"Okay then."

He watched her eel her way through the throng and then out onto its periphery where, here and there, people from the group were taking photos. She moved easily; no one could tell what was under her long coat.

He stayed within the heart of the group, which was beginning to move on toward the Pyramid of the Sun. Keeping one eye on Maricruz and the other on the lookout for Juan Ruiz, he went down the Avenue of the Dead.

Ahead of him, Maricruz had stopped at the corner of the stone wall that wrapped around the structure. To her left were the central steps, filled with awestruck people, ascending and descending, that rose up to the pyramid's peak.

A short time later, a slim, almost effeminate man came up to where Maricruz stood. Diego de la Luna. Maricruz, keeping her hands in the pockets of her coat, turned to him and they began to talk. De la Luna looked extremely nervous. His tongue kept flicking, serpent-like, from between his bloodless lips.

Bourne kept moving, and when he spotted the big man Maricruz had described, he moved out from the shelter of a herd of Italian tourists. He strolled until he was behind Juan Ruiz. The assassin's presence was proof enough for Bourne that Matamoros had lost faith in Maricruz and what she promised to do for him.

Juan Ruiz might be big, but he stalked Maricruz like a cat. He had small feet, and like a dancer he seemed to glide over the ancient paving stones of the avenue as if he were death itself.

He was very good at his work. Though he had fixed on his prey, he was acutely aware of his surroundings and those people coming within his proximity. Bourne knew he needed to be extremely careful. If Juan Ruiz spotted him too soon, the plan would fail.

He kept circling, keeping himself out of range of the big man's peripheral vision. Juan Ruiz was very close to de la Luna, who had engaged Maricruz in an argument that, as Bourne had suspected, was designed to keep her fully occupied.

Bourne had to admire Juan Ruiz, even as he was working his way toward Ruiz's broad back. He was close enough now that Maricruz became aware of him. Her head jerked, as she began to turn, but it was too late. Juan Ruiz already had his gravity knife flicked open.

As Maricruz opened her mouth in surprise, he plunged the blade into the soft spot just beneath her sternum.

45

WHEN MINISTER OUYANG was angry or at a crossroads in his life, he inevitably withdrew to the Kunlun Mountain Fist training facility in Beijing. As he traveled by car to the facility, Ouyang could not remember a moment in his life when he had been as enraged as he was now.

Being told that he had to form an alliance with his nemesis was bad enough, but that this order came from the mouth of Deng Tsu—his mentor and, in the parlance of the West, his rabbi—was a humiliation not to be borne.

He needed to clear his mind, and the only way he knew to do that was to fight.

The Kunlun Mountain Fist training facility was located within sight of the Great Wall. This site was deliberate, as the elders were quick to point out to their novitiates. The Great Wall was a symbol, they preached, of the walls we built inside our minds to keep us from seeing the Truth—a Truth that practicing Kunlun Mountain Fist wushun would in due course illumine.

Ouyang was welcomed within the complex as the first-draft master he was. With great deliberation, he changed into the loose-fitting uniform reserved for all wushun practitioners. He chose a *jian*—the slender double-edged gentleman's sword he had wielded to such fine effect in the Kunlun Mountain Fist training facility in Shanghai.

Assigned an opponent, he moved out onto the mats. He began, as he almost always did, with Sacred Stone Form, standing immobile and steadfast while the opponent attacked, employing the White Snake Form, an advanced method often favored by Ouyang himself.

At first it was interesting to counter the moves he knew so well. But it wasn't long before his opponent's blade started slipping through his defenses. He was half a step faster than Ouyang, and at the four-minute mark his weapon slapped Ouyang hard on the chest.

Rocked back a pace, Ouyang felt himself overcome with a blind rage. Out the window went no-mind, the sense of calm and order in a world filled with disharmony. A whirlwind of chaos devoured it all in a heartbeat. Without another thought, he switched to the little-used Fire Ghost Form, performed a vicious lunge as his opponent withdrew his sword.

Ouyang's *jian* passed through his unprepared opponent's defenses. The point of the sword pierced the man's chest. Instead of withdrawing it, Ouyang completed the lunge, skewering his opponent upon the *jian*'s blade.

The man cried out, blood bloomed like a field of poppies, and soundless footsteps came running.

Juan Ruiz had just worked out that something was wrong. Then Bourne was on him. He reacted by reversing his bloodless gravity knife and stabbing backward with it. He almost caught Bourne—the blade pierced his jacket, but not his flesh. Bourne delivered a vicious blow to Juan Ruiz's kidney, which would have felled anyone else. Juan Ruiz was unfazed. He withdrew the knife and slashed backward a second time.

Bourne was prepared. He twisted Juan Ruiz's forefinger at the apex of the strike, when his hand was farthest from his body. Jamming it backward, he broke the finger, then the one next to it.

Ignoring the pain, Juan Ruiz turned and delivered a massive blow to Bourne's shoulder, almost spinning him completely around. Juan Ruiz, a street fighter by nature, grinned as he smashed his fist into Bourne's side. Bourne staggered, the breath fairly knocked out of him. He felt like he broke his hand on the next blow to Juan Ruiz's ribs. A sharp stab of pain shot through his wrist, all the way to his shoulder.

Juan Ruiz clamped a hand as large as a meat hook onto Bourne's throbbing shoulder and squeezed so hard the bones beneath his fingers ground together. Blackness formed around the edges of Bourne's vision, the center of which was ablaze with showers of sparks, each one accompanied by pinpricks of electric agony.

Determined to crush Bourne's shoulder, Juan Ruiz became convinced he was on the verge of victory. He was unconcerned when Bourne twisted, assuming he was continuing to writhe in pain. He never saw the blow that felled him: a hand-edge kite to the place on his neck protecting the carotid artery.

Bourne caught him before he could fall to the ground. Diego de la Luna stared from Bourne to Maricruz, his mouth half open in shock.

"How," he stammered. "How?"

"Show him," Bourne said.

Maricruz opened her coat, revealing one of the Kevlar vests Bourne had gotten from the armorer.

"You were going to fuck me over, Diego." She stepped up to him. "Now I'm going to have to hurt you."

She took her right hand out of her pocket. A small blade in the shape of a beech leaf protruded from between her forefinger and her middle finger—a gleaming push-dagger that Bourne had also requested.

De la Luna, staring fixedly at the blade approaching his nether regions, swallowed convulsively.

"There's only one punishment for a traitor," Maricruz said in a soft tonal burr.

"Wait, Maricruz. Think of where we are," Bourne said, still holding Juan Ruiz's bulk.

"I don't care." Maricruz grabbed hold of de la Luna. "This fucker deserves a radically altered life."

"She has a point there, Diego."

"She's crazy. Do something," de la Luna implored.

"Sorry," Bourne said, continuing their play-acting. "At the moment, my hands are full."

"There must be something—"

"Give me Matamoros."

De la Luna was clearly terrified. "What?"

"You give me Matamoros and I'll see what I can do about changing Maricruz's mind."

"Fuck that." Maricruz pressed the point of the push-dagger against de la Luna's trousers.

"Oh, Jesus God," he breathed. "I'll do whatever you want."

"I don't care now," Maricruz said.

De la Luna looked as if he was about to vomit.

"Maricruz," Bourne said soothingly. "Keep your eye on the prize. We came for Matamoros."

"This cocksucker already lied to us once, what's to stop him from lying again?"

"She's got a point, Diego. I guess there's no recourse. She's going to carve out a part of you—"

"Stop!" De la Luna was trembling like a newborn lamb. "I'll do whatever you want. I swear it."

"He swears it, Maricruz," Bourne said. "Can you accept that?"

Maricruz moved the tip of the blade so that it pierced the fabric. "He's full of shit."

"Please!" De la Luna looked ready to jump out of his skin. "Just tell me what you want me to do and I'll do it."

Bourne waited a moment. "Let him use his mobile, Maricruz."

"Really?"

He nodded. "But keep the push-dagger where it is."

De la Luna closed his eyes, licked his dry lips. His hand was shaking when he took the phone out.

"Call Matamoros," Bourne said. "Tell him you and Juan Ruiz have Maricruz."

"And?"

"Come on," Bourne said. "You know he's going to want to get the hell out of Mexico City the moment he has her. Tell him you'll meet him at the airfield where his plane is located."

De la Luna nodded. "Anything else?"

"If you tell him anything else," Maricruz said, "you'll be singing a permanent high C."

In the moments before his mobile rang, Felipe Matamoros was contemplating completely wrecking the hotel room. He had to do something; the waiting was driving him out of his mind. He had started drinking—the bottle of mescal he had ordered from room service was already nearly empty, but such was his distress he scarcely felt the effects of the alcohol.

Then his mobile buzzed, he saw it was de la Luna, and he accepted the call.

"This had better be good news."

"It is, *jefe*. Juan Ruiz and I have found the Encarnación bitch."

"You have her?"

"We do, *jefe*. Tied up as neatly as a Christmas present."

A wave of relief washed over Matamoros so profound he nearly staggered. "Excellent work, Diego. Bring her to the airfield. I can't bear another moment in this accursed city."

Before leaving, he took the bottle of mescal, unzipped his trousers, and urinated into it. He had drunk a lot, so the stream went on and on, steaming like that of a racehorse. When he was finished, he zipped up, screwed the top back on the bottle, and replaced it in the bar.

Then he went out of the room, and never looked back.

46

THE POLICE WERE CALLED, but due to Minister Ouyang's exalted position, what inquiry had been anticipated quickly dissolved, much to the disgust of the Kunlun Mountain Fist elders. Theirs was not a world normally constrained by the necessities of political corruption, and while they were not unaware of Ouyang's place in the Middle Kingdom they never for a moment believed it would impact them.

Now that it had, they were in something of an uproar. Blood spilled in anger within the precincts of their martial arts monastery was unthinkable. There was even some thought of burning down the entire complex and moving elsewhere. Fortunately, cooler heads prevailed, but the knowledge that they were not immune from the evils of the real world forever changed their view of both their art and the candidates who came seeking to share their knowledge.

Shen, the head wushun master, was designated as the one to represent the complex in confronting the murderer before he left the training ground where the crime had been committed.

"Ouyang," he said, addressing the Minister in deliberately demeaning fashion, "please do not take off your *gi*. The bloodstains are your responsibility. You must wear it out of the complex."

"I understand, Master Shen."

"I don't believe you do. What you have done here today is unforgivable."

"It was a tragic error. I was not in my right-mind."

"Tragic it was, Ouyang, but we cannot countenance it as an error. The taking of a human life is never an error."

"But isn't that what we're training for?"

Shen looked at Ouyang as if he had never seen him before. "Our training is a pathway to another plane of existence, a higher plane, where—"

"That's just plain bullshit." Ouyang was fed up with these people. "You preach a higher plane of existence while teaching your students how to make war. You have taught me how to make war, Master Shen. You have done an admirable job, and

I'm grateful. But now it is time for me to leave this isolated hothouse, to apply what you have taught me to the real world."

Felipe Matamoros used a carousel of private airstrips on the outskirts of Mexico City to fly in and out of the Distrito Federal. His plane was fueled and waiting for him on the northwest outskirts of the city, where buildings were still few and low.

He arrived with six of his hardened gunmen, nerves still stretched taut as a drawn bow. The mescal was finally starting to kick in, making the world look brighter and slightly surreal, like a candyland of sorts.

The brutish men stood guard, assault rifles at the ready, while he entered the plane and spoke to the pilot, giving him their destination and the route least likely to be observed by radar. In any case, the pilot always flew low enough to keep out of range of the normal elevations regularly monitored by the police.

He turned to the window when he heard several bursts of machine-gun fire, but could not see who his men were firing at. Pulling an assault rifle off the rack on the cockpit wall, he stepped into the cabin. In a half crouch, he was heading toward the door when the entire tail section of the plane exploded into a fireball inferno.

Matamoros, hurled onto his back, was fortunate to be lying in the aisle as pieces of the fuselage and tail flew by over his head. As soon as he was able, he scrambled to his feet. Incredibly, the forward door and gangway were still intact. Hurling himself out of the plane, he scrambled down the gangway.

Four of his six men were dead, caught in the conflagration. The other two, seeing him, clustered around him, facing outward. He saw Jason Bourne emerging from behind a stucco building and cursed under his breath. Bourne was holding something at waist level.

Matamoros started to fire and his men followed suit. Then something inexplicable happened. A jet of superheated flame shot out toward him. His men screamed as their clothes caught fire. The stench of burning flesh was enough to make anyone gag, but Matamoros ignored it.

Stepping between his two writhing, shrieking men, he kept his assault rifle aimed at the hated figure behind the horizontal column of flame, squeezing the trigger, the bullets spewing out at a horrific rate. "I'll kill you!" he shouted. "I'll kill you!" But the thick tongue of fire kept advancing, and he left it a moment too late.

The flames reached him, covered him, and began to devour him with an unnatural greed. He tried to scream, but the fire rushed down his throat. Everything turned bright purple. Then something popped inside his head, and all was fire, smoke, and the char of scorched bone.

Book Four

47

YOU LOOK SO PALE, Eli. I can see the toll this is taking on you."

The Director shook his head. "It's devastating."

Reuben Yadin nodded. "It's one secret I fervently wish didn't exist."

"I know, *abi*. The ordeal has been so difficult. But I can't think of myself."

Reuben studied his son's face as they exited the Tel Aviv Sourasky Medical Center. Weizmann Street was still burdened with traffic and bustling people, even at this hour of the evening.

He glanced around. "You're certain no one followed you?"

"I took the usual precautions, but even if someone did, there's no way they can suspect."

They snaked their way through the crowds on their way home from a long day. Here and there, army personnel could be seen, strategically placed, looking at nothing and everything.

Eli's hands were jammed in the pockets of his coat. "Let's talk about something else."

"Shall we talk about the plan, then?"

"There's nothing to talk about. Every piece is in motion."

"But the plan is as fragile as a thin sheet of glass," the old man said.

"At least no one but us can see through the glass."

"This isn't a time for jokes, Eli," his father admonished.

"I disagree. This is precisely the time for jokes, *abi*. A little levity allows you to take a step back, imagine the plan from different angles, look for any flaw—no matter how tiny."

"And what have you found?"

"If there's a flaw, I can't see it," the Director said. "If there's a flaw, there's nothing I can do about it."

"You can recall Bourne."

"You try recalling Bourne," Eli said. "The mountain won't move; the mountain won't even acknowledge your existence. But you see, *abi*, this stubbornness and this absolute will to move forward are two of the things that elevate him above all others in his trade."

"Eli, I worry you're putting too much faith in this one man—a man who's proven himself to be the enemy of organization and tradecraft rules."

"And yet he has his own tradecraft rules."

"The trouble is he invents them as he goes along. He takes too many chances."

"Ah, but, *abi*, this is where Bourne is most misunderstood. Where his former bosses fear him because they can't control him, I *know* I can't control him. I seek only to guide."

"He's damaged, Eli."

"Well, yes. That's irrefutable. But the prevailing wisdom—if you want to call it that—is the damage he has suffered has made him dangerous and unreliable. I see his damage in another light—it has made him harder, faster, wiser." The Director looked across the street into a darkened shop window filled with mannequins—sleek and smooth and anonymous—awaiting a new shipment of clothes. "He's also sad, *abi*. Very sad."

"Aren't we all." Reuben pulled at his ear. "I don't know about you but I need a drink—maybe two."

"What about your gout?"

"Fuck my gout," the old man said as they headed

diagonally across the street toward a restaurant. "Fuck everyfuckingthing."

When they were settled at a table with a clear view of the front windows, Reuben said, "Dani Amit?"

"He's in the Sinai," Eli said. "Happily soaking up useless intel for our American friends."

"Good, then we have a clear field interrogating the Chinese nationals Bourne brought back with him."

Reuben accepted the slivovitz from the waiter, downed half of the fiery liquid in one gulp, then set the small glass down. He watched his son sipping at his Yarden, a wine grown on the Golan and Naphtali Ridge, where the winter weather helped the grapes ripen fully.

"When did you start drinking wine?" the old man said gruffly.

"When you weren't looking. I'm not old school like you, Pop."

"What did I tell you about calling me 'Pop'?" When his son didn't respond, he tipped his head back, let the rest of the slivovitz slide down his throat, then called for another. After the waiter refilled his glass, he said, "Do you think you'll get anything useful out of the Chinese?"

"Bourne said it was simply a matter of *how* we got the intelligence out of them, not *if*."

Reuben made a face. "Treat them like lost children, you mean."

"There's a time to intimidate, a time to spill blood, and a time for compassion."

Reuben leaned forward, his elbows on the table. "These people are our enemy, Eli."

"Because they're Chinese?"

"That's right." The old man nodded. "Have you thought about the possibility of them being moles?"

"I've thought about that and many other scenarios," Director Yadin said. "I've rejected them all. The girl has admitted working for Cho Xilan; the man has worked both sides of the street. They're done, *abi*. They want out, and they're willing to sing for their exit."

"I don't believe that."

"Well then—" The Director threw some bills on the table. "—why don't you accompany me when I interrogate them?"

Yue and Sam Zhang were playing mah-jongg when the Director and his father entered the safe house, on a backwater street in a blue-collar residential neighborhood of Tel Aviv.

"Whatever that is," Zhang said, looking up from the tiles, "it smells good."

Eli set down the two shopping bags of take-out food he had purchased on the way, walked over to the table, and sat down between the two.

"Who's this?" Zhang said, using his thumb to indicate Reuben.

"I have questions," the Director said.

Zhang pursed his lips. "And I have answers—for Jason Bourne, not you."

"Bourne isn't here." Eli laid his hands flat on the table. "I will have to do."

Zhang sat back, arms crossed defensively over his chest.

Turning to Yue, the Director said, "This attitude isn't helpful for anyone—especially the two of you."

Yue eyed him for a moment, then said, "Who's the old guy?"

"My father."

Zhang guffawed. "You need your father to hold your hand?"

"He was the Director of Mossad before me. He taught me everything I know."

Zhang turned away, but Yue seemed to be considering. "Ask your first question," she said.

"Little sister!" Zhang looked scandalized.

She held up a hand to forestall his protest. "I want to hear it, Sam."

The Director opened a thick folder he had before him, ran his forefinger down the first page. "Who killed Wei-Wei?"

"A man posing as a police officer," Yue said without hesitation. "He knew that Wei-Wei had been ordered to meet Bourne at a certain tea shop at a certain time. He killed Wei-Wei, then sent a boy with a note to lure Bourne to Wei-Wei's apartment."

"What happened?"

"I killed the fake cop, Bourne witnessed it and took off after me. He caught me and, well, you know..."

Frowning in concentration, Eli flipped over a number of pages. "This man who killed Wei-Wei"—he glanced up at Zhang—"who did he work for?"

Zhang glanced over at Yue, who nodded at him ever so slightly.

"The same man who owned Wei-Wei," Zhang said. "Ouyang Jidan."

"You're saying Wei-Wei was working for Ouyang at the same time he was working for us."

"That's right."

"Then why did Ouyang have his own asset murdered?"

"He'd become a liability," Zhang said with a sigh. "Cho had men nosing around Shanghai.

Given the chance, he could have used Wei-Wei's contact with the Mossad against Ouyang."

"With any luck," the Director said, "Ouyang and Cho will eat each other alive."

"Not much chance of that."

This from Yue, small, wounded creature that she was. Even had he not been briefed by Bourne, Eli would have quickly cottoned on to the young woman's innate intelligence. Combine this with her street smarts and obvious expertise in trade-craft, and he knew he was looking at someone who could easily become a top-notch field agent, should she choose to, which, by her own admission, was highly unlikely. But then in this business you learned never to take anything for granted— especially human motivations, which were often as changeable as the weather.

"Explain," he said now.

"There are too many factions involved, too many powerful people—more powerful than either Ouyang or Cho—for that to happen. Though they hate each other, and profess to want to destroy each other, that will never happen. Each man has too much power aligned with him. It's a matter of checks and balances. Besides, with the Party Congress days away, the Politburo would never al-low that level of dissension—these days it would inevitably be picked up by the social media, then spread to the press, even against the Politburo's wishes. The Party could hardly recover from such a loss of face."

Eli considered this for some time. "Tell me, Yue, how would you disrupt the Party Congress?"

"We're kinda hungry."

She tapped her fingertips together while Eli signaled for two of their guards to bring the bags to the table and take out the food—vegetables, couscous, stewed chicken, and pots of freshly brewed tea.

They sat in silence while the food was doled out and Yue and Zhang began to eat. After a while, Eli said, "Please answer my question."

"I don't know if I can." Yue laid aside the chopsticks they had brought along with the food. She rinsed her mouth out with a swig of tea. "What I mean is, I don't know if it's possible. I mean, first you'd have to have someone who could get past all the safeguards put in place around the area, then he'd have to somehow infiltrate the venue itself." She shook her head. "It's flat-out impossible."

"You see," Reuben said softly in his son's ear, "I told you."

Christ Jesus," Maricruz breathed as she surveyed the battle site. "Now I know why you needed the services of that armorer."

Picking her way across the field strewn with blackened bodies, twisted shards of metal, and half-melted blobs of plastic, she came at length to the crisped corpse of Felipe Matamoros, left in its final grotesque pose, clawed hands raised in front of him, as if to ward off the inevitable; clothes and skin incinerated by the flames; bones protruding rudely from the blackened muscle. The fat had burned away first, leaving a nauseating stench, horribly like that of a large-scale barbecue. His nose and eyeballs had been burned away, leaving only the deep hollows seen in horror films featuring zombies. But for all that, it was clearly Matamoros, clearly the man who would be king, the man who had been reduced to the aftermath of a fire.

At length, Bourne took her elbow and gently led her away from the carnage. "This chapter of your life is over, Maricruz," he said. "Time to concentrate on the future."

"There's still Jidan to think of. I'd better call him."

Bourne handed Maricruz his mobile. "What will you tell him?"

"I have no idea." She punched in the number. "One thing's for sure, he's going to want me back right away."

"Do you think that's wise?"

She shook her head. "I don't know, but there's

a life there. I can't just jettison it." Finished dialing, she listened for him to pick up. After a moment, she frowned. "His mobile number has been disconnected. Maybe I misdialed." But when she punched in the number again and got the same result, she dialed the number of the Chinese embassy in Mexico City.

"I'd like to speak to Ambassador Liu, please...I don't care if he's in a meeting, tell him it's Maricruz Ouyang...yes, I'll hold." She closed her eyes for a moment. "Yes, I'm still here...what?...did you tell him—? Minister Ouyang Jidan's wife... what?...All right, yes, I..."

She took the phone from her ear; she looked stunned.

"What's happened?" Bourne said.

"Apparently I've become persona non grata in China," she said in a voice that seemed to come from her chest. "I've been exiled." She turned to him. "Jidan loved me; he wouldn't do this to me. He couldn't."

He said nothing, knowing she was working the situation through herself.

"He must be under orders, some form of extreme duress."

She looked to Bourne, but he deliberately kept his expression neutral.

"You don't believe that, do you?" She put her

head back, stared at the blackened sky. "Christ, the bastard. He didn't even have the guts to tell me himself."

"His attention is elsewhere."

She was shaking. "The Party Congress. That's all that's on his mind now."

"It's his future—his everything. Without maintaining his membership in the Politburo, he's finished in China, a nobody. His name will be expunged from every document he ever signed, every law he put forward. His power will evaporate as if it had never existed."

"Gone," she said. "Like I am now. From visible to invisible with the snap of two fingers."

"His use for you is over, Maricruz."

"But he loved me!" she cried to the stars gathering overhead.

Bourne led her out of the field, into the woods, where they would be safe for the time being.

She put her head down. "Now I see no one ever loved me."

"Why would you discount the people here, Maricruz? Angél, Lolita, Constanza. Their love is real; you can't buy it, which is what you've been trying to do ever since you left home. You have family now—a family that cares about you, people who want nothing more from you except to know that you love them."

She turned to him. "What about you?"

"I want something from you. I don't count."

"No, no, that's *your* problem. You made yourself invisible so you could slip through the cracks between emotions. Massively great trick, but what are you left with? Nothing. What kind of life is that?"

"The only one I know."

"Then find another." She leaned across, kissed him on the lips. She drew back, a small, wry smile on her face. "You see? You won't give yourself to anyone."

"I made that mistake once," Bourne said.

"Ah." Maricruz nodded. "At last, a clue to who you really are. Well, the next time you encounter someone—and there will come a time—someone you don't want to be without, maybe you'll leave the past behind."

"I have no past."

"Oh, but you do, Bourne. And it's a fucking heavy weight to bear. What, ten, fifteen years expanded out into a lifetime of memories anyone else would have? It's too much—too much for anyone, even a warrior like you."

"Let's get back to what I want."

"Ouyang." She'd stopped using his given name. "You can have him."

"Tell me."

"Political expediency." The bitterness in her voice was unmistakable. "The Party Congress meets in three days. It was moved from Beijing because the Politburo is afraid of demonstrations and riots. Another cultural revolution is about to happen, but this time it's coming from the bottom instead of the top."

"Do you know where the Congress is being held?"

"Beidaihe—a small seaside city in Hebei." She looked at him. "That's where Jidan will be."

"Then that's where I'm headed."

"I'm going with you."

"No, Maricruz. Your path lies elsewhere. You have your family to think of now, and the freedom for all of you only the future can bring."

"But I want to help you."

"And you will. On the way back to the city, you'll tell me everything about Ouyang Jidan—his likes, dislikes, his predilections, his fears and expertise, his friends, his enemies, and his allies."

She nodded as they began to retrace their route to the car Bourne had hijacked. "It will be my fucking pleasure." She reached into her handbag and brought out a bit of colored cardboard, handed it to Bourne. "And here's where we can start."

As Bourne took it from her, he said, "What is this?"

"Colonel Sun's diplomatic documentation. I grabbed it before I slipped out the hospital window. I think a man of your abilities will find a good use for it." She smiled. "Although it won't be any good until we find you a new face."

48

Everything is packed and ready to go, sir," the adjutant said.

Ambassador Liu nodded, distractedly. He was gathering up the last-minute items he required for the flight to Beijing, and then to Beidaihe. As he strode out of his office, down the wood-lined corridors of the embassy, he felt a swell of pride puffing up his chest. True, he was first cousin to Deng Tsu, the Patriarch; true, his mother and Deng Tsu's mother were sisters; true, it was Deng Tsu who had ensured he had received the plum assignment here in Mexico City; true, he had been Deng Tsu's eyes and ears in the drug trade, sending back detailed reports on the pipeline Ouyang Jidan had negotiated with the late Maceo Encarnación; and, true, it was he who had informed

Deng Tsu of Maricruz Ouyang's arrival, of her involvement in the cartel wars between the Sinaloa and Los Zetas; but the personal invitation to the Party Congress delivered by Liu's cousin himself was a reward beyond imagining. It surely meant an elevation in rank into the elite levels of the Chinese inner circle, where all decisions were made, the vortex of power.

He had reached the front door. One of the two armed guards flanking it was about to open it. Nodding his assent, Liu stepped forward, the wide, heavy iron door swung open, and he went down the marble steps onto the sidewalk in front of the embassy's elaborate entrance.

His adjutant hurried after him. "Sir," he said, "there's been a change of plan. You'll be making a stop before Beijing."

"What?" This news brought Liu up short. "You know I despise last-minute changes."

"Minister Ouyang's orders, sir."

"Min—"

"It *is* his plane, sir."

The ambassador sighed. "All right, all right, as long as it doesn't make us late to Beidaihe."

"Not to worry, sir," his adjutant said. "You have plenty of time."

"Where are we stopping?" Liu inquired.

"Moscow, sir. You're to take on a passenger."

"He's going to Beijing, I assume."

"Beidaihe, sir. Though technically he'll be staying on board the plane after it lands."

"Why?" the ambassador said. "What's this all about?"

"I have no idea."

"Fine." Liu made a dismissive gesture with the flat of his hand. "I always do as I'm told." He regarded the adjutant, and said with an audible trace of sarcasm, "Any other last-minute orders?"

"No, sir." The adjutant inclined his head. "Safe travels, sir."

"I'll give Minister Ouyang your regards." This last was said with a heavier layer of sarcasm.

"That would be appreciated," the adjutant said with the hint of a smirk.

Liu was so light-headed, he almost cracked his forehead on the gleaming side of the waiting SUV. Only the driver's hand on the top of his head saved him, but he was too self-absorbed to thank the man or even to register his face.

On the way to the airport, he did not glance up once from the papers Deng Tsu had asked him to bring with him—his final report on Maricruz's last known movements, whom she had been consorting with, and how a string of murders had been left in her wake, including that of Colonel Sun.

When Liu finally did glance up, he realized he

did not recognize the driver. "Where's Wen?" he said.

"Driver Wen fell ill last night," the driver said. "I'm his replacement."

"You're not even Chinese," Liu said without thinking.

"Half Chinese, actually," the driver said. "My father." He wove the car expertly through the traffic. "Do you find my Mandarin inadequate, Ambassador?"

"Not...not at all." Embarrassed, Liu lowered his gaze to his report. "Carry on."

Forty minutes later, the limo pulled into the airport's VIP area and rolled to a stop. The driver jumped out, opened the door for the ambassador, then busied himself removing the ambassador's luggage from the gaping rear of the SUV.

Ambassador Liu was welcomed aboard the diplomatic jet by a flight attendant, who tried to take the luggage from the driver. The driver refused, and the attendant shrugged—he was used to the unusual requests made by diplomats. Besides, it was less work for him. He took one last look around to make certain no one else was coming, then he trotted up the stairs and busied himself with stowing the food carts that had been loaded at the last minute.

"I'll be staying on as bodyguard," the driver said.

Startled, Liu glanced up from his reading. "I need a bodyguard on board Minister Ouyang's plane?"

"For afterward," the driver said. "In Beidaihe."

The ambassador frowned. "What is Ouyang expecting?"

"I'm simply following orders," the driver said.

"Oh, well." Liu waved a hand. "Take a seat. You might as well make yourself comfortable. It's a long flight."

When the attendant went up and down the aisle, he saw the ambassador, his work spread out around him, and his driver sitting across from him. He approached the doorway and pulled the cord, swinging the stairs up, locking them in place. Then he went up to the cockpit to inform the flight crew that they were all set.

After fetching the ambassador a glass of sherry, he went to his seat, strapped himself in, leafed through a magazine on shopping in Beijing. Five minutes later the pilot released the brakes, the plane rolled to the head of the runway, turned, and, engines ramping up, raced midway between the tiny blinking lights. They lifted off dead on time, rising above the thick, brown industrial soup of Mexico City, heading for the same thick, brown industrial soup eight thousand miles away, on the other side of the world.

* * *

Bourne sat back in the plane's plush seat and, with eyes half closed, watched Ambassador Liu's every move with hawk-like acuity. Maricruz had done an admirable job with the theatrical latex, face paint, and glue he had purchased at the actors' supply store recommended by Anunciata. There was, of course, no way to make him look Asian, but mixed race was a different story altogether. What was needed was a deft hand and hints and racial cues here and there, especially around the eyes and nose. He himself was excellent with disguises but, as it turned out, Maricruz was a magician. During the process, he could see how much pleasure she was deriving from altering his appearance so that he could slip through the concentric rings of security guarding Beidaihe.

While she was working on him, she had told him everything she knew about Ouyang, Cho Xilan, and Deng Tsu, known as the Patriarch, the leader of the historic families, who still held so much sway in modern-day China.

"*There is one other man I must tell you about,*" she had said. "*The trouble is I know next to nothing about him. His name is Kai.*"

"*Is that his family name or given name?*"

"I don't know. I've only heard Jidan call him by that name."

"Have you seen him?"

"Once, briefly. He came to the apartment. It was the dead of night. All the lights were off. I was asleep; I thought Jidan was, too, but when I turned over, he was gone. As I lay in bed, I heard voices, muffled and low. I rolled out of bed and, not even bothering to slip on a robe, I padded silently out of the bedroom.

"A single lamp was on in the entryway. I stood in the darkened living room, willing myself to become just another piece of furniture. By the lamplight, I saw the outline of Jidan's face in profile. He was speaking to a tall, thin man. From what I could see of his face it looked rich with Manchu blood. He used his hands when he spoke, which is not a typical Chinese trait. Anyway, they were extraordinary, those hands—impossibly narrow palms, long, delicate, spider-like fingers."

"What were they talking about?"

"A man. I couldn't hear his name. Maybe they never mentioned him by name. Kai said, 'It's done, neat and clean as ever.' That was the only clear sentence I heard."

"Anything else?"

"Nothing that made sense."

"What was your takeaway?"

"That Kai had killed someone, that Jidan had ordered it."

During the long flight, Bourne dreamed. He dreamed of swimming in the ocean in Caesarea. The water was as warm as blood and nearly the same color. As he moved farther and farther from shore the water changed, became less murky, turning the color of aquamarine, until it was as clear as glass.

Sand crabs scuttled across the floor of the ocean, small fish curled and snipped around his bare ankles. Seahorses hung on bits of coral, nibbling and slowly blinking at him. Gradually, he became aware that the blinking held a pattern. It was Morse code.

Follow on, the seahorses blinked in unison. *Follow on*.

What did that mean?

He struck out, following the flow of the tide. A ribbon of ink passed by below him, like an arrow, its shape distorted beneath the waves.

He followed on.

And at length, he saw her. She was lying on the bottom of the sea, arms and legs spread like a starfish. Her eyes were closed, her hair swung about her, pushed and pulled by the tide. Her lips and nails were blue.

Follow on.

He had followed on, and he had found her, not alive as he longed for her to be, but dead, as she had to be. Diving down, he unwound the necklace with the star of David he wore around his neck and gently locked it around hers. The gold six-pointed star gleamed and glittered like a real star in the night sky.

A sky that swallowed him whole.

Bourne woke with a start, his heart pounding. The sweet taste of Rebeka's breath was in his mouth, on his lips. He tried to breathe her in, but received instead the plane's flat recycled air. Dead as a doornail. Just like Rebecca. He turned his head to stare out at the nothingness through which they were passing.

He rose, went back down the aisle to the re-stroom. His rage was so powerful, so concentrated, he felt he could break the necks of everyone on the plane within a matter of minutes and still not be satisfied.

He wanted to splash cold water on his face, as if that would help dissipate the tendrils of his dream in which he was still entangled, but he did not dare disturb his makeup. Instead, he stared at his al-tered countenance, wondering who he was, where he was going, and why.

49

BEIDAIHE IS A FAMOUS and scenic summer resort located at the southwest of Qinhuangdao Municipality a few hours by rail from bustling, overcrowded Beijing. A scenic coastal village providing a soothing change from the capital's hectic pace, it encompasses both beaches and tidal woods home to an astonishing number of bird species. After the Mao Revolution in 1949, the Party leaders developed a love for the resort. Mao himself had a summer villa built there. The views of the sea are magnificent, the long stretches of beaches relaxing, and the proliferation of small coves offering perfect nesting places for any number of shorebirds.

Ouyang Jidan journeyed to Beidaihe by private train. He was accompanied in the plush car by Cho

Xilan, Deng Tsu, and Kai. Naturally, there was
also a large security contingent. The red silk seats,
the tinkling miniature chandelier, the pair of cast-
silver foo dogs all served to give the interior the
appearance of a Party conference room or a hotel
lobby.

These three men were the last people Ouyang
had imagined as his traveling companions to the
Party Congress, and after the confrontation in
Deng Tsu's limo, he made the 185-mile journey
on edge, not knowing what to expect or whom to
trust. Not that he wasn't going to get his revenge
on Cho and Deng for making him relinquish his
hold on Maricruz. The agent of this revenge was
even now on his way from Moscow.

Rageful though he was at his core, he showed
none of his bitter enmity to the men in the train
carriage. He was still coming to terms with the
reality of never seeing his wife again. It seemed
to him an absurd impossibility, an unimagin-
able loss that had altered his life forever. There
would be hell to pay, of this he was absolutely
certain.

"Now that we're all together, snug as dung bee-
tles in a rug," Deng Tsu said, "I'd like to discuss
the situation vis-à-vis Israel." He crossed one leg
over the other, Western-style. "Jidan, I believe
you're best qualified to start us off."

So this is what it boils down to, Ouyang thought. *This is what it's all about: Israel.*

"What would you have me say, Patriarch?"

"Why don't you start at the beginning?" Deng Tsu said easily.

"You remember Brigadier General Wadi Khalid, don't you, Jidan?" Cho Xilan interjected.

"Khalid was my contact inside the Syrian government."

"Oh, he was more than that," Cho said, relishing each word. "You were the architect behind what came to be called the Torture Archipelago; you taught Khalid everything he knew about torture. And you know so much, Jidan, so very, very much."

"I appreciate the compliment, Cho, but this is old news."

"And yet it's the genesis of your personal animus toward Israel and the Mossad, in particular."

This from Deng Tsu, which caused Ouyang to listen carefully to not only the words but also the intonation.

"True enough," Ouyang said, nodding. "But the Israelis were a thorn in our side even before that. Reuben Yadin, then the Director of Mossad, first spearheaded the electronic surveillance of entities in Africa and Southeast Asia controlled by us, then masterminded the first virus attacks on our military computer cores. His son, Eli, has only built upon the foundation his father put in place."

Deng Tsu shifted uneasily in his seat. There were times when his aging bones discomfited him.

"Mossad has been using a more sophisticated form of the Stuxnet worm used to periodically shut down Iran's nuclear project generators," Ouyang concluded.

"And you can't stop it," Cho Xilan said smugly.

"On the contrary, we not only have stopped it, but we have launched our own cyber counterattack against Israel. We're currently at a stalemate, but if history is any guide, that won't last long. We need more programmers, which," Ouyang emphasized, "is why I was in Shanghai." He shook his head. "What puzzles me is why Cho Xilan did his best to impede my recruitment. Don't you want us to succeed against the Israelis?"

There was silence between the men as the train rocketed along, the wheels *tick-tock*ing over the tracks like a clock, the carriage swaying gently. Ouyang noted Kai's gaze flicking back and forth between Cho and himself. Was he trying to assess the winner in this battle, or had he already been ordered to take a side by Deng Tsu? Impossible to say.

"That question is unworthy of you," Cho Xilan

said. "So far as I know, we all want the same thing."

"Then why send your people to Shanghai to spy on me?"

"Is this true?" Deng Tsu said.

"Of course not, Patriarch," Cho Xilan said.

"He's lying."

Everyone turned to look at Kai, who had spoken.

"Cho Xilan sent a young woman named Yue, along with one of his men, acting as her husband, to Shanghai."

Cho Xilan clucked his tongue. "It was a fact-finding mission, nothing more."

"Then," Kai said, "how to explain the death of your man and the disappearance of Yue?"

Cho Xilan remained as still and silent as the seat on which he sat.

"This matter," Deng Tsu said, "illustrates the time and energy wasted on this rivalry." Suddenly he sat forward. "I'll have none of it. Do you hear me? It appears to me that neither of you took to heart what I told you before we left Beijing. This distresses me greatly."

So this is to be a contest of sorts, Ouyang thought. *Will one of us be among the two members of the Politburo Standing Committee ousted at the Party Congress to whittle the committee down to seven?*

The Patriarch bent over, opened a briefcase, withdrew a slim dossier. Its cover was crimson with three diagonal black stripes in the upper right-hand corner. Top secret, highest priority. It contained a single sheet of onionskin, which Deng Tsu perused before he spoke.

"What annoys me, Cho, is that you spoke up when you should have kept your mouth shut."

Ouyang could not resist the tiniest of smiles as he registered the effect of the direct rebuke on his rival's face. If he was right about the contest, then surely he was winning. However, his elation was short-lived, because now Deng Tsu speared him with his unwavering gaze.

"Cho Xilan was wrong when he said this affair began with Brigadier General Wadi Khalid, isn't that so, Ouyang Jidan?"

Ouyang's heart seemed to freeze in his chest. It was a very bad sign when the Patriarch addressed him by his full name. He looked to the silver foo dogs, who grinned at him mindlessly, then back to the gaze that seemed to penetrate to the core of him.

"Well," Deng Tsu said authoritatively, "we are waiting for an answer." Though no further emphasis to his words was needed, he plucked the sheet of onionskin out of its jacket and held it aloft.

"No, Patriarch." Ouyang had to pause to clear his throat, which was as clotted as his emotions. "It began with Sara Yadin." He looked around the rail carriage at each man in attendance. "The Mossad agent known as Rebeka."

50

T HE MAN WHO BOARDED the plane at Moscow's
Sheremetyevo airport was shaped like a bullet,
said not a word to anyone, and had a small reinforced metal case chained to his left wrist. That he
was FSB was indisputable. Ambassador Liu eyed
him with ill-concealed terror. Bourne merely observed. He had met many men like him; he'd even
known a few.

The FSB operative looked at no one, stared
straight ahead. Just before takeoff, the attendant
made the mistake of asking if he would like something to drink. The FSB agent regarded him with a
look that backed the attendant off as if he had been
scalded by boiling water. Bourne continued to ob-
serve.

The operative wore a gray, worsted suit that fit

him well but was made of inferior materials. A thin white line where the left sleeve was attached to the body of the jacket attested to a strip of mis-sewn padding.

Half an hour after takeoff, when the plane had achieved cruising altitude, Bourne unstrapped himself, walked up the aisle to the galley, got the attendant to pour him a container of coffee, and plunked himself down into the seat next to the operative. He smelled of camphor and cheap tobacco. His cheeks were blue with stubble but his scalp was as shiny and smooth as a bowling ball.

"How's the weather in Moscow?" Bourne said in Russian.

Nothing.

"Hot or cold, it still stinks there. But at least the girls put out for people like us, eh, comrade?"

No reply.

"So how's my friend Boris?"

The operative stared at him with the same dead-fish eyes that had terrified the flight attendant.

"General Karpov," Bourne said. "Boris Illyich Karpov. Short, roly-poly fellow with an unerring political sense. Surely you've met him."

A faint flicker in those dead-fish eyes. Then a slight smile that showed feral incisors. "Please."

"He's your boss, isn't he?"

The operative went back to looking at nothing.

"If he's not, your career is screwed."

"And you would know that how?"

"I told you."

The operative grunted. "Man like you, you have no friends."

"I think," Bourne said, "you're talking about yourself."

Now the operative's eyes engaged his fully. "Fuck you, *comrade*."

"Boris and I last worked in Damascus. We were after the same terrorist, Semid Abdul-Qahhar, the head of the Munich—"

"I know who Semid Abdul-Qahhar is."

"Was. Boris and I took him out."

At this point, the operative looked at Bourne as if in an entirely new light. "If that's true—"

"It is true." Bourne went on to describe the incident in detail, leaving out only Rebeka's role in it. When he was finished, he said, "What are you doing on this flight? Delivering your package to someone in Beijing?"

"I'm going all the way to Beidaihe. You?"

"I'm taking the ambassador there," Bourne said. "Orders from Minister Ouyang. If you don't mind my saying I'm surprised a Russian is being allowed into the seaside inner sanctum."

The operative leered at Bourne with his yellow

teeth. "You know something, *comrade*, you talk too much."

Eli Yadin's daughter, Reuben Yadin's grand-daughter." The Patriarch waved the sheet of onion-skin back and forth like a flag over a battlefield. "With these people it's family—always family. Isn't that so, Ouyang Jidan?"

"That is my experience with the Mossad, Patri-arch."

"And yet you managed to entangle yourself in that family. Please enlighten us as to the circum-stances of your error." He waved the onionskin more vigorously. "And please do not omit your reason for doing so."

Ouyang stared up for a moment, as if gathering his thoughts from the curved ceiling. He began his narrative in a voice that harked back to his past. It was a lighter voice, less crusted with cyn-icism, less hardened by time. "Rebeka came to my attention almost by accident. Reading through daily intel on Syria, Iran, and Oman, I came across an item that, though brief and sketchy, piqued my interest. One of our operatives re-ported a rumor that military secrets were being stolen from Syria. Who was doing this? Was it, in fact, being done, or was it simply a rumor, one of thousands that drift through intel reports every day of the week?

"In any event, I was intrigued. If Syrian military secrets were being stolen I wanted them. I ordered this operative to investigate further. Within a week, he reported that he had discovered proof that the rumor was true. I ordered him to send me the proof, but I never heard from him again. Whether he was killed, abducted, or thrown into a Syrian prison remains an impenetrable mystery.

"I set another operative onto the case. Two weeks later, he informed me that the secrets were being transported from Syria to Oman. Where were they going from Oman? I asked him. He did not know, but he was determined to find out. Again, nothing. No follow-up, no news, no body. Nothing. He had followed the first operative into oblivion."

"That doesn't say much for your operatives, Ouyang," Cho said.

"Must I?" Deng Tsu said, turning a wrathful face to him.

Cho subsided, trying his best to become invisible.

"Please continue, Jidan," the Patriarch said in an altogether different tone of voice.

Ouyang gave the old man a deferential nod. He was determined not to look at Cho Xilan at all.

"For us, the disappearance of one operative was unusual enough. Two was unheard of. As a result, I determined to take matters into my own hands. I flew into Oman under diplomatic cover, with a legend worked up by one of my people.

"All I had to go on was a name: Fisal. Fisal was a bedouin, an itinerant merchant who traveled from country to country, buying and selling all manner of goods, legal and illegal. He knew everyone in every city in which he did business.

"It was Fisal with whom the second operative had made contact in Muscat. Fisal was still there when I arrived in the capital. Gold and diamonds were his specie of choice. Forearmed, I had plenty of both.

"It was through Fisal that I learned about Rebeka. She was a flight attendant on a regional airline, on the run from Damascus to Muscat and back again. It was she, Fisal believed, who was the courier.

"But who, I asked him, is this woman working for? Through his contacts at the airline, he had discovered her nationality to be Saudi, so she was probably working for them, though, he admitted, it could just as easily be the Americans. '*All sands shift*,' I remember him saying. '*None more so than here*.'

"I asked him to find out for me. He was reluctant,

knowing the fate of my second operative. I showed him more diamonds and we struck a deal."

For a time, Ouyang fell silent, until Deng Tsu prompted him. "And?"

By way of reply, Ouyang stood. Shrugging off his suit jacket, he folded it carefully on his seat. Then he took off his tie.

When he began to unbutton his shirt, Cho Xilan said, alarmed, "What are you doing?"

Ouyang made no reply. Instead, he finished unbuttoning his shirt. As he took it off, he turned his left side to them so they could see the three-inch scar between his second and third ribs. It was nasty looking—discolored, ropy, and raised from the rest of his flesh, as if it had been treated hastily and incompletely in the field.

"This," Ouyang said, "is where the Mossad agent Rebeka knifed me the third time we met."

51

T HERE WAS THIS one girl," Bourne said in a confidential tone of voice. "Her name was Olga. Blond, blue-eyed, from the Caucasus, in sight of the Caspian." He gave the FSB operative, who had at last confessed his name was Leonid, a knowing grin. "A robust girl, if you know what I mean." He shook his head. "Boris and I had some memorable nights with Olga and her friends. Maybe you remember her?"

"They all tend to run together, those girls," Leonid said. "Interchangeable as cogs, and about as memorable. Their intense neediness makes them ugly. All of them are steeped in poverty and ignorance, all of them think you're their ticket out. For them, you're nothing more than a rung on the ladder out of the cesspit."

That was the most Leonid had spoken at once since the plane had taken off from Sheremetyevo. For Bourne's purposes, it was a major break-through.

"There is that," he said now. "The problem: too many beautiful girls."

Leonid nodded grimly. "All wanting the same thing."

Bourne glanced down at the container he was holding. "This coffee is terrible. Tea suits me better."

"Tea would be welcome."

"A generous pour of first-rate vodka would make it perfect." Without waiting for a response Bourne rose and went back down the aisle to the galley to give his order.

The attendant brought out a large tray of small bottles, then set a pair of china cups and saucers out on the narrow counter. "Here," he said, "take your pick of vodkas while I find the tea."

On his first trip to the galley, Bourne had noted the medical cabinet that all such planes carrying dignitaries had on board. While the attendant knelt down to fetch the tea canisters from a lower drawer, Bourne rummaged through the cabinet until he found a sedative powder. He poured some into one of the cups, then added the contents of one of the small vodka bottles, stirring it with his forefinger until the powder dissolved.

"English Breakfast or Oolong?" the attendant asked.

"No Russian Caravan?"

"I'm sorry, no."

"English Breakfast will be fine," Bourne said.

Moments later he brought the teas back to Leonid, but when he handed him one cup, Leonid, looking up with a wolfish smile, said, "I'll take the other one."

Bourne handed him the cup he indicated, then sat down and began to sip his tea. Leonid, keeping his eyes on Bourne, put his lips to the rim of the cup and tasted the tea. He wrinkled his nose. "English Breakfast."

"Not Russian Caravan," Bourne said, "but at least it's brewed strong."

The two men sat in companionable silence for a time, until Bourne set aside his cup. Pressing a button on the side of his seat, he lowered the back, crossed his arms over his chest, and closed his eyes. His breathing soon slowed.

Beside him, Leonid's eyelids began to droop, his eyes losing focus. He set his cup and saucer on the seat tray and, as Bourne had done, lowered the seat back. His lids flickered closed and he was out.

Bourne counted to one hundred to be certain

Leonid had succumbed, then checked the lock on the case affixed to his wrist. It was one of those that could be opened only by a key that could not be duplicated. He set about searching Leonid for the key.

It took him some moments, but at length he found it in a thin leather case strapped to the inside of Leonid's left ankle. He was reaching for it when Leonid stirred. Bourne waited, patient, until he was certain Leonid was still deeply asleep.

Extricating the key, he fit it into the lock, turned it to the right. There was an odd sound, not of lock tumblers opening but of a mechanism arming. Bourne froze. He had encountered locks like this before. They were triggers for a booby trap set inside the case—a fail-safe mechanism to destroy the contents before it could fall into unfriendly hands.

In his experience, there were two ways to disarm the mechanism. The first was to pull out the key and reinsert it; the other was to turn the key to the left. The problem was if it was the latter, removing the key would detonate the fail-safe. Crouching down, Bourne peered more closely at the lock. He had seen one of these before—in fact, Boris had showed it to him. It was a favorite of the FSB.

He had to be right; there would be no second chance. Holding his breath, he turned the key to the left. He heard the tumblers click into place, at once disarming the fail-safe and releasing the lock. Gingerly, Bourne opened the case.

The interior was entirely made up of a thick pad of dense gray foam interspersed with lines of dull metal. In the precise center a cutout, approximately four inches by two inches, had been made. Resting in this cutout was a small rectangular object. Its metal top gleamed dully in the airplane light.

The object was made of solid lead, which could mean only one thing: It was a protective shell that contained a radioactive substance. It was far too small to be a nuclear warhead, and this tiny a bit of uranium, even if it were weapons-grade, would be useless. What then did the lead shell contain?

Bourne's mind raced back to the locking mechanism Boris had shown him. It was guarding a case not unlike this one, containing a lead shell in which resided a tiny vial of polonium-210, *"our new silent weapon of choice for assassinations,"* Boris had said. Bourne remembered the death of former FSB agent Alexander Litvinenko, who died in London of polonium poisoning after having leaked secrets to MI6. The radioactive substance had been put into his tea.

Was that what Leonid was bringing into the Party Congress? Why? On whose orders? Bourne relocked the case with the same care with which he had opened it, returned the key to its miniature "holster," and, lying back in his seat, closed his eyes.

Behind lowered lids he considered the possibilities. This plane belonged to Minister Ouyang, so there was a high probability that it was Ouyang who had ordered the polonium-210. Who was it for? The obvious choice was Cho Xilan, his nemesis, but Bourne knew that choices like these weren't often obvious.

With an iron will, he cleared his mind of questions he could not as yet answer. He detached it from the moorings of consciousness, and, soon enough, drifted off to sleep.

The first time I met Rebeka, she was curious as well as courteous," Ouyang said as he slipped on his shirt and began to button it up. "The second time, we had dinner, and a more charming companion could not be imagined." He wrapped his tie around his neck and slipped it underneath his collar. "The third time, she almost killed me."

Having neatly knotted the tie, he put on his suit jacket, and sat. "That she didn't succeed was a simple matter of happenstance."

"Blind luck," Cho said sourly.

"If you wish." Ouyang sat back, shot his cuffs,

resettling himself. "There is no easy way to describe this creature. She was far too complex a personality for that. And perplexing."

"She caught you off guard," the Patriarch said.

"This was before I understood what she was."

"You were never able to understand her."

"No one did. She's inscrutable." Ouyang picked a piece of lint off the sleeve of his jacket. "As to her being a field courier, I allowed myself to be swayed by her gender. I didn't credit her enough. I treated her with disdain."

"She made you pay for your arrogance." Deng Tsu slid the onionskin back into its file, stowed it away in his briefcase. "You couldn't leave well enough alone. You had to have your revenge. You had her killed in Mexico City when she was with Jason Bourne. You had her knifed in the side, as she had knifed you." Deng shook his head. "So began Mossad's personal feud with you. And all for a courier, Jidan." He sighed. "You have put us in a perilous situation."

"With respect, Patriarch, I have done nothing of the kind," Ouyang said. "Eli Yadin's increasing desperation to get to me has finally led him to make a mistake. He has enlisted Jason Bourne to be his proxy."

"How has he managed that?" the Patriarch said.

"Ever since he was manipulated by the American

Central Intelligence Agency, Bourne notoriously hates the clandestine services."

"Eli Yadin is smarter than the CIA. He never would have been able to persuade Bourne to do his bidding if Rebeka hadn't been murdered. Eli is canny enough to know that Bourne will only respond to personal loss. Rest assured, it will be Bourne who comes after me."

Cho Xilan shook his head. "How is this good news?"

"The devil you know." Ouyang crossed one leg over the other. "Instead of being faced with the daunting task of monitoring every member of Mossad's Kidon section, I can concentrate on Bourne. Best of all, I don't have to lift a finger because I know he'll come to me."

"What? In Beidaihe?" Cho laughed uneasily. "Surely you're joking."

"He isn't," Deng Tsu said.

"But Bourne is a Westerner," Cho protested. "No Westerner will be allowed within fifty miles of Beidaihe."

"Clearly, Jidan knows Bourne better than you do, Cho Xilan. Have a care."

"Bourne is a master of infiltration and assassination." Ouyang put his hands together, much in the manner of a priest at prayer. "But I am forewarned—and I am prepared."

52

THE SEAT BELT LIGHT came on as the plane headed into the old military airport outside of Beidaihe. The new, ultramodern civilian airport was still a year away from completion. Bourne could see its skeleton as they overflew it, continuing their descent.

Leonid awoke when the attendant touched him on the shoulder and indicated that he needed to fasten his seat belt and put his seat back in the upright position. Some time ago, he had come along and taken away their cups and saucers.

The first thing Leonid did, even before locking himself in, was to check the integrity of his case. Confirming that all was as he had left it, he buckled up and looked out the window.

"Been to China before?" Bourne asked.

"Who would want to come here?" Leonid said. "The women..." He shuddered.

"Stick with me. I know where all the best spots are."

"I'm not getting off the plane, thank fuck. My meeting's here on board. Then, the moment the crew gets some sleep and the plane's refueled, it's back to Moscow for me."

The shadowy outlines of the inland side of Beidaihe became clearer as the plane came in for a landing. Leonid's gaze seemed pinned to the view, though Bourne felt certain it was something else he was looking at.

At length, Leonid said, "There comes a time when you have traveled so far from your beginning it seems to belong to another person. Then you travel farther, and that beginning fades completely from memory, and there you are, left stranded on a farther shore."

"I expect all the passengers on this plane are on a farther shore."

Leonid turned to Bourne, studying him. "If circumstances change and you want to join me on the return flight—" He held out a slip of paper with a number on it. "I'll hold departure for you." He smiled—the first physical sign of a normal human emotion he had shown.

* * *

When Ouyang arrived in Beidaihe, he and his traveling companions were immediately transported via limousine to the compound Mao had had built for his summer sojourns. The Patriarch and the president installed themselves in opposite wings of the sprawling main villa. There were six villas in the compound, the main compound's inner sanctum, all built on the model of Russian seaside dachas.

Ouyang and Cho Xilan had their own satellite villas. Kai stayed with the Patriarch, as if they were old friends, increasing Ouyang's suspicions. Kai had asked several days ago how the Patriarch was doing, as if he had had no recent contact with him. Now Ouyang knew the truth, and he felt the bitter gall of betrayal. Kai lied as a way of life, but why had Kai lied to him, the man whom he presumably worked for, the man whose wet work he did? Which led him to the billion-yuan question:

Why was Kai here?

Unfortunately, Ouyang hadn't the time to contemplate Deng's internecine agenda. He had prearranged to have a car pick him up outside his villa; he didn't want to use one of the military jeeps at his disposal. The car was waiting for him when he arrived, and after he had set down his luggage in the entryway for his people to put away as instructed, he went back out, down the steps, and ducked into the backseat.

It took off the moment he was seated. As they drove through the outer compound, Ouyang saw how well the small army of architects and builders had re-created the Great Hall of the People in Beijing where the Congress was normally held. No one would miss the Congress in Beijing this year, especially not with the very real specter of protests.

For the past fifteen months, he, as well as the other Politburo members and their staffs, had been closely monitoring Weibo, the leading Chinese microblogging website. The traffic, repeatedly calling for multiple protests both outside the Great Hall of the People and along the major thoroughfares leading to the hall, had reached a pitch that had alarmed the elite.

The decision to move the Congress to Beidaihe had not been difficult. It was November—deep into the off season for the resort. And it would hardly be difficult to block access to the compound, whereas managing such a feat in Beijing would mean calling out the army. With the entire world watching, that would lose the ruling party immeasurable face.

Within fifteen minutes Ouyang's car had reached the military airport, which was, not to put too fine a point on it, somewhat of a shambles. All the effort in the area was on the new civilian airport, leaving this one to slowly rust away in the shadow of its past.

The car slowed, came to a stop parallel to his airplane. He got out, hurried across the tarmac and up the folding stairway, into the interior.

He found Leonid intent on his meal. Without preamble, Ouyang sat on the seat across from him.

"Enjoying yourself, I see."

"I might as well," the courier replied. "There isn't much else to do around here." He looked around. "The crew are sacked out for the next four or five hours, the plane is being refueled, and I'm waiting for Minister Ouyang."

"I'm Minister Ouyang."

"Prove it."

The tone was so peremptory and lacking in respect, Ouyang stiffened. *But then*, he reasoned, *this is a Russian. Moreover, he's FSB, where you get reprimanded for displaying good manners.*

When Ouyang made no reply, Leonid looked up from his rapidly disappearing food and rattled the chain locked onto his wrist. "With what I've got, I'm not about to hand it over to just anyone claiming to be Minister Ouyang."

"They didn't give you a code phrase?"

"They did not."

"But they must have showed you a photo of me."

The courier smirked. "They sure did. You look like the fellow, but..."

Ouyang made a sound in the back of his throat, produced his Party card, and handed it over.

Leonid studied it as if it were an abstract painting he was trying to decode. At length, he looked at Ouyang. But instead of handing back the card, he held it up, flicking it back and forth. "Minister Ouyang," he said, "what are you without this card?"

Ouyang stared at him, barely restraining himself from launching out of his seat.

Leonid shrugged. "It's just a question." He handed back the card.

Ouyang reached out for it, but let it go the moment the courier did. The card fluttered to the floor of the plane.

"Pick it up," Ouyang said.

"Is there a problem?"

"You dropped it. Now pick it up."

Leonid appeared about to reply, then thought better of it. He smiled thinly, bent down, and retrieved the card. When he held it out, Ouyang took it, slowly and deliberately.

"Now," he said, "the item."

Leonid never took his eyes off Ouyang as he unlocked the bracelet around his wrist. He pushed the case across the floor to a place between the Minister's knees.

Ouyang did not move a muscle. "Open it."

Leonid held out the key. "Not in my job description."

"Humor me."

Several moments of silence were followed by a shrug from Leonid. He hoisted the case flat on his lap. Inserting the key in the lock, he said, "Watch."

He turned the key first to the right, then to the left. The top sprang open, and Ouyang peered inside.

"That's it?"

"That's it," Leonid affirmed.

"It's very small."

"You wouldn't want to have possession of any more of it, believe me."

Ouyang nodded. "On that point, at least, we can agree."

A moment."

Kai, a step from walking out the door of the lavish villa, turned back to Deng Tsu.

"Close the door," the Patriarch said.

Kai complied, then picked his way across the exquisite Isfahan carpet to where the Patriarch stood.

Deng Tsu gestured, and the two men sat on fac-

ing wooden, highly lacquered Mandarin chairs.
Kai was acutely aware that the room was devoid of
the Patriarch's ubiquitous bodyguards. No tea being brewed and served: another oddity. Light spun
off Deng Tsu's black-dyed hair as if it were made
of acrylic.

"What are Minister Ouyang's plans regarding Jason Bourne?"

Kai was a little taken aback. "Do you credit his
contention that Bourne will seek to infiltrate our
compound?"

"Please answer the question."

"I don't know."

Deng Tsu's eyes narrowed. "That hardly seems
possible, given your relationship with him."

"I think today that relationship has been rup-
tured."

"I sincerely hope so." The Patriarch looked
searchingly at Kai. "If Minister Ouyang has any
hope of rising out of the Standing Committee into
a true leadership position he cannot have any contact with you. He cannot use you as he has done in
the past—the danger is too great for all of us, including you." He laced his fingers together. "You
understand."

Kai felt the strong beating of his heart. It seemed
to echo in his throat, like a fluttering bird he had
swallowed whole. "Perfectly."

"Good. As for Minister Ouyang's plans..."

"I am not privy to them."

"That is troubling. You were my only window."

Kai took a breath, wondering which way Deng wanted him to go. "I would have no trouble monitoring the situation."

"Well," Deng Tsu said, "that would put my mind at ease."

Kai smiled.

When he was alone, Deng drew his briefcase onto his lap and opened it. Inside was a locked compartment, which he opened by pressing his thumb onto the pad of a fingerprint reader. The interior of the compartment consisted of six pockets, each holding a phone—three mobiles, three satellite. Deng plucked the one from the sixth pocket—a satphone—and turned it on. Each phone had only one number stored in its memory.

When it had booted up, he tapped in the code that unlocked the phone, then pressed the numeral 5. Placing the phone against his ear, he listened to the hollow electronic clicks—a kind of music—as the scrambler kicked in. A moment later the line connected, ringing distantly, as if through water.

"Pasha," he said, "has the package been delivered?"

Pavel Mikhailevich Zhukov, colonel in the FSB, said, "My good friend, I sent my best man. Leonid has never let me down."

"Nevertheless," Deng said, relentless, "you have heard from him."

"I have. Minister Ouyang has the case containing the payload."

"And this payload is as we discussed?"

"Yes. A special isotope of polonium, one that is fast acting. The victim will begin to experience the deleterious effects within hours after ingestion; most likely he'll be dead by tomorrow morning or, at the very least, incapacitated."

"Meaning he won't under any circumstances be able to attend the Congress."

"If the payload is delivered accurately." A slight pause. "Tsu, you sound anxious."

Deng Tsu looked out the villa window, at the broad back of one of his bodyguards. "Minister Ouyang must never know my hand in guiding his plan."

"This was agreed upon at the outset," Pasha said. "You *are* jumpy."

"The course for the next ten years is to be decided over the next several days," Deng said snappishly. "There is a degree of tension to every move made now, no matter how seemingly inconsequential."

"This particular move is anything but inconsequential."

Deng tilted his head back as if he could see the stars of a velvety night sky, and closed his eyes. "It will cement my legacy for the next decade."

"It will clamp down on your restless populace, which has become decadent and a nuisance due to the Western plague of social media."

"A week after the new general secretary is anointed, he will announce reforms that will resonate with the populace—cutting down on meetings, the length of those meetings, feasts, flower arrangements, expensive cars and homes, frivolous or showy spending—but for us will mean nothing. Nothing substantive will change."

"Except cementing the link between China and elements within Russia that has for decades been crumbling into disuse," Pasha said.

Deng Tsu thought briefly of Jason Bourne, but knew that even if Ouyang's fixation on the rogue agent had a basis in fact, if against all logic Bourne were to somehow infiltrate the compound, Kai would put an end to him once and for all.

53

PROTECTED BY TIERS of diplomatic protocol, Bourne accompanied Ambassador Liu through the massive gates of the Party compound, entering the movable inner sanctum of the modern-day Middle Kingdom. The sight of the opulent villas set on cliffs overlooking Beidaihe's beaches and the Bohai Sea was so transporting it seemed to exist in some other, less politically oppressive country.

The streets between villas were alive with soldiers, both on foot and in jeeps, some with dogs, others with machine pistols, but despite the manpower and armament there was no discernible tension, which seemed to have been left behind in Beijing.

Ambassador Liu had been assigned a relatively modest villa only steps away, the ambassador informed Bourne with ill-concealed pride, from the far larger one housing Minister Ouyang and his staff.

Bourne carried the ambassador's luggage up the steps and into the villa.

"I won't be needing you from now on," Liu informed him in his typical officious manner.

"I am meant to guard you, Ambassador."

"I have my own security in place here. Return to the plane, which is your transport. I, myself, will be going on to Beijing after the Congress to meet with the new leaders and map out any changes in foreign policy before I return to Mexico City."

Dismissed, Bourne was freed from any duties associated with the ambassador, and he immediately exited the villa to begin work on his own agenda, which was focused solely on Ouyang Jidan.

Sit down," Minister Ouyang said. "Make yourself comfortable while I brew the tea. I have some beautiful Long Jing I brought with me."

Cho Xilan stood in the living area of the villa assigned to Ouyang, watching Ouyang's back as he prepared the tea at a sideboard. The space was studded with six thick columns of highly polished cedar, each one containing carvings of two animals of the Chinese zodiac. Low divans, tables, and chairs were placed in precise places and at precise angles in accordance with the feng shui master who had been in charge of situating the villas and aligning the furnishings in their interior.

"The Dragon Well would be much appreciated," Cho said in an uncertain voice.

Noting his tone, Ouyang turned and, smiling, said, "There's no point to us being formal with each other, Xilan."

"I'm afraid I don't know how else to act."

Ouyang nodded knowingly. "That comes from being at each other's throats for too long."

"It comes from wanting different paths for the future of China."

Again his tone, now steely, gave Ouyang pause. "The Patriarch has given us a directive. Now neither of our envisioned paths for China is relevant. Together we must forge a third path, a middle ground, and we must accomplish this before the Congress opens tomorrow morning."

Cho Xilan pursed his lips. Even, as now, when in Western attire, he seemed to be dressed in traditional Chinese robes. "Do you find this a realistic goal?"

"Anything is possible," Ouyang said, "between us."

"Then let me be frank, Minister Ouyang. I doubt that we can."

"We certainly can't, Xilan, if we don't try."

Ouyang turned back and, careful as a handler of mercury, poured the polonium into one of the two cups he had laid out on the sideboard. Just a couple of drops, the courier had said, but Ouyang had other ideas. The polonium dribbled out like liquor.

"If we don't try, Xilan, what will we tell the Patriarch tonight at the banquet?"

The water, just under boiling, was at the right temperature. Ouyang poured it into the teapot into which he had spooned the Dragon Well tea leaves. Now to let it brew for three minutes, no more, no less. Maricruz used to brew his tea. It never ceased to amaze him how a Westerner had learned to brew each kind of tea separately. It was as if she were born with the understanding. This talent, among many others, he missed with a terrifying fire that branded itself across his mind's eye. Never to hold her again, never to feel her lips searching his body for all the secret places she knew gave him pleasure. Never to hear her salacious whispers in his ear as she lifted her dress around her sleek, powerful thighs to straddle him. Never to plunge into her secret grotto, never to feel the exquisite ecstasy only she could bring him. As if of their own volition, his fingers curled into fists. How he despised everyone around him, none more than this piece of shit polluting the very air he breathed!

"I'll inform the Patriarch that we tried and failed."

"You propose we lie to Deng Tsu?"

Cho barked an unpleasant laugh. "As if you've never done that before."

Ouyang turned back to him. "You're making this exceedingly difficult."

"Minister, I am making it as difficult as it needs to be." He spread his hands. "On the matter of China's future, I simply refuse to compromise."

Ouyang frowned. "Do you understand the gravity of your position, the gravity of the cracks in the system? Do you want to be plowed under?"

"By whom? The masses? Don't be absurd."

"They wield power now."

"That so-called power is an illusion."

"Ah." Ouyang brightened. "Then this discussion *is* about self-interest."

"Feel better now that we're on your home turf, Minister?"

Ouyang grasped for a semblance of tranquillity, but Maricruz was gone—lost to him on the other side of the world. He felt like an entrained oxen suddenly woken up to the misery of his imprisoned life. His position was intolerable.

"Time for tea," he said in as steady a voice as he could manage.

He poured the Dragon Well into the two cups,

careful not to spill a drop. Then he brought them over to Cho Xilan. He held out the one laced with the polonium, and his implacable adversary took it.

Ouyang raised his cup. "To self-interest."

"To stability for the Middle Kingdom."

He watched over the lip of his cup as Cho sipped the poisoned tea. A tiny circle of calmness, if not serenity, in the maelstrom of his emotions lapped at him at the thought of the horrible death awaiting his rival.

"Can we at least sit down and be civil to each other," he said, "if nothing else?"

"I prefer to remain standing," Cho Xilan said, reflecting his inflexible stance, "but by all means sit if you're weary."

Ouyang then experienced a moment when he imagined himself leaping at Cho, digging his thumbs into his eyes until they turned to jelly. How satisfying that would be! How utterly delicious! Then the crest of the rage passed, leaving him certain that sticking to his plan was the best course of action.

"The only thing I'm weary of, Xilan, is your intransigence."

"Intransigence is the only way to turn one's beliefs into reality. No matter the people left in its wake, the sword must be wielded."

"And this sword of yours will be wielded—"

"Tomorrow at the start of the Congress."

"Why are you telling me this?"

"Because it pleases me. Because those who wish to destabilize China through change will be not only defeated but annihilated. Because you can't stop it," Cho said. "The train has already left the station."

Something in his tone made the hairs at the back of Ouyang's neck stir, but he showed none of his uneasiness. "Well, here's to ambition." He tipped his cup. "Let us finish our tea and go our separate ways."

Cho nodded, drained his cup, and set it down. "The next time we see each other my victory will be complete."

By the time Bourne saw Cho Xilan exit Ouyang's villa he was dressed in the uniform of the patrolling guard he had overpowered. Creeping up behind him, he had jammed the crook of his right arm against the guard's throat, thus preventing him from uttering a sound. A moment later, the guard was unconscious. Bourne had dragged his body into a clump of evergreen bushes, stripped him of not only his uniform, but his weapons and his identification.

He then crossed the road to Ouyang's villa. Outside two guards stood, automatic weapons slung across their chests. Bourne trotted up the steps and, as they closed ranks in front of him, drew out a slip of paper.

"Message from Deng Tsu," he said in idiomatic Mandarin, "for Minister Ouyang."

"I'll take it," the guard on the left said, holding out his hand.

Bourne shook his head. "My orders are to deliver it to Minister Ouyang in person."

"Have you met the Minister?" the left-hand guard said. "Do you know what he looks like?"

"I do."

"We wouldn't want you to deliver your message to the wrong individual."

"I told you—"

A pinprick on the side of his neck caused Bourne to turn. It was a slow-motion turn, taking all his effort. He stared into a face unknown to him. He opened his mouth, but his blood seemed to have congealed into ice. He tried to gesture, but this seemed to overbalance him, and he fell into a sunless void.

54

A JADE DRAGON, translucent green, pale as shallow water, stared at him with a baleful eye that seemed nevertheless curious. It was curious as to where he was and what he would do next. The dragon spoke to him, but its voice never seemed to penetrate the fog swirling around him. It was the mist of dreams that had followed him out of unconsciousness into this place of talking dragons and Ming vases shot with blue chrysanthemums and more dragons, ethereally floating between clouds that looked like sticky buns. He could smell incense, but it couldn't quite mask the stench of alcohol and medication. His head hung on his chest and he half coughed, half gagged.

"He's awake, Minister," someone above him said.

"Leave us." Even through the fog, he recognized Ouyang Jidan's voice.

"But, Minister—"

"I said leave us!"

The military tramp of booted feet over the floor, then the sounds of a door opening and closing.

Apart from the call of the birds from outside, silence.

Then, abruptly, a hand was placed under his chin, and Bourne found himself looking into the eyes of Ouyang Jidan.

A bitter smile split Ouyang's face. "I've been anticipating this meeting ever since Rebeka died in the back of the taxi you were desperately driving around in Mexico City." The smile widened. "She bled out, Bourne, while you watched, helpless as a baby. My only regret is that I wasn't there to see it."

Bourne's eyes lost focus for a moment, and Ouyang slapped him hard across the cheek.

"That woman caused me an endless amount of grief. She was always one step ahead of me. How did she do that? Tell me."

Bourne looked at him. Ouyang seemed to be wavering through a candle flame, going in and out of focus. *What did they inject me with?* he asked himself. He felt the sluggishness of his pulse, the slow thoughtless beat of his heart, and he began to work

on overcoming them. That would require adrenaline and lots of water to flush the drugs from his
system. He licked his dry lips.

"Ah, yes, what a poor host I have become."
Ouyang moved away from him toward a sideboard. "I have just the thing to return you to health.
The best Dragon Well tea. It's your good fortune
that I already have brewed a pot."

He returned to Bourne, who now realized he was
strapped to a chair, hands tied behind his back.
Just in front of him was a low lacquer table on
which Ouyang set down the two translucent cups
of tea. Ouyang sat to Bourne's left, hands clasped
together like a priest.

"We have a long history, you and I. We're bound
together with the agent named Rebeka. One of you
is dead; soon the other will be." He cocked his
head. "The only reason you aren't dead now is that
I want something from you."

Bourne looked at the tea in its cup. He remembered the polonium. His interior processes were
slowly breaking free of the drug's shackles.

"I want you to tell me about Rebeka. I want to
know what I missed. I want to know what made
her so dangerous."

A small smile came to Bourne's parched lips.

Ouyang frowned. "I find nothing funny in your
situation."

"I think I know something you don't," Bourne said. "Especially about Rebeka."

Ouyang leaned in. "And that's another thing. I'm interested in why you still call her by her field name. Surely she must have confided her real name."

Bourne said nothing.

"So as it turns out, we both know something about Rebeka the other does not. Would you agree to an exchange of information?"

"Why should I? Either way, you're going to kill me."

"On the other hand, you'll go to your grave knowing Rebeka's real identity. I know that must have meaning for you, Bourne. Even a man like you."

"A man like me?"

"A man without human connection, a man who has risen above day-to-day concerns, a man at home in the shadows at the margins of the world." He tapped his fingertips together. "Like me."

Picking up one of the teacups, he held it beneath Bourne's mouth. "Now a drink of tea, and then the exchange will begin." The edge of the cup was about to touch Bourne's lower lip. "What d'you say?"

"You don't want to know about Rebeka; it's

Maricruz you want to know about—what happened to her, how badly she's hurt."

Despite his best effort, a tremor of intent passed through Ouyang, and for the space of a heartbeat his eyes flickered closed. Then he recovered. "She's dead to me."

"Just as well," Bourne said. "She's dead for real. She got caught in a crossfire between Los Zetas and the Sinaloa."

Ouyang put down the teacup. "You're lying."

"What d'you care? She's dead to you."

The two men glared at each other without another word being said.

At length, an evil spark flickered in Ouyang's eyes. "Well then, we have something else in common. The women we loved are dead." The corners of his mouth turned up, but there was only a perverted hint of a smile. "Yes, I know you loved Rebeka. That provided me with added incentive to have her killed." He leaned forward. "My only regret is that I didn't have the chance to torture her before she died."

Bourne, who had been calculating the vectors ever since his mind had begun to clear, now closed his eyes, conjuring the dimensions of the room, the table in front of him, the angle of Ouyang's chair in relation to his.

In the next blink of an eye three things happened

simultaneously: Bourne moved his head back, his eyes flew open, and his left leg upended the table, so that the pot, tea, the table itself flipped up and over onto Minister Ouyang.

The edge of the table caught Ouyang on the point of his chin. He toppled over backward and lay unmoving. Unlocking his arms from the chair back, Bourne picked his way into the kitchen. Grabbing a carving knife out of a wooden rack, he reversed it in his right hand, began to methodically saw through the ropes that bound his hands together. The instant they were free, he sprinted back into the living room. Everything was where he had left it, except Ouyang, who was nowhere to be seen.

Cho Xilan, looking out at the sea, stood on the deck of his villa. At either end of the deck was an armed soldier, the presence of whom made him feel queasy in the pit of his stomach. The soldiers took their orders from Deng Tsu, who had pledged to personally protect both him and Minister Ouyang. Cho, who longed for his vision of the old China, the real Middle Kingdom, chafed at the inexorable march of time. He imagined Deng Tsu wished to engender this very unease in him as a reminder of who held all the cards. But Cho had amassed an unshakable coalition of like-minded

Politburo members that, he was certain, even the Patriarch and his coalition of ancients and younger members could not stand against.

Still, he had felt a chill enter his body the moment he had stepped off the special train and been whisked into the compound at Beidaihe. That chill had now entered his bones, and would not be dislodged despite his best efforts. He thought of Wan, his son of seven years. Wan was a great birder. He and Xilan would go birding every other Sunday, starting out before sunrise, light packs on their backs, treading their way through forests, across streams, up hillocks, and into swales thick with marshy undergrowth.

Wan had been most excited when he had learned his father was going to Beidaihe, and had begged him to take him along. Beidaihe was a birder's paradise, even at this bleak time of year. Shorebirds, terns, and gulls abounded. Inland, he might come across Siberian rubythroats, Siberian blue robins, and others. But he most fervently wished to capture the images of the Chinese grosbeak and the large hawk-cuckoo, photos of which Wan would prize most highly.

That was why Cho had brought a fine digital camera, having promised his son he'd take time out from work to digitally capture as many birds as he could. Even though he was tired, even though it was late in the afternoon, he determined to make good on that promise. To him, his promise to Wan was no less important than the promise he'd made himself to be the guardian of the Middle Kingdom's new path going forward. If no one else would speak for the people of China, it would be him. He wasn't afraid of standing up and speaking within the Congress's conclave. He had the votes, he had the backing. He had made himself invulnerable to Deng Tsu's disgustingly cynical machinations that would inevitably lead to the demise of the Middle Kingdom. He wanted a stable future for Wan and Wan's children still to come.

Lacing on hiking boots, donning a light windbreaker, he took Wan's camera and headed down the wooden stairs to the seashore. An onshore wind ruffled his hair, scrubbed his face clean of the cares of civilization. A bird lifted off from the place where sea met sand, soaring across his vision, and all at once he understood with an immense clarity his son's fierce love of birds. How free they were! Masters of sea, sky, and land, they went where they wanted, when they wanted.

The slanted light was coming from behind him, and he lifted the camera to his face, staring at reality through the view screen. Over the next hour, he took many photos of myriad birds, all of which, he was sure, would thrill Wan. By that time the light was falling into the sea and shadows lengthened across the shore, distorting its contours.

As he turned to retrace his steps he felt a heaviness in his chest, a difficulty breathing. He slowed his pace so that by the time he reached the wooden stairs that would take him back to his villa, he was walking very slowly, indeed.

He grasped the railing, almost pulling himself up. But a third of the way to the top, his right foot missed a tread, and he slipped backward. Arms pinwheeling, he fell into the sand.

Stunned and somewhat afraid, he lay, staring up into the rapidly darkening sky. He heard the surf rush toward him and then, as if fearful of touching him, retreat, sinking back into the black sand, leaving only a ruffle of dirty white foam speckled with minute sea life. A crab emerged from the damp sand, scuttled to feast on the foam. When it was done, it headed toward where Cho lay.

One leg was still on the lowest tread of the stairs, twisted but not broken. He felt no pain in his legs, but his chest seemed to be seized by a giant fist. All at once his stomach rebelled, he turned his head to the side and vomited.

He tried to pull himself to his feet, but he lacked the strength. In the last of the light, he saw Wan's camera half buried in the sand where it had fallen. He turned on his side, one hand reaching out to scrabble for it. At that moment something let loose in his bowels and diarrhea spilled out of him, immersing him in a foul stench.

Tears came to his eyes. They were curiously heavy and, though he could not be certain, appeared to have the same consistency as mercury.

Ouyang's mouth filled with the salty, coppery taste of his own blood. He wiped blood off his lips, as offended as if it were a gobbet of sputum. His head spun and he fought to think clearly. Bourne was free. All he had to do now was call his guards. They would find him, surround him, and shoot him dead. But maybe not. And in any event, that wasn't what he wanted. The almost mystical victories Bourne had pulled off in the field were still vivid in Ouyang's mind, not the least of which was the assassination of Brigadier General Wadi Khalid. Khalid had been the perfect mark for Ouyang—he was greedy and corrupt, but he had an insatiable appetite for underage boys, a commodity in short supply in his circles, though not in Ouyang's. His relationship with Khalid had been a particularly fruitful one until Bourne had cut it short in the full flower of its success. The military secrets Ouyang had obtained from Khalid had, in good measure, been responsible for

Ouyang's election to the Politburo Standing Committee.

And then there was the time in Rome, when Bourne's interference had not only snatched Rebeka away from him but also murdered three of his men, a loss of face difficult to overcome. Colonel Sun, who had run that mission, was dead, too, at the hands of Jason Bourne.

Now, as he grabbed his shining steel *jian*, he removed his mind from everyday considerations. He sank deeper and deeper into that state he had perfected within the precincts of Kunlun Mountain Fist; slowly, inexorably, he gathered the wushun magic around him until the layers of strength and victory made him invulnerable.

Then, crouched and barefoot, he went hunting for Bourne.

Bourne, aware the guards had been alerted by the table's crash, had returned to the kitchen. Searching under the sink, he found bottles of ammonia and bleach. He poured one into an empty glass jar, then the other, and quickly screwed on the lid. The toxic chloramine gas swirled around the top half of the sealed jar.

Behind him, he heard the sound of boots running toward him. Voices shouted at him—he counted three—but he waited until the guards were all in the kitchen before he turned. Their automatic weapons were leveled at him. They were shouting at him, but two were speaking at once, and their orders weren't clear.

Bourne slowly lifted his right hand above his head, drawing their attention, then he swung the jar from behind his back, held his breath as he hurled it at the floor. The glass cracked and the thick vapor escaped its prison, rising up toward the soldiers' faces. They reared back, but too late. They had already inhaled the toxic fumes.

Bourne sprinted forward, pushed past them, through the living room and down a short hall that led to the sleeping quarters. Behind him, the soldiers were dead or dying before they hit the floor. He would dearly have liked to grab one of their automatic weapons, but the chloramine gas was notorious for clinging to metal surfaces, especially oiled ones.

Ahead of him the hallway split into a T—left and right presumably led to separate en suite bedrooms on either side of the villa. Bourne turned right, went silently down the short hall. The bedroom door was open, and he could see a wide swath of it without entering. Pushing the door back until the inner knob struck the wall, he went in. Both the bedroom and the bath were empty, but he saw a small stand, lacquered black, which was also empty. He knew it held a kind of sword known as a *jian*. Maricruz had told him that Ouyang was a fifteenth-level master of Kunlun Mountain Fist wushun. In the bathroom, he found a straight razor, which he pocketed.

He went back down the hallway, past the base of the T, heading toward the second bedroom. Two doors on the left, one on the right were narrower than room doors and most likely opened onto closets. He tested his theory and found he was correct. One contained linens and towels. Grabbing a hand towel, he wrapped it around his left forearm.

Again, using the method he employed in the first bedroom, he pushed open the door all the way to make sure Ouyang wasn't standing behind it. The bedroom, which looked like the mirror image of the first, stood empty, as did the closet. There was only the bathroom to check.

There he found a pebbled-glass window as tall as a man, a shower behind a glass door, a Western-style toilet beside a sink, a stack of large bath towels atop a small glass-and-metal table. That was it. Ouyang wasn't in here, either.

Bourne waited a moment to see if he could discern movement behind the pebbled-glass window, but not even the shadow of a passing bird showed itself. This shower was contained in a bathtub, which was concealed by a vinyl curtain hanging from a metal rod.

Taking a step toward it, Bourne pulled it back from left to right. Ouyang, who had pressed himself back against the side wall of the shower, sprang at Bourne, the *jian* held before him in the Fire Mountain grip.

55

BOURNE FLEXED HIS protected left forearm, but the strike by the *jian* was a feint. The edge of Ouyang's hand slammed into his shoulder. He staggered back, expecting Ouyang to come after him, to allow him to break inside his defenses, but instead Ouyang hung back, his feet solidly on the floor. Sacred Stone Form.

For the space of several heartbeats, the two men faced off, still and silent, sizing each other up.

Then, as if he were made of air, Ouyang slid forward with such breathtaking speed he was inside the span of Bourne's hands. The *jian* flashed out, carving an arc through Bourne's uniform and into the flesh on the left side of his chest. Hot blood ran down Bourne's front, darkening the tunic.

He fought off Ouyang, only to have Ouyang

spring in again. This time the point of the *jian* flicked a circle of flesh from Bourne's right shoulder.

"We can keep this up all evening," Ouyang said. "Death by a thousand cuts. You'll bleed out just like Rebeka."

Bourne flicked open the straight razor, which only made Ouyang laugh.

"Please," he said, "you're making a mockery of your demise."

Ouyang's *jian* was thirty inches long and double-bladed, far more deadly than Bourne's straight razor.

Locking the blade in place, Bourne made a run at Ouyang. Ouyang flicked the *jian*, using the White Snake Straight Sword Form. This time Bourne was ready, lunging down and away on his front leg, stabbing diagonally upward toward Ouyang's belly. The tip of the razor's blade severed a piece of cloth from Ouyang's jacket, forcing him to step back into the tub.

Bourne wasted no time, bringing a flurry of short sharp stabs to Ouyang, in the Seven Stars Form. Ouyang, momentarily startled, failed to block the fourth of the strikes, and the razor blade cut horizontally across his white shirt, immediately staining it with a crimson line that expanded outward on either side of the cut.

Pent up in the small box of the bathtub, Ouyang found himself at a disadvantage. White Snake Form required long, sweeping passes of the *jian* in order to be effective. The tile walls cut off his best attacks and parries.

Dropping his *jian*, Ouyang switched to the open-hand Red Phoenix Form: his forearms vertical, like a pair of columns protecting either side of his body. He stamped his left foot, his right hand blurred out, smashing into the inside of Bourne's right wrist. The razor went flying. Ouyang struck Bourne in the solar plexus, forcing him back several paces. In a flash he had grasped the hilt of his *jian* and stepped out of the tub.

The long blade came whistling toward Bourne, and only a last-second move saved Bourne from having his throat slit. As it was, the blade passed so close to him the glare off its surface momentarily blinded him.

Ouyang took advantage, and struck at Bourne's right arm. The blade bit in, blood bubbled up onto the blade's surface, ran down the blade as Ouyang withdrew it. He had switched to the White Crane Form, normally employed with a saber. He was gripped by the same red haze that had washed over him in the Kunlun Mountain Fist sanctuary just before he killed his unwitting opponent. There was no possible future he could conceive of where he would not defeat Bourne and send him into the infinite void of death.

Bourne, under relentless attack, retreated from the bathroom. In the hallway he took a blow on his left forearm, and the towel he had wrapped around it, completely severed, fell to the floor in two neat sections. Blood spurted from the wound the blade had made.

The farther Bourne retreated, the faster Ouyang pressed his attack, so that by the time they reached the living room the two men were fairly sprinting. All at once, Bourne reversed himself, bulling his way toward Ouyang as if in one last desperate attempt to turn the tide.

Ouyang jabbed the *jian* outward, forcing Bourne to leap back. He hit the sideboard. Glasses slid along the top and something rolled toward him. Out of the corner of his eye, Bourne saw the vial that contained the polonium vibrating perilously close to the edge of the sideboard, and he whirled away, nearly being decapitated in the process.

Grinning, Ouyang once again swung the *jian*, this time in a shallow arc, but with such viciousness it used all his strength. The blade headed directly toward Bourne and would surely cut deep into flesh and bone, but at the last instant Bourne darted away, and the *jian* sliced off a section of the sideboard's top. Bottles of liquor shattered, glasses disintegrated, and the teapot split apart. The vial of polonium jumped, shivering, then began to roll wildly toward Bourne.

Ouyang delivered a horizontal strike. Bourne ducked down, the blade passing just above his head. The vial was headed straight for him. Ouyang kicked out, pushing Bourne up against the sideboard with such force that what bottles remained standing split and spilled their contents.

The vial reached the edge of the sideboard and rolled off. But Bourne had pulled out a drawer into which it dropped. He slammed the drawer shut.

Enraged all the more, Ouyang swung a massive, two-handed blow. Bourne whirled away at the last instant and the singing blade of the *jian* struck one of the cypress pillars, burying itself so deeply in the dense wood that when Ouyang tried to pull it free it would not come. He yanked it again and again, until Bourne delivered a blow to his thorax that knocked him off his feet.

Bourne threw himself on Ouyang. The two men were locked in a grim struggle where inches and fractions of inches would tell the tale between life and death. Their muscles bulged, their sinews stretched, their bones cracked with the strength, energy, and sheer willpower each brought to the fight. Arms were twisted painfully back, punches delivered to ribs and kidney. Sweat and a terrible silence were the only manifestations of the road they took toward death. There could be no turning back, no deviation whatsoever.

At length, Bourne struck an unexpected horizontal blow that nearly took Ouyang's nose apart. Ouyang slid backward, blood spurting from the center of his face. Fetching up near the opening to the kitchen, he felt the bulk of an assault rifle dropped by one of his dead guards.

He grabbed the weapon, but the moment his hands closed around the oiled metal he felt a searing pain so acute it paralyzed his arms. Rising, Bourne took hold of Ouyang's *jian*, slammed a two-fisted blow that broke the blade in two. Taking control of the freed stub, he picked his way to where Ouyang was still struggling with the assault rifle.

Kicking him into a supine position, Bourne dropped to one knee.

"It doesn't matter what you do to me," Ouyang said.

Bourne drove the stub of the *jian* into Ouyang's heart. Ouyang stared up at him. His hands were bleeding, red as raw meat, burned from the toxic mixture Bourne had brewed up. He convulsed as his system started to shut down.

"What was the point?" he whispered in a glottal voice.

Bourne stared down at him without an ounce of pity. "Retribution," he said.

"But do you have her back?" Blood poured from between his lips, partially obscuring his words. "Does her father, her grandfather? The Yadins are without their child."

Bourne bent down. "What?" he was fairly shouting. "What did you say?"

Ouyang regarded him or the image of him, which was all his fast-dimming eyesight allowed him to see. "Sara. That's her name. Sara Yadin." He tried for an expression, either to laugh or to cry, but he had nothing left. Blood bubbled out of every orifice, as if even his bones had turned to red liquid.

With one last effort, he grabbed Bourne's shirt-front and pulled him closer. For just an instant, his entire body trembled and his eyes rolled in their sockets, as if looking for the way out. Then they refocused on his nemesis.

"You see how it is," he whispered. "It'll be the same for you." He convulsed again, gritted his teeth to hang on just one more moment. "It's just as well she's dead. There is no happiness in this life. We're shackled by loss...terrible losses... one after another. Until there's nothing left...but tears...drowned...in a sea of blood."

56

LEONID," BOURNE SAID into his mobile, "I'm on my way."

"We're rested and refueled and ready to go."

Night, in the form of a stifling darkness, had enclosed Beidaihe like a swaddling cloth. Bourne could scarcely hear the Bohai Sea coming ashore down below the ragged lip of the cliff. A wind was picking up, cool and wet, and far out on the horizon jagged bolts of lightning could be seen threading their way through clouds the color of gunmetal.

Dressed in the suit Minister Ouyang had chosen for tomorrow's Congress, Bourne was driving one of the jeeps through the compound, away from the sea and the opulent villas that clung to its edge.

The darkness interspersed with twinkling lights recalled to him the evening in Mexico City when he drove a commandeered taxi across town to try to save Rebeka from bleeding out from the knife wound in her side. He had done everything he could, applying a makeshift tourniquet, placing her hands over the wound and telling her to press down, to keep her life inside her, to keep safe until he could reach a hospital.

He came to the compound's outer gate and was allowed through. The guards, bored, tired, at the end of their shift, were none too interested in who left the compound. Their bickering over the latest ministerial sex scandal—more salacious than most—occupied the bulk of their attention.

Out onto the road, he took the left-hand fork, toward the tumbledown military airfield, where Ouyang's private plane was waiting to take Leonid back to Moscow. He drove very fast, even though the terrain was rough, the road rutted and in ill repair. Once, he had to slow, take a detour around a wide crack in the tarmac that seemed to be many feet deep. A light rain began to fall.

Just then he thought he spotted a pair of headlights paralleling him on a narrow cut through the trees on the ridge above the road. He put on speed, and was soon within sight of the airfield. Its lights cut through the thickening darkness like diamonds, smeared by the rain.

He was nearing the gates when a shot plowed

into the side of his vehicle. A moment later a second shot shattered the window on the passenger's side. Bourne swerved off the road, threw the vehicle into neutral as it rumbled down a rocky embankment, coming to rest on sandy soil.

Bourne was out of the jeep in an instant. Keeping the vehicle between him and the origin of the shots, he moved to the rear of the jeep and, crouching down, vectored the immediate area in an attempt to ferret out the marksman's place of concealment.

He was close enough to the airfield to hear the jet's engines whining to life as it prepared to lift off. Scrambling obliquely up the embankment, he reached the lip of the road, hanging there for a moment, waiting to see if his presence would draw another shot. The jet's engines roared louder, and he launched himself up onto the road. The gate was only a hundred yards away. He sprinted toward it.

Leonid, confined within the metal tube of the plane, was slowly going crazy. If it wasn't for the prospect of having an intelligent companion on the way to Moscow, one who, furthermore, could put in a good word for him with General Boris Karpov, already a legend in the FSB as well as in the hallowed offices of the Kremlin itself, he would have roused the flight crew to get him the hell out of here well before this.

But now his friend was coming, just as he said he would, and now all would be well. He stared out the Perspex window on the stair side of the plane, and within moments saw the twin headlights of a vehicle run along the tarmac, pull up just before the folding stairs.

A man jumped out and headed straight for the stairs. Leonid, his mood lightening with every step the man took toward the doorway, went to greet his friend.

The figure mounted the stairs, taking them two at a time, but as soon as he was swept up in the plane's interior lights, Leonid took a step back. It wasn't his friend who was coming on board; it was someone he'd never seen before—a Chinese national who nevertheless possessed all the hallmarks of Manchu blood.

"Who are you?" Leonid said, frowning.

"*Cào nǐ zǔ zōng shíbā dài.*" Fuck your ancestors to the eighteenth generation. "You were expecting Bourne." Kai drew an S&W Bodyguard 380 ACP and shot Leonid twice in the chest. As Leonid lay in the aisle, Kai shot him a third time between the eyes.

As he stepped over him, he took the time to kick him in the face. "*Pìyǎn!*" he spat. Asshole!

Having heard the shots, the navigator emerged from the cockpit, a standard-issue 9 mm Glock in his hand. "What the hell—!"

Kai shot him in the chest, and he fell back into the cockpit, where the screaming started.

"We're taking off now," Kai said, aiming his S&W at the pilot's head.

"We were told to wait for another passenger."

"And here I am." Kai waved the S&W. "Take us up now."

The flight attendant, crouched in the corner farthest away from the blood and mayhem, whimpered. His arms were clutched around his drawn-up knees.

"This is a direct order from Minister Ouyang."

"I can't, sir. The folding stairs are still deployed," the pilot said.

Kai moved the handgun toward the flight attendant, and he made an involuntary animal sound deep in his throat. "Go back up the aisle and pull up the folding stairs." He waggled the barrel threateningly. "Do it now!"

At the sound of his raised voice, the attendant jumped up and, with a strangled cry, forced himself to step over the body of the navigator. He went down the aisle to the doorway, but when he encountered Leonid's corpse he almost turned back.

Kai, keeping one eye on the attendant's progress,

shouted at him to get the damn stairs folded back into the fuselage. Trembling, he picked his way over Leonid's bloody body and, at last, reached the open doorway. As he was about to haul the stairs up, Kai forced the pilot to take off the brakes. The plane began to roll forward, picking up speed as the jet engines built revs.

The attendant had just begun to haul the stairs up when he saw someone running alongside the plane. He recognized him as one of the passengers they had picked up in Mexico City—Ambassador Liu's bodyguard and Leonid's friend. He ran toward the stairs. Clearly, this was the passenger they had been waiting for.

The attendant could see by the gathering speed of the aircraft he was never going to make it. Gingerly, he stepped down onto the stairs, descending each step with the utmost care, lest he slip and go hurtling off onto the tarmac.

The running man was close now—as close as he was ever going to get. His upper body was fully extended, his right arm outstretched. The attendant descended to the lowest step and, leaning over, offered him his extended hand.

They missed the first time, their fingertips just grazing. Then the man grabbed onto the attendant the second time; his weight almost dislocated the attendant's shoulder. His body was whirled around and, had it not been for the solid aluminum side of the steps, the attendant would have been spun off with him.

Instead, the attendant held on, pulling hard in stages, his muscles straining, his breath coming in ragged gasps, until Bourne's other hand grabbed hold of the top of the stairs. He swung his legs, vaulted up onto the stairs, then, taking the attendant's hand, ascended into the plane.

"There's a Chinese man with a gun," he gasped in Bourne's ear. "He looks like a Manchu—acts like one, too. He shot Leonid and the navigator."

Where is he now?" Bourne said.

"In the cockpit with the pilot."

Bourne saw Leonid's body, sprawled and bloody, where he had fallen near the doorway. Keeping the flight attendant's body between himself and the cockpit, Bourne helped him pull the folding stairs up into the fuselage. The attendant was about to lock it in place when Bourne stopped him.

"Not now," he whispered, and the attendant shivered, understanding what he had in mind.

"Go lock yourself in the toilet," Bourne said softly, "and don't come out until you hear my voice."

The attendant's alarm escalated. "What if I don't hear your voice?"

"Go on now," Bourne said. "Hurry!"

Up in the cockpit, Kai was arguing with the pilot. The rain had increased in intensity and now a low fog had come in off the sea, rising up the cliffside. The pilot was reluctant to take off; Kai wasn't interested in what the pilot wanted.

The instant he saw the flight attendant slip into the toilet and lock the door, Bourne wiped down the rain-slick floor to cover his tracks, then stepped to the galley, quickly foraged through cabinets until he found a full-size bottle of wine and a warm can of beer. Then he went back to the last row of seats forward of the door and crouched down, hidden by the seat backs.

Kai must have won the argument. With a lurch, the jet sprang forward, rolling down the runway at speed. A moment later he heard the Manchu's voice raised as he stuck his head out the cockpit doorway.

Bourne knew Kai could see that the stairs had been drawn up, the door closed, but there was no sign of the attendant. All at once the plane's pitch steepened as it rose into the nighttime sky. With a rumble, the wheels retracted into the belly of the fuselage.

Bent forward as if battling a stiff wind, Kai came

down the aisle toward the aft area to find the attendant. Bourne shook the can of beer. Just before Kai reached the open area in front of the door, Bourne raised himself, swung the bottle of wine into Kai's leading knee. Kai grunted, the leg crumpled, and as he was about to pitch over against the last row of seats, Bourne shoved the can of beer into Kai's face, popped the top.

The warm beer geysered out, covering Kai's face, momentarily blinding him. Bourne used a kite on Kai's clavicle, causing him to lose his grip on the S&W. Kai, on hands and knees, lunged for it.

Bending forward, Bourne drove a fist into his side. Kai reached the butt of the pistol, slammed it back into Bourne with such force that Bourne stumbled across the aisle directly toward the door. At the last instant, he braced his arms on either side of it, stopping himself from plowing into it.

However, this gave Kai time to recover. He struck with the muzzle of the S&W, swiping a long track of ripped fabric and, beneath it, a length of Bourne's skin. Blood welled up. Bourne maneuvered back across the aisle, as if trying to get away, until he was directly across from the door. Raising both arms, he gripped the edge of the overhead rack, then levered the rest of himself up until his legs scissored around Kai's neck.

Kai struggled, but his arms could find no leverage to pull Bourne's legs apart. With a titanic effort, he clawed his way to Bourne's face, trying to gouge out his eyes. There was blood on Bourne's face. He tried to turn his head away, but Kai had it locked in the vise-like grip of desperation.

Extending his body fully, Bourne kicked the door with his feet. It flew open. Bourne let go of his grip and kicked hard, his shoes striking squarely in the center of Kai's chest. Kai was launched backward. His left foot went over the lip of the door frame, he lost his balance, and, arms pinwheeling wildly, he was sucked out of the plane, immediately enveloped by the wind, vanishing into the clouds, leaving only a single shriek, like a distant rumble of thunder.

Epilogue

A PURE BLUE SKY, devoid of even a single cloud, greeted Jason Bourne as his commercial flight settled onto the runway at Ben Gurion Airport.

To his surprise, Director Yadin was waiting for him inside the immigration section, leading him around the long lines and, accompanied by an escort of Mossad agents, out onto the arrivals concourse, heading for the front doors.

"My apologies for the delay," Yadin said as they strode along. "I, myself, was in a bunker until an hour ago. Mortars from Gaza."

"Have you retaliated?"

"Oh, yes. Pinpoint strikes. Two of the Hamas leaders are dead. Then the missiles came. Don't be concerned if you hear air raid sirens. They go off all the time now."

Their escort held the doors open for them and they went out into the blinding sunlight, the baking concrete slabs. An immense, bulletproof SUV was waiting for them by the curb, guarded by soldiers with submachine guns.

"Ouyang is dead," Bourne said as he followed Yadin into the dim, capacious interior.

"I expected nothing less." Eli leaned forward to give the driver an address, then settled himself on the backseat. His men piled into the front, and the SUV pulled away from the curb.

"Cho Xilan has vanished," the Director said. "It's as if he never existed."

"Ouyang murdered him," Bourne said. "Poisoned him with polonium."

"Polonium?" Eli appeared startled. "That's a KGB trick."

Bourne told him how Ouyang's plane had stopped in Moscow on the way to Beidaihe to pick up Leonid. "The FSB was the source," Bourne concluded, "but I think Cho's death was Ouyang's personal retribution."

"All to Deng Tsu's great good fortune." Yadin rubbed his chin. "With Ouyang dead and Cho's coalition leaderless, Deng has gained the freedom to handpick the next president. Another reactionary. The reforms he enacts will be entirely cosmetic."

Bourne stared out the window at the shadowed buildings, the silhouettes of passersby. "The more things change, the more they stay the same, especially in China."

At that moment, the air raid sirens began to scream.

"Sounds like another war," Bourne said.

"Short-lived, thank God. Short-lived because of the success of your retribution." Eli smiled. "Minister Ouyang was funding the Hamas jihad through elements in the Sinai. With that source of funding gone, a cease-fire will be negotiated in a matter of days." He nodded. "We—I—owe you a debt I'll never be able to repay."

Bourne put his head back against the seat and closed his eyes. He felt unutterably tired, as if he were a sprinter who had been compelled to run a marathon.

"You look like shit, by the way."

"I feel like shit," Bourne said. "Maybe I'm getting old."

Director Yadin laughed. "Never, my friend! Never! But you're bleeding all over my seat cushions. You will have a thorough medical checkup and then some rest."

The SUV drove on through the thick Tel Aviv traffic.

"Eli, I'm sorry."

Yadin turned to him.

"I know Rebeka was your daughter. I know what a terrible loss Sara's death was."

Yadin made no comment. He stared straight ahead as the SUV turned onto Weizmann Street. Bourne had been here once before, following the Director into Sourasky Medical Center.

As the SUV pulled up to the entrance, Yadin said, "Come now, Jason. You really do look a sight."

Twenty minutes later, in a surgery on the third floor, Bourne, stripped naked, lay on a table while a surgeon checked all his wounds. Several of them required stitches. He was given shots of local anesthetic and was duly sewn up. His lesser cuts and contusions were administered to, he was given a prescription for an antibiotic, then was released to get dressed.

All the while he had lain naked, Eli Yadin had stood guard, staring out the window, hands clasped loosely behind his back, as if in deep contemplation.

"I followed you here once," Bourne said as he buttoned his shirt.

"Did you? I never knew."

"I was concerned you were ill."

"I am ill." Yadin turned back to him, his expression bleak. "Life has made me ill, Jason. I am dying of the ten thousand lies I am forced to tell in order to ensure the safety of my country. I am a patriot, Jason, but I am wounded to my soul by the lies I utter."

He lifted an arm, ushering Bourne out of the surgery. They began to walk slowly down the hall dotted with nurses, patients on gurneys, an occasional doctor, hurrying from one catastrophe to another.

"None of my wounds has struck deeper than the one caused by the lie I was forced to tell you."

Bourne stopped, turned toward the Director.

"That the lie was absolutely necessary. That it served to protect a number of people, including you, makes it only nominally more palatable."

He shook his shaggy head. "You see, the lie I told you goaded you into hunting down Ouyang. He was a serious threat to me, to Mossad, to the State of Israel, but try as I might I could not get to him. Then you fell into my lap, as it were. Because of Rebeka. Because of your work with her, because of your feelings for her.

"God sent you to me, Jason, and I had no choice but to use you. And you accomplished the impossible." His smile was wan, almost transparent. "I know I have given you reason to hate me now, but I have faith that in time you will find it in yourself to forgive me."

"Why would I?" Bourne said coldly. "You've done to me what every other agency has done."

Eli gestured and they continued down the hallway. "Because whether you choose to believe it or not I consider you a friend—a good friend I am honored to know."

"Enough with the bullshit, Director."

"I mean it, Jason, with all my heart."

"How can you mean it when you lie to friends?"

"I lie only when it's absolutely necessary."

"The trouble is it's you who decides when it's necessary."

"I think I've earned the right."

"Everyone thinks that."

Eli grunted. "Let me know if you feel the same way when you leave this unit."

He pushed open the double doors to critical care. Inside, the atmosphere was as hushed and sepulchral as a funeral parlor. Solemn nurses and PAs moved from patient to patient like bees pollinating flowers.

Each patient was housed in a separate room. The sighs of breathing tubes and beeps of electronic monitors were virtually the only sounds, a kind of doleful electronic music.

They stopped in front of a door. "The measure of my trust in you, Jason, is that I have taken you here, that in a moment I will allow you to walk into this room, because in there is my one true secret and your gift."

There was silence for some time.

"Will you come in with me?" Bourne asked.

Eli Yadin's smile seemed to brighten. "Another time."

Bourne opened the door.

"I'll be here, Jason."

The room was large and bright, more like a diminutive living room than a hospital cubicle. The door sighed shut behind him and he was alone with the person sitting up in the bed on the far side of the room.

"Hello, Jason."

For a moment he felt rooted to the spot, absolutely disbelieving despite what his eyes showed him. It was as if his stunned mind was suspicious that this was another of Eli Yadin's superbly tailored lies.

"Won't you come here?"

Bourne could find nothing to say. Was this a dream? He had such a powerful sense of unreality he nearly staggered. He felt blood rush to his head. His heart beat painfully in his chest, and he could scarcely breathe.

"Rebeka," he said at last, "for all this time I thought you were dead."

"My real name is Sara. Sara Yadin." She held out her hand. "If you touch me you'll know I'm not dead."

"I've been..."

"I know, and I'm so sorry."

"All I could think of was..."

Her hand was so thin, so pale, almost translucent.

Bourne was aware of a great heat inside himself, a rageful trembling in his soul. His fist slammed into the wall so hard, the plaster groaned, cracking. The door opened, and it was all he could do not to rush through it and crush Eli Yadin's windpipe.

"Get out!" he yelled.

"It's all right," Sara called. "Everything's fine."

The door subsided, sighing shut.

Bourne's face was a frightening mask. "Your father lied to me, time and again he lied."

"He lied to everyone, Jason. It was to protect me while I was vulnerable lying here, without strength, recovering."

Her words did nothing to dispel his fury. "But it was me he manipulated. He used my anguish at your death—"

"To kill the man who ordered me dead."

"I would willingly have—"

"Of course," Sara said, "but you might have

failed. Even you." She smiled sadly. "If he'd told you the truth you would have insisted on seeing me. And having seen me, part of you would have remained here with me. Your attention would have been divided. Your effectiveness would have been compromised."

Apart from the rhythmic beeping of the heart rate monitor, there was silence.

"You know it's true, Jason."

She was right, Bourne thought. Knowing she was alive, lying here helpless, would have made him crazy. He would not have been thinking clearly. Ouyang was far too dangerous a foe to engage while his concentration was divided.

"Please." She waggled her outstretched fingers. "I want to touch you. I want to hold you. I want to know you're real, that you've returned from China alive and well."

Like a sleepwalker, he approached the bed. He recognized her, yet she looked vastly different. She was painfully thin, and so ashen she appeared almost ghostly. In some places, the blue of her veins shone through her translucent skin with a venomous lucidity. She had the appearance of someone who was still in the grip of an exceptionally grave and painful illness.

As he came close, she parted her gown, revealing the ugly scar on her side where she had been stabbed the night they had escaped Maceo Encarnación's villa in Mexico City. He had had to carry her the final yards, and then...

He took her to him, enfolding her, cradling her, rocking her gently. As the tips of his fingers ran along the still-livid scar, he felt his heart well up to the bursting point. And he whispered, "I saw you bleed out in the back of the taxi. I left you a corpse in Mexico City. I stood by while they buried you here in Tel Aviv. And now..."

"Now here we are. Everything is good." She smiled.

He remembered that smile, and the feelings it engendered rose up in him like a cresting wave.

"You were so brave, Jason. So resourceful. I never would have made it if it weren't for you." She took his head in her hands, kissed him tenderly with lips soft as clouds. "My love, you saved my life."

For a seemingly endless time, they held each other wordlessly, content just to feel each other, to assure themselves that this reunion was real, not a dream from which they would wake, heartbroken and in despair.

"Jason," she said at length, "I was so frightened for you. When my father told me his plan, I was livid. I wouldn't speak to him for days. But he kept at me, repeated over and over what I told you, and at last I relented. And he was right. You were the only one who could get close to Ouyang, who could kill him. The only one. And of course, he had given you the perfect motivation: my death."

There was anguish in her voice, as well as love. But there was also unmistakable pride.

Holding her now, hearing her speak, having once again felt her lips against his, the rage leached out of Bourne's heart, and he calmed. As always, her touch was like a balm against the betrayals the world had, time and again, heaped on him. And as this process continued, he understood that though Eli had used him, he hadn't betrayed him. On the contrary, Eli had trusted him to commit the most sacred act a father could set in motion: retribution for his gravely wounded daughter.

Rebeka—Sara; it would take some getting used to before he could call her that—shifted against him, and he realized that she must still be in pain.

"Lie back," he said gently.

"Only if you keep hold of me."

He lay her down, held her hand in both of his while she smiled up at him, and sighed deeply.

"Now listen, my love, while I tell you a story. When we met I was a flight attendant. You were heading for Damascus and so was I. But some time before, I met with Ouyang. It was all part of the plan. I presented myself as a courier, moving military secrets from Damascus to Oman. He saw me as a mule—as he was supposed to.

"The fact was, I was the one stealing the secrets. I was hiding in plain sight. From that moment on, his attention moved off me to find the people running me. But he never could find them, because they didn't exist. He wasted untold time and money chasing the invisible honeypot while, one by one, I killed off his people."

"Until he discovered the truth."

"Yes."

"And then he wouldn't rest until you were dead." Bourne wanted to scream. All at once, he hated his life of secrets and lies, hated the despicable life that had put her in harm's way.

"At the outset of the mission, I was outfitted with a hollow tooth," she continued. "Inside was a fast-acting capsule. It wasn't a death pill, but one that would ensure my life under extreme circumstances. I swallowed a drug our scientists have perfected that slows the metabolism to simulate death. If I'm found in time, I can be revived, though the return to life is a long and painful one."

For some time, Bourne sat holding her hand.

Tears leaked from the corners of her eyes. "How many times have I imagined this moment, Jason; longed for it with all my heart and soul."

Leaning over, Bourne kissed her tears away. "You're not going out into the field again."

"Could I stop you?" She searched his face. "Be honest. What else would either of us do?"

For a long time, they stared into each other's eyes. At length, he took the gold chain from around his neck. The small star of David glimmered between them, a comet in the night sky. The moment she saw it, the tears came again. But this time her eyes were shining. She bent her head forward and he affixed the chain at the nape of her neck. The emblem of her he had carried with him from the moment of her supposed death lay on her chest as it had on the afternoon he had met her, heading to Damascus.

"You see, you were always close to me," he whispered.

"Jason." Tears lay heavy on her eyelids, reflecting tiny prisms. "Oh, Jason, what are you waiting for?"

He leaned toward her, and Sara Yadin burst into delighted laughter.

"Yes," she sighed just before his lips covered hers.

Acknowledgments

My thanks to:
Sinocism and *The Financial Times*
for insights into China.

About the Author

ROBERT LUDLUM was the author of twenty-seven novels, each one a *New York Times* bestseller. There are more than 225 million copies of his books in print, and they have been translated into thirty-two languages. He is the author of *The Scarlatti Inheritance*, *The Chancellor Manuscript*, and the Jason Bourne series—*The Bourne Identity*, *The Bourne Supremacy*, and *The Bourne Ultimatum*—among others. Mr. Ludlum passed away in March 2001. To learn more, visit www.Robert-Ludlum.com and Facebook.com/ RobertLudlumBooks.

ERIC VAN LUSTBADER is the author of numerous bestselling novels including *First Daughter*, *Blood Trust*, *The Ninja*, and the international bestsellers featuring Jason Bourne: *The Bourne Legacy*, *The Bourne Betrayal*, *The Bourne Sanc-*

tion, *The Bourne Deception*, *The Bourne Objective*, and *The Bourne Dominion*. For more information, you can visit www.EricVanLustbader .com. You can also follow him on Facebook and Twitter.